THE SEER

THE SEER

DRAGONSLAYER
BOOK TWO

JULES CORY

Copyright © 2020 Jules Cory

The moral right of the author has been asserted.

Apart from any fair dealing for the purposes of research or private study, or criticism or review, as permitted under the Copyright, Designs and Patents Act 1988, this publication may only be reproduced, stored or transmitted, in any form or by any means, with the prior permission in writing of the publishers, or in the case of reprographic reproduction in accordance with the terms of licences issued by the Copyright Licensing Agency. Enquiries concerning reproduction outside those terms should be sent to the publishers.

Matador
9 Priory Business Park,
Wistow Road, Kibworth Beauchamp,
Leicestershire. LE8 0RX
Tel: 0116 279 2299
Email: books@troubador.co.uk
Web: www.troubador.co.uk/matador
Twitter: @matadorbooks

ISBN 978 1838592 387

British Library Cataloguing in Publication Data.
A catalogue record for this book is available from the British Library.

Printed and bound in the UK by 4edge Ltd.
Typeset in 11pt Minion Pro by Troubador Publishing Ltd, Leicester, UK

Matador is an imprint of Troubador Publishing Ltd

For those who still believe.

Chapter One

The day had started so perfectly. The smooth peaks of Cloud Mountain hovered over the trees. The dawn mist was still clinging to the hills, softening and blending the edges. The woodcutter's cottage nestled in a sea of green as the forest started to show its autumn finery. A few leaves had turned to scarlet or gold, a striking counterpoint of colour in the lush canopy. The winds had been light that season, allowing the foliage to stay on the trees and provide shelter for the creatures that took advantage of the available food bounty before winter. Birds, squirrels and small rodents feasted on the berries, grains and nuts. My basket was full of the mushrooms that were thickly carpeting the ground.

But something was wrong. The cabin was too quiet; no birds sang in the branches around the low-lying timber building, no squirrels foraged along the garden borders. The dwelling was a little too still. The doorway was slightly ajar, and I knew I had closed it. Old habits returned easily. I stayed within the shadows of the treeline as I crept closer to the cottage. I was approaching the front of the dwelling, so I could not see if a horse had been tied to the rail along the right of the building. I strained to listen for the noise of restless hooves, but heard nothing. A headache was forming between my eyes as my heart increased its pace. I tried to convince myself that it was just Kennig, the woodcutter, come to check on me before winter seized his joints. My mind dismissed this train of thought in favour of more ominous possibilities. It was unusual for Lindvane to raid this far into Faulknar, but not unheard of. More likely possibilities involved bandits and petty criminals searching for plunder. While not as violent as the Lindvane raiders, they still posed a serious threat to a young woman on her own. I cursed myself for leaving my sword in the cottage, but rejected obtaining a branch to use as a weapon. My belt dagger would suffice, and hunting had kept my throwing skills fresh.

I watched the wooden hut, assessing the danger before sneaking up to the left side, avoiding the single window so I would not be seen by anyone inside. The breeze must have carried my scent around the building, causing the horses to snort anxiously. I identified two. It seemed the bandit had not come alone. I concentrated on slowing my breathing, but my heart refused to calm. Drying my sweating palms on my leather trousers, I moved around to the front window and peeped into the single room. I could only see one stranger. He had his back to me, kneeling in front of the fireplace. I had a clear shot but was loath to relinquish my only weapon. I did not know where the other rider was. I bit my lip as I considered my options and eased the shutters open a little further to allow a wider view. The man stood and started to turn. Instinct took over as I drew back my arm and threw the blade.

I had released the knife a heartbeat before I recognised who was turning to face me. Anxiety for my own safety turned to concern for my visitor as the blade flew straight towards his throat. A flash of blue light deflected the dagger a hand-width from his neck.

Drey smiled. 'It's good to see you have retained your skills.'

I stared at him for several heartbeats, my mouth falling open as my brain tried to understand what had just happened.

'For the love of Mobis, Drey!' I spluttered eventually. 'What are you doing here?'

'I'm about to make a cup of tea. Would you like one?'

The pressure from my headache was added to by the ache of a deepening frown, as my mind tried desperately to catch up. I walked round to the door as Drey rummaged around the cottage. I stood in the doorway watching him.

'What are you looking for?'

He turned to face me, his forehead creased by his own puckered brow. 'Do you keep anything in this place?'

'There's rose hip and mint on the shelf above the fire. Behind the cups.'

He raised an eyebrow. 'And food?'

'I've some mushrooms outside.' I had left the basket of wild fungi at the edge of the forest: I would have to go and retrieve that.

'Anything to go with the mushrooms?' He resumed his rummaging. 'Eggs? Bread? By the Goddess, Tallen. How can you live in this mess?' He looked up. 'And what have you done to your hair?'

I pulled at the ragged strands of my hair that had been irregularly shorn with my dagger when they grew too long. 'What's wrong with my hair?' I grumbled. 'It's functional. And I don't get many visitors.' I moved to tidy some clothes off the bed and straighten the sheets. 'Have you come here just to complain about my housekeeping skills or was there another reason?'

His frown deepened. 'No. I'm here for other reasons.' He gave a thin smile. 'But tea first.'

I had fetched the mushrooms and we had both finished our drinks before Drey explained why he was here.

'It's time to come home, Tallen.'

'I am home. Kennig is happy for me to stay here and maintain the place. He doesn't get up here so much since the accident.'

Drey scowled at me. 'This is hardly a home.'

'It suits me fine,' I persisted.

'Humph. That may be, but you are needed back at Liegeport.'

It was my turn to glower. 'I'm no longer welcome there.'

'Nonsense.'

'Not according to Breya.'

'And you just went along with her temper tantrum. It's not like you to back down in the face of a bully.'

I studied the small scratches on my hands from picking blackberries two days before. 'People change,' I said quietly.

Drey hesitated. His tone was gentler when he continued. 'You can't hide here forever.'

'I can try.'

He sighed and rubbed his eyes. 'Well, the world has continued to turn while you have been here. Kyllian has declared war on Gallowgla and Hilman, as well as Lindvane. This summer's fighting has been the heaviest I've seen. The king has had to introduce conscription, against his wishes. Liegeport is bursting with new recruits. But still Faulknar is looking a little isolated at the moment.'

'And what has that got to do with me?'

Drey glared at me and I was careful to avoid eye contact. 'You have been called to serve your king,' he said harshly.

The tea suddenly felt as heavy as soaked soil in my stomach. I had no desire to fight the Lindvanes. I feared going back to Liegeport. 'Where am I to fight? Can I go straight there? If I am permitted to request a posting, I would fight alongside Keenan.'

'I'm sure the Lord General would welcome you with him. But Kyllian feels your talents are required away from the front line. For a more secretive role.'

I hesitated as I felt my past catching up with me. 'And if I refuse?'

'I would not want to test Kyllian's temper at the moment.'

I closed my eyes, feeling trapped. It would seem that the deal I'd made as a ten-year-old child was valid for the rest of my life. Shelter and protection in exchange for non-negotiable service to the king. I would steal at my king's command in repayment for the food and clothing I had required when growing up. I owed Kyllian a debt, and was therefore owned.

'Then I have no choice.'

Drey remained very still. 'No,' he said quietly.

My dream that night was set on a misty battlefield. The colours were garishly bright, painfully vivid. Glistening golds, ruby reds, emerald greens and deep sapphire blues stood out on the billowing banners scattered across the two armies. Shouts and curses ebbed and flowed as the wind and mist swirled the noise in erratic patterns over the fields. Horses stamped and whinnied, unsettled by the nervous energy of their riders and the soldiers around them. The scent of blood and waste had yet to appear, but the sense of fear was palpable in the air. The two armies faced each other, the wide, open space seeming pitifully small in the presence of the hordes of fighters. On the far side, the archers, pikemen, foot soldiers and cavalry rallied under the tusked boar standard of Lindvane. The left flank carried the standard of Hilman, a rearing stag with a golden crown nestled in its antlers. The right flank displayed the majestic eagle of Gallowgla, carrying the salmon of wisdom. Facing them were the armies of Faulknar, the lion standard flapping in the wind as if the big cat was impatient to start the battle. Mixed in with these troops were small groups of soldiers carrying no banner, declaring no fealty to lord or king. An unknown element. We were still outnumbered three to one.

I stood on a small rise overlooking the flat land. I pulled my cloak a little tighter, the material scratching at my neck. Tears stung the corners of my eyes. 'I can't do this.'

I turned to the only other on the rise. A tall figure, enclosed in a midnight-black robe, stood next to me. Her face was covered by her hood as she continued to look forward over the battle. Her delicate pale hands were clasped loosely in front of her. Her continued silence added to my guilt.

'You offer me an impossible choice.' I took a shaky breath. 'How can I choose between my heart and my soul?'

I turned back to the developing scene below me. The order to advance had been given by both sides. The horses thundered across the ground while the foot soldiers ran, bellowing, behind them. The ring of metal as swords were pulled from their scabbards sounded like a mournful sigh heralding the coming of death. It was followed by the soft exhale of breath as the archers let fly the arrows from their longbows. The graceful, curved flight before the lethal impact. The wet *thwack* as iron heads bit into muscle. The screams of the injured and dying spread chaos through the ranks of both armies. Iron shrieked as swords clashed. Wood cracked as shields were pierced.

I closed my eyes, clenching my fists in frustration. 'I won't do this.'

At the soft rustle of silk, I turned. I looked into a serene face as the cloaked woman turned towards me, her pale face glowing slightly. Her long silver hair framed her delicate features, escaping from the bottom of the hood to spill over her shoulders; a sharp contrast with the black robe. She looked at me with the palest blue eyes, small beads of clear glass protecting the unprepared from the depth of knowledge and compassion lying within. Her rose lips curled into a sympathetic smile.

I know you will do the right thing. Her voice flowed like water trickling over rocks. *The fate of the Gods rests on your decision.*

I awoke before dawn and retreated to my place of calm. I reached the lake as the dawn broke, the sun still unseen behind the trees. A thin mist clung to the water, but Cloud Mountain caught the morning light. The smooth rocky peaks turned silver in response to the Sun God's touch. Small birds hopped along the shoreline searching for grubs as I sat, motionless, on the gravel pathway leading to the water. Dark brown roe deer came to drink, cautiously scenting the air for danger, flicking their tails in agitation as they licked moisture off their whiskers. The calm of the forest and the stillness of the lake infused into my mind, soothing my restless soul and melting the nervous tension in my muscles. I felt small and insignificant compared to the splendour of the nature displayed before me. My concerns were mere wisps of spider silk when set against the unimaginable time represented by the trees and the hills. I was contained in a bubble of tranquillity.

Drey joined me around mid-morning. I smiled as he noisily crunched the gravel path to ensure I would not consider him a threat. I continued to look out over the lake as he stumbled up behind me, complaining of uneven ground that could turn an old man's ankle.

'For the love of Mobis, Tallen. Why must you pick the most remote of places when you need peace and quiet?'

He slumped down beside me, letting out a deep sigh. My smile widened as I turned to face him. His shirt was open at the neck and his rose quartz pendant was clearly visible. He placed a long bundle covered with sacking beside him, opposite to the side on which I was sitting.

'I think the clue is in the words "peace" and "quiet".'

He chuckled. 'True enough.' He sighed again. 'By the Gods, this really is a beautiful place.'

I turned to look back over the water, my smile slowly melting. 'I think so.'

Drey paused for several heartbeats before continuing. 'After our talk yesterday, I feared you had run again.'

'I thought about it,' I admitted.

'What stopped you?'

I turned to face him and saw a hint of an apology in his hazel eyes. 'Where could I go where you couldn't find me?'

He dipped his head in acceptance.

'How long have you known that I'm here?'

His lips twitched in a small smile. 'You came straight here after leaving Liegeport the winter before last. I had to make sure you were safe.'

Turning back to the lake, I watched the birds skim low over the water to collect insects. I needed the calm of the scenery as the silence became a little less comfortable than before.

Drey broke it first and changed the subject. 'You're still having your bad dreams, I see,' he said, referring to the night terrors that had tormented me since I was a child.

I closed my eyes momentarily; it was a poor subject to change to. I shook my head and sighed. 'At least I don't feel Villermir's presence any more. Although, maybe he's just getting cleverer.' I turned at Drey's sharp intake of breath, and grimaced as I realised my unconscious admission. 'I hadn't told you about that bit?'

Drey's face was set in a stone mask of contained rage. 'No,' he snapped. 'You did not tell me about that bit.'

I brought my knees up and hugged them to my chest as I remembered the way Villermir had easily manipulated my fears to orchestrate my dreams. I talked to the ripples rather than face Drey with my darkest secrets. 'Apparently Villermir can gain access to my head any time he chooses.'

Drey kept very still.

'He used my fear to get around my protective barriers. He'd been controlling my dreams for years. Playing with my insecurities and shortcomings. Amplifying my guilt.' I took a shaky breath as I remembered his easy manipulation. 'He mainly used Laken to point out my many faults. Sometimes it was Kade. Sometimes others.' I took a shaky breath. 'Now my dreams appear to be my own. Normal stuff. The war with the Lindvanes. Being trapped underground. Searching for something.' I breathed a bitter laugh. 'Last night's involved a massive battle between Faulknar and Lindvane. Seems I had to make a big decision that would decide the outcome of the war. I wonder what triggered that?'

I turned to smile at Drey, but he was in no mood to be teased. His face was pale and his jaw muscles tight. A dangerous glint lay deep within his eyes.

'Did he just access your dreams?' he asked quietly. 'Could he enter your mind when you were awake?'

I looked at the textured pattern of scars radiating from my hands and up my arms. I had managed to ignore them during the time on my own, but became self-conscious again now someone else could see them. I traced a vein of raised tissue with my finger, biting my lip as I recalled my time as Villermir's prisoner at Burford Hythe.

'He could make me see things. Things that weren't there. Weren't real. Although they seemed real to me.' I hugged my knees a little tighter to my chest as I started trembling. 'He tried to break my inner barriers. The very core of me. I fought him. I don't know how, but I somehow managed to keep him out.' I frowned and closed my eyes, not wanting to remember any more. 'He used my connection with the Empathy Crystal. He followed the link to hidden parts of my head. Bits I didn't know were there. Things I still couldn't see, but he could. He saw where my magick came from. Saw the birth of whatever talent I have. He called me a child of the Ancients. A protector.'

I stopped. I would remember no more. I closed the lid on that box of bad memories, keeping it sealed deep within me.

Drey was quiet for a long time. When he finally spoke his voice held no hint of anger, just one of tiredness. 'I'm sorry, Tallen. I failed you.'

I shook my head. 'It's not your fault.'

Drey continued as if I hadn't spoken. 'I got it wrong. I thought that by shielding you from magick I would avoid drawing attention to you. But it just left you vulnerable. I was naive.'

I was embarrassed that Drey felt responsible for my problems. I tried to dismiss his concerns by changing direction. 'Villermir called you that,' I said, turning to smile at the ageing Druid. 'I thought you were too old to be naive.'

Drey narrowed his eyes at my comments, but smiled. 'I think I shall have to speak to Villermir regarding his low opinion of my character.'

Our smiles widened as the tension drifted away on the breeze. I relaxed my grip on my knees, letting the warmth of the sun soften the muscles of my shoulders.

'You can see why I'm reluctant to return to Liegeport,' I conceded. 'And that's without mentioning how much fun seeing Kade is going to be.'

Drey hesitated. 'Kade has... mellowed since you last saw him. He has had to adapt to a lot of changes. His may not be the path he would have chosen for himself, but he understands his responsibilities.'

'I notice you didn't use the word "accepts" his new responsibilities.'

Drey raised an eyebrow. 'He hasn't changed that much.'

We lapsed into a more comfortable silence as I studied Cloud Mountain, thinking again how strange it was to have this one mountain in the flatlands. How it should dominate the landscape, but a quirk of nature had caused it to give the impression of a rugged cloud floating above the treeline.

I felt Drey watching me. Mentally sighing, I turned to face him. 'What?' I asked, using my expression to soften any accusation in the word.

He hesitated for a few more heartbeats before deciding to proceed. 'I thought you might need some persuading to return to Liegeport. So, I brought this.' He reached for the package beside him and presented it to me.

'Bribery or blackmail?' I asked.

He shrugged. 'Whichever works.'

I took the long, thin bundle: it was heavier than I was expecting it to be. My heartbeat strengthened in anticipation. I slowly unwrapped the outer layer of rough woven sacking. The material separated to reveal a layer of midnight silk. My stomach flipped, instinct responding to a fragment of memory I couldn't fully recall. My hands trembled as I placed the sacking on the ground beside me. The silk shimmered like ink, catching the sunlight. The shape was revealed. I frowned as I tried to force the memory to the surface of my mind.

I carefully folded back the cloth at the heaviest end. Red light flashed into my eyes as the sunlight was captured and forced out as a blood-red flare. The ruby eyes of the dragon seemed to bore into my soul as I gasped in recognition.

'My father's sword,' I breathed.

'*Your* sword,' Drey corrected quietly.

I traced the embossed design with my fingers, reconnecting with the teeth, nostrils, horns, scales, wings, talons, tail. Warmth spread from my fingertips deep into the core of me. The sensations of home and safety that words could not express. A feeling of acceptance and belonging. I removed the rest of the silk, tears stabbing at my eyes as I bit my lip to prevent the onslaught of emotions that was threatening to shatter me. The smooth leather of the scabbard brought back so many memories. As clearly as if it had happened yesterday, I remembered the bargain with Laken when the scabbard was given in exchange for me going to Liegeport with him. His big hands as he adapted it for my seven-year-old body.

The sword slipped easily from the protective sheath, releasing a whisper of air as the metal slid along the oiled leather. The blade seemed covered with a thin layer of smoke as the light played over the iron. The engravings writhed in response to the touch of the Sun God. Scratches I couldn't read but had seen before. Shapes that I knew belonged to the old ways. The time of magick and of the Ancients. The time of the Gods. I held the sword out, testing its weight and balance. It seemed shorter and lighter than I remembered. I smiled as I realised that this was probably due to my having been a child when I had last seen it, held it, used it. Drey remained silent and still as I admired and caressed the sword. My smile melted slowly as I turned to him.

'Thank you.'

He shook his head in dismissal. 'It's your sword. You're old enough now to be able to hold on to it.'

I ran my fingers over the characters engraved on the blade, then reluctantly re-sheathed it and placed it across my knees.

'It's part of your heritage,' continued Drey. 'It may help protect you.' I ignored the catch in his voice as he said those words. 'I have done extensive research. Most of the information comes from myths, legends and rumours. Nothing factual. No reliable accounts—'

'Drey,' I interrupted kindly. 'What did you find?'

He hesitated. 'There were five swords forged in the fire mountains of the south. Each represented a virtue that was required by those entrusted with the weapons. The Ancients infused the swords with spells and blessings so that the blades would protect against magick and mystical creatures. They were bound to the holder, accepting only those who were deemed worthy. Forever linked to their kin. Passed down through countless generations, but staying true to the bloodline of the original bearers.'

Drey paused to make sure I was giving due respect to the sword I held in my hands. That I appreciated the history interwoven with the sword, and understood the responsibilities of owning it.

'Tallen. The swords were given to one of the favoured, by the Ancients. A small number of humans to whom the Ancients bestowed real magick so that they could watch over creation and protect from daemons and evil spirits. They acted as overlords. Stewards of the Gods.'

He paused again, making me look up from the ruby stare contained in my sword. 'You may be the direct descendant of an original sword-bearer.' His eyes glistened brightly as he appraised me. His breathing was rapid, and blotches of red had appeared on his cheeks and down his neck. 'I believe you are a Dragonslayer, Tal. You have the ability to destroy dragons.'

Chapter Two

We left later that day. Drey had brought a battle-trained gelding for me to return to Liegeport. He was well trained and allowed me to ride him, although he displayed his discomfort with frequent snorts and one ear constantly turned in my direction. I spent the journey considering all that Drey had said regarding the sword now tapping at my hip in time with the gelding's steps. The baldric fitted well enough now I had grown, and it felt good to have its reassuring presence again, but I couldn't dislodge the heavy weight of responsibility that sat in my abdomen. It seemed, once again, that fate had plans for me. I suspected that I would not enjoy what they had in store.

As we neared the city my thoughts were dominated by those I had left behind. There would not be many to welcome me home, but plenty who would have preferred me to stay away. Breya would be married to Kade by now, making her Queen-in-Waiting. She would be more powerful and more dangerous than before. I had hoped that she would no longer carry a hatred for me now I had nothing left for her to take, but our enmity had lasted many years, so I prepared myself to face her displeasure. More of a threat was her personal bodyguard, Rolyan. His hatred for me was mean and spiteful. It had festered while I had the protection of Kade into something that frightened me. I knew that he gained pleasure from my fear, and I did not like to admit that I was truly scared of him. I would do all I could to avoid him.

And then there was Kade. I had no idea how I would feel about seeing him again, or how he would react to me. It had been nearly two years since we had last seen each other. I could still clearly picture his face. The sprinkling of freckles over his nose. The creases at the corners of his mouth. The melting chestnut eyes. The unruly hair that refused to obey court standards of conformity. I smiled as I remembered his face and was rewarded with the image of his easy, open-mouthed grin that revealed small, perfect teeth. The memory infused a warmth that flowed through my guts to be immediately turned into a searing flame that pierced my heart as I recalled how we had parted. His acceptance of the betrothal to Breya. A marriage of state, to honour a treaty rather than fulfil the romance in his bard's heart. The weight of responsibility on becoming his father's heir after his brother's violent death, and having to suppress his free spirit. The look of fear in his eyes after I had retrieved his soul from Mobis's Hells. The hurt from being faced with something so beyond his understanding in someone he thought he knew so completely.

I would not think of that either.

Instead I remembered the colours, sounds and smells of the royal city. The market stalls covered with brightly coloured material. The goods for sale ranging from practical footwear and eating utensils, to fine silks and bejewelled statues. My fingers tingled at the memory of gold, sapphires, rubies and emeralds. Of coloured glass and shiny metal. Of pendants and brooches, daggers and goblets. I thought of the times I ran the clifftops with Tawpin. His quick humour and love of mischief kept me amused and infuriated in equal measure. We would watch the ships tie up at the docks, wondering what treasures they had brought from faraway lands. We would help the fishing folk with the morning's catch before returning to the city, where the smell of hot pies made our stomachs grumble and saliva flood our mouths. More often than not we would 'obtain' a couple of pies before returning to the royal residence. Tawpin had been my only true friend left in Liegeport. I wondered briefly if that friendship still remained, before smiling at the memory of him in the Blue Boar, chasing the barmaid for a kiss while she beat him off with empty tankards. Somehow, he always got the kiss.

'We're nearly there.'

Drey's voice made me startle after so long in silence. The light had started to fade, and the landscape was dotted with tiny fires. I stared at the scene that had changed so much since I had left. Extending in a half-moon from clifftop to clifftop around the clan capital were the signs of an army's presence. Sleeping shelters could be seen surrounding the fires, covering several fields around the city and two fields deep from the city walls. Cleared spaces had been left for mounted drills, while others had been provided for close combat skills. Several soldiers were fighting in numerous small, circular arenas, the flames from the torches intermittently reflected on their blades as they twisted and turned. I could hear the repetitive clang from the blacksmith's forge, as far away as we were on the rise. The camp was organised and active. The war had come to Liegeport.

'So many men,' I breathed, shocked at the number of soldiers present.

Drey's voice remained quiet and steady. 'Kyllian's conscription has called for every young man over thirteen summers to present himself to his lord. Half of those were sent here. This is the second intake. The first recruits were sent to the front in the spring. This lot will be ready for next summer's campaigns.'

I turned to face him. 'This must be killing the kingdom.'

Drey looked at me with sadness tugging at the corners of his eyes. 'The king had no choice. While you were hiding in the woods, Faulknar lost more territory. Our border has been pushed back so that the front line now stands along the estates of Neasden and Crowhill. Almost a fifth of the kingdom has been taken or is no longer habitable.'

There was no blame in Drey's tone, but I felt the shame anyway. The loss of that much land would have cost so many lives.

'And Villermir?'

Drey snorted in contempt. 'Rumours and gossip. Nothing substantial. But earth tremors are frequently reported. Areas far from rivers have been flooded. Large cracks have appeared in fields. Trees have fallen without the aid of strong winds.'

'He's gaining control of the Empathy Crystal.'

'I believe so.'

I shivered as a cold hand touched the base of my neck and sent tendrils of chill down my spine. Lindvane had the advantage of numbers with Hilman and Gallowgla as allies. The last thing Faulknar needed was a traitorous priest using an ancient magickal artefact to undermine the very ground our troops were walking on. I knew it would erode the confidence of the superstitious experienced campaigners as well as the fearful new recruits.

The sun had set by the time we reached the main gate. Despite the garrison camped outside, the gates were bolted and Drey had to bang on the wood repeatedly before the guard arrived to allow us through. Although it was still early evening, the streets were quiet. The markets had closed, with only a few of the merchant houses still selling their goods. There was an air of suspicion in the hurried glances and the bowed heads. People were busily finishing up the tasks of the day so they could return to the safety of their homes. The atmosphere in the stables was less inhibited and the familiar sights and smells of the men and horses confirmed that I had, indeed, arrived home. The soldiers and grooms went about their tasks efficiently, paying little attention to the presence of Drey and his as-of-late-errant apprentice. The horses were taken from us and my gelding shook out the tension that had tightened his back muscles before I had even walked away.

I had barely made it halfway across the courtyard when a familiar voice called out.

'Magpie!'

I turned to see Tawpin striding across the courtyard. He had grown a little in the time I had been away, but more noticeably had added bulk to his frame. He was wearing the black uniform of the senior staff, with a gold sash displaying Kade's heraldic banner of a white lightning spear. His ridiculous smile was reassuringly familiar, and I found myself responding with a wide-mouthed grin of my own.

'Magpie,' he repeated as he raised me in a suffocating embrace. 'You're home.' He nuzzled his head into my neck and repeatedly kissed the skin.

'Tawpin! Put me down, you big ox.'

My attempt at chastisement was ruined by the giggles I couldn't keep restrained. He squeezed me tighter, giving me one final, noisy kiss before placing me back on the floor.

'You've lost weight,' he commented, ruffling my ragged hair.

I ignored the snort of agreement from Drey and slapped Tawpin's hand away from my hair. 'And you've gained weight. Where'd those muscles come from?'

His smile grew wider as he beamed with pride. He flexed his bicep so that the material of his tunic strained against it. I raised an eyebrow to show I was not impressed. He was not fooled, and it was good to hear him laugh.

'And you've been promoted,' I continued, lightly slapping him on the chest over Kade's crest.

He bowed dramatically. 'Duke Tawpin of Kingsport. Equerry to His Grace Kade Faulknar, heir to the throne of Faulknar. At your service.'

I returned the bow in courtly style. 'Suits you. Kade must be very pleased with you.'

Tawpin groaned. 'I doubt it. There's always something I haven't done right. Or just haven't done. The other day he complained that I wasn't fitting his armour properly. How else can you fit armour? Should have put his helm on first and then I wouldn't hear him complain.' He grinned to take the judgement out of his words. 'Anyway, I'm not the only one to have changed. You appear to be carrying a sword. And a very nice one at that.'

I followed his gaze to the sword at my hip. My cloak had caught on the hilt when Tawpin had lifted me up. The red stones in the dragon's eyes caught the torch-flame and flickered malevolently. I slowly replaced the material over the hilt, breaking Tawpin's view. He looked up, with disappointment clearly shown on his face. He glanced back down towards the sword, now hidden by my cloak, then returned to look at me. I did not say a word as I held his gaze.

He sighed. 'Well, if that's not a clear statement telling me not to ferret about in other people's business, I don't know what is.'

I smiled. 'Clever boy,' I said, as patronisingly as I could.

He stuck his tongue out at me, and I returned the gesture. It was a nice reminder of our younger selves.

'Have you two finished catching up?' Drey interrupted as he passed me the saddlebags from my gelding.

Tawpin's face crumpled into a picture of disappointment. 'Oh, Drey. I wanted to take Tal to the Blue Boar. We've got so much to catch up on. I've got *so* much gossip to tell her. Please let her come. *Please*.'

Drey shook his head in defeat. 'Fine.' He took back the saddlebags. 'It's not like I'm going to collapse under the weight of taking your belongings to your room.'

I smiled in gratitude, and in acceptance of the fact that I had only brought a few clothes from the cottage. 'Thank you.'

'Don't be back late. I've grown accustomed to the quiet.'

He walked off as Tawpin grabbed my hand and dragged me to the Blue Boar.

The tavern was crowded, and it was several moments before Tawpin saw an available table. We squeezed past the regular drinkers; an assortment of dockers, soldiers and merchants. There were few farmers present, and I suspected that the fields of new recruits discouraged the workers from the surrounding villages from entering the city. The mood was loud and jovial and I felt my grin widening at the familiarity of the inn.

Tawpin elbowed me as we negotiated our way through the crowd. He leaned close to my ear so he could be heard. 'The dockers will kick off later,' he said, nodding towards a small group of well-built men. 'Soldiers receive regular pay to spend on the merchants' wares. Business is booming for both. The dockers, however, are getting less work with the Gallowglass pirates helping themselves to what little is traded with us. They are getting more and more frustrated. Tempers are getting shorter.' He grinned. 'Should be a good show later.'

I hit him on the arm, shaking my head in mock disappointment. His grin grew wider. I shoved him towards the table that was tucked into a far corner, away from the bar. The table was still covered in dirty plates and empty tankards from previous customers. I pushed them to the edge and sat opposite Tawpin.

Despite the crowds, it was not long before Shanna noticed us and came over to clean the table.

'Two large jugs, please, Shanna, and two bowls of your delicious stew.'

She laughed at Tawpin as she picked up the plates and balanced them on one arm, placing the tankards on top. 'Flatter all you like, Master Tawpin. You'll be getting no discount.'

Tawpin stuck out his bottom lip and sulked, crossing his arms over his chest as he slumped further into his chair. Shanna raised a mocking eyebrow at him, not fooled at all by his dramatics. She turned to me and placed her free hand on my shoulder.

'It's good to see you back, Tallen,' she said, gently squeezing my shoulder.

I was momentarily shocked that she had noticed I had gone, before accepting that I had spent a lot of my time in the Blue Boar. 'Thank you.'

She nodded and left, instructing a young girl to fetch two tankards of ale.

Tawpin grinned at me.

'What?'

'See?' he said smugly. 'I wasn't the only one to miss you.'

The girl returned before I had a chance to reply and I was instantly distracted by the size of the drinks.

'Tawpin, are you trying to get me drunk?'

Tawpin perfected the look of innocence. 'Would a gentleman do that?'

'You ain't no gentleman.'

He grinned at me, but did not deny his intention to get me drunk. The ale tasted so good after seasons of spring water. The alcohol rushed pleasantly to my head on the first taste. I removed my cloak, making sure I tucked it around my waist so my sword remained covered. My fingers were tingling slightly already. The food arrived soon after, with a generous portion of meat among the vegetables and grains. A chunk of coarse bread was provided to soak up the dark gravy.

'Mmm,' I sighed contentedly. 'This tastes so good.'

'What have you been living on?' Tawpin asked around a mouthful of bread.

'Anything I could find.'

He sniffed. 'No wonder you've lost weight, then. You're a rubbish cook.'

'Yeah? Well at least I can hunt. I don't jump up and down with excitement every time I see an animal and frighten it away.'

Tawpin frowned miserably. 'I only did that once.'

'That was because you were banned from going on hunts after that.'

He nodded his head in defeat. 'True.'

We raised our tankards and saluted good times.

'So, have you invited me here to mock my cooking skills or did you have some gossip to tell me?'

He smiled. 'My dear Tallen. I always have gossip to tell.'

I lost track of time as I listened to Tawpin recounting colourful stories of life at court. Lord Fenwick had been caught with his wife's maid. Apparently, he had walked with a limp for several weeks after his wife found out. Lord Impingden had been beaten up after failing to repay his gambling debts. He had sold his estate to fund his habit and now had to rely on the charity of his brother. Not a comfortable situation. Lady Kell married, combining the estates of Tule and Lowland to make one of the biggest in Faulknar. I only paid slight attention to the gossip of minor lords and ladies; enough to nod at the appropriate places and keep Tawpin talking. The tavern remained busy as customers came and went. Some stayed and got steadily more drunk. As Tawpin had predicted, the dockers were getting louder as they consumed more alcohol. Insults were occasionally exchanged between them and the soldiers.

Tawpin eventually paused in his ramble to take a large mouthful of ale, draining the jug. I seized the opportunity to ask about those I was interested in hearing about.

'And how's the king?' I asked quietly.

Tawpin stared at the empty tankard. He hesitated for so long I was starting to think he was not going to answer. 'Kyllian is still grieving,' he said without looking up. 'He has a quicker temper than before. Takes most of his frustration out on Kade. He knew it had to be done, but he was angry at having to call for conscription. Says he's betrayed his people's trust, forcing them to lose their sons. He looks old.'

'And Breya?'

Tawpin looked up and rolled his eyes at me. 'She is as annoying as ever. Prancing around the place like she's the queen already. Rearranging furniture and ordering more drapes.' He leaned forward. 'She's even changing some of the tapestries, replacing the more depressing ones with pretty flowers and fluffy animals. Would you believe it? There's a war on. Says it's times like these when it is the royal duty to raise the morale of *her* people. *Her* people! She's never had a moment's concern about *her* people before. I find it hard to believe she has suddenly developed a conscience.'

'And what about Kade?'

'Oh, Kade ignores her. Happily married couple, those two. If they say two words to each other it's declared a state holiday. I'm sure the temperature in the room drops when they are forced together for formal functions.'

He stopped, watching me closely as if to judge whether to continue. 'He misses you.'

'He does not,' I denied instantly, but not before my stomach had twisted sharply.

'He's miserable.'

'Being married to Breya would do that to anyone.'

Tawpin's lips flickered in a small smile. 'True. But Kade is really miserable.'

'Times are hard for a lot of people.' I drained my tankard. 'That's why we have friends and ale.'

As I intended, Tawpin smiled and the mournful mood dissipated. I turned to order more drinks.

Just then, a docker leapt onto a table, using it to launch himself onto a soldier. The muscular docker easily flattened the young guard, who had the upper arms of an archer but little bulk elsewhere. The encounter acted like a stone being dropped in a puddle. Ripples of drunk, angry men spread in all directions. Fists flew. Heads connected. Legs kicked. Chairs smashed. Tables toppled. The merchants seemed to have left earlier, and the whole tavern appeared to erupt.

I looked back at Tawpin, who was laughing. 'Breya can keep her tapestries. There's nothing like a good brawl to boost morale.'

'Duke Tawpin, you give wise counsel. I suggest we do our duty and join in.'

He stood up, neatly avoiding a tankard that had been thrown. He bowed formally to me, indicating that I should proceed. I inclined my head in acknowledgement, before rising and turning in the same movement to punch the soldier standing next to me.

We were soon enveloped in the fighting melee. Dodging more punches than we threw. Always keeping an eye on the other to ensure the situation did not get too serious. Merrily changing allegiances depending on who surrounded us. It was a riotous end to my first day back in Liegeport.

'Are you planning on getting up at any point today?'

Drey's disapproval bore into my sensitive head to join the stabs of light from the window I had failed to shutter the previous night. Keeping my eyes closed, I cautiously touched my swollen cheek. The movement tugged at my tender ribs, making me groan as I tried not to breathe. The sound echoed around the cavern of my head, adding new discomfort to the crushing ache I already had there. My stomach flipped as I sat up, and I swallowed repeatedly to relieve the nausea.

I vowed to kill Tawpin the next time I saw him.

I had slept in my clothes, so changed into a new tunic that was slightly less crumpled, pulling the sleeves down to cover my scars. It seemed I had mislaid my cloak, but I was relieved to see my sword lying on the chair. The cold stone made my feet tingle as I walked into the main room and saw Drey sitting at the desk. He turned to face me.

'Oh. You are alive, then.'

I grimaced, whispering, 'Would it be all right if we talked very quietly for the rest of the day?'

'No,' he replied flatly. 'You brought it on yourself. You should know better than to go drinking with Tawpin.'

I sank into one of the padded chairs near the fire. 'I know,' I sighed. Then smiled. 'It was a good night.'

'Humph.' Drey rose and walked over to the fire, where a small kettle was gently steaming. He poured the hot water into a beaker that had been resting on the hearth, releasing an aroma of mint from the leaves. He agitated the tea, crushing the leaves with a spoon until the desired colour was achieved. Throwing the used leaves onto the fire, he passed the cup to me before sitting in the chair opposite.

He nodded in acknowledgement as I thanked him, watching me take a few sips before continuing. 'I have to go out for the rest of the day, but I've left some work for you to do.'

I groaned dramatically.

'Be grateful it's quiet work. I'm sure you have questions, so I have left out all the scrolls and ledgers that mention the Ancients and their use of humans.'

He indicated the desk where he had been sitting. Two large ledgers were placed at the far end, with four smaller ones next to them. The leather was cracked and faded, making them look old and used. A number of scrolls were scattered over the surface of the desk. I stared at them for several heartbeats as the implications spun around inside my head. Information on the Ancients who had made the Empathy Crystal and my sword. The favoured humans who were empowered with divine gifts. The Dragonslayers. The protectors, as Villermir had called me. Answers to the many questions I had about my own talents that lay latent, waiting for the trigger to release them into my control. The secret of who I was. What I was.

I turned back to Drey, who had remained silent, watching me. 'Don't get your hopes up. There's not much information, but it's more than you have at present. I should have told you before.'

'I wouldn't have believed any of it. Not sure I totally believe it now; that somehow I am involved with all this.' I paused to ensure Drey understood what this meant to me. 'Thank you, Drey.'

He stood up, waving his hand in dismissal. 'Just make sure you eat something.'

I smiled at his concern as he left our chambers. I finished my tea, thinking of all the questions I wanted to ask. What powers would I have? What were the dragons like? Would my sword have special properties? But mainly, what powers would I have?

As Drey had told me at the cottage, there was little information on my sword. Five swords were forged, identical but for the different stones set in the dragons' eyes. Rubies had been placed in the sword that currently lay in my room. The others boasted emeralds, amethysts, yellow diamonds and jet. The iron was cast in the fires of Mount Khaluea, folded and layered for days before the Gods were satisfied. Runes of power were engraved on the blades by senior Druids; the breath of the Gods used to blend the characters into the metal, so no scratch could be felt. Each sword possessed a different power, but I could find no reference to what those powers were. A sword each was given to the five chosen by the Gods to protect the land and those who lived upon it. The Dragonslayers.

I could find no more information on the swords.

The Ancients were discussed in detail; an advanced civilisation living with the physical presence of their Gods. The people lived in harmony with the land and the animals with which they shared their environment. All things were respected as having a soul, including mountains, rocks, plants and trees. They were times of plenty, with the seasons controlled by the Gods to ensure bountiful harvests. Animals offered themselves as honoured sacrifices so that others could eat. Culture developed, resulting in a society full of philosophers, poets, bards and sculptors. Disease was controlled with the use of plants and herbs, and ordinary people were skilled in the healing arts. It was a time of spiritual completeness, a paradise of compassion and joy.

Within the ancient society were those chosen to be more than human. Druids and priestesses catered for the spiritual well-being of those in their care. The Druids were the keepers of knowledge. They were singers and storytellers, ensuring the oral traditions were remembered. They represented the earth, able to nurture the plants and harness the powers of rocks. The priestesses provided compassion and temperance. They were healers of the soul as well as the body. Their element was the air, drawing strength from the winds. These favoured humans acted as stewards for the Gods. They oversaw the day-to-day life of the people, animals, plants and rocks to ensure all thrived.

But not all Gods were benevolent and respected free will. Some considered humans as playthings to be used and disposed of at their whim. They obtained energy from the souls of those taken. Created daemons to terrorise and subjugate. Required obedience and sacrifice.

Favoured humans were needed to protect from these threats. While Druids and priestesses were numerous, the higher orders were very selective. Few humans were deemed worthy and capable of receiving the power of the Gods. Four groups were selected to serve against the malevolent deities and their daemons; men and women tasked with ensuring survival. The Aqualine took the element of water. They could control rivers and oceans. They had the power to create torrential storms or cause a drought. They could breathe under water, swimming as fast as a seal, and battled sea serpents. The Firewalkers controlled fire, from the small spark of anger in a lost temper to the erupting fire mountains that spewed molten lava. They could provide warmth in the freezing depths of winter or devastating firestorms during the heat of summer.

The final two were beyond the call of the elements, having full mastery over all. The Empaths had a telepathic link to all aspects of the created world. They communicated directly with the Gods as well as humans, animals, plants and rocks. They connected to the spirit of all living things, whether that individual's spirit lasted moments or aeons. Permissions could be granted. Knowledge could be obtained. Structure could be changed. The Empaths controlled the life force of all. Only seven individuals were permitted to control the power of the Empaths. And this was two more than those selected as Dragonslayers. Such was their power that only five were needed to protect the world from the dangerous, vengeful Gods and their daemons. The Dragonslayers were the Gods' personal bodyguards, tasked with protecting humans from all threats, including the Gods themselves if necessary. They could level mountains. They could drain the oceans. They could tear open the sky. They mastered the most powerful creatures ever to have existed: the dragons.

My mind whirled with images of dragons and Dragonslayers. How could I possess one of the five swords forged for these mythic warriors? If the stories were true, how could I hope to control even a fraction of their powers? Abilities direct from the Gods, capable of defeating Gods. I rubbed my eyes to ease the headache lodged in the middle of my forehead. This was so far beyond my understanding. It was a faerie tale, a story told to amuse children. How could Drey be taking this seriously? Why would Villermir believe that I held the key to these ancient talents? I could not begin to comprehend all the information, much less the implications. I chose not to follow this line of enquiry any further. I turned my attention to dragons.

Information on dragons was sparse. It seemed that very few people had seen a dragon, and most of those had been killed by the beasts. The accounts told of destruction of villages and livestock; people consumed by rivers of fire breathed from the dragon's mouth. The draught from their wings could topple a horse. Their talons could pierce rock. Despite their size, they could fly almost without making any sound. Descending on their victims without warning, tearing great chunks with rapier-sharp teeth and claws. The muscles of a dragon's neck could rip limbs from joints as it shook its prey like a terrier, its roar of challenge carrying enough force to fell trees.

Other reports told of their beauty. Iridescent scales rippling with colour. The grace of their movement as the giant creatures soared over the mountains and lakes. The effortless power contained in the contoured muscles of their chests and thighs. Their delicate wings that belied the immense resilience needed to support the massive weight of the dragon during flight. The intellect behind their jewelled eyes. I was very glad that the dragons had disappeared along with the Ancients and the Dragonslayers. Grateful that I would not have to face one; that any potential skills I possessed would not be tested on such a beast.

I rubbed my eyes again, closing the ledger. The room had darkened, and the fire had died back to smouldering embers. I stretched my cramped back muscles before building up the fire and heating the kettle for some peppermint tea taken from Drey's room. I curled up in the padded chair to try to make sense of all the information I had read. The tea grew cold in my hands as I gazed into the fire, my mind conjuring images from the flames of flying dragons. Diving over villages. Pouring fire over the small wooden huts. Grasping livestock in their powerful claws. Leg muscles bulging as they took the strain. High-pitched calls splitting the air as the creatures called to each other; a sound that chilled the bones of those hearing it. An animal perfectly designed for terror and destruction.

The images faded as my stomach grumbled in response to the smell of cheese. I blinked away the scenes of burning within the flames and turned to see Drey standing in front of me with a plate of cheese and biscuits.

'I presume you didn't eat,' he scolded as he passed the plate to me.

My mumbled thanks were a clear confession. He watched me eat for a few heartbeats as I cleared the final images from my mind.

'What did you see?' he asked. 'In the flames?'

I smiled guiltily. 'Dragons.'

He nodded. 'That would be right.' He sat down in the chair opposite me and relaxed into the seat. 'They were strange times.'

I shook my head. 'How can you believe in those tales? They're just stories.'

'True. The accounts are myths and legends. Facts have been exaggerated. Inconvenient truths have been removed. Political statements have been added by those in power. But strip away the decorations and there will always be a grain of truth within these stories. The difficulty lies in determining which part is truth and which is exaggeration.'

I shook my head, still disbelieving. 'But...'

'You've seen the power of the Empathy Crystal,' Drey persisted. 'You know what those like Villermir... like me... are capable of. You know what you did to rescue Kade.'

The silence became heavy as I tried to combine the world I had grown up with – the daily life of Liegeport and the war with the Lindvanes, everyday survival – with the fantasy of dragons and Gods and people who could breathe under water. Could I dare to believe such things had existed? That such talents could still exist? Could exist in *me*?

Chapter Three

My preparation began the next morning. I was to report to Langdon for a review of my fighting ability. I had hunted at the cottage, so I knew my throwing and archery skills had been maintained, but I had not wielded a sword since leaving Lindvane. Over two years had passed since I had fought. I knew my reactions would be slow and my muscles would no longer support sustained tension.

Walking through the streets of Liegeport from the royal house to the practice arena was so familiar it was almost as if I had never been away. Almost. The roads were quieter. People hurriedly went about their business. Idle conversation was rare. There were more soldiers about, and most of them were unknown to me. A small number had darker skin than those native to Faulknar. Their long black hair was braided with coloured cord. Their close-fitting, brightly dyed tunics were fastened with cross-straps of leather. Their heavy swords were clearly displayed within the walls of the city. A few soldiers had skin tones similar to that of the three heraldic kingdoms, but were mainly blond or had light brown hair. These soldiers wore fur-lined gambesons over plain shirts. The stitching of the leather suggested great care had been taken over the items. Each one was uniquely embroidered with intricate patterns and designs, interwoven with animals from the hunt. Their swords were shorter and finer than the heavy weapons preferred by Kyllian's troops, but longer than a rapier. These men watched closely as I passed by.

I entered the arena via the underground tunnel. The sand had been raked smooth, with lines made by the teeth of the rake drawing numerous shallow slashes across the open space. No footsteps had crossed the sand since it had been combed. I could see no one in the stands. I frowned in confusion, wondering if Langdon had forgotten our arrangement or if he had been called away on urgent business. I returned through the stone archway under the stands. Two soldiers were leaving the courtyard, but otherwise it was deserted. I decided to go into the armoury on my left, assuming this was the best place to find someone who would know where Langdon was.

The armoury smelt of waxed leather and oiled steel. I breathed in deeply, savouring the familiar scents while my eyes adjusted to the softer lighting. Benches were lined up down the centre of the long, thin room to allow soldiers to dress in plated hauberks, wrist bracers and shin guards. These protective items, along with padded tunics and helms, were stacked neatly along the walls. Each size was represented by several sets. A solid oak desk, standing against the far wall, effectively split the room into two and bore numerous scratches and chips that been gouged by armour and weapons.

'Sir,' I began, as I approached the armoury clerk. 'I'm looking for Langdon. Do you know where I may find him?'

Nemy continued to write in the ledger, not bothering to look up and acknowledge me. 'The Master of Arms is training at the fallow training ground.'

I took a breath, endeavouring to remain polite. 'I'm afraid I don't know where that is.'

He sighed noisily through his nose, clearly displeased with the interruption. He raised his gaze to look disdainfully at my ragged hair and patched clothing. He sniffed. 'Some of us have been busy while others deserted the family who took them in and supported them.'

'That's not fair,' I snapped, before clenching my teeth against further protest. It was not his fault that he knew nothing of the attack by Villermir. It wasn't his fault that I failed to retrieve the Empathy Crystal.

'I have a training session at the fallow,' said a slightly accented female voice to my right. 'I can show you the way.'

The second half of the room stored the swords, knives and crossbows. The clerk's desk was positioned so that no one could obtain a weapon without his permission. I knew he had a loaded crossbow below his desk, ready to use if necessary. I turned to see a female soldier dressed in a rusty orange tunic that fitted closely at the waist and forearms but allowed free movement at the shoulders. The cross-laced fastenings were similar to those I had seen earlier, and her long black hair was plaited with orange ribbon. Her warm brown eyes twinkled with mischief as she smiled at me.

'We wouldn't want to disturb Nemy for longer than we need to, would we?'

The clerk shot a glare at the soldier, suspecting some insult, but could find no fault with her words or manner. I watched as she collected three throwing knives and walked over to sign out the weapons in the ledger. Female soldiers were occasionally found in Kyllian's ranks, but it was unusual. Her appearance suggested she might have come from the Travellers' lands to the south, although I was unaware of these traders using women fighters any more than in Faulknar.

She introduced herself as we left the armoury. 'Erula,' she said as she concealed the knives within her tunic.

'Tallen.'

'Pleased to meet you, Tallen. What was the Nemy on about back there? He got a personal grudge against you or something?'

I shook my head. 'I don't think so. It's a long story but the short version is that I left Liegeport several seasons ago, just as it started to get busy around here.' I nodded towards the armed guards walking the streets. 'Seems there are soldiers on every corner.'

'Mercenaries, mainly. Hired hands to boost the numbers and provide some experience in a company of new recruits.'

'So, are you a mercenary?'

Her laugh was light and musical. 'I prefer to think of myself as a freedom fighter.'

I frowned. 'What's the difference?'

'I'm more choosy about who I will fight for. I have some morals. I fight for the cause, not for the glory.' She shrugged. 'It means I get paid less.'

I smiled as we continued to talk comfortably about the changes in Liegeport as we walked towards the makeshift military camp outside.

The fallow training ground was a small clearing within the centre of the nearest field to the right of the main gates. We passed through rows of sleeping shelters where men mended clothing, cleaned tack or sharpened weapons. I was surprised at how young they all looked. Barely older than me, they all carried a hint of bewilderment in their eyes. The combat area was circular, about forty paces in diameter. The ground had a sprinkling of sand on top to delay the earth turning to mud as it was churned by numerous boots. There were three pairs of female soldiers arranged around the outer boundary of the ring. Each was armed with a sword and a belt dagger. Two had their swords sheathed along their backs so the blades could be drawn over their heads. All wore leather trousers and a close-fitting coloured tunic. I noted that most had sleeves that finished at the elbow, while two had sleeves of the same design as Erula's. Half the women had dark hair gathered into a tail with coloured ribbons, while the other half had fair hair.

Standing next to the pair on my left were Langdon and his captain. Langdon had his back to me, but I smiled as I recognised his broad shoulders and bare, muscled arms. Captain Casial nodded in acknowledgement, placing a hand on Langdon's shoulder to get his attention. Casial had been a soldier in Laken's company and had risen rapidly through the ranks. His amiable nature ensured he was well liked, despite several times being promoted over those that were older and had more experience. His skill had always been evident, and I was not surprised that Langdon had made him his captain.

Langdon smiled broadly as he turned and walked towards me. 'Tallen,' he boomed from across the arena, making everyone turn to look at me. 'So good to have you back.'

I smiled self-consciously. 'It's good to see you too, sir.'

'Pah!' He threw his hands up in dismissal. 'Enough of the "sir" malarkey. You know I can't be bothered with all that.' He grew serious, nodding to where my hand was resting on the hilt of my sword. 'Let's see what you can do with your new friend.'

My hand instinctively gripped tighter, reluctant to draw attention to the sword in case he wanted to claim it. A heartbeat later I conceded that, as Master of Arms, Drey had probably entrusted it to Langdon when I had first arrived at Liegeport and was too young to keep the blade. I forced my fingers to release their hold and removed the light cloak from my shoulders. My tunic had long, loose sleeves that flapped around my wrists. I tightened the laces at the cuffs, but still frowned at the irritation. I took a deep breath to calm my turbulent stomach and drew my sword.

Erula gasped as the sunlight flashed on the polished silver metal. The rubies in the dragon's eyes sparkled as if eager to engage in combat. The air hummed as I sliced the blade. Up and down. Left and right. Loosening taut ligaments in my wrists, elbows and shoulders. My two-handed hold fitting comfortably on the handle. I saw Langdon frown as my cuffs caught on the pommel.

'That's a nice weapon,' Erula breathed.

I looked up to see her staring at the blade with the obvious desire I had seen in others when they first saw the sword.

'I know,' I replied flatly.

My tone broke the hold of her gaze and she lifted her eyes to look at me. She smiled. 'Let's see what she can do.'

Erula released her own sword and cut at my raised blade in one fluid movement. The force of the contact sent concussive waves up my arms. I had to tighten my grip to avoid dropping the weapon as my fingers tingled. I turned the angle of my sword to slice at Erula's legs, but she easily blocked my move. I smiled as I stepped back, and she returned the gesture. We had assessed each other's skills and knew we would be evenly matched.

I flicked my cuffs away from the hilt and attacked Erula's shoulders, slashing left, then right, then left again in quick succession. I forced her to take several steps backwards. She twisted out of my reach before launching her own attack and reclaiming the lost ground. The cuffs again tangled around my sword handle.

'Oh, this will never do,' grumbled Langdon. 'Tallen, fold your sleeves up. You can't fight with those laces flapping everywhere.'

I hesitated. 'Langdon, I…'

'Come on, child. Hurry up.'

I clenched my teeth against further protests, realising how feeble they would sound. Gripping the sword tightly with one hand, and keeping my eyes fixed on the ground, I rolled one sleeve up to my elbow, repeating with the other. I heard Langdon and Erula draw in their breath. I could feel their stares on the ruins of my arms. Spider-web patterns of raised pink welts, where damaged tissue had healed, covered my arms from hand to elbow. Angry red blotches filled in the gaps where the skin had been burnt. Small black pits dotted the blotches where vessels had been seared away. I rounded my shoulders protectively as the silence dragged on.

Langdon cleared his throat. 'I'm sorry, Tallen. I didn't know.'

I looked at him and tried to smile. 'It's all right. It's fine.'

'Wait here,' he said as he walked briskly away from the arena and disappeared into a nearby shelter.

'Is that the reason you left Liegeport?' asked Erula quietly.

I shrugged. 'One of many reasons. I needed time to heal. It was easier for all concerned if I did that away from the city.'

We stood, suddenly uncomfortable in each other's presence. I ineffectually tried to cover the scars by folding my arms or crossing my wrists. I was about to suggest that we should continue to spar when Langdon reappeared carrying two archer's wrist bracers.

'Here,' he said, passing the leather bands to me. 'They may be a little big but there's room in the straps to punch more holes if needed.'

The dark brown leather was well worn and soft. The brushed inner layer covered my scars comfortably, extending from my wrists to three finger-widths below my elbows. The scars were still visible on my hands and above the leather bracers, but they were a lot less noticeable. Langdon used the point of his belt dagger to gouge new holes higher up the restraining straps, so the buckles could tighten and prevent slippage. I executed a few warm-up exercises with the sword to check their position, smiling at Langdon in approval.

'Right then,' he bustled. 'Let's get some work done. Erula, work her hard. I want to see how much stamina has been lost these past seasons.'

Erula smiled, her eyes sparkling with mischief again. 'With pleasure.'

By the time we broke for the midday meal I was on my knees. Erula had pushed me continuously, with occasional adjustment or correction from Langdon or Casial. She had tested my strength and reaction speed as well as my knowledge, mixing in moves I had not seen before with the more familiar attacks. My shoulders felt like they were being pierced by a red-hot poker. Sparks of flame shot down my arms whenever I moved them. My thighs throbbed painfully in time to my racing pulse. I panted as I sucked in lungfuls of air, but was pleased to see Erula breathing hard as well. The final move came when Langdon called for an end to the morning's practice. The soldiers walked towards where I was kneeling in the sand.

I was distracted for less than a heartbeat.

Erula sliced her sword under mine. The blades screamed as she dragged the edge of her blade along mine, twisting it out of my grip. The blade flashed briefly as it flew through the air to land a few paces away from her.

She smiled triumphantly. 'Seems we've found the limit of your stamina.'

I groaned in defeat as my muscles protested at the sudden movement. Erula turned to pick up my sword. Her hand stopped just above the hilt; frozen in place. Her fingers trembled as a small frown creased her forehead. Her head tilted slightly to one side. She closed her fingers above the sword and stood, then checked to ensure I was watching her before using the toe of her boot to flick the blade back to me. The dragon eyes glinted eagerly as it returned to my hand. I dipped my head in acknowledgement and gripped the hilt tightly, grateful to feel its weight again.

Langdon walked past me, placing a hand on my shoulder. 'Well done.'

I smiled.

'Same time tomorrow.'

The smile faded as I anticipated more painful muscles. I closed my eyes as Erula laughed at my discomfort.

'Come,' she said. 'Share a meal with us, and you can tell me the long story you avoided telling earlier.'

She offered her hand, and I was grateful for the assistance with rising. Erula led us out of the arena and past several rows of sleeping quarters before stopping at a circle of shelters around a small hearth. One of the women who had been training with us earlier prepared and lit a fire while Erula indicated for me to sit. I groaned as my muscles protested and I landed heavily on the ground. Erula laughed, sitting lightly next to me with no obvious ill effects from our earlier fighting. The soldiers disappeared inside their shelters. Each returned a handful of heartbeats later carrying plates, mugs, bread or cheese. A tall woman with straight black hair and green eyes introduced herself as Parin as she placed a pan of water over the newly lit fire, adding some leaves to make a tea. Erula introduced everyone and we chatted easily about the morning's session.

She was not distracted for long. 'So what's your story, Tallen? How did you come to be at Liegeport?'

I took a mouthful of tea, buying some time while I decided how much I could tell her. Her face was open and her eyes direct: I could see no deceit or motive hidden there. Regardless, I told only the selected highlights that most people in the city would know. I talked about Laken and how he took me in after my parents died. I spoke of how he was killed. My time spent in North End, running wild through the streets with cut-throats and thieves. I recounted how Drey had offered to raise and educate me in exchange for loyalty to Kyllian and Faulknar.

Erula interrupted me for the first time. 'Just your loyalty?'

I turned to look at her, trying to judge her motive for asking such a question. Her face remained relaxed with only an eyebrow raised enquiringly. The others also showed interest, but not overly so.

'I was required to provide certain… services.'

Erula's eyebrow raised higher as Parin choked on a mouthful of bread.

'Oh really?' Parin spluttered. 'Dirty old man.'

Heppra, a slim, fair-haired woman sitting next to her, slapped her playfully on the arm. 'Parin. Get your filthy mind out of the bedchamber. Not everyone has your low standards.'

I smiled as the others laughed at their friend. 'Nothing like that,' I amended quickly. 'I'm good at being invisible. I can get into places without being seen.'

Etard leaned forward. 'A spy,' she whispered, her green eyes flashing excitedly.

I shook my head, shrugging with a little embarrassment. 'A thief.'

Etard leaned back again, less impressed now I wasn't a spy. Erula watched me closely and I suspected that she had stored this information for future use.

I changed the subject. 'But what about all of you? How did you come to be in Liegeport? I can't believe Kyllian is conscripting women now.'

Parin huffed dismissively. 'It seems our liege does not feel women are suitable for battle. We should stay at home like good, obedient wives.'

Heppra nodded in agreement. 'Needs us to stay behind and do all the work that should be done by the men he's taken for his war.'

Tiny Iffan played with a strand of her light brown hair. 'Seems we're not "man" enough to fight for our kingdom, but we're "man" enough to toil the fields and fish the oceans.'

'Think he's scared we might cry if we get hurt,' added Etard. 'I'd like to see a man deal with giving birth to a child. That would teach him about pain.'

'I don't think it's the pain Kyllian's worried about,' I said quietly, thinking of the night terrors that tormented me. The deathly faces and vacant eyes of those I had killed. 'War is an ugly business. Wounds heal but the memories remain.'

'We fight because we have something to offer.' Erula spoke for the whole company. 'Lindvane has to be stopped. Hayton rules through intimidation and subjugation. We have to make a stand.'

The soldiers nodded their heads in sad agreement.

'We've learnt to fight to defend ourselves from the raiders.' Muris was a small, delicate woman from the borders of Faulknar. 'There is no distinction of gender there. They come to kill all. I have no one left to defend. I make my stand where I'm needed most.'

'As do we all,' confirmed Erula, smiling encouragingly at the quiet older woman.

The conversation faltered as the soldiers became lost in their private thoughts of why they had come to the capital and pledged their lives to the war against Lindvane. All except Erula, who continued to watch me, as if to determine my reasons for being here. Did I also believe that Lindvane should be stopped? Or was I merely fulfilling an old obligation? I began to feel uncomfortable under such scrutiny.

'I must be going,' I said sharply, breaking the silence. 'Thank you for the food. I'll see you all tomorrow.'

I hastily left while the mood was still sombre. I sought out Kennig to let the woodcutter know I would no longer need his cottage in the forest.

He was wintering in a small wooden shack, easily overlooked between its larger neighbours. He welcomed me enthusiastically and, having few visitors, kept me longer than I had intended. It was growing dark by the time I left. A few light brackets had been lit. Shadows had begun to dance at the edges of the streets as the light wind caused the flames to flutter. I pulled my cloak a little closer around my shoulders to prevent the chill creeping down my neck. Kennig's lodgings were on the far eastern side of the city and I had to walk down several darkened alleyways before reaching the market in the centre of the town.

I eased the tension in my shoulders when I reached the market, scolding myself for jumping at shadows when I was safely within Liegeport. The market was deserted, the coloured stall covers slapping against the empty wooden frames. I took a deep, steadying breath and forced my legs to move at a slower pace, mocking myself for being frightened of the dark when there was nothing to be fearful of.

Then I was grabbed.

Strong hands grasped my cloak and pulled me into a darkened recess. With the dim light from the street torches in front of me, I could not make out any features but was confident that it was a man who attacked me. He stood several hand-widths taller than me. A thick arm pressed against my throat; the other hand knocked my arm away as I reached for my sword. I scratched at the arm against my neck, but it was covered by padded leather and my short nails made no impact.

'Welcome home, Tallen.'

Panic settled into my stomach like a large boulder as my head flushed with sudden heat in recognition of who was restraining me. I struggled desperately against the painful pressure at my throat, using my free hand to jab, club and gouge at any piece of him I could find. I located no skin, my punches and kicks bouncing harmlessly off padding and leather until my wrist was grasped and slammed against the wall. My knees buckled as I fought for air.

'Rolyan, you stinking heap of horse dung,' I rasped. 'What are you doing?'

'I told you not to come back.' His face was so close to mine that I could smell his stale breath as he spoke. 'Things could turn out badly for you.'

He pressed harder on my neck. Black specks dashed erratically across my vision as the pressure in my head grew. He released my wrist and I immediately used it to claw at his arm. I scrabbled for purchase, trying to ease the constriction. My fingers lacked the power to press against the tendons of his wrist and the pressure held. The blood pounded behind my eyes and at my temples.

I suddenly froze as Rolyan stroked his free hand down my chest, lightly brushing each of my breasts. My vision dimmed as my heart raced out of control. My body trembled, while my fingers had turned numb. I could no longer fight him as he moved his hand down my stomach to rest between my thighs.

'Keep looking over your shoulder, Tallen,' he breathed in my ear. 'I'll be watching you.'

He released his hold and I collapsed to the floor, gasping for air, my abused throat seared as I sucked in each breath. My head swam with dizziness as I shook uncontrollably against the wall.

It was a long time before my mind was calm enough to realise that Rolyan had gone.

Drey returned to our rooms late that night. I was still curled up in the chair in front of the fire, watching the flames dance as they consumed the logs. I tried to concentrate on the practice session with Erula, to remember the new moves so I would not be caught out by them the next day. But my mind kept returning to the attack by Rolyan. It had unsettled me more than I cared to admit. Despite all that I had been through in Lindvane, despite all the training I had received from Langdon, I was still reduced to a helpless, quivering girl. It made me feel vulnerable and afraid. It made me feel sick.

I rhythmically stroked my thumb over the smooth surface of the disc nestled safely in the inner pocket of my cloak. The shiny surface had reflected the light of the street torches as I lay crumpled on the ground after Rolyan's attack. As I picked it up, I saw small engravings on a gold pendant the size of a silver coin. The fine-link chain must have snapped during the struggle. I knew it belonged to Rolyan. For as long as I had known him he had shown off the runes promising luck in battle at the slightest opportunity. I traced the markings with my thumb as I sat by the fire. A small smile played at the corners of my lips, knowing he would miss the charm. It gave me the smallest feeling of power over him. That I had something he would want returned. That it was my choice whether to grant him that concession. That tiny hint of power was enough to provide me with an element of control. It would have to be enough.

I looked up to see Drey standing in front of me. His eyebrows were raised questioningly.

'Sorry, Drey.' I felt confused, as if I had just woken up. 'Were you saying something?'

He raised his eyes to the ceiling and shook his head. 'I said, are you cold? You still have your cloak on.'

I avoided answering the question and lowered my eyes to the floor. I shrank a little further into the chair, tucking my chin into the collar of my cloak. Drey remained silent until I raised my eyes to look back at him.

'What's happened?' he asked.

I mumbled a barely audible reply. 'Nothing.'

'Tallen.' His tone held a more commanding tone. 'What happened?'

My hand reflexively went to my collar to ensure it still covered my neck and the bruises Rolyan had given me. It was as good as a confession.

'Show me.'

I did not respond.

'For the love of Mobis, Tallen. Do I have to repeat everything tonight? Show me.'

Reluctantly I removed my cloak and revealed the discoloured skin. The whole area was tender, but I had not looked at the damage. Drey's sharp intake of breath, sucked noisily through his teeth, confirmed the worst.

'Who did this?'

I hesitated before sighing. 'Good news travels fast. Rolyan went out of his way to welcome me home.'

Drey growled. 'That rotting piece of ferret dung. That weasel is without a single shred of decency. I should have wrung his stinking neck when I had the chance.'

I shrugged. 'Rolyan being a bully is nothing new. He just caught me by surprise. It won't happen again.'

Drey's demeanour instantly calmed. He looked at me for several heartbeats. 'No. No it won't.'

He folded into the chair opposite me and steepled his fingers as his elbows rested on the arms of the chair. A slight frown crinkled his forehead. I shuffled in my chair, feeling uncomfortable under his scrutiny. Eventually, he sighed, having made his decision.

'I've put this off for too long. I can delay no longer.' His hazel eyes looked deep into mine to ensure I was paying attention to him. 'We start your training tonight. Let me into your mind.'

I blinked at him. 'What?'

'I need you to allow me access to your mind. I need to assess your abilities and limitations before I show you how to use your magick.'

'But, Drey,' I spluttered, 'I can't let you in. You know this. I have no control over the barriers to my mind. You've always had to hypnotise me before. I can't just open up.'

'Then that is what you have to learn. If you cannot control your protective barriers, you will not be able to harness your magick. Now try.'

I did not know where to start. Feeling foolish, I took a deep breath and settled into a comfortable position. I closed my eyes and concentrated on my breathing. Slowly breathing in. Holding the breath. Slowly breathing out. I tried to empty my mind of the distractions of the room. The smell of the smoke as the flames popped quietly against the burning wood. The feel of soft leather below my fingertips as they rested on my trousers. The dull ache in the muscles of my lower back.

I felt a pressure build behind my eyes, extending into the bone of my left cheek. Instinctively I tensed, pushing against the pressure as I scowled at the pain.

'Don't resist me,' commanded Drey.

It was like the healer telling you to relax just before they cause you pain. I could not refrain from resisting any more than I could stop my heart from beating. Drey tried again and was repelled as before. He sighed softly in defeat.

'Let's try something different. Imagine a room in your head. A room full of doors. Each one will lead to a different memory, a different grain of knowledge. As your magick progresses, more doors will be available to you. Doors that lead to other worlds. Doors that will allow you to communicate with others via the mind. Doors that will allow you to look into another's soul.'

As Drey talked, his smooth, familiar voice eased the tension in my shoulders and back. My breathing deepened as I concentrated on his voice. I pictured the room in my head and removed the furniture piece by piece. I removed the rugs to leave the floorboards bare. The room stayed like that for a couple of heartbeats before the stone walls slowly moved outwards. As the corners separated, bright white light shone into the room. The light spread as the walls and floor moved away so that I was eventually standing in the middle of a pure opal sphere. Gradually, pale grey rectangles appeared randomly. The shapes slowly darkened to reveal doors of different styles floating around the space. They appeared above each other, continuing as far as I could see. They lined up behind each other, disappearing far into the distance. There were ornate doors with decorative carvings next to plain panelled ones. Dark wood doors between light ones. Tall doors twice my height stood next to doors as small as my hand. All gently floating around my vision, slowly moving so that they continually changed position.

A door shimmered in my peripheral vision, attracting my attention. I turned towards a hazy portal. Iridescent colours swirled across a rectangle slightly taller than me. I watched as the colours faded until I could see through the sparkling rainbow mist. A golden shadow formed into the basic outline of a man. Broad shoulders narrowed to a lean torso and straight hips. No features were visible, but I felt a warm, comforting feeling as I watched him approach. He reached out a hand that did not extend through the portal. I confidently reached through the door, grasped the hand and gently pulled the shadow through into the white room.

Drey emerged from the swirling mist. He was taller, straighter, and younger than the man who sat across from me in the royal house. His mousy-brown hair was cut short to his head, framing a smooth face with only a few fine lines at the corners of his eyes that would extend to become the wrinkled face I knew. He stood several hand-widths taller than me and I was forced to look up to see into his face. A slight frown creased his forehead as he looked down at me.

'Is this how you see yourself?' asked Drey within my head. 'You must be – what? – nine, ten years old.'

I looked at my hands held out in front of me. They were smaller than I had expected, and I realised that they were the hands of a child. I was not surprised that I had imagined myself as a nine-year-old, particularly after my encounter with Rolyan had made me feel so vulnerable. I longed to have the protective presence of Laken again, as I had when I was that age.

I smiled at Drey. 'And is that how you see yourself?'

'Well,' he spluttered, 'it seems my body has grown older before my mind is ready.'

I surveyed the white sphere filled with drifting doors. 'This room is amazing, Drey. Is it always this beautiful?'

'Each room is different, reflecting the mind of the individual. Yours is particularly… eccentric.'

'Is that good or bad?'

'It's you.'

We looked at the many doors, noting the different styles and textures of the wood, for several moments before Drey asked me to recall a memory. He started with the training session that morning. As I remembered my meeting with Erula, a plain door moved from behind two others to float directly in front of me. I cautiously lifted the latch and opened the door to reveal the armoury. Drey took my hand and led me through the opening. The memory played out as if we were observers on the morning's activities. I watched my conversation with the armoury clerk, and Erula's offer to take me to Langdon. I recalled every detail of the training session, an onlooker to each stroke and feint.

Drey watched closely as Erula bent to retrieve my fallen sword, paused, and then used her foot to return the blade to my hand. He gave a small grunt, but I could not determine whether he was surprised, pleased or had just had a suspicion confirmed. He turned me around to find the door hovering behind us, ready for our return to the white room. As we stepped through the portal, the door gently closed and floated off to return to its place amongst the others.

'Let's try something a bit harder,' said Drey quietly. 'Show me the first time you held the sword.'

My stomach fluttered in dread as I understood that I would have to recall a time before Liegeport. Before Laken. A time of painful memories involving a cherished family who had been lost in the most violent way. Drey squeezed my hand in support as I hesitated.

As soon as I had decided to retrieve the memory, a large oak door drifted towards us. The panelling was finely carved with patterns intertwined around acorns and berries. There was no latch, but a small area, worn smooth, where I was to push the door open. Drey followed a pace behind as I walked through into a small forest glade. The smell of the tree blossoms brought tears to my eyes as it invoked treasured memories of Methhold. Of home. Small birds darted over the tall grass as they hunted insects on the still spring afternoon. I looked over the meadow to the treeline to see two people emerging from the darkened woods.

My heart constricted painfully, and I could not breathe as I recognised the pair. I was five or six years old, dressed in grass-stained breeches and a torn overshirt. There was dirt on my face as I walked next to my father. He was a tall and rangy man, with black hair like mine and gentle hazel eyes. He chatted away to me as we crossed to the centre of the glade. He was carrying a narrow bundle wrapped in a cloth.

I knew it was the sword.

My father knelt in front of me and removed the material, exposing the sword to the sunlight. Both the remembered child and the one observing gasped as the blade flashed and the rubies glinted in the sun. My father moved to stand behind me and placed the hilt in my small hands, helping to hold the weight that was obviously too heavy for me. We twisted the weapon to make the sunbeams dance over the silver metal. I grinned with sheer joy.

'This is your blade, Tallen.' My father's voice reverberated deeply as he spoke. 'Many generations have held it in trust for you. And now you will use this sword to fulfil your destiny.'

Another person walked slowly from the forest. My father and I did not seem to notice as we focused on the sword. This person was completely covered in a black cloak, the hood covering their face. Slender white hands were softly clasped in front. The hairs stood up on the back of my neck. I had seen her before. In my dreams.

My father continued talking. 'This sword comes with a great responsibility. You must strive to be worthy of its legacy. You have much to learn about your heritage.'

My younger self frowned as I tried to understand what my father was saying. The observer-me was repeatedly drawn to the silent, cloaked figure walking towards us.

'Little one. You will not understand now, but one day you will. One day you will be great.'

The cloaked figure halted five paces from the pair holding the exquisite sword. The fine-boned fingers released their clasp as she slowly raised her hands to reveal pale, delicate wrists.

'You will be remembered in the legends of our age. Tallen, this is the sword of a—'

The cloaked figure clapped her hands together, but it made no sound. The image of the forest glade vanished. For several heartbeats there was nothing but black. No sight. No sound. No smell. No texture.

I blinked and found myself in front of the fire, back in Drey's chambers. Drey sat opposite me, looking surprised and pale.

'What, in all that is holy, was that?' he asked.

'I was hoping you could tell me,' I countered quietly. The sudden removal of my father was felt as a physical wound deep in my chest. I trembled as my mind raced to catch up with what had just happened. I tried to recall what my father had been saying, but could no longer remember the encounter. What I had seen through the oak door slipped from my conscious thoughts as water flowing through fingers, leaving a hollow emptiness that was hard to breathe around.

Neither of us spoke for a very long time.

Chapter Four

I managed to avoid Kade for three weeks. I was not invited to state occasions and I had no formal meetings with the king, and I was kept busy with my daily training sessions with Langdon and evening lessons with Drey. Free time was generally spent in the Blue Boar with Tawpin, and it wasn't long before we had convinced Erula and several of the other female soldiers to join us. Those evenings were frequently rowdy and for a while I was glad to be back in Liegeport.

It was late afternoon and the shadows lengthened as the sun sank behind the town walls. Despite the deepening gloom, few street lights had been lit as fuel was being diverted to the military campaign. It was easy to remain in the shadows and avoid being seen by the townspeople, Faulknar guards and hired mercenaries. Habit ensured I watched everyone with suspicion. I was returning from the west side of the town so that I passed the Temple of the Holy Baila. The coloured tiles were muted in the fading light, but the building had lost none of its majesty. The winged figures stood proudly within the large windows, while the candles burning inside the building emitted a warm glow through the coloured glass. I stopped for a while to watch the shadows flicker over the statues closest to the light, and it was easy to imagine their faces animated. I shuddered as a chill brushed the base of my neck. The place unsettled me, and even though Villermir was no longer in residence, his presence remained. His magick still protected the building and the secrets locked within, giving me pimple-flesh if I walked too close and an unwelcome feeling that encouraged me to walk away.

I was so busy convincing myself of the evil magick within the temple that I startled like a flushed rabbit when one of the large wooden doors opened smoothly on its iron hinges. I quickly pressed a hand against the pretty glass beads in my pocket to prevent them making a noise and alerting the two men to my presence. I was close enough to hear them talking. My stomach clenched painfully when I recognised the pair.

The one furthest from me was the new High Priest of the Holy Baila in Liegeport; a small, weaselly man named Coen who had been rapidly, and unexpectedly, promoted from Villermir's scribe. His light brown hair hung two finger-lengths straight from his scalp. He had a natural tonsure, so that the long hair formed a horseshoe around his bald crown. The hair was fine and lifted easily in the light breeze. He wore the grey robes of the religious order, and I could see the seven silver bands denoting his high rank. His hands disappeared into the hanging sleeve of the opposite arm as he held them loosely in front of him. His shoulders were slightly rounded, adding a hunched posture to the characteristic pointed nose and chin that reminded me of the sly creature.

Standing next to him was Kade.

The prince had grown since I had seen him last. His tall frame had gained muscle, so that all was in proportion. No longer the lanky adolescent, he carried himself with the confidence of the heir apparent; unconscious of the grace shown with each stride, each hand gesture. His hair was cut short but still retained a hint of curl to ensure a tousled effect. The index finger of his left hand bore the white gold signet ring that sealed his marriage to Breya.

'The teachings of the Truth from the Holy Baila would suggest your ideas may hold some credence.' Coen's voice was unexpectedly mild. It held none of the power that had been clearly evident when Villermir had spoken. 'Although I have to admit my personal doubts.'

Kade did not appear concerned by these doubts. 'But you admit that the legends are based on fact.'

'I believe they are true accounts.'

'And that the Holy Prophet Abrexyrtle called on the power of the One God to rain fire from the mountains of Castern Ring.'

'I believe the prophets performed many wondrous feats.'

'So, there should be a way to harness the magick of Baila.'

Coen smiled as if teaching a child who failed to understand a complex subject. 'The holy prophets were chosen by the One God as vessels for his majesty. They did not command the power. The power passed through them by the will of the Holy Baila.' Coen stopped walking and turned to face Kade. His smile slowly faded. 'To desire the power of the One God suggests a flawed soul. That path leads to obsession, greed, lust for control, unnatural ambitions. The pursuit of magick results in corruption and abomination. The old ways must be denied. Salvation lies in placing your trust in the higher consciousness that is the One God.'

Kade sighed, frustrated at the familiar sermon. 'Even to defeat a threat to the freedom of free choice?'

Coen's face clouded. 'Your Grace. You mean to release the fury of the Holy Baila onto your enemies. Lindvane is committed to the teachings of Baila. I do not believe the One God would consent to the destruction of believers of the Truth.' His tone turned rock hard, suggesting the inner strength of the man beneath his mild exterior. 'Do not presume to confuse the concerns of the One God with those of his subjects. He answers to no royal line.'

Kade dipped his head in acknowledgement of the reprimand, but did not apologise. 'Would you at least consent to my access to the holy texts? I'm simply looking for a way to end the fighting, to prevent the suffering of our people as well as Hayton's. Surely that is in everybody's interests?'

Kade maintained direct eye contact while Coen considered his request. The two men silently challenged one another for several heartbeats before Coen lowered his gaze.

'I suppose there can be no harm in you familiarising yourself with the sacred teachings.' He resumed eye contact. 'But please. Forget your quest for his power. No good can come of that search.'

A door banged in the alleyway behind me. Kade turned in my direction, and the breath caught in my throat as he seemed to look directly at me. I retreated further into the shadows, suddenly dizzy as my heart hammered against my ribs. I stayed pressed against the damp wall until my heart rate slowed, then waited several heartbeats longer before moving to where I could observe Kade and Coen once more. The pair had moved on and I could no longer see them in the courtyard in front of the temple.

I couldn't believe what I had heard. I understood that Kade was desperate to end the war with Lindvane, but I could not accept his easy manner around a priest of Baila. Villermir had been a traitor who had tried to kill Kade. Why would he trust any priest from that religion? I had been shocked when Kyllian had pledged his kingdom to Baila after his eldest son's death, but I never thought Kade would accept his father's decision. It appeared that not only had he accepted the king's commitment, but he had lent his own support to the priesthood, seeking the counsel of the High Priest. I felt a strong suspicion that the religion could not be trusted. I also knew that I would have no opportunity to talk to Kade about his new adviser.

The next day I was late for my training session with Langdon. Having stayed up late the previous night, I had overslept that morning. The women were already sparring when I ran onto the training ground. I was bent over, trying to recover my breath, when I noticed Kade standing next to Langdon. The Master of Arms slapped Kade on the shoulder and the two of them walked towards me. Kade was already scowling.

'Kade will be practising with you this morning.'

Langdon gave me a big smile as I widened my eyes in a silent plea. Kade looked to be in a foul temper, and that could not bode well for me.

Langdon patted me on the shoulder as he walked past. 'Play nicely, children.'

I closed my eyes for a heartbeat before meeting Kade's stare. His dark green jacket fitted closely, although slits at the shoulder seams revealed pale green silk beneath. He would be able to move his arms freely, and would have full use of his noticeably large biceps. I bit my lip as I tried to control my rushed breathing at the thought of the power those muscles were about to direct at me.

Without saying a word, Kade drew his sword and advanced, bringing his weapon up across my body. By instinct alone I stepped back to avoid the blade, which sliced so close to my face that I felt the puff of air as it whistled past. I drew my sword and blocked his follow-through, retreating another two steps as he sliced at my abdomen. I tried to halt his attack with a slicing move of my own, but it was easily deflected and he followed with a swing to my face. I overbalanced as I moved to avoid the blade and landed heavily on my bottom.

'Merciful Mother, Kade,' I snapped. 'What's wrong with you?'

I was angry at the ferocity of his attack. He had not held back, fighting with the full force of his ability. A talent that far exceeded mine. His face remained impassive as he stepped back, allowing me the space to rise without the threat of attack.

'Why were you outside the temple last night?'

I blinked at him, surprised by his question. He had seen me. 'Don't flatter yourself, prince. I was just passing by.'

He came at me again, quick slashes to the left and right, and I lost more ground as I tried desperately to block him. Whirling his sword around his head to gain extra momentum, he crashed his blade down onto mine. The two pieces of metal screamed in protest as concussive waves travelled painfully up my arms. I kicked out at the side of his knee, knocking him off balance, buying time while I waited for the tingling to leave my hands.

'And yet you lingered long enough to hear the entire conversation.'

I cursed myself for being so careless. Not only had he seen me, he knew I had been there the whole time.

'It wasn't that interesting a conversation.' I tightened my grip on my sword, ready for the next assault. 'I'm just surprised at your choice of company these days.'

He lunged to my left, swinging his blade round to hamstring me. I caught his steel against the edge of mine, twisting as the force wrenched my wrist. I continued the spin to add strength, and slashed at his neck. He stopped my blade easily enough, but I slid my weapon down his to defuse the concussion. Aiming for his calves, I forced him to skip backwards.

'On the contrary,' he continued. 'I think my company has improved now I have removed myself from base distractions.'

My arms responded to my anger as I charged towards him. The steel rang as our blades connected again and again. I forced him back a few paces before he regained the advantage. He drew my lunge to expose my right shoulder, then slammed the pommel of his sword onto my shoulder blade. My right hand went numb and my left was required to grip tighter to compensate as I retreated out of range.

My tone turned nastier. 'I'm sure you get all your base distractions from Breya.' I leaned in to taunt him. 'Does she make you beg?'

I had always harnessed my anger to enhance my abilities. It added strength and speed. It sharpened my reflexes. Kade's anger impeded his skill. Normally calm and methodical, he became impulsive and overconfident when riled. As I had planned, he came at me with a flurry of erratic strokes, although instinct did more to protect me that any talent I had. I batted each slice away, relinquishing ground, waiting for the opening that would inevitably come. Two strikes at my head. One aimed at my abdomen to disembowel. One feint to the knees before striking back at my head. He stretched for my bruised shoulder, but slipped on the loose footing and overbalanced. I slammed my elbow into his ribs, satisfied at his grunt as the air was forced from his lungs.

He recovered quicker than I expected. I was vaguely aware we were drawing a crowd, but was soon absorbed again by the need to defend myself. My stamina was fading and my shoulder felt as heavy as a boulder, the prickling fingers of my right hand preventing any finesse. I wiped sweat from my upper lip as Kade advanced once more. We twisted round and round, a lethal dance with sharp steel rushing past exposed flesh, both of us aiming for known weak spots, both knowing each other's style so well. I blocked his moves again and again, as he blocked mine.

Inevitably, I finally responded too slowly and Kade's blade caught me on my left bicep. I stepped out of reach as I clutched my upper arm. My fingers came away red and sticky as the blood seeped into the material of my sleeve. I glared at him while I panted for breath.

'I'm sorry,' he mocked. 'Do you need to run away again like the coward you are?'

I lunged for his neck, but he turned my blade with ease and I was forced to take the defensive role again. As my strength failed, tremors rippled through my leg muscles and my steps descended into stumbles. It was not long before he cut me again, just above my right bracer.

'I may be a coward but at least I don't consult with traitors.' I rushed at him, using my words to distract while wildly swinging my blade. All pretence at strategy had been abandoned and I succumbed to the desperation of blind anger.

'The priests of Baila are not traitors.' He parried my attacks, but was by now also displaying less talent and more reactive moves. 'One person's actions do not condemn the whole religion. The Teachings have much to tell us.'

'Oh, please. Now you sound like your father.'

Kade roared with anger. He kicked out at my legs and knocked them from under me. I fell heavily onto the ground, the air forcefully expelled from my lungs. My wrist hit a stone, numbing my hand and releasing my sword, which flew out of reach. Kade fell to his knees on top of me, each knee slamming into one of my elbows to pin me down. With a two-handed hold he held his blade high over my exposed neck.

'*Kade!*' Langdon's voice shouted from a short distance behind me.

Kade and I ignored it. I was focused on the blade that had been lowered to rest against my skin. I could feel it trembling when I breathed in, so I was careful to take shallow breaths.

Kade's jaw was clenched tightly, but the anger was leaving his eyes. 'You're dead,' he said flatly, before rising and leaving the arena without acknowledging Langdon.

I closed my eyes while I tried to get my breathing back to normal. Both arms tingled with needle-stabs, while the muscles of my legs jumped in time with my heartbeat. It was some time before I opened my eyes to see Langdon standing above me. I sighed to see another angry face in front of me.

'I'm sorry, Langdon.'

A rumble rattled deep in Langdon's chest. 'He's the King-in-Waiting. He should show more restraint in front of the troops.'

I smiled to ease the tension. 'At least he restrained himself from slitting my throat.'

Langdon's scowl informed me that he would not be easily placated.

'It was as much my fault as his. I wanted to hurt him as much as he wanted to hurt me. Only I lacked the skill to get anywhere near him.'

'Even so—'

'Even so, I know how to spark his temper, Langdon. I provoked him on purpose.'

The Master of Arms huffed in acceptance and the scowl melted from his face. He offered his hand and I gladly accepted the help in rising. Langdon's frown returned briefly as I winced at the pull of sore muscles.

'All the same, I'll be having a quiet word with His Grace.'

I checked to see that the crowd was dispersing. 'Why is he so angry, Langdon? Tawpin had mentioned it, but he was really easy to provoke.'

Langdon watched Parin walk over to my fallen sword. 'That's not for me to say, Tallen. You should talk to him.' He scowled at me again, but no longer in anger. 'But not on my training field.'

I smiled as I nodded in agreement. I was in no rush to face Kade with a weapon again.

'Go get those cuts cleaned up,' Langdon said gently, turning me towards the city.

We both turned as Parin cursed. My sword was still on the ground, but Parin held her fist cupped in her other hand.

'Wretched sword bit me,' she whined, opening up her hand so I could see a bleeding slice across her palm.

I laughed. 'How can a sword bite you?'

'I swear by the twelve Gods of the Lower Hall. I was definitely holding it tight enough for it not to fall.'

'Perhaps you held it too tightly.'

'I have handled swords before,' she snapped.

I held my hands up in submission. 'Very well. It bit you. Let's get some of Drey's ointment for your cut.'

I picked up the sword, making a point of holding it by the hilt. Langdon chuckled softly as Parin and I left the arena.

I was restless that night, tossing and turning as I recalled the fight with Kade over and over again. I was angry at Kade. I was angry at myself. I was mostly angry that I continued to obsess over the incident. I could not place it to one side, box it off in my mind and move on. Eventually I got out of bed, dressed and went to walk the streets. I had soon fallen into my old habits, feeling more comfortable when walking the town at night. Few people roamed the markets and alleyways, and those who did were keen to avoid conversation. We all stuck to the shadows, moving silently to avoid attention. I thought it ironic that I was more relaxed in the company of cut-throats and thieves than I was around the honest people of Liegeport. Maybe I had just never felt good enough for them.

I wandered where my feet sought to take me, aimlessly walking with no particular destination. I was unsurprised, however, to arrive at Renis's trading house. I had stolen many beautiful items from Renis over the years. He traded in the best quality goods. Decorative treasures from exotic lands far to the south and east. Gold. Silver. Precious stones. Coloured glass. Things that sparkled when they caught the light. I smiled at the thought of seeing his latest supply of goods that had arrived two days ago.

I slipped into the shadows at the side of the trading house and crept into the small courtyard at the rear. It took several moments to open the back window, using my belt knife to prise the locks on the outer shutters, the glass-panelled window and then the inner shutters. Despite the stiffness in my muscles from the bout with Kade, Langdon's training had left me toned and limber and I easily climbed onto the inner ledge. I opened the window as little as I dared and listened for any sounds that would suggest Renis and his wife were still awake. After waiting several heartbeats, I was satisfied that it was safe to enter and squeezed through the narrow gap. Taking care not to catch my clothing on the rough wooden framework, I balanced lightly on the inner ledge before silently dropping to the ground.

A shadow moved.

I froze. Trying to listen past the blood pounding in my ears for the sound of movement. Trying to think of the quickest escape route out of the building. The shadow moved again with a soft swish of air. I felt my eyes growing large as I strained to see in the darkness. Whoever stood there was small; too well hidden for me to discern more than a darkened shape in the shadowed doorway leading to the living quarters upstairs. Another thief? My hand tightened on the handle of my dagger.

The shadow moved a third time, stepping into the faded light cast by the unshuttered window. Renis's dog wagged its short, stumpy tail at me as its eyes reflected an unnerving red hue. I sighed silently with relief, cursing myself having forgotten the hound. Renis had reacted to my thefts by obtaining a dog to guard the premises at night, but the dog was lazy and I had easily bought its silence with meat when it first appeared. I knew it would leave me alone and not raise the alarm as long as I remained in the store and did not venture in Renis's private apartments.

Then I realised that I had no bribe for the dog. I had not planned to visit Renis and therefore had not brought the usual fee of meat jerky. The dog's body was lowered as if in fear, and it hesitated before taking the two steps into my reach. The tail wags grew slower as the dog waited for its food. A small grumble started deep in its throat. Trying to think of what to do, I remembered the small packet of sugar sweets that Tawpin had given me earlier to cheer me up after the incident with Kade. I retrieved the sweets from my tunic pocket and inspected the offering. The hard, yellow sweets had melted slightly as they rested next to my body heat. The packet had torn, so that where the surface of the sweets had become sticky, several cloth fibres had stuck. Dark veins traced over the rough coating. They looked totally unappetising. I threw the sweets onto the ground in front of the dog. They had barely touched the floor before it had snatched them up. I flinched as it noisily crunched the bribe. The dog turned and quietly padded back into the shadows, and I heard no further sounds.

I returned to surveying the small room that ran the width of the house. The fire had been stacked to ensure that the smouldering embers would prevent any damp spoiling the goods. A warm, flickering orange glow bathed the room. I smiled with pleasure at the shiny metals and polished stones blinking at me as I slowly walked along the rows of trinkets and ornaments. Letting my fingers gently caress the treasures as I walked by, my fingertips tingled with the sensations from engravings, embossing, worked edges and pitted metal. Warm surfaces melded with cool as I explored the texture of each piece, savouring the sight of the gentle sparkle that filled the room with numerous tiny glazed-honey stars.

About two thirds of the way along the second aisle was a small rock, about the size of my hand. The outer layer was rough and appeared as any other. But this rock had been cut in half, so the centre could be seen. There were jagged spikes with smooth surfaces encircling a cavity in the middle. I picked it up in order to turn the inner face to the light. It felt heavier than I expected one that size to weigh, particularly with the hollow centre. As I walked towards the window, the pale light seemed to smother the stone like a protective blanket. I bit my lip to prevent myself gasping in surprise and joy at the highlighted jewel. I could not suppress the wide grin that exploded onto my face. Deep purple ringed the middle of the rock. Spikes of crystal poked into the dark central cavity. Each spike had five sides, seeming to reflect the light as the smallest glimmer bounced around the rock. Tiny purple flashes winked as I twisted the stone to enhance the effect. The rows of crystals radiated from the centre, each getting smaller and paler as they neared the edge. The final layer was almost clear, and blended with the gravelly beige outer surface.

I slipped the crystal into the pocket that had not previously held the sticky sweets, as I could not allow the stone to get covered in sugary slime. As I turned to leave, the moon emerged from behind a cloud, sending a spear of bright white light into the trading house to highlight an object I had not seen before. The breath caught in my throat as I looked upon the most beautiful lute I had ever seen. The body and neck of the instrument were a deep, rich brown, the colour seeming to ripple in the moonlight as the grain swirled around the dark wood. The frets on the neck were made of oyster shell, brightly reflecting the light. The shell highlighting was continued on the body of the lute, where patterns were finely entwined to enhance the impression of fragility. There were twelve bone pegs to tune the fine wire strings, which, as I touched them, I realised were made of silver. I had the urge to pluck the strings and hear the voice of the lute; to hear a note so pure that it matched the exquisite beauty of the instrument. The urge was easily ignored: I would never be able to do this masterpiece justice. I removed my hand from the strings.

There was only one person I knew who would be able to make the lute sing as it should. And I would not give him a stolen lute.

Later that morning, I lay awake listening to the sounds of Drey pounding herbs in his rooms. I spent several moments trying to decide what to say, rejecting each question as I rehearsed it in my mind. I finally accepted that there was no right way to say it, so I rose to confront him. Drey let me stand, leaning against the door frame, for several heartbeats before acknowledging my presence. I was a little sad that the comfort I had taken from watching him work had ended.

'What's on your mind, Tallen?' Drey asked without turning from his task.

I spoke quickly. 'How would I get some money?'

Drey stopped crushing the plants and slowly turned to face me. 'Do you need something?'

'No. No, it's not that. You have always provided everything I needed. And I'm really grateful. It's just…' I took a breath. 'I want to buy someone a present.'

Drey smiled and returned to his pounding. 'Ah. Yes, I heard about your incident with Kade.'

I frowned in annoyance at Drey's back. 'Who said it was for him?'

Drey glanced at me over his shoulder. 'Who else would you *buy* a present for?'

The emphasis on the word was not lost on me. Most of my gifts had been taken from someone else before I presented them. Drey was right. Kade was the only person I wouldn't steal for.

'How much do you need?'

I hesitated. 'Three sovereigns.'

Drey spun round. 'How much?! Are you buying him a horse?'

'No, I'm not buying him a horse! He has a horse.'

Drey studied me to see how serious I was.

'I'll pay it back. Everyone else seems to get wages, but you've always provided for me. Tell me how I can repay you and I'll do it.'

Drey looked at me for a moment longer. 'Are you sure he's worth it?'

I nodded and Drey dipped his head in acknowledgement. Leaving the pestle on the bench, he disappeared up the small staircase that led to his private chambers. He returned a short while later carrying a small leather purse. I could hear the coins knocking together as he passed it to me.

'I dare say you've earned half of this already. And the other half will be earned soon enough, I fear.' He narrowed his eyes at me to ensure I took his words seriously. 'I'll inform you when the debt has been repaid.'

'Thank you, Drey.'

He huffed as he released the purse into my palm. The pouch was heavy, suggesting the sum was made up of lower-value coins. It would take thirty crowns to total the three sovereigns. Sixty half-crowns. I estimated that Drey had given me a mixture of crowns and half-crowns. I wondered if there was a sovereign contained within the pouch. I had rarely seen the large gold discs that were embossed with the Faulknar crest surrounded by a circle of small diamonds. But I felt it would be rude and appear untrusting for me to check in front of Drey.

I rushed directly to Renis's trading house, concerned that the lute may have already been sold. The store was empty of customers when I arrived, and as soon as I entered Renis narrowed his eyes at me from behind the small counter in a corner of the room. I dipped my head in greeting before aimlessly walking along the aisles as I had done the night before. The treasures looked very different in the daylight; an explosion of colour as the sun sent shards of vivid light reflecting off the polished surfaces of the stones, glass and metal. A rainbow of reds, yellows, greens and blues danced throughout the shop. My fingers itched as I lightly touched each faceted surface.

'Can I help you with anything?' asked Renis gruffly. His displeasure at having me in his store was clearly evident.

I smiled sweetly. 'Just browsing.'

'Checking my place out for your next thievery is more like it,' he grumbled.

I let my smile slip as I stared at him directly. 'Can you prove that?'

He huffed noisily in reply. I resumed my amble around the trading house, picking up random items. I could feel his suspicion press on me like the air before a thunderstorm. He watched me closely, but I was confident he could not do anything about his concerns. His jaw was tense and there were small spots of colour dappled over his cheeks by the time I made my way around to the counter.

I spent several moments looking at the lute behind his left shoulder, being careful not to let any desire show in my face.

'How much for that?' I indicated the instrument with a nod of my head.

Renis barked a quick laugh. 'You couldn't afford it.'

'How expensive can it be?' I sneered. 'I suppose it's pretty enough, but it's not even a proper lute. It's got too many strings.'

Renis rolled his eyes at my ignorance. 'That is an altissimo lute. The extra strings allow more complex harmonies. There are only four in the whole of Faulknar. Only ten are known of in all the three heraldic kingdoms.'

'And you just happened to have one?'

Renis succumbed to his pride. 'I only trade in the highest quality items. I have a reputation for trading valuable oddities.'

'Is that so?' I sounded unimpressed, although I knew his boasts to be accurate. 'How much, then?'

'Four sovereigns.'

I spluttered dramatically. 'How much? You must be jesting. That's not worth a crown.'

He stared levelly at me. 'Like I said, you cannot afford it, much less appreciate the fine workmanship that goes into a piece such as this.'

I looked at him thoughtfully for a moment. 'I'll give you a sovereign for it.'

'Steal me blind with that offer. You may as well give in to your thieving fingers and take it one night.'

'Is that an offer?'

He growled. 'Three sovereigns.'

'So, you admit it's not worth four. I doubt it's worth three. I'll give you one sovereign, three crowns.'

Renis's eyes narrowed again. 'That would hardly cover the item taken last night. You insult me with that price.'

I held his gaze. 'It's a shame you lost things last night. But that does not concern this transaction. Two sovereigns.' Feeling confident, I decided to push the trader a little harder. 'You should get a dog to protect your goods. Then again, it would be very embarrassing if that dog slept through anybody raiding your store.'

The muscles along Renis's jaw rippled as he ground his teeth in frustration. Despite his suspicions, he could not accuse me of taking the rock crystal, and he would not admit that his hound had failed him. 'Two sovereigns, two crowns,' he said finally.

I made a show of considering his offer, knowing it to be a good price for the lute. I nodded agreement and emptied the leather purse onto the counter. I watched as Renis counted out the seven crowns and two half-crowns that would remain mine. I retrieved the coins, feeling a small stab of disappointment as Renis collected the two golden sovereigns and the smaller coins. He reluctantly passed the precious instrument to me. I took it graciously, feeling no triumph in his defeat.

Kade was not free until later that day. The sun had set hours before he left his final meeting. His evening meal was being served in his private apartments, and I followed the serving girl to his room. I gambled that he would not be discourteous to me in front of the servant. The fragile truce lasted until the door closed behind her, his face clouding with anger immediately.

'I wanted to apologise for yesterday,' I said quickly. 'I said some things that I should not.'

Kade ignored my apology. The silver points on the ties of his tunic flashed in time with his rapid breathing. 'Get out of my rooms.'

'Kade, please. I don't know why you are so angry with me. I know you don't want to be King-in-Waiting and that Breya is not your choice of consort—'

'None of which concerns you,' he interrupted.

I held up the wrapped bundle as a shield between us. 'I've brought a peace gift, Kade.'

He hesitated. His liquid brown eyes were suspicious, but after several heartbeats he snatched the lute and ripped open the light cloth covering. I was watching him closely, so I saw the fleeting look of wonder cross his face. His eyes betrayed how much he liked the lute. They drank in the detail of the delicate shell highlights; the rich, dark wood; the twelve silver strings.

The moment passed quickly and was soon replaced by his mask of anger. 'Do you think this is an appropriate jest?'

I frowned in confusion. 'No, Kade. I...'

'You think it funny to remind me of all that I've lost? Of what I can never be?' His voice grew louder. 'Some peace gift, Tallen. You offer a stolen token to poison my heart and drive me more insane.'

Without considering his actions, Kade threw the beautiful instrument across the room. As soon as it left his hand he was aware of what he had done. We both held our breath in dread of the destruction that was about to occur. Kade had aimed for the padded chair in front of the fire, but the force of his throw caused the lute to bounce and fall on the floor. The silence hung for several moments as we absorbed the fact that the lute had landed on the thick rug, a hair's breadth from the stone hearth. The lute was undamaged.

It was now my turn to get angry. 'I didn't steal it. I sold my soul to Drey to borrow the money. I would not give you a stolen gift.' I threw my hands up in frustration and paced the floor to release some of the furious energy swirling inside me. 'I'm sorry life didn't turn out the way you had planned it. I'm sorry Kerk died. I'm sorry you had that responsibility thrust upon you. I'm sorry you've had to make sacrifices. But so does everyone. People make what they will of the choices given to them. We all live with the fates the Gods give us. Why should you be any different?'

I was only partially aware that Kade had moved to retrieve the lute. I was no longer looking at him as I stamped around his room, releasing frustrations that had been simmering for some time.

'It's not my fault that you have been caged here. It's not my fault that you can no longer get drunk at the Blue Boar. It's not my fault that life moves on. But nobody said you had to give up living. Nobody forced you to stop playing. You always said that you played your music for you, and if other people liked it that was a bonus. Seems you need an adoring audience more than you care to admit.'

I turned to face him, no longer concerned with how he cradled the instrument protectively. How his eyes had darkened to midnight pools. How he trembled ever so slightly.

'I'm sorry I saved your miserable life at Burford. If I'd known it would make you this unhappy, I wouldn't have bothered. I would have left you in Mobis's Fourth Hell to be sport for the daemons.'

I stormed out of the room, letting the heavy wooden door slam behind me. I was shaking as I marched the long hallway back to Drey's apartments. I was furious at Kade for being such a spoilt child. His temper had been fuelled by a thwarted desire to be a bard; by the fact that he wouldn't get to do what he wanted to do. What made him so special? Everyone else had made compromise and loss part of their lives. Drey's door received equally harsh treatment as I crashed into his rooms.

'Go well?' he asked, looking up from his book.

'No,' I snapped as I stomped past him into my room.

I threw myself onto my bed. Too angry to shed the tears that welled in my eyes, I slammed my fists into the bedding, frustrated that there was even more animosity between Kade and me after my disastrous peace gift.

I was too restless to settle, so I climbed onto the roof. Almost immediately the cool breeze from the ocean calmed my turbulent mind. I could hear the waves crashing onto the rocks of the harbour, the dull, rhythmic tone slowing my rapid pulse. I took a deep breath of the salt-tinged air, exhaling my turbulent emotions.

Soft. Exquisite. Soul-capturing. Heartbreaking music slipped from Kade's window. Intricate harmonies interwoven with a haunting melody, played all the more beautifully for the heartache behind the plucking fingers. The tears spilled over my eyelids and ran unhindered down my cheeks. My heart burned with the pain displayed in Kade's music. All his sorrows and loss became melded with mine, draining over the chasm in the centre of my chest like a turbulent waterfall. The chasm where forbidden dreams were sent to fester.

Chapter Five

I looked at myself in the mirror. My face was too long, my mouth was too small, and my amber eyes were still unsettling, but even I had to admit that Erula had done a good job. Breya had decreed that, despite the increase in hostilities with the Lindvanes, the midwinter parade would be held as normal. To increase the morale of the townspeople, she had organised a festival to follow the more formal procession of the royal family and their more important retainers. I had declined Erula's invitation to watch the chosen few display to the common people, but she had been insistent that I attend the evening feast.

My dress was made of the softest cloth available in Liegeport. The main panels of the front and back were a pale lilac, studded with small glass beads that reflected the light in a rainbow of colours. The narrow side panels were cream and extended from the armpit to the hem. The lilac sleeves contained cream slashes that could expand to accommodate the sword-fighter's muscles of my upper arms. Below the elbow the sleeves clung to my forearms, with a triangle of material covering the backs of my hands. A thin strap of lace hooked round my middle finger to hold the triangle in place. The dress was delicate and highlighted my small waist, as well as covering the scars on my arms. I smiled as I swayed my hips and made the material swish around my ankles. The toes of the matching lilac slippers peeped out from under the hem, the tiny glass spheres joining the symphony of colour created by the beads on the dress.

My smile widened as there came a loud knock on the door to Drey's apartments. Tawpin did not wait for an answer before bursting into the room, calling out to see if I was suitably clothed. I fussed with my hair one last time; the oils Erula had given me had made my black hair shine, with ribbons of dark blue swirling through it like spilt ink.

Tawpin crashed into my room before I had taken one step away from the mirror. His face was brightened by the toothy smile he gave me. 'Looking good, Magpie.'

I raised my eyebrow at his use of my nickname. 'You scrub up quite well yourself.'

Tawpin had chosen a black tunic with slashes of red running the length of the sleeves, his undershirt revealed as a scarlet contrast within the collar and open V of his tunic. His black trousers were brushed leather, as were his boots. His unruly blond hair had not been tamed, so that the roguish street rat I had grown up with was still visible under all the fine clothing.

'You ready?' he asked, offering me his arm like a gallant gentleman.

I took it and grinned at him, knowing he shared my thoughts of feeling like a child dressed up to pretend at being grown up. He escorted me out of the royal house and into the ribbon-covered streets of the royal city. Vibrant banners hung from trees and buildings. Waxed-paper lanterns were roped between the street-torch brackets, while roaring braziers kept away the chill of the early-evening air. The courtyards were full of muted colour that gave a hint of the spectacle that would develop as the sun set. Golds, crimsons, violets, emeralds, ceruleans: an explosion of vivid colour to defy the dark, cold nights of midwinter.

The townspeople had taken the theme of colour and reflected it in their choice of clothing. Tunics, cloaks, hats and dresses competed to distinguish their wearers in the rolling sea of vibrant hues. Any weapons that were carried were well hidden beneath folds of fabric. The atmosphere was jubilant and companionable as children ran about energetically, excited from eating too much sugar. Any hint of the suspicion and hostility that was readily seen on other occasions was abandoned on this day of celebration. I reluctantly accepted that Breya had brought a sense of community back to Liegeport. Something that had been missing for some time.

Tawpin guided me to a corner of the market where a large hog was being roasted. Erula and Parin were waiting for us. The women were sitting on benches that had been placed around the courtyards so that people could sit and eat. A large platter of roasted vegetables and meat was placed on the bench between them. The scents of succulent food mixed with the spices that were being burnt in the lanterns. An exotic mix of aromas floated on the gentle breeze to add an extra element to the occasion.

Tawpin grabbed a handful of the greasy food as we joined them. Parin glared at him, before passing him a plate.

'You'll get grease all over your nice clothes,' she chastised him gently, before turning to me with a wide smile. 'Greetings, Tallen. Nice dress.'

I returned the compliment as I took the plate that she offered. Parin's long black hair, normally contained within a plait, fell freely over her shoulders, curling softly around her tanned face. Her tall frame was elegantly covered in padded gown of pale green with delicate lace at the throat, waist and wrists. The colour was a shade lighter than her eyes. She looked beautiful. Erula had chosen to be more modest in her appearance. She wore a fitted tunic of peach that contrasted pleasantly with her dark colouring. Her cream leggings finished in the middle of her calves, where soft leather boots tucked under their hems. Her black hair was bundled into a nest at the back of her head. Trailing strands fringed her face, with peach- and cream-coloured ribbons braided into the edges to make the creation look delicate.

I raised an eyebrow at her. 'You made me wear a dress and you get to wear leggings?'

She smiled sweetly. 'And don't you look beautiful? Doesn't she, Tawpin?'

I turned to see Tawpin fill his mouth with crusty bread, wondering when he had managed to obtain that. He nodded enthusiastically at Erula's comments. I glared as I snatched a large bread roll that was resting next to him. I filled my plate with meat and vegetables before sitting next to him.

'You're not helping,' I grumbled as I nudged him with my shoulder.

His sea-green eyes sparkled as he grinned at me. 'I only tell the truth.'

I huffed. 'Since when?'

'Since it is in my interests to do so.' He stole some meat from my plate. 'I think you all look beautiful.'

Parin was sitting the other side of Tawpin, and nudged him as he lifted the meat to his mouth. Grease smeared over his chin. 'Aren't you the charmer tonight?'

We teased each other with easy-flowing banter as the evening's festivities got under way. Street minstrels wandered amongst the crowds, accompanied by flute and drum. The noise level rose steadily as ale was consumed and people joined the minstrels for the choruses of popular songs. Dancers swirled and swayed, adding further brightness to the already colour-rich scene. Acrobats tumbled and flipped, twisting their bodies into unimaginable shapes and positions, being thrown impossibly high to land on the shoulders of others. Jugglers balanced balls, batons and banners, throwing them to each other as well as tossing them around their bodies and high into the darkening sky. The items moved at breathtaking speeds, with the jugglers' hands becoming blurred as they responded to the movement. Trained dogs spun and danced amongst the crowd, followed by giggling children. There were even a few small monkeys performing alongside the dogs. These appealing creatures were very good at begging food from the onlookers.

The jugglers changed to fire sticks as night closed in. The flames carved arcs of fire as they flew through the air. One group had dressed in black so that the orange shapes drawn by the flames were all that could be seen of the entertainers in the darkening marketplace. The sight was mesmerising, and I found myself drawn into the dance made by the fast-moving patterns.

Tawpin nudged my elbow. 'Time to join the grown-ups, Tal.'

I looked up and saw him and the women waiting for me.

'There'll be more pretty things for you to look at in front of the main house.'

We made slow progress through the crowds. There were numerous people who were more than halfway to being drunk, and they wanted to dance with us as we negotiated our way across the marketplace. The atmosphere, however, had remained friendly and I felt no threat from the close presence of people. The party mood continued along the side streets, with the lanterns providing a mellow glow of lemon, mint and peach. People's faces were bathed in a flattering light so that everyone looked like the sculptured creations on the Temple of Baila. Peaceful expressions were highlighted by eyes full of joy. These were people I had seen on the streets of Liegeport for years, but they seemed different that night. I felt accepted.

Parin bumped into me as I stopped suddenly on the edge of the courtyard in front of the main house. I felt my mouth drop open as I saw the arrangements that had been made for the important people of the royal town. All the important vassals had arrived at the capital for the parade earlier in the day. They and their families were being hosted by Breya, and she had produced quite a scene for them. I was amazed by the amount of work that had to have been done in the few hours since I had left with Tawpin.

There was a large area in the centre of the courtyard that had been reserved for dancing. The paving had been scrubbed and coated with a thin sheen of wax to make the stones shine in the lamplight. The lanterns surrounding the dance floor and extending across the open space were exclusively white, so that it appeared that stars had been captured to illuminate the dancers. Several couples were already waltzing to the tunes played by the musicians who sat at the base of the steps leading to the royal house. Arranged to the side of the musicians and around the outer edges of the courtyard were benches and tables, so that the honoured families could enjoy an uninterrupted view of the dance floor as they ate. Only one side of the courtyard was free to allow non-invited guests to join the celebrations. I smiled at Breya's cleverness. The etiquette of rank had ensured that the higher layers of society bordered the courtyard while the rest of the townspeople were relegated to the side streets. No one had been specifically excluded, but only those who were deemed socially acceptable would be able to take part in Breya's ball.

I turned my attention to the high table, sited at the top of the steps so that all could see the chosen few. Kyllian was not in attendance, so Kade and Breya took the honour of the central positions. I took a deep breath as I looked at the heir to the Faulknar throne. While his scowl had been softened for the occasion, his expression was tightly controlled as he surveyed the festivities in front of him. So different to the easy joy of festivals he had enjoyed as boy. His brown eyes were hidden by shadow, but his breathing was regular, causing the silver buttons on his slate-grey tunic to flash rhythmically. The responsibility of hosting social occasions had clearly dampened his enthusiasm.

To his right sat Breya. She looked regal and radiant in a rose-coloured gown. Unlike her husband, she had risen to the challenge of being Queen-in-Waiting. She soaked up the attention given to her, and almost glowed with it. She smiled indulgently at the dancers in front of her, inclining her head to listen to her father talking beside her. I frowned to see Coen sitting on Kade's left. His plate was frugally arranged with bread, cheese and fruit, and it was clear that he drank only water. I scanned the top table for Drey, my frown deepening when I could not find him there. I extended my search and located him halfway along the left side of the courtyard. My frown melted, and I smiled as he loudly shared a joke with Herron and Langdon at a table full of military advisers. Ale and wine flowed freely, and the advisers were clearly having more fun than those at many of the more prestigious tables.

I was distracted by an energetic Sergeant Jorge soliciting Etard and inviting her to dance. I nudged Tawpin and grinned as the normally confident woman became shy and self-conscious. She finally accepted his offer and allowed him to lead her onto the dance floor.

Erula rolled her eyes. 'So easily impressed.'

Tawpin laughed. 'I'm sure I've seen you looking at Captain Skellen. Tonight would be the perfect opportunity to ask him for a dance.'

She glared at him. 'You are not even remotely funny, horse boy.' She lifted her nose imperiously. 'I'm saving myself for a wealthy lord.' She winked at me.

'Such a shame.' Tawpin shook his head sadly. 'To spend your whole life alone.'

Erula leaned over and punched him on the shoulder. 'I could get a lord!'

'Ah,' continued Tawpin. 'But the question is, could a lord handle you?'

Erula and I nodded to each other in acceptance that it would take a very strong man to woo the self-contained soldier. I watched the dancers turn and swirl, my shoulders swaying in time to the music. The scene was so pleasant and relaxed it was easy to forget the worries of war; to be drawn into the whirling colours and fragrant scents of the food, wine, candles and lanterns. People laughed easily as they twirled their troubles away. I smiled as I happily left my cares and concerns for another day.

My view of the dancers was interrupted as Tawpin moved to stand in front of me. I raised my eyebrows as he bowed formally and offered his hand.

'Tallen nic Duane, may I have the pleasure of this dance?'

I coughed a laugh of surprise. 'You have got to be jesting.'

He did not remove his hand.

'I can't dance.'

He smiled reassuringly. 'It's easy. I'll show you.'

'Is that before or after I've broken your toes from stomping on them?'

'I have sturdy leather boots and you have soft cloth slippers. How much harm can you do?'

I hesitated, looking at Erula for an excuse not to dance.

'Don't worry about me. You go and have a good time.' She smiled broadly at my frown, waving towards the dancers and encouraging me to go.

I knew Tawpin would not back down, so reluctantly I took his hand and he escorted me onto the dance floor. He was a good teacher, patiently guiding my steps. I initially concentrated so hard on our feet that I was no longer aware of anything else, but, as the steps repeated themselves, the rhythm of the music began to dictate my movements. I began to predict the requirements, so my feet placed themselves in the correct positions. I looked up to see Tawpin smiling broadly at me, causing me to lose the beat and bring my heel down on his toe. He laughed freely at my expression, taking me by the waist and lifting me up. He turned me in a full circle before placing me gently on the ground. He skilfully guided me back into the rhythm, and by the end of the dance I was beginning to enjoy myself.

As we performed our courtesies, Tawpin bowing over his stretched leg while I curtsied awkwardly, a silver-haired gentleman in finely tailored clothing came over to whisper in Tawpin's ear. Tawpin gave a small nod and guided me back to Erula.

'It appears I have to perform my duties as the lord of a ruined estate further up the coast.' He kissed my fingers before releasing them. 'Seems there are a number of ladies awaiting my favour.'

Erula laughed. 'Serves you right for being such a rogue.'

He sighed dramatically. 'This gift is such a burden sometimes.'

'Oh, please,' I mocked as I shoved him gently backwards. 'Go and see to your adoring ladies.'

He bowed a final time before disappearing into the crowd. Erula passed me a drink.

'Having fun?' I asked.

'Oh, yeah.' She grinned, indicating a couple with her glass. 'You see that couple underneath the lantern? They have to be married. She's been sniping at him all evening and he has completely ignored her.' She indicated another couple. 'While that gentleman with the awful orange tunic has been simpering at the pretty girl in yellow. She's been desperately trying to think of a way to escape him.'

Erula continued to describe the power play that was unrolling among the people apparently enjoying the festivities. Men forging allegiances. Couples courting favours. Disagreements becoming exaggerated as alcohol continued to be consumed. False appearances for the public while frosty relations simmered below the surface. My first impressions of everyone being happy, relaxed and friendly were convincingly stripped away under Erula's keen observations.

'And as for your prince—'

'He's not my prince,' I protested.

Erula raised an eyebrow. 'Really? Then why has he been staring at you all night?'

'He has not.'

She continued to silently challenge me, raising both eyebrows to convey her point. I looked towards the top table where Kade was sipping a glass of wine. My stomach twisted to find him looking at me. In less than the time it took for me to blink, he had looked away. My festive mood evaporated as I realised Erula was right.

'And now look at Lady Faulknar.'

I moved my attention to Breya. She was furious. Her delicate mouth was pinched, so that her lips had become a white line in her pale face. In contrast, two blotches of colour stained her cheeks, extending along her jawline and down her neck. Her violet eyes had darkened to dangerous shards of black glass. Her attention moved from me to Erula, and I turned to see the soldier raise her glass in a mock salute to the Queen-in-Waiting. I thumped her on the arm hard enough to hurt.

'Thank you very much,' I snapped. 'Like she doesn't hate me enough already.'

'Relax.' Erula sipped her wine. 'What can she do about it?'

My mind immediately obliged with a number of ways Breya could get back at me. My carefree mood had gone for good. I grumpily mumbled my excuses and escaped to my room, taking two bottles of wine on the way.

How much Breya disliked me became evident the next day. I was cleaning out the stables for Baden, the Master of Cavalry. As usual I was having to dodge the horses within the stalls as they barged me with their shoulders or tossed their heads at me in irritation. Most showed no hesitation in demonstrating how much they wanted me away from them. I was still grouchy from the previous night, as well as the effects of the two bottles of wine, so I was in no mood for the big black gelding currently trying to dissuade me from his stall. I took my frustrations out on the soiled straw, while muttering about people who made my life difficult by insisting that I cleaned the stalls that had horses in them rather than giving me the empty ones. Horses had always hated me. That wasn't going to change because they saw me keeping them clean.

Movement at the corner of my vision stirred my instincts. Without thinking I moved as two hooves crashed into the wall beside me. I cursed the beast as it whipped round to bare its open mouth at me. I snarled back, knowing that my actions would not help the situation but no longer caring. My patience was noticeably absent by that point, and I raised the rake in threat.

'I hope you get a splinter in your foot and it gets infected,' I grumbled childishly.

'Tallen nic Duane.' A man's voice calmly called my name.

I looked over the black horse's shoulder to the passageway that ran between the stalls. The gruff voice belonged to a middle-aged man dressed in the colours of the Queen's Guard. The thickset man was unsmiling. His short hair and piercing blue eyes added to his effortlessly intimidating manner.

'You are requested to attend the Lady Faulknar,' he continued.

I lowered the rake, sighing at another unwelcome distraction. 'What does Breya want now?'

His scowl deepened. 'Your presence is required immediately.'

Keeping as far away from my equine antagonist as possible, I moved around the stall and ducked under the rope barrier. The man was accompanied by another of the Queen's Guard. This one was equally muscled and lacking in humour. His arms were folded across his chest. I dismissed the second guard, returning to address the first.

'Well, you can tell her that I'm a little busy right now.'

The guard did not move, showing no sign that he had heard me. His companion moved to stand behind me so I was positioned between the two men. His posture was only mildly threatening, but I knew they would not leave without me.

'You will follow me,' instructed the guard who had addressed me initially.

He turned on his heel and walked towards the door of the stables. He had taken a single pace before the second guard shoved my back to get me moving. I quickly regained my balance, managing to turn and glare at him as I cursed loudly. That earned me a more forceful shove towards the exit that required me to concentrate in order not to fall over.

A young stable boy ran into the barn, carrying empty feed buckets. He stopped, his eyes growing large as he took in the scene before him. I thrust the rake at him as we passed.

'If I'm not back by midday, send someone to look for my body.'

The lad snatched the rake and nodded without saying a word. I received another shove in the back to quicken my pace and was escorted out of the stable yard.

Breya was waiting in the Queen's Garden. She was seated on a wooden bench under a trellis covered with climbing plants. In the spring the plants would produce scented blooms of blue and white, although the evergreen leaves still added some dark emerald colour to the overcast grey morning. Breya wore a fur-trimmed white cloak that covered her from neck to ankle; white brushed leather boots peeked out from under the hem. Her blonde hair framed a calm face. Standing behind her right shoulder was Rolyan; his hand resting on the hilt of his sword and a smug look on his face suggesting that he was not here by accident. The guards stopped several paces from Breya, then moved to the side so my view of her was unrestricted.

'Is this necessary, Breya?' I asked impatiently.

Rolyan's eyes flicked to the guard beside me, and pain exploded from the back of my head where he struck me.

Rolyan's voice was almost purring as he addressed me. 'You should show the appropriate respect to your Queen-in-Waiting.'

I glared at him. 'My apologies.' I let the sarcasm in my voice heavily colour my words. 'How can I be of service, my lady?'

Breya hesitated to make sure my full attention was turned back to her. 'Yesterday saw many of my subjects renew their fealty to Faulknar.' Her violet eyes silently challenged me. 'I believe it is time you formally declared your loyalty to this family. I would have you swear fealty to me. Now.'

Cold water rushed through my intestines like the spring rains flooded the river. My mind whirled with the consequences of Breya's command, and I shivered as I comprehended the depth of her vengeance. If I refused to swear allegiance to her I could be charged with treason. Breya could have me executed. I also knew that if I did swear fealty to her, she would demand some task of me that would have equally dire consequences. If I refused her orders, I would again be accused of treason. Breya had neatly presented me with a situation in which I clearly could not win. Rolyan's eyes flashed with triumph, and I suspected his involvement.

'Breya, please.' My head snapped forward as the guard struck again. I closed my eyes in frustration. I was starting to get a throbbing headache. 'My lady,' I began again. 'This is not necessary. You know I am loyal to Faulknar.'

'Then you should have no objection to swearing your fealty to me.'

My mind spun in dizzying circles, trying to find a way out of Breya's trap. Rolyan could not contain his smile as he watched me struggle with the dilemma. The cold water slowly turned to the boiling steam of anger. I chose my words carefully when I replied.

'I'm flattered that you would consider my allegiance.'

Rolyan's smile faltered at the confidence of my tone.

'It is with regret that I cannot oblige you.'

Rolyan took a step towards me, but was halted by Breya's hand on his arm. He continued to glare at me but did not advance.

'On what grounds do you refuse me?' she demanded.

'On the grounds that my loyalties are already sworn.' There was no challenge in my voice as I spoke the truth. 'I have always been, and will continue to be, loyal to only one. I would have it no other way. I cannot swear allegiance to another and risk a conflict of duty. No matter how small that risk may be.'

I took a breath. Breya gave a small smile that accepted she was about to lose this battle. Her eyes, however, held a steeliness that left no doubt that the war was far from over.

'My fealty lies with His Grace, Kade Faulknar.'

Rolyan fumed with frustration, confirming my assumption that his desires had been at the heart of the ploy. Breya rose from the bench. Her cloak gaped open to reveal a small bump rounding a belly that had always been flat. My eyes widened with comprehension, and I lifted my attention to her face. She returned my gaze evenly, knowing I had seen the first signs of her pregnancy. She closed her cloak and walked towards me.

'As it should be. A hound can only serve one master.' She lowered her voice as she reached me so only I could hear her next words. 'Serve him well.'

I was unsure whether it was a request or a threat.

As I turned to follow her, each of the two guards escorting me placed a heavy hand on my shoulder to restrain me. I turned back to question Rolyan. He waited until Breya was out of sight before strolling towards me. A cruel smile spread across his lips as he approached, causing the cold hand of fear to grip my stomach again. He stopped within an arm's reach of me and paused for several heartbeats, savouring the effect he was having on me. Appreciating how my breathing had become fast and shallow; how I was unable to control the small tremors that chased through me.

He raised his hand. I clenched my fists and braced for a punch. The guards flanking me instantly reacted by restraining my arms. Their immobile holds on my shoulders and forearms effectively prevented me from moving.

Rolyan gently stroked the side of my face with the back of his hand. The action froze my heart in a way a punch would not have done. My lungs spasmed as I fought to get air into them. I felt dizzy and nauseous, my mind filling with unidentified fears more damaging than if he had hit me.

'You think you are so clever.' He wandered slowly around me. 'I will convince Lady Breya that you have no loyalty. I will find evidence to prove you are a traitor.' He stopped in front of me, leaning in to emphasise his point. 'I will see you hang.'

He leaned back and turned to leave, then changed his mind, turning back to add, 'Oh. And don't think I have forgotten about your sword. I will have that.' He raised his hand again, laughing as I flinched. 'I'm always watching. Always waiting.'

He patted my cheek as the guards released their hold on me and followed Rolyan out of the gardens. I stood alone, trembling from more than the cold wind that blew across the low shrubs. I stayed where I was for a long time before trusting my legs to carry me without collapsing.

Rolyan was true to his word. I started seeing him everywhere. When I went to the market to get supplies for Drey, Rolyan would be leaning against a wall, watching me. My practice sessions with Langdon were distracted by his presence. He would bump into me as I walked around the royal house. He never spoke. Never threatened me. He was just always there. I felt like a length of cord that was being twisted, tighter and tighter. I scanned constantly to be able to see him before he saw me. I jumped at every noise. I snapped at everyone. I felt ready to smash into pieces.

I avoided wearing my sword. I would borrow a sword from the armoury rather than risk Rolyan taking it from me. I was torn between wanting it in my hand to know it was safe, and risking losing it to Rolyan. I stored it with my other treasures: checking the cache was always my first action on returning to my room. It had taken weeks to chisel the mortar from below the stone windowsill, allowing a slab to be removed by sliding it from between the corner bricks and a small dowel of wood to hold it in place when returned. A long, narrow pit had been excavated beneath the windowsill that held all the treasures I had obtained over the previous weeks. Gold and silver trinkets sat amongst coloured glass and precious stones. Ornate daggers lay next to finely decorated pendants on glittering chains. The sword rested on top of them, wrapped in soft cloth. My hands trembled with anxiety each time I pulled back the plain material to see the dragon eyes looking back at me.

It was ridiculous. I was supposed to be able to slay dragons and I could not protect the sword from one man. I needed to control the magick that was hidden inside me. I needed to learn how to access the energy that Drey believed was within me. It was time to use my magick as a weapon.

I was waiting for Drey when he returned to his chambers. He sensed my mood as soon as he walked through the door, stopping to look at me as I sat beside the fire, before removing his cloak. I held his gaze for several heartbeats. He sighed and placed his cloak on the desk.

'What's happened?' he asked as he walked over to join me in the comfortable chairs.

'I need you to teach me how to use my powers.'

'What has happened?' he repeated quietly.

'Nothing.' I shifted, suddenly uncomfortable in the soft chair. 'I just think that it's time I knew how to use magick to protect myself.'

'I've shown you how to protect your mind from intrusion.'

'I know. But I think I need to move on.' I avoided his enquiring eyes. 'I need to know how to protect myself from more natural threats. Physical ones, not ones in my head.'

'Not magickal ones?'

I looked up and nodded.

'You want to attack rather than defend. Is that what you are asking?'

I bit my lip. 'I can stop people entering my mind. I can fight with a blade. But I'm still weaker than most. I can't fight on equal terms. I need another option.'

Drey hesitated. 'What happened?' he asked again.

I took a deep breath to summon the courage to tell the truth. 'Rolyan is making moves for the sword again.'

'So, you want to frighten him off?'

'No.'

'You want to hurt him before he hurts you?'

'No!'

'Then why do you need this other option?'

'I want to stop being scared all the time,' I replied, harsher than I had intended.

Drey nodded. 'So that's why you've stopped wearing your sword. You are afraid you cannot hold on to it.'

'When we went to fight Villermir, you used some sort of invisible shield to force him back. I may be able to fight Rolyan off, but not if he brings his men with him. Not if he demands it in front of Breya and the royal court. I can't fight the whole of the Queen's Guard. If I stay in Liegeport for much longer, he *will* take the sword.'

Drey was silent for a long time, trying to find clues to a motivation in my face. I thought about all the reasons he could give for not teaching me. Did he trust me enough not to use my power to victimise Rolyan? Did I have the strength to control the magick, or would it control me? Would I be a danger to everyone if I could access my inner resources?

I felt a gentle pressure against my mind. I closed my eyes and concentrated on the sphere of light in my head that held numerous entrances. Doors of many shapes and colours floated around me. I thought of a plain door with a round knob made of bronze. The metal had been worn smooth by countless hands having turned it. As I pictured the door I wanted, it floated closer to me, stopping within my reach. I extended my arm, once again seeing the thin limb with the child's hand grasping the handle and pulling the door towards me. The portal shimmered with an iridescent mist, swirling with bright yellows, blues, reds and greens. Drey's familiar golden shadow was hazily visible on the other side. I showed no hesitation in reaching through the mist and pulling him through.

'Show me Rolyan,' instructed Drey.

I hesitated for a couple of heartbeats before calling a large oak door to me. The sturdy wood was plain but bound by heavy iron rivets. I bit my lip as Drey approached the portal to all my memories of Rolyan. I watched as he extended his hand and grasped the iron latch. A sharp crack accompanied a strong smell of burning. Drey's projected image faded until it was almost transparent before returning to a more solid form when he removed his hand from the latch.

He looked at me with clear annoyance. 'Tallen. I am well aware of your powers of defence when it comes to your thoughts. That is not what we are here for. Please lower your barriers and allow me access to your memories of Rolyan. I would examine your motivations before we proceed with teaching you how to attack with magick.'

I had not been aware that I had set such protections around my thoughts, but apologised quickly and concentrated on allowing Drey access. I stood uncomfortably, my nine-year-old self hugging my chest against the trembles that were chasing each other around my body. I watched Drey witness my early memories of Rolyan. His persistence in trying to obtain my sword. His frequent bullying, involving taunts and shoves at every opportunity. I remembered his intimidation. Threats whispered. Bruises given. I showed Drey the exchange between Breya and me. Admitted my suspicions of Rolyan's influence in planning the trap. The fear I felt at the gentle touch of his hand.

Drey grunted and vanished from my mind. I closed the door on the memories, adding a heavy lock before sending the door to the depths of my mind. I returned to Drey in his apartments.

'What do you want to know?' he asked quietly.

'At Burford Hythe, you used some sort of air-shield to push at Villermir. It seemed to protect you when he attacked you; deflect it off to the side.' I paused. 'Would you teach me that?'

Drey studied me as if searching for an answer to an unspoken question. Eventually he gave a quick nod. 'Come with me.'

He led me into his back room that was stacked with herbs, dried and stored in jars. I paused by the table where I had assisted in pounding and grinding the leaves. The surface was as clean and organised as always, and I smiled at Drey's fastidious habits. I looked up to see that he had left via the small, plain door that led up to the tower. I had been forbidden to enter this most secret of places, but had long suspected that Drey performed his magick up there. That he kept his magickal artefacts stored safely there. I quietly walked over to the open door, unable to resist a quick peek. The stone was worn in the centre of each step where countless feet had worn away the pale rock. A glow illuminated the top of the straight stairway as Drey lit a candle and impatiently called for me to hurry up and join him. I grinned and rushed up the steps before he had the chance to change his mind.

The stairway opened into a large, circular room. Drey had finished lighting the candles and a chamber of wonder greeted my eyes. The outer walls were filled with large leather books and stacks of rolled scrolls. Any spare wall was covered with aged maps. On the wall to my right was a painting of an emerald dragon breathing fire as it flew over a burning town. The windows were tightly shuttered, and below them was a faded leather couch that may once have been black or dark brown, but over the years had been worn to light brown on the seats and cushions. Darker seams ran across these areas like veins and the original colour still seemed to reside in the corners. A dark oak table stood to one side of the room. Papers were weighted down with large chunks of uncut crystal. A polished stone the shape of an egg and the size of my hand lay cradled in a brass stand. The colour was such a light blue that you could almost see through it.

'Tallen,' Drey barked.

I blinked and dragged my eyes away from the crystal egg. Drey was standing in the middle of the room. A circle covering half the floor had been chalked onto the rough wood. At four points of the circle, smaller discs had been drawn, dissecting the larger circle. Each contained a symbol: a series of three wavy lines, a triangle within a square, a pentagram and an inverted arrowhead. A circle large enough for me to stand in was placed at the centre, with more characters drawn within it; boxes and lines that seemed to belong to a language that I vaguely recognised but didn't understand. To the north of the inner circle was a chalk drawing of a waxing moon, while the sun with its stylised rays was drawn to the south.

Drey retrieved four brass dishes from a shelf before moving to the table. He opened the lower drawer and removed a small leather pouch. He poured the contents into one of the dishes, half-filling it with dark, peaty earth. Replacing the pouch, he removed a small bottle and poured clear liquid into another dish. The third dish was coated with another clear liquid, with an acrid smell that irritated my nose when Drey carefully poured the small volume into the container. The last dish remained empty. I watched as Drey placed a dish in each of the small circles along the perimeter of the identified space. Above the image of the moon he placed the fuller bowl of liquid. The odorous liquid was placed below the sun image. Drey extended his fingers over this second bowl and bright yellow flames erupted from the liquid. He placed the empty bowl in the circle to the left of the flames, while the final bowl was placed opposite that.

Drey indicated the four bowls. 'The essential elements at the cardinal points of the circle. The moon governs the north. Her element is water. The sun masters the south. His element is fire. To the east is earth. To the west, air. Each pair are equals, one providing temperance for the other. Fire and water. Earth and air. Water douses fire, but fire evaporates water. Earth smothers air, but air blows away earth. Equal and opposite. Perfectly balanced.'

Drey indicated that I should sit opposite him within the large circle, both of us between the moon and the sun images. I was seated in front of the empty dish. Drey sat in front of the earth. We sat facing the small inner circle with the strange language. Another circle within a circle.

'The centre contains the element of the spirit world. The energy that holds everything together.'

Drey's voice lowered as he spoke; a resonance that gently vibrated through the room and caused the brass dishes to hum quietly. He started to chant, the same words over and over again. *Gealbhan. Deuraich. Blàthaich. Talamh. Tathasg.* The humming of the dishes grew louder. Small sparks of blue light flashed from the bowls along the chalked outer circle. After several attempts the sparks connected with the other dishes and the whole outer circle blazed with blue flame before subsiding to a glow along the chalked line.

'The circle is protected,' explained Drey. 'Anything you conjure will be safely contained. Nothing can leave the circle.'

I took a deep breath, suddenly remembering to breathe. I still found it hard to accept that magick was real and I was a part of it. I still had doubts that I would be able to perform the simplest of spells that Drey demonstrated so naturally. I tried to concentrate on everything he did. The position of his hands. The focus of his eyes. The tone of his voice.

'We will start with something visible so you can see what you are creating. Clear your mind of all distractions. Concentrate solely on my voice and what you are forming.'

Drey had drilled me in the exercises of emptying my mind and concentrating on a single point. We had worked, with varying degrees of success, on moving small objects and identifying an individual's thoughts. This was the first time that I would be creating something new. Drey instructed me to visualise the air within the central circle as tiny spheres of energy. Each small orb was to vibrate. I was to make them move as fast as I could without touching another sphere. A headache developed in the crease of my forehead as I frowned in concentration at controlling countless balls of energy.

'Compress the energy. Mould it to the size of an apple.'

Closer and closer. Faster and faster. The spheres were forced into an impossibly small area. Two orbs touched, causing a cascade of explosions as the effect knocked other spheres together. A fireball stayed suspended over the inner circle. In my surprise, I lost focus and the fireball dissolved into transient sparks.

'Again. Maintain the concentration.'

I repeated my actions and recreated a fireball. Adding more tiny orbs of energy, the fireball grew to the size of my head. I held it in place while admiring the waves of flame that raced over its surface. I could feel the heat on my face. Smell the faint odour of burning. I smiled. I had created fire from nothing except my imagination.

The fireball trembled as the door at the bottom of the stairway banged against the wall.

'Concentrate,' barked Drey.

The fireball stabilised as heavy feet pounded the steps, suggestive of someone taking them two at a time. Kade burst into the upper room. In my surprise at seeing him I jumped up and took a step backwards. I noted his eyes growing wide as he extended a hand towards me. Drey also rose with a look of shock on his face, his mouth opening to say something that he never said.

I took another step back to regain my balance. This step took my foot almost to the chalked outer circle, leaning back over the barrier as momentum carried me backwards. A strange sucking sensation seemed to muffle all sound as the blue flame erupted into a blazing inferno. My body buzzed with the stabs of uncountable wasp stings as I fell backwards. My breath caught in my throat as my vision became crystal sharp, colours becoming more vivid for an instant, before I was enclosed in darkness.

Chapter Six

My vision was blurred and there was a persistent ringing in my ears as Drey applied a salve to my face that had a sharp, clear scent. I had small burns on my nose, ears and fingertips. My lower back was sore in a thin strip that ran from hip to hip. I could see that Drey had a dark bruise starting to discolour his left temple. Kade stood in the corner of Drey's lower room, next to the dried plants. He absently rubbed his shoulder while holding a compress to the back of his head with his other hand. Both men had small scratches all over their faces and hands. I had several similar marks on my arms, and I had scratched at a few scabs on my face that were probably the same.

My back itched, and I tried to rub it on my shirt. Drey tutted at me, and instructed me keep still while he finished applying the salve to my fingertips. Taking a deep dip into the pot, he turned me sideways on the chair and lifted my shirt to reveal the damaged skin. I twisted and could just see a reddened stripe as wide as my thumb was long. It looked like a bad case of sunburn. Small welts traced across the surface. Drey gently applied the cream and the itchiness cooled into numbness. He wiped his fingers clean of the salve by rubbing at the old scars that were visible below my bodice. He carefully lowered my shirt and I turned back to face the room. Kade's jaw was tightly clenched but he remained silent.

'What happened?' I asked quietly, making an attempt at an apology. 'Did I do much damage?'

'Much damage?' Drey's tone seemed more exasperated than angry. 'Tallen. Only you could take a simple fire spell contained within several layers of protective wards, and cause enough damage to blow out my windows, shatter my shutters, dislodge several tiles from the roof and remove a number stones from my walls.'

'But how…?'

Kade pushed away from the wall and placed the scented cloth on the workbench. 'You broke the circle, you dolt.'

I bit my lip in embarrassment; it was a basic mistake. The protective ward would remain intact for as long as the circle was complete. As I had fallen backwards, my body had broken the ethereal barrier and released the energy contained within, leaving my body to escape at the peripheral points. It explained the burns on my nose, ears and fingers.

'Your back landed on the chalk line,' Drey continued. 'It's the focal point for the containment ward. You smudged the line and the sudden release of energy burned your skin.' He turned to Kade with a hint of a smile. 'That released your fireball.'

Kade resisted for a couple of heartbeats but was finally defeated and broke into a wide grin. 'The good people of Liegeport will be telling tales for generations to come of the night a comet blazed over the royal city.'

I groaned as I imagined the damage a fireball could do to the precious artefacts kept in Drey's tower. 'Your books…'

Drey shrugged. 'The thick volumes seem to have absorbed most of the energy. Other than being forced off the shelves and a few torn pages, they survived with very little damage.' He narrowed his eyes at me. 'You will have plenty of tidying up to do in the morning.'

I sighed, accepting that was a more-than-fair judgement. 'I didn't mean to,' I said lamely. 'It was just that Kade came rushing in as if all of Mobis's Furies were after him.'

'Oh. So, I'm to blame now?' Kade protested.

'Well, you should know better than to burst in on Drey's tower.'

'I didn't expect someone to be so incompetent that they couldn't control a simple fireball.'

I opened my mouth to respond, but Drey halted the exchange by holding his hands out between us.

'Children. Behave,' he mocked. 'The damage has been done.' He looked pointedly at the two of us to ensure we understood that the discussion about who was to blame was finished. He held Kade's gaze. 'Tallen will need help to board up the window.'

Kade's mouth fell open. 'But… but I'm the King-in-Waiting.'

Drey remained unimpressed. 'Who bickers like a child. Both of you will repair the damage. And that's the end to it.'

Kade scowled childishly at me, causing Drey to roll his eyes in frustration. 'Perhaps Your Grace would care to explain why you rushed into my tower without an invitation?'

Points of red coloured Kade's cheeks at the rebuke, but he could not hide the excitement in his voice. 'I found it, Drey. I found it.'

'Found what?' I looked at Kade and then at Drey, finding matching smug grins. 'Found what?!'

Kade looked at me with a very satisfied expression. 'I have found the name of your sword.'

I forgot to breathe. Then compensated by breathing too rapidly as my heart attempted to hammer out of my chest. A wave of heat flooded through my body. My hands trembled. 'Tell me.'

Drey raised a hand. 'Perhaps you should start at the beginning, Kade.'

I silently raged with impatience as Drey settled back in the chair beside me and Kade moved a stool to sit in front of us. I jiggled my leg in frustration as Kade purposefully took his time before starting.

'As you know,' he began, 'I managed to talk Coen into lending me the holy teachings of Baila.'

I interrupted. 'So that's why you wanted the scriptures.'

Kade gave me a condescending look. 'What? You thought I was so upset at your leaving that I decided to change my religion?'

'Well, I didn't know,' I protested. 'You were so angry at everyone. And you do seem very close to the weasel.'

Kade frowned at my description of Coen before shrugging. 'He has some interesting things to say.'

I snorted.

'But the Teachings were required for research. And if you keep interrupting, we will never get to your sword.'

I sat on my hands to keep them still, but could not stop my leg jumping with impatience. Kade settled himself again, smiling at me teasingly before continuing.

'My main purpose was to study the texts to see if there was any information that would prove helpful in the war against Hayton. The teachings tell of the prophets raining fire on their enemies. Boiling seas. Unleashing plagues and disease. I looked for ways in which magick could be used to perform these feats.'

'And did you find any?' asked Drey.

Kade shook his head. 'Frustratingly little. The writings seem more concerned with what they did rather than how they did it. There are vague hints at the use of crystals. Maybe the Empathy Crystal or one like it. Mainly deeds are achieved through prayer, so maybe chants or spells.' He shrugged again. 'I don't know. It was all a little vague and suggestive.'

I bit my lip to avoid prompting Kade to tell me about the swords. He saw my movement and smiled.

'The holy texts reflect the common teachings with regard to the prophets. But not everything has been translated for the eyes of the worshippers. The versions given to the faithful are rather lacking when it comes to details regarding the old religion and the Gods. The original texts go into great detail about the God and Goddess, and the Halls of the Lower Gods. Most of the rhetoric is about how depraved and corrupt they were.'

Drey grunted his displeasure.

'How the use of magick was evil and stole souls. But there were some useful teachings not in the common text. There is information about rituals and spells that are still practised by a few wise ones.' Kade inclined his head towards Drey in acknowledgement. 'And some scattered information about the swords.'

I moved one hand to bite down on a knuckle in anticipation. I knew very little about the history of my sword. Drey and I had explored my memories of my time in Methhold but details of the sword had remained elusive. There were tantalising clues that it was special. The quality of the blade in both form and function. The dragon on the hilt containing precious rubies. The runes etched into the blade. I could not explain the significance of any of it.

'There was a lot of bluster about how the swords were made by daemons wielding unnatural powers: the usual propaganda. Each sword was given to control the destiny of man. But it contradicts itself by claiming the sword-bearers displayed the virtues of their blades. They acted as protectors against malignant spirits and fearsome beasts. The teachings talk about the use of the swords to control the dragons and protect the people.' Kade turned to look at Drey. 'They talk of how the blades remained in the hands of those upon which they were bestowed. The swords were magickal and therefore desirable. But the daemons had charmed the swords so that the blades would disarm any who sought to possess them. The swords could only be safely handled by those who had been chosen, and their selected descendants. The blades would cut any who did not have a true claim.'

I looked at Drey to find him looking at me. Twice someone had tried to take the sword, and both had been bitten by its blade deep enough to incapacitate. It seemed the charm was still working.

'The swords were given to the five chosen. Each had a virtue, demonstrated by the selected humans but also contained within the blade. The virtue was intensified by the sword, each blade carrying the sigils of virtue as well as the spells for protection that would ensure that the blade never broke and always remained lethally sharp.'

Kade looked at Drey, pausing before revealing the names. I tasted blood as I bit my lip hard enough to split the skin. I leaned forward, desperate to learn the name of my sword.

'The first sword had emeralds in the eyes of its dragon. It was named *Ceartas*.'

'Justice,' Drey translated quietly.

'The second had jet in its eyes and was named *Ìobair*.'

'Sacrifice.'

'The third had eyes of amethyst and carried the name of *Dlighé*.'

'Duty.'

'The fourth had yellow diamond eyes. The sword was named *Firinn*.'

'Truth.'

My heart pounded painfully, and I swallowed as my mouth went dry.

'The fifth sword had rubies in its dragon's eyes. It has the name of *Saorsa*.'

'Freedom.'

A strange calmness settled on me like a warm blanket. I knew the name of my sword. *Saorsa*. The word sounded like a sweet chime in my mind, and I smiled at the sensation.

'Freedom,' I breathed.

Kade huffed. 'Explains why you are always running away.' He shrugged as I glared at him. 'Well, you have to admit that you do have a tendency to disappear when you want *freedom* from some problem or another. *Freedom* from certain responsibilities.'

'You are seriously going to lecture me about responsibilities?' I spluttered.

'Enough!' interrupted Drey. 'Did you find anything else?'

Kade shook his head. 'Not really. There were a few references to the blades scattered throughout, but the naming of the swords was the biggest section.' The prince frowned as he tried to recall all the information from the scriptures. 'There was one comment that the swords would deliver certain death, but it was unclear whether this would be for dragons, daemons or Gods.'

We all fell silent as we each considered the implications of the weapon's legacy. What did it mean that I was a bearer of a dragon sword? What was expected of me? How could I possibly understand the ancient magick involved in creating the blade, or the requirements of the person wielding it? My mind was swirling with so many questions that I had no hope of formulating a beginning to any of the answers.

'Carries the virtues of the sword...' mused Drey, lifting his gaze to look at me and smiling. 'What virtues do you have, I wonder?'

Kade snorted a quick laugh. 'What, apart from running away? I would say the ability to steal anything she can lift, the ability to ruin anyone's peace of mind, and finding it really easy to get angry.'

'Hey!' I complained, falling into his trap.

'I'm not sure that was the aim in mind when making the swords,' Drey countered calmly. 'I was thinking about more positive characteristics. Somehow associated with freedom.'

'Running away,' Kade muttered.

I ignored him and tried to think of any virtues I might have. I soon gave it up as impossible, as my mind gleefully offered up all my faults but was less willing to identify any favourable traits. The only other that I knew who had carried *Saorsa* had been my father, so I tried to think about the traits I knew he held. Memories of him had always been difficult, so I recalled a more general scene involving my family. My mother was preparing the evening meal, scrubbing roots in a pail of water on the smooth earth outside our round hut. My father was sitting next to her whittling a new toy for my sister, his face crinkled in amusement as she waited impatiently for him to finish. I looked towards his waist to see if he carried the sword, but my attention drifted to Ciarnan as her face clouded in a prelude to a toddler's tantrum at the wait for her toy. As usual, my mother deftly diverted the youngster's focus away from her distress by carving a small figurine from a carrot and allowing the child to crunch noisily on it.

I shook my head and reminded myself of why I was remembering the scene. I turned back to my father, industriously shaving the wood into a stocky pony; his hazel eyes intent on his work, his black hair gently curling away from his forehead. As I tried to concentrate on his personality rather than his physical features, I found myself repeatedly distracted by other aspects of the memory: birds flying overhead, the sounds of other families preparing food, the crease of my mother's gown as she leaned forward to place the scrubbed roots in the water bubbling over the fire. The harder I tried to focus, the more my father slipped away like a fish from the grasp of wet hands. All I could remember of him was that he was lean and agile like me, but also calm and patient, which was most unlike me. I frowned in frustration as the only sense of him I could rely on was that I felt safe around him. Protected.

Unwilling to continue that train of thought involving the tainted label Villermir had given me, I changed direction and thought about the potential influences the sword had on me. Did I feel different when I held *Saorsa*? When I used her? It had been several years between Drey taking the sword on my first journey to Liegeport and her return at the lakeside near the cabin. Had I felt any changes since then? There was a growing impatience, a sense that I should be doing something, a task needing to be completed, although that could just be the ever-present reminder that the war was getting closer, and that we would all be needed to defeat the forces of Hayton and Villermir. My night terrors of being trapped under a mountain had haunted me for as long as I could remember – perhaps they were linked to the sword. What if it had been forged by daemons? Were dreams the way they manipulated my fears in order to control me? Could this influence somehow be connected to the deaths of my family and Laken? Was this the reason why I was able to follow Kade to Mobis's Hells? Had they allowed me to bring him back for their own purposes?

'Merciful Mother,' I breathed, covering my mouth with my hands as if that would somehow protect Kade from my thoughts. I turned for the reassurance of Drey to find him looking at me with concern.

'What is it?'

I quickly glanced at Kade, but could not meet his eyes as he scowled at me.

'What if the blades were made by daemons?'

Drey shook his head. 'That is just one theory. They could just as easily have been made by the Gods. I doubt that the swords would have been given names such as Justice and Sacrifice if they had been designed by daemons.'

'But we don't know whether the swords were named to promote these virtues or corrupt them,' I persisted. 'What if the blades were created to control the Dragonslayers? Surely the daemons would want to control something as powerful as an Ancient favoured by the Gods.'

Drey calmly shook his head. 'You are letting your imagination run away with you. There is no evidence to suggest that the sword is influenced by either daemons or Gods. It is just a very old weapon, that may or may not be connected to a Dragonslayer. All we have are accounts written by people who would have had no way of knowing where the swords came from. They were generations removed from the Ancients, and an unknowable length of time from the forging of the blades.'

I balled my hands into fists in frustration at trying to get him to understand. 'But what if they were—'

'Tallen,' snapped Drey. 'Enough of this.'

I stood in sudden anger at his dismissal. 'No, Drey. Listen to me. How can I be trusted if there is even a hint that the blades can be used to cause harm? You were right to deny me the magick. I can't be given that power.'

Drey raised his voice to match mine as he rose to stand in front of me. 'I refuse to believe that you are in any way compromised by your ownership of that sword. You have resisted the temptation to do harm, despite some severe provocation by the likes of Villermir. The teachings of magick will provide you with the tools to protect against any malign influence that you may face in the future.'

'How can you be so certain?'

'Because I'm certain of you. The Goddess has a hand in your future, and I'm sure—'

'Listen to yourself, Drey. I'm not sure whether that's blind faith or wishful thinking. How would the Gods benefit from sending me to Mobis's Hells? How could I retrieve Kade unless the daemons wished it?'

I jabbed a finger at Kade to emphasise my point, turning to see him glaring at me; his brown eyes flecked with black. A wave of cold doused my temper as I saw how hatred twisted his face, and I took a protective step backwards.

'I knew it,' he snarled. 'You've befouled me with daemonic visions. You've corrupted my nature and left me vulnerable to attack.'

I tripped over Drey's chair in my haste to get away from Kade as he lunged towards me, convinced that he was going to kill me. As I scuttled backwards to cower in a corner, Drey stood firmly between us, unfazed by his prince's temper. An unspoken conversation took place as the two men locked stares – one calm, one raging. It took several tense heartbeats before Kade pushed past Drey to leave the room, angry but no longer murderous.

'I didn't mean to hurt him,' I whispered.

'Oh, stop the self-pity,' Drey snapped, before taking a deep breath. 'You were not the one who sent him to Hell, Tallen. Any blame falls on Villermir, not you.' He offered a hand and helped me stand, taking my chin when I refused to look him in the eye. 'We are all influenced by daemons and Gods. What is important are the choices we make in each moment. Your choices are your own and you must fight to ensure they stay that way. In that you are no different to anyone else.'

'But—'

'But nothing. Until I see any evidence to the contrary, I refuse to believe that evil forces hold sway over you, and I will continue to use what talents you have in order to fight those forces. Can you commit to that?'

I reluctantly agreed, still feeling uneasy at the prospect of *Saorsa* having an influence on me, but accepting that analysing every decision I made for malicious intent would prevent me from doing anything. I returned to my room and retrieved the heirloom, placing it reverently on my bed. I gently stroked the embossed dragon that seemed too beautiful to have been created by the dark designs of daemons. The blade felt as much a part of me as the hand that touched it, and I knew that for good or ill I would never part from it for long. I would do its bidding and hope that I would not destroy everything as a consequence.

Chapter Seven

The cold winter months slowly mellowed into the brighter days of early spring. The city gradually increased its activity as Liegeport got ready for the summer campaigns. The army gathered greater supplies of wood, clothing and grain. The blacksmiths' anvils rang deep into the night. Trade caravans from all over Faulknar gathered in the city as merchants tried in vain to supply the garrison's growing demands. The markets for the remaining population were sparse, with items generally being restricted to those that were necessary or functional. Very few pretty trinkets were available, although I scoured the stalls daily; people were hoarding their treasures. There was little to buy so money was commonly forsaken in favour of bartering for goods. There was also the fear that money devalued during war: gold, silver and gems held their value no matter who ruled.

I returned to Drey's apartments from another disappointing search, with even Renis's stocks getting depressingly low. I had the afternoon free and was planning on spending it sulking in my room.

I walked in to find Rolyan sitting in the comfortable chair by the fireplace. He had draped one leg over the arm of the seat. A wine bottle dangled from a relaxed hand.

I took a deep breath but stayed within one pace of the door. 'What are you doing here, Rolyan?'

'Waiting for you.' His words were a little slurred and I suspected that he had drunk more than the one bottle.

'And helping yourself to Drey's wine store while you waited, I see.'

He raised the bottle in a mock salute. The sound of the liquid sloshing suggested that there was less than a cupful left. ''S very good wine,' he said, before draining the last dregs and throwing the empty bottle into the fireplace. I flinched at the sound of breaking glass.

'What do you want, Rolyan?'

His lips curved into a cruel smile. 'I want the sword.'

I calmed my breathing, putting my faith in the exercises Drey had taught me. I should be capable of defending myself against one man. 'You can't have the sword.'

The smile faded. 'Where have you hidden it?'

'You can't have it,' I repeated.

Rolyan sprang out of the chair and rushed towards me. I raised my defences. A bubble of air surrounded me that I was sure would be strong enough to repel any strike. I braced for the impact, but Rolyan stepped around me and slammed the door closed. He now stood between me and my only means of escape. Distracted, I lost focus on my shield. It faded and could no longer protect me when Rolyan backhanded me across the face. I was thrown across the room. I tasted blood from a split lip as I landed heavily on the floor near to the door to my room. The contents of my drawers had been scattered; clothes on the floor, books lying open on top of them. The small vials of oil that Erula had given me had smashed and spilled their contents over my clothes, and my large mirror had been pushed over.

Rolyan grabbed the front of my tunic and twisted me round. He easily picked me up and slammed me against the door frame. My barely healed back protested painfully as it hit the wood, Rolyan's face looming in front of me close enough that I could smell the alcohol on his breath. I desperately tried to conjure a fireball or slam a wall of air into him, but my panic made it impossible to focus long enough to create anything more than a few spheres of energy. Rolyan did not even notice them.

'Where have you hidden it?' he growled.

'You won't find it,' I spluttered, more to convince myself than Rolyan.

He sneered. 'Really? I found this.'

He held up the thin chain from which hung his battle charm. The swinging gold disc reflected the light, highlighting its engraved runes. I silently cursed myself as a fool. I had removed it from my cache two days earlier, tempted to return it to Rolyan. It was a sour note amongst the beauty of my treasures and I had left it in my top drawer while I made my decision. It would have been easily found when Rolyan ransacked my room.

Enraged by my silence, Rolyan punched me in the face hard enough to send me sprawling onto my discarded clothes. Tears of defeat leaked from my eyes as a sharp pain radiated along my cheek and into my nose. Spots of black jumped in the centre of my vision, making it impossible for me to gather my thoughts. Rolyan grabbed a fistful of my hair, pulling me back onto my knees and twisting my neck so I could look at him.

'Where is it?'

The twisting of my head had constricted my throat so that when I tried to speak I could only produce a croak. Frustrated, Rolyan lifted me up by the hair and slammed me into the wall, the muscles of my shoulder screaming as they were wrenched beyond their natural limits. Before my legs failed and I fell to the floor, Rolyan grabbed my tunic. The pressure of his large fists and my poorly supported weight were enough to rip the seams at the collar and shoulders.

'I'm losing patience with you,' he roared into my face. 'Tell me where it is!'

Warm tears ran down my swollen cheeks as I gritted my teeth against the pain that I knew would come. 'You can't have it.'

He threw me across the room. I landed on the small wooden nightstand, which smashed easily; splinters of wood mixing with shattered porcelain and spilt water. I held my breath against the pain that ran through my ribs, spine and shoulders. I closed my eyes tightly, not wanting to see the next blow.

It never came.

I carefully opened my eyes to see two royal bodyguards and Lord Kehoe, Kade's chief steward. Kade was squeezing Rolyan's neck as he held him against the wall; Rolyan was having to stand on the tips of his toes in order to support his weight. The two men glared at each other. Fear had widened Rolyan's eyes, while Kade's were dark shards of anger. The prince's face was held rigidly tight, with the pulse of an artery along his jaw being the only movement for several heartbeats. They seemed to remain motionless for an impossibly long time before Kade finally spoke. Little more than a whisper, the words were smothered in razor-sharp danger.

'You lay one finger on her again,' he purred maliciously, 'and I swear I will remove the head from your shoulders.'

Kade threw Rolyan at the bodyguards as Rolyan coughed and wheezed air into his lungs.

'Get him out of my sight.'

The guards manhandled Rolyan out of Drey's chambers. They were closely followed by Kehoe, concluding that his meeting with Kade was over. Kade stared at me for several moments without speaking. I could see he trembled as badly as me. He left without saying a single word to me.

I was called to a Council of War the next day. The bruises I'd received from Rolyan had darkened and I was acutely aware of the glances in my direction. I had tried to dismiss them as a result of a tavern brawl. Langdon and Herron readily accepted my story, although I doubted that they believed it. Duke Ryburgh believed the story a little too easily and proceeded to give me a long lecture on the dignified behaviour expected of a lady. Tawpin's face crumpled in concern before he glared at Kade, confirming my suspicion that Kade had not told him of the attack. Kade ignored us as Drey guided me protectively to my seat.

It was an uncomfortable wait before Kyllian joined us, and I was dismayed to see that he was accompanied by Coen. Wasting no time on introductions or informalities, the king proceeded immediately to inform us of the purpose of the council.

'The spring campaigns have commenced already.' His voice held the clear tone of command. 'Keenan will again defend the middle border and the direct route to Liegeport. My brother will be needing new recruits to cover the gaps in the defences near Rymer Point. Langdon, you are to send two companies to station there.'

He did not wait for Langdon's nod of agreement before continuing. 'Ryburgh. You are to create a diversion at the south-west border. Your aim is to take Lindvane territory along the Teag River. I want to bite back at Hayton this year, and we will start with the poorly defended areas to the south. See if we can get some of his Hilman allies to move from our northern lines.'

Ryburgh mumbled his acknowledgement, but Kyllian had already moved on.

'Herron. You will take men into Lindvane. Take what you can and destroy the rest.'

My heart dropped lower in my chest at the thought of Herron going into dangerous territory. He was one of a decreasing number who had a link back to Laken. Herron had been with Laken when I had been found at Methhold, and he had been Laken's sergeant, confidant and friend. Another of Laken's men, Gheth, was fighting with Keenan on the border. His carefree face, remembered from my childhood, had been aged and scarred by the war. Herron's scars had been carefully hidden by growing his hair long and shaggy and cultivating a full beard, but I knew they were there. I hated the thought that more could be added. I would not think about the possibility of him not returning.

Kyllian continued. 'Langdon. Six companies will accompany Ryburgh and Herron. Organise the appropriate supplies and the means to send them south. There will be little to support them on their journey down.'

He turned to Tawpin. 'Duke Kingsport. It is time you returned to your estates. Kingsport is the only port, other than Liegeport, large enough to support seafaring ships. If we arrange trade, we need a port less strategic than the capital to carry the risks. In addition, the Fenlanders have managed to resist the advances of Hayton's troops. Mainly due to the marshes, but I would have them supported by more than neglected buildings and field turned to fallow.'

Tawpin had gone very pale and I saw the muscles of his jaw ripple as he ground his teeth. He stayed silent, nodding his acknowledgement as I suspected that he would not trust his voice to remain steady.

Kyllian turned to his son and I saw Kade tense a notch tighter. 'Against my better judgement, I have been advised to send you on an ambassadorial assignment. Perhaps you can serve the kingdom in this role. You are serving small enough purpose here.'

In contrast to Tawpin's pale face, blotches of red coloured Kade's cheeks. His clenched fists betrayed the force of will required to remain silent. I looked at Langdon to see him exchange a confused frown with Herron, and knew he was as shocked as I was that Kyllian was sending Kade away from the relative safety of the royal port.

'Recent developments,' Kyllian continued, 'have made it desirable that you remove yourself from the city. You will accompany your equerry to Kingsport and determine how the remains of his people have managed to resist the advances of Hayton's troops. You will be required to learn all you can about the Fenland sabotage tactics, to see if we can utilise their methods elsewhere along the border. You will be tasked with convincing these renegades to actively join my forces in the campaign against Lindvane. Drey will go with you as adviser to ensure that you do not embarrass the kingdom, and your personal guard will try to make sure that you don't get yourself killed.'

The Fenlands were on the far side of Kingsport. It was an area partially submerged in marshland and I could see little relationship between the situation there and the rest of the kingdom. There was no reason why Kade would be needed to create links with the few people who lived there, despite their success at harassing the Lindvanes.

'Why the Fenlands? It's just a swamp.' I asked Drey in a too-loud whisper.

My comment carried easily across the room and, while Kyllian declined to elaborate for me, I had succeeded in gaining his attention. I shrank a little further into my chair as he turned a reptilian stare towards me.

'Ah, my thief. As you seem intent on repeatedly creating holes in the buildings of my city—'

'Twice!' I blurted out before I could stop myself.

'...it is desirable to remove you from Liegeport as well. It has been suggested to me that the stealth attacks used by the Fenlanders would appear to suit your skills. You are to join their raiding parties and learn all you can of their methods. You will be used beyond the border to sabotage supply lines or disrupt key garrisons.'

It would appear that Herron was not the only one Kyllian was willing to send to the enemy.

'Any questions?' The king had already risen from his chair, confirming that the question was rhetorical. He would not expect to hear of any concerns regarding his assigned tasks; it would be for us to determine how to carry out his requirements. 'You leave tomorrow.'

No one spoke as Kyllian swept out of the room. I suspected each one of us was slightly stunned by the enormity of what our liege had just charged us with achieving. Coen closely followed the king. He had not spoken a word during the meeting, and I wondered what his motive was for attending.

In the end it took over four days for us to be ready to leave. The sun had barely risen, and the morning mist still blanketed the courtyard as our party finished its final preparations. We travelled light, but supplies still required bulging saddlebags on all our horses as well as on the four extra mounts that were needed. The sharp ring of metal on stone was repeatedly heard as the restless horses stamped their feet, jostling their neighbours and causing further irritation. Curses were barked as fingers were pinched and feet were stepped on. There was an undercurrent of tension snaking through the company, dulling the edges of the normal excitement and anticipation when setting out from Liegeport.

We were to number fifteen in total. Already three distinct groups had been identified. The mood between the groups was companionable but there were subtle differences in the way tasks were performed and in who assisted whom. All of us were dressed in functional travel clothing of dark leather trousers and plain tunics that would be appropriate for the changing terrain as well as different social occasions, with only the small embroidered patches on the left side of the men's chests and their horses' numnahs to indicate any rank or status. Five of Kade's personal bodyguard were to accompany the prince. These men were quietly efficient as they teased their colleagues and cursed their horses. Their saddlebags had been loaded in a logical manner so that each pouch was uniformly filled and laid neatly against the mount.

I wondered at the choice of men selected from Kade's personal guard. All were skilled swordsmen and their loyalty was beyond question, but Kade had included the youngest members of his guard as well as one of the oldest. Dru and Kutan were brothers but as different as two men could be. Dru was the elder by seven years. His hair was prematurely greying, and his face carried the scars of many battles fought in service of his king. He was surly and short-tempered, but everyone was happy to have him at their left shoulder. Kutan shared his brother's fair colouring with an unruly thatch of blond hair, but while Dru looked many seasons older than his age, Kutan always seemed younger than he truly was. His easy smile and exuberant gestures easily won him many friends. Much of his humour was aimed at his older sibling, with the jests made funnier by comments made about Dru that nobody else would dare utter. Despite their near-constant bickering, the brothers were very close and virtually inseparable.

The oldest guardsman travelling with us was Mace. It was widely rumoured that the only reason he had not been killed in battle was because he was too stubborn to die. Mace was an ox of a man, with shoulders that were more than twice the width of mine. His clothing always seemed to strain against the muscles of his arms and legs. He had dark hair and patchy stubble, but it was his piercing green eyes that stopped many a conversation. Mace obtained respect purely by his presence, but he could also crush a man's skull with the aid of the spiked mace that he always carried, and which gave him his name.

A few seasons younger than Mace was Slicer. His real name had long been forgotten, so that even his mother called him Slicer. He was a tall, lean man and many underestimated his strength. He carried a broadsword and used it with lethal ease. His character was similarly easy to overlook. He was a quiet member of the group, but I watched as he walked among the other guards; sharing a story, helping secure a saddlebag, or giving a touch on the shoulder. I suspected that he was useful in maintaining the cohesion of the group and balancing its many forceful egos.

Hagan was Kade's captain. The tall man was well liked and well respected. He was a daemon on the battlefield and ruthless with his enemies, maintaining discipline within the guards with just a look. His sharp eyes observed everything and, when combined with his quick intelligence, ensured he was frequently three paces ahead of everybody else when it came to sensing trouble. I liked Hagan. I respected his abilities, but I liked the man. He was fair and compassionate to his men, as well as being fiercely loyal to those he cared about. I trusted him to protect Kade no matter what threatened him.

Sudden laughter turned my attention to the second group. Parin was laughing at Muris, who had turned very red in the cheeks. I smiled at the easy manner in which the women jested with each other. While Hagan's men were organised, orderly and professional, Erula's women were more chaotic. The supplies had been divided unevenly between their horses so that some carried little more than sleeping mats, while Etard's horse was burdened with so much equipment that the saddlebags bulged beyond the ability of their straps to contain them. Pots, boxes and bedding were being attached with frayed lengths of twine. I suspected that the supplies a horse carried reflected the role the rider had been assigned, and it appeared that Etard had volunteered for the cooking duties. Iffan and Heppra were already mounted. Heppra was offering unhelpful comments while Parin struggled to tighten the girth on her 'swine-headed' horse who refused to breathe out. Iffan was calmly plaiting her horse's mane, seemingly oblivious to the mayhem surrounding her.

I turned to Erula and found her already watching me. She winked as she caught my attention and I shook my head in disbelief at her obvious pride in her ragged company.

I was starting to get bored before the final group arrived in the courtyard.

The cold, damp air had penetrated my cloak and I huddled deeper into the wool. I shivered, causing my loaned mount to shy in alarm. He snorted nervously as both ears turned in my direction. I tried to calm the bay by talking softly as I had seen the grooms do to frightened animals. The horse remained tense and kept one ear constantly turned towards me.

By the time I felt I had the horse under control again, Kade had entered the courtyard. The mood immediately changed to one of sober efficiency, with even the horses quietening as if they understood the sense of occasion. Kade was dressed similarly to the rest of us in dark leggings and a plain tunic, but there was no question of his authority. The quality of his clothing was clear, from the neat stitching to the small silver thread at the hem and collar. His cloak was folded back over his shoulders but held in place with the Faulknar lion; frozen in silver with one paw raised. He wore his customary scowl, but carried his head high and strode towards us with a purposeful step. Drey and Tawpin walked either side of their prince as the grooms held their horses. Tawpin remained at Kade's side while Drey moved his skewbald Mupp to stand next to me, allowing my horse to relax a little in the company of the older equine.

In a heartbeat it seemed we were ready to go. Kade led us out of the courtyard and towards the main gate. Despite the early hour there were still plenty of townspeople sombrely watching us leave. My horse shook his head in annoyance as I reflexively tightened my grip on the reins.

Drey leaned towards me. 'So? Are you ready for another adventure?'

I turned to see the sparkle of mischief in his eyes. It had the desired effect and I smiled at his enthusiasm, instantly relieving some of my anxiety and melting the tension in my shoulders. Drey winked and we settled into a gentle trot out of Liegeport.

The mist lifted slowly and seemingly only rose to an arm-length above my head, mixing with the grey clouds that covered the day. A persistent drizzle blurred the edges of the horizon, trees and hedgerows melting into low cloud as dye dissolves into a pail of water. The road quickly turned to mud as the horses' hooves cut through the patchy turf. The previous days of steady rain had left a reservoir of water barely hidden under the grass of the verge. Mud was being thrown up by the horses in front, so that everyone behind Kade and Hagan was soon covered in a splattering of dirt.

Despite all this, I found my mood lifting as we rode away from Liegeport. A tension that I had not realised I was carrying was lifted from my shoulders as my hand rested on the familiar curves of my sword's hilt. *Saorsa*. My forehead softened its customary scowl as I smiled at the new-found name. My back straightened and I relaxed into the saddle.

I noticed the small details in my field of view. The patterns made by the mud on the hocks of the horse in front. The rhythmic squelch as hooves were sucked out of the mud. The smell of wet earth; warm and musky, satisfying and comforting. The perfect clear pearl of a raindrop balanced on a leaf. I took a deep breath and exhaled the remaining Liegeport air from my lungs.

I had never travelled the coast road before. Methhold lay to the southwest of the capital, and we had journeyed south to the Travellers' lands. The coast road ran almost directly west from Liegeport to the Fenland borders. The track stretched to the east of the kingdom as well, along the clifftops to the eastern port towns currently being raided by the Gallowglass. The route had brought goods from all the coastal towns to the royal city, both for taxes and for trade. It had been a thriving river of animals and carts, full of colour and chaos almost every day. With the attacks from the north, the stream of trade had faltered to a trickle and we were the only travellers on the road to Kingsport.

We travelled through wild meadows that would be full of yellow, blue, red and white petals on a background of green during full spring. That morning the flowers hid from the rain while the grasses bent in the wind. The mud of the roads leading from Liegeport gradually gave way to the sandier terrain of the cliffs. The horses found the ground easier and we picked up our pace. We maintained a steady gait until we were forced further into the meadows by the soft sandstone cliffs being eroded by the wind and rain, causing the path to dissolve into crumbling sand onto the pebble beach a long way below. Although I had no fear of heights for myself, the cliff face reminded me of the journey down the chalky cliffs into the Travellers' lands when Nalya, my beautiful grey horse, had slipped on the cliff and I had been suspended by her reins to dangle far above the ground. I trusted this horse a lot less than I had Nalya, so ensured we remained safely away from the cliff.

The midday meal was taken on horseback. Dried meat and biscuits were eaten in the saddle, with warm water taken from the water skins. The fine rain had finally stopped, leaving a washed-out scene of grey sky melting into a darker grey sea. The wind had dropped and barely rustled the blades of the coarse grass. My mount had taken all morning to decide I wasn't a threat and I was finally able to stop concentrating on being relaxed. Consequently, I relaxed deeper into the saddle, matching the rhythm of the sway as the bay placed his feet; his dark mane bouncing gently against his red-brown neck. I scratched at a clump of mud that had matted his coat, causing his ears to finally relax.

Emboldened by my success in getting the bay to trust me, and my own sense of well-being on leaving Liegeport, I decided to speak to Kade. He had dropped back a little, leaving Hagan and Slicer to ride ahead by a couple of horse-lengths. Tawpin had fallen back to ride between Erula and Iffan, and was chatting quietly with Erula while Iffan rode in comfortable silence beside them. Drey was deep in a conversation with Parin and Muris that involved a lot of gesturing with his arms.

I nudged my mount into a trot, bypassing Erula's group to join Kade. I saw that Tawpin had noticed my destination but did not break his conversation. I felt a flutter of nervousness as Kade scowled at me. Unlike me, leaving Liegeport had done nothing to reduce the tension in his shoulders or the strength of his grip on the reins. He barely grunted an acknowledgement before returning to look ahead at the road.

I took a deep breath. 'Kade, I'm sorry if I got you into trouble with your father.'

He turned to face me, the scowl replaced by a frown of confusion. 'What are you talking about?'

'The other day. When we were called to the meeting with your father.'

He still looked confused.

'The sudden need to get us all out of Liegeport.'

'What does that have to do with you?'

The angry scowl had returned, and I bit my lip, suddenly unsure of what I had been thinking. I hesitated for several heartbeats before continuing.

'Your father mentioned something about "recent developments". How you need to be away from the capital. Suddenly sending you on this mission to Kingsport.'

'And?' There was a hint of a threat in the growling of the word.

I spoke faster in my nervousness. 'Well, your father has hardly championed your diplomatic abilities before, and I doubt he sees you as the silent soldier, plotting ambushes behind enemy lines.'

'Thanks for the insults, Tallen. But you still haven't explained how all this is connected to you.'

'Oh.' I hesitated again. 'After the... incident... with Rolyan, I thought maybe Kyllian had given you a hard time about it. Behaviour unbecoming for the heir of Faulknar and all that. I'm sorry if I've caused more trouble between you two.'

Kade snorted dismissively. 'Not everything is about you, Tallen.'

He kicked Mael a little harder than was necessary and the horse jumped forward to join Hagan and Slicer. Tawpin moved into the space left by Kade.

'That went well, then.' He grinned.

I glared at him in what I hoped was clear exasperation, but it only made him grin wider. I sighed dramatically. 'The more I try to make things better between us, the worse I seem to make them.'

'It's not easy for him,' Tawpin continued quietly. 'Kyllian is fiercely against everything that makes Kade who he is. Give him time. A couple of days away from his father and we'll see the old Kade again.'

'You think?'

'I know.' Tawpin winked. 'I have a plan.'

I groaned. 'Oh, Merciful Mother. Why does the idea of you having a plan fill me with dread?'

He laughed easily, effortlessly lifting my mood as his sea-green eyes sparkled with mischief. We rode in a comfortable silence for a while.

'At the risk of annoying another friend,' I began tentatively, 'would you mind if I asked you a question?'

Tawpin raised his eyebrows. 'Well, that depends on the question.'

'How do you feel about returning to Kingsport?'

He was quiet for so long that I thought I had offended him as well. He sat very still and concentrated on the point between his horse's ears.

'Ashamed,' he said quietly.

My forehead crinkled in confusion. 'Why would you feel ashamed?'

'I have not been back since my family was killed. I am the Duke of Kingsport. I have a responsibility to the people of the city and the surrounding estates. Yet, I was scared of their ghosts. Scared of failing my father's legacy. I've been a coward.'

The shame in his face caused pain deep in my chest. 'You are not a coward, Tawpin. You have responsibilities to your prince. You are needed in Liegeport.'

He shook his head sadly. 'Doesn't change the facts. I abandoned Kingsport because I didn't want to remember. Didn't want anyone to know

I can't be like my father.' He raised his eyes to the sky. 'I can't manage an estate. I can't decide fair taxes. I know nothing about trade.' He turned to look pleadingly at me. 'How can I run a city?'

'Oh, Tawpin. No one is expecting you to be your father. Luart was his own man, and you are yours. You bring your skills and people will help you with the rest. That's why you have advisers and other people. You get them to do all the boring stuff while you sit like a spider in the middle of the web.'

A hint of a smile flickered at the corners of his mouth.

'You know you're good at that.'

He reluctantly gave in to the smile. 'It will be a disaster.'

'It will be fine,' I insisted. 'Now tell me what Kingsport was like when you were growing up.'

His smile slowly faded as his eyes grew distant. 'The best way to approach Kingsport is by the sea. I returned home from Liegeport on a trade ship once. I must have been… nine or ten. There's a hook in the coastline, a sandbank that forces you away from the shore, so you approach the harbour straight on. The cliffs form a natural bowl as the sea funnels into the tidal river. The incoming tide carries the smaller boats deep into the flatlands. The outgoing tide carries the silt and deposits it at the outer edges of the bowl. The harbour is gradually getting larger and deeper.'

He glanced sideways at me, ensuring he had my full attention; relaxing into the story he was telling. 'The first thing you see of Kingsport are the trade houses lining the docks. Massive buildings declaring the wealth of their owners, with giant carvings of sea creatures and ocean birds. Some of the richer merchants had these carvings covered in gold, ensuring their warehouses were seen by the fleets of trading ships floating at anchor. Oh, Tallen. It was a riot of colour as you approached from the sea. Vibrant reds, blues, greens and golds.' He grinned at me mischievously. 'Your magpie heart would have exploded.'

I hit him playfully on the thigh. 'And these glorious buildings were just the warehouses?'

'The ground floor of each warehouse was used for storage, although these caverns were as tall as a ship's mast and contained curving archways and decorative carvings. But the families and their servants lived above, in the two storeys that sat above the warehouses. We were the centre of trade for the three kingdoms at one point. These merchants were ridiculously wealthy and declared it to all. It was beautiful on a sunny day. Approaching the harbour from the sea, it was truly breathtaking.'

'So,' I asked innocently, 'were you fabulously rich as well?'

He laughed easily. 'Unfortunately not. The tension between the kingdoms had stifled trade well before my family governed the port. We were comfortably rich,' he boasted with a cheeky grin. 'But not to the level of the merchants who built the dock houses.'

'And was the rest of Kingsport this opulent?'

'As with any city, we had the full range of society. The docks were the top of the heap, but the city spread from the harbour like ink in a bucket of water. The town grew in two halves, one either side of the river. A series of bridges connected the two as they flowed down the riverbank. The colours became more muted as you travelled from the docks, but people still took pride in their dwellings. Even the smallest house would have simple carvings above the doorway and windows. Personalised touches painted onto the walls.' He sighed softly. 'It was a beautiful place.'

'And what of the town away from the water's edge?' I prompted.

He turned to frown at me. 'There was no town beyond the water's edge. All business was conducted within easy reach of the docks or the river. Everything was connected to the sea trade and transported by the river. Farming is difficult in this area. The land on the east side is sandy, making it hard to maintain crops. Most farming involves pigs and orchards. The deep roots of the trees are able to withstand the strong winds in fragile soil. The west side is very fertile, but marshy, and floods regularly. There was some trade in reeds for thatching, but crops were frequently drowned and livestock would easily get foot rot.'

'Sounds fabulous,' I commented drily.

He grinned. 'It was. Toughest people in the kingdom. Could make you gold out of sand.'

I smiled at his obvious pride; the smile slowly fading as I quietly asked my next question. 'How long has it been since you were last there?'

Again, he was quiet for several heartbeats before answering. 'That was my last visit. I caught a ride with a ship carrying timber from Liegeport to Kingsport. It was Elin's birthday. She was three.' A sad smile flickered over his mouth. 'She was so full of energy. Running around the gardens in her cornflower-blue dress. All frills and bows. Her strawberry-blonde hair in curly pigtails with matching blue ribbons. She held my leg for a whole day, not wanting to let go of her big brother for fear I would go away again.'

He stopped as his voice trembled. His lips pressed into a thin white line; his eyes suspiciously bright.

'I'm so sorry, Tawpin.'

He took a deep, quivering breath. 'No, that's what I'm here for. Time to put these ghosts to rest.'

I shook my head. 'You should remember your family fondly. The blame lies with the Lindvanes. Your anger should be directed at them. You did nothing wrong, Tawpin.'

I cowardly neglected to add that the blame also lay with me. My deeds had caused the Lindvanes to look in that direction, and had led to the raid that had taken Tawpin's family's lives and destroyed their city. I allowed Tawpin his grief as I silently accepted my guilt in his pain.

The rain returned with force in the late afternoon. Heavy drops stung as they bounced off any exposed skin. Our company huddled together, and conversation ceased as we tried in vain to avoid the cold water trickling down our necks. Moisture wicked up our sleeves and soaked into our boots, and droplets dripped from my nose onto my numb hands. The journey became progressively more miserable as the short evening faded into dusk.

Hagan led us away from the coastal road to a large tavern sited at a crossroads. The horses snorted warm plumes of steam as they smelt the dry straw in the stables, their pace increasing as they heard the whinnying of the horses already stabled there. We needed no encouragement to settle them quickly and enter the tavern. Although there were several spare rooms, most of the soldiers bedded in the stables above the horses where they were able to keep an eye on their mounts and the supplies. Rotas were quickly established to ensure everyone stood guard, and everyone had time for a bath and a hot meal. The privileges of rank were awarded to Erula and Hagan, with the pair joining Kade, Drey, Tawpin and me in the tavern.

The main room was effectively split into three areas by thick wooden barriers. Each section could be easily seen from the main bar, but allowed some privacy for smaller groups of drinkers. I breathed in the familiar smells of wood, stale ale, smoky fires, and the musky scent of damp humans and dogs. The building and furnishings were plain and functional but well maintained. There were five groups already in the tavern. Most were in the area nearest the door, happy to sit where they could see and be seen by those entering. One group remained hidden until we stood near the bar. Two men were sitting close together in the section furthest from the door. They looked at us suspiciously but did not appear hostile or threatening. Their unshaven faces displayed the hardships of life on the road, and I suspected their cautious mood was just a product of a difficult job. They quickly returned to their conversation and I paid them no further attention.

I slumped into a booth within the middle section, groaning loudly as I stretched my legs and rested my back against the smooth wood. 'I'm refusing to move for the next three years,' I declared.

I closed my eyes, savouring the stillness of the seat, the way the warmth of the room was drawing out the dampness from my clothes, and the returning of sensation to my fingers and toes. A tankard was banged onto the table. I opened one eye to see Tawpin grinning at me.

'I'm willing to bet that you move before then. Prompted by your bladder after consuming several rounds of ale.'

I grinned back, saluting him with the offered drink. 'You know me so well.'

Erula joined us with her own tankard, bumping her hip next to mine as she sat down. 'Move over. The rest of us want to sit down too.'

Grumbling dramatically, I shifted along the bench to allow Erula and Tawpin to sit down. Drey, Hagan and Kade sat opposite and we relaxed into a comfortable silence, allowing the ale to warm our bellies as the room was warming our faces.

I was drowsing, halfway to sleep, when the food arrived. The smell of hot vegetables and meat in a rich gravy was almost too much for my mouth to bear, with saliva flooding in anticipation. Two serving girls brought us six small bowls and spoons, two large, coarse loaves of bread, and a steaming pot of stew. The older of the two ladled each of us a bowl, while the younger split the loaves. She blushed and scuttled away when Kade winked at her. The older girl was less impressed, merely raising an eyebrow. He attacked her with his full grin, and I watched unsurprised as she surrendered with a shy smile.

The evening passed with friendly chatter and the tension between Kade and I was easily ignored. The tavern filled with local villagers as news spread that we were there. The noise levels rose as the ale was consumed, but the atmosphere remained companionable. It was not long after the meal, however, before Drey began to doze.

I winked at Tawpin. 'Looks like it's past the old man's bedtime.'

'I heard that,' grumbled Drey without opening his eyes.

Tawpin grinned, unable to resist joining in. 'Perhaps it's time for a nice bath to ease your aching joints.' He winked back at me. 'I'll come and tuck you up later.'

Drey opened his eyes to glare at Tawpin. 'You do that, Master Tawpin, and I'll break open that thick skull of yours to see if I can put some sense in there.' He rose stiffly and squeezed past Hagan, muttering about the lack of respect shown by young people, while grudgingly accepting that a bath sounded like a very fine idea.

'I'll check on you later,' I called after him. 'To make sure you haven't drowned.'

Drey turned to look at me with an expression of equal measures of condescension and exasperation.

I couldn't help but laugh. 'Sleep well, Drey.'

He replied with a huff. 'Just make sure you don't wake me when you finally retire, Tawpin.'

Tawpin smiled fondly. 'I suspect my head will be too delicate from the ale for me to risk it getting hit by your staff. Sleep well.'

As Drey walked past the central area on his way to the stairs, he placed a hand on Kade's shoulder as the prince entertained the crowds with bawdy folk tales and sea shanties. My attention lingered, once again noting the sharp change in attitude Kade showed whenever he was surrounded by villagers and labourers. Their lack of expectation allowed his youthful character to be released. The crowd adored him, and he returned the sentiment.

Erula nudged my arm. 'I'm going to check on the girls. You want to come?'

I smiled, appreciating her obvious attempt to distract me from Kade. 'I'm fine. Thank you anyway.'

She squeezed my arm before clumsily pushing past Tawpin, apologising as she deliberately stepped on his toes. He playfully slapped her out of the way as she sat on his lap before finally escaping the booth. Tawpin shifted over so that he was next to me, draping an arm around my shoulders.

'So, my morose Magpie.'

I rested my head against his shoulder. 'Is it that obvious?'

He gently kissed the top of my head. 'I'm afraid so. Hiding your emotions is not one of your many talents.'

He removed his arm as Kade sat heavily in front of us. His face was flushed but I was unsure whether it was from the heat, the ale or the attention. He dragged the giggling serving girl onto his lap. She had obviously changed her mind about him as she laid her arm across his shoulders, playing with the buttons of his tunic with her other hand.

The atmosphere around the table instantly changed to one laden with danger. Tawpin scowled in disapproval.

'Do you think this is appropriate, Your Grace?'

Kade's eyes darkened as the muscles around them tightened. 'To what, exactly, are you referring?'

Tawpin's jaw rippled as he clenched his teeth. His voice was very low as he replied. 'You are married, Kade.'

Kade barked a bitter laugh. 'Ha! Finally, somebody's noticed!'

Tawpin clenched his fists in frustration at what he wanted to say but did not dare. The serving girl had the wit to feel uncomfortable at the exchange and tried to rise. Kade tightened his grip, keeping her in place. Giving Tawpin a challenging stare, he turned her face to his and kissed her forcefully on the lips.

It was too much for Tawpin. He stood violently, knocking over an empty tankard. Without a word, he stormed out of the tavern, slamming the door against its hinges as he left.

'I never believed you to be a fool,' I said quietly as Kade played with the girl's hair. 'It seems I was mistaken.'

Kade's fingers stilled. 'And who are you to pass comment?'

I shrugged. 'Nobody. But I don't think Breya will be too impressed.'

Kade stood quickly, supporting the girl while she regained her balance. 'Perhaps she should have considered that before she started this game.'

He turned and marched away, leading the girl to his room and taking any chance of a restful night for me with him.

Chapter Eight

As expected, my rest was hard to find that night. I tossed and turned, turned and tossed, and quietly huffed in frustration while trying not to wake Erula. Hating myself for listening to the small sounds coming from the next room, while straining to hear the slightest creak of the floorboards. Watching the light grow imperceptibly brighter as dawn crawled nearer.

I had given up on any chance of sleep when I finally succumbed to a fitful slumber. The dream embraced me almost immediately. I was standing alone on the plateau halfway up the mountain. The sun was behind me, warming my back as I hesitated in front of the dark shadow that was the entrance to my private hell; the opening silently challenging me to acknowledge the beauty of the rugged stone. I took a deep breath and shuddered at the familiar scent of the ocean, hidden from my view by the grey rock that softly glinted in the light of the sun. The gentle breeze ruffled the small, coarse plants that clung tenaciously to the crevices, while the cries of the seabirds sounded like shrieking jeers to my sensitised ears. I took another long inhalation in an attempt to calm the turbulence in my queasy stomach. I knew I was delaying the inevitable: there was no turning back, so I took a final, steadying breath and clenched my fists against their trembling.

I stepped into the darkness and instantly the mountain slammed down on me. Ice formed in my guts, freezing my diaphragm and paralysing my lungs as sweat beaded on my upper lip. My heart raced faster and faster as every fibre in my body strained to turn around and run from the cavern. I willed myself to remain still. I knew the exit would have already closed and I would not turn to confirm this. I would hold on to the slightest glimmer of hope that I could leave if I wanted to.

The pressure built in my head as sparks of light danced behind my closed eyelids, but still my lungs refused to relax. An extra layer of panic quickened my pulse at the thought of suffocating. The white spots in my vision were joined by dots of red as the trembling in my legs increased to the point where they could no longer support my weight. My knees slammed into the ground as I collapsed, causing a reflexive gasp of air.

My chest heaved breath after breath, the points of light fading and the pressure in my head easing. My fingers dug into the gritty dirt that covered the floor of the cavern, concentrating on the texture of the soil under my nails while my heart slowed to a less frantic pace. I slowly opened my eyes. The light was dim but I could clearly see the boundaries of the cavern and the wide-open space before me. The air felt damp but not stale, suggesting there was an exit somewhere in the heart of the mountain, although I could see no trace of it. It was enough for my brain to gain control over my body and I was finally able to rise and start forward. Towards the centre of the mountain. Towards the daemon that lurked within.

The sound of my footsteps was muffled by the loose soil so there was no echoing from the stone walls that gradually drew closer together. My rasping breath was the only sound in the blanketing darkness to confirm I had not lost my sense of hearing. I resisted the urge to reach out my arms to touch the rock as it narrowed into a tunnel five paces across. I refused to look at the ceiling even though it was easily an arm-length above my head.

In the way of dreams, I had just thought of the first junction when it appeared in front of me. As always, two options were offered; one left and one right. There was no decision to make and I did not slow my pace; I chose the left passage. The floor sloped smoothly downwards, leading me deeper into the depths of the mountain.

Two further junctions were presented, and at both I took the left-hand pathways. The fourth junction, however, caused me to hesitate. The left led further into the mountain, deeper into the dark as before, but the right offered me hope. A light could be seen a few paces within the tunnel; a bright shaft of white arrowing from the ceiling. A puff of fresh air gently lifted strands of my hair, with the promise of an exit only a handful of steps away. I knew it was a false hope. I knew the dream would close the tunnel as soon as I walked into it. But it was so tempting. What if the dream wanted me to escape this time? What if this was my last hope of escaping the mountain? I lacked the strength to resist and I started down the right path.

I had not taken three steps before I slammed into a solid wall of stone. I stood frozen in despair and miserable resignation, my forehead resting against the cool rock. That small suggestion of hope was terminally blocked, along with the passageway. I was destined to repeat the recurring dream yet again. My muscles somehow felt heavier than before as I futilely slapped my hands against the wall, returned to the junction and followed the inevitable left path. The inescapability of the situation thickened the air, requiring a little more effort just to keep walking.

The path continued down, with more and more junctions being presented. The left path was automatically taken each time, my mind no longer attempting to resist. My world compressed to the small bubble of space surrounding me as I forcefully ignored the darkness ahead, actively refusing to turn back the way I had come. I concentrated solely on placing one foot in front of the other, on breathing in and breathing out, nothing more. Resisting the urge to hunch my shoulders as I imagined the ceiling pressing down on me.

It seemed that I had travelled to the centre of the earth when the final element of my nightmare arrived. I stopped abruptly, closing my eyes as my trembling leg muscles refused to move at the presentation of the final stage. I clenched my fists a little harder to stop them shaking, desperately trying to convince myself that I had not heard the chilling scrape of scales against stone. The harsh hiss came again as the creature slithered further up the tunnel. It was impossible to tell how far away it was, and my panic would no longer be denied. Knowing the outcome, I turned anyway and ran back the way I had come. I ran as fast as I could to beat the dream, the fastest I had ever run, but I was too slow. The tunnel closed in front of me, blocking my retreat. I banged my forearms into the barrier of stone, tears of fear and frustration streaming down my face as I yelled at the injustice. I yelled until my throat was raw, but I could still hear the scrape of the scaled monster sliding ever closer.

I awoke with my heart pounding painfully against my ribs as my brain fought to make sense of the retreating dream and the approaching reality. My arms were pressed against my chest as a strong arm hugged me against a warm body, my head held against a shoulder. A female shoulder. Erula's shoulder. I relaxed with the realisation that I was safe. Erula loosened her grip and gently stroked my hair. My tears were slow to cease and the fabric over her shoulder was soon saturated. Eventually I took a shuddering breath and got myself under control.

'I'm fine, Erula. You can let go now. I'm fine.'

Erula reluctantly released me. My hands were finally free to rub at my eyes, itchy with dried tears. I avoided her gaze, embarrassed that she had seen such vulnerability in me. I fussed at the blankets, but she refused to move, waiting for me to raise my eyes and look at her.

'Do you want to talk about it?' she asked softly.

I shook my head with a levity I did not feel. 'It's nothing. Bad dream. That's all.'

Erula was not convinced. 'How often do you get these "bad dreams"?'

'I'm sorry,' I said quickly. 'I should have warned you.'

Her expression darkened.

'They're not that regular. I don't have them every night. It didn't occur to me that I would disturb you. I'm sorry.'

'Tallen!' Erula snapped, halting my nervous rambling. She continued more gently. 'How often?'

I shrugged. 'There have been times where it's been weeks between them.'

'And now?'

I hesitated, reluctant to admit it. 'Three or four nights in a moon cycle.'

Erula sighed in sympathy, and the tears threatened to start again. I looked up at the ceiling and concentrated on a dark knot in the timber while Erula waited patiently.

'Always the same dream?'

'Pretty much.'

She gently held my chin so that I was forced to look at her. 'My people believe that recurring dreams foretell your destiny.'

I laughed bitterly. 'I truly hope not.'

'No.' She shook her head. 'It's a blessing. The Gods offer the dreams so you can prepare. So that you'll know what to do.'

'That's not a comforting thought, Erula.'

She released my chin to softly stroke my cheek, smiling sadly. 'Let's get some breakfast.'

The day stayed fine as we travelled along the coast road towards Kingsport. The sun warmed our shoulders as the spring flowers exploded in celebration. Bluebells and snowdrops carpeted the meadows, claiming their share before the grasses grew too tall and blocked the sun's energy-giving light. To our right, the sea lay as still as azure glass. Small streaks of white were all that we could see of the swell from our point high on the cliffs, strands of foam as the water travelled over the sandbanks to the shore. Seabirds danced over the water as their harsh caws floated to us on the mild breeze.

I was left to my own company for most of the morning. I was unsure whether my dark mood was due to the dream or because Erula had seen me at my most vulnerable. Either way, the set of my shoulders and the frown on my face were enough to discourage others from lingering. It was late morning before Drey was the first to position his horse next to mine. He waited patiently for my shoulders to relax and the muscles of my face to soften.

I turned towards him, smiling to take the sting out of my word. 'What?'

'Erula is worried about you.'

I sighed, but Drey held his hand up to stop me.

'I know. But she is, so learn to live with it.'

'She says that my dreams are showing me my destiny.'

'It's a belief held by many peoples,' he agreed gently.

I gripped the reins tighter to cover my suddenly trembling hands. My bay objected, shaking his head and jostling me in the saddle. I concentrated for several heartbeats on relaxing my hands and calming my horse.

'I don't want to die under a mountain.'

'Tallen. Look at me.'

I continued to look ahead, biting my lip and avoiding acknowledging my words.

Drey repeated his words with a more commanding tone. 'Look at me.'

I reluctantly obeyed.

'Dreams, visions, portents, omens. None of them should be accepted as facts. Their meanings can be interpreted a number of ways. The full story is rarely revealed. Dreams are often only our fears, played back and magnified.' He looked at me and held my gaze. 'Did you feel Villermir's presence?'

'No,' I mumbled, terrified of the thought that the traitor priest was controlling me through my dreams again. 'But I never could tell.'

I was desperate to believe that the dreams were simply my own harmless fears, but the heavy weight lodged in my abdomen refused to lift. The suspicion that they foretold my doom proved resistant to hope. I could not think about what, if any, involvement Villermir had in them.

'Anyway,' Drey continued after a handful of heartbeats, 'that's not why I'm here.'

I turned to raise an eyebrow at him. 'Why do I sense that I'm not going to like this?'

Drey tried to look innocent, but I was not fooled. 'I don't know what you are talking about. I just think it's time we continued your studies.'

'Ha,' I crowed. 'And there it is.'

'Well, it will do you good to focus on something more constructive than feeling sorry for yourself.'

I turned to face him, my jaw hanging open for a sharp retort as soon as I could think of one. His face had crinkled into a small smile, pleased with the way I had reacted to his jest. I frowned at his easy manipulation of me as we moved to the side of the track and allowed the others to pass us. Drey held back until we were several horse-lengths behind the others before rejoining the road and slowly following.

'So,' I asked once I was sure we would not be overheard. 'What would you like me to learn?'

'Elemental control.'

'Oh, good. I liked playing with fire.'

Drey harrumphed. 'I noticed.'

I cringed in mock contrition. 'Yeah. Sorry. I will replace that rug. Did I ask if it was special?'

'Yes, you did. And no, it wasn't. But I think we'll leave fire until we're in a less public situation.'

'Probably best.' I nodded, but I could not contain my rising excitement and had to resist the temptation to bounce in the saddle. 'So, what am I to learn?'

'Air,' he said. 'I should be able to keep you under control with that.'

I grinned. 'Is that a challenge?'

Drey became serious. 'Remember, there is always a balance. Moving too much air will change the world's winds. Rain-laden clouds will be dragged from the sea so that areas suffer floods. Dry wind from the deserts will carry to farmland so that crops wither from drought. People could die because of your folly.'

'I know, Drey,' I whined at the familiar lecture. 'I'll be careful.'

It was Drey's turn to sigh. 'Very well. I want you to lift your horse's forelock.'

'Without scaring him halfway to Mobis's Hells?'

Drey looked at me with clear exasperation. 'Preferably. Now concentrate. Feel the air all around you. The spiderweb-thin currents swirling around Bolt's head.'

My concentration shattered. 'Bolt? He's called Bolt?'

Bolt tossed his head at the sound of his name. He jogged a few paces in response to my surprise as Drey rolled his eyes at me.

'Did you not even bother to find out your horse's name?'

'No,' I snapped, exasperated that he had totally missed the point. 'But *Bolt*, Drey. They've given me a horse that likes to bolt!'

The corners of Drey's mouth kinked upwards. 'I think it was Bow's idea of a jest.'

'Oh yes. Very funny. Remind me to congratulate the Head Groom on his humour. That is if I don't sneeze, causing Bolt to panic, who then runs off at full speed, and I fall and break my neck.'

'Don't be so dramatic. The horse trusts you fine. Now concentrate. Feel the air. Gather the strands. Weave them like lace.'

I slowed my breathing and relaxed the focus of my eyes. I caught the silver glimmer of spiders' webs in the periphery of my vision. Wished for them to come together; to twist and turn. The coarse hair of Bolt's mane lifted. I glanced sideways at Drey to see his raised eyebrow; he was not fooled, not for a heartbeat.

'That was the wind. It had nothing to do with you. And I said forelock.'

I smiled. 'It was worth a try.'

I slowed my breathing again, relaxing my focus and gathering the silver strands. Weaving them into a fine net. Watching as it glided in the air, folding this way and that so it caught the light. Playing with it like a gossamer butterfly, as fragile as a breath. I drifted it towards Bolt's head; careful not to touch his skin, careful not to brush his coat as his head moved up and down with each step. I moved the net backwards and forwards in time with his head, moving slowly closer. Small sparkles of light flashed like tiny diamonds, glinting enchantingly as the net gently swayed. I held my breath as I moved it under the dark hair of Bolt's forelock, biting my lip as I lifted the net and the hair rose from his forehead. The air moved so gently that the nervous bay did not even twitch his ears. I held the forelock away from his head, cradling the hair in the delicate mesh of air.

'Well done,' murmured Drey. 'Good control.'

My concentration faltered at his voice, and the net dissolved into the sea breeze. Bolt tossed his head as the forelock dropped back onto his forehead. I turned to grin at Drey, pleased with his praise.

'What next?' I prompted.

'I think that will do for now.'

I would not be dissuaded. 'Oh, come on. I was good. Let me try something else. *Please.*'

He hesitated while I contorted my face into something I hoped was pleading and appealing at the same time. Eventually, he gave a small nod.

'All right. Try lifting a pebble and holding it in the air.'

I smiled my gratitude and composed my thoughts before he had time to change his mind. Slowing my breathing and relaxing my focus, I gathered the silver strands as before. The currents of air were as thin as a single thread, only visible when reflecting the light. I opened my senses, trying to detect the tiny presence. My ears heard nothing over the rustle of the grasses and the background hush of the sea. The smell of the meadow flowers was carried away from me by the incoming sea breeze. All I smelt was salt.

While gathering the fine strands, I was able to divert some of my attention. I became aware of my own presence; the slight pressure that surrounded me; a part of me but distinctly separate. I gently pushed part of this presence towards the gathering mesh of air currents. As my presence grew closer to the net, the strands swelled. The hair-like threads grew to twice their size, then bigger still. Although still barely visible, the currents were now the size of my finger, bending and twisting as the lace became a solid ball. With barely a thought, I was able to flatten the captured air into a shimmering disc.

I slowly guided the disc under a small rock. It felt like handling water in a skin; too much pressure at one end would cause a bulging at the other. I bit my lip as I concentrated on feeding the air under the stone. My breath faltered as the rock wobbled, then rose. My lip was released as I smiled at my achievement.

The stone settled level with my foot in the stirrup, two arm-lengths away from me. Once in the air, the feat took very little concentration and I wanted to see how far I could push my new skill. Pinching off another portion of my presence, I weaved another ball of air current, flattening it as before, and guiding it under a rock the size of my clenched fist. It was soon hovering next to the first. Still not content, I aimed for a third. I produced another silver disc with surprising ease, slowly lifting the third rock to join the others. As it rose to an arm-length above the ground, I saw a slight crack in the stone; a small imperfection that caused the silver disc to deflect into this small space. Intrigued by the strange occurrence, I concentrated on this area, somehow resulting in more of the swollen strands of air current rushing into the crevice.

The stone shattered from the pressure of air inside the rock. Pieces smashed into the other pebbles, causing them to burst apart and shower tiny shards of rock into the air. Startled by the noise and peppered by shingle, Bolt stayed true to his name. He bolted, kicking his hind legs out behind him to force me forward over his neck. I grabbed handfuls of his mane as the hind legs connected with the ground and powered him towards the safety of the group of horses further along the track. I heard Drey grumbling about those who have the slightest talent always having to be the most reckless, as he followed me at a more sedate pace.

Mace led us away from the coastal road as the sun touched the trees in the distance. He had grown up in the area and his family still lived in the nearby village. He confidently led us towards the cliff and onto the track that provided access to the beach, sheltered by the curve of the cliffs. The way down involved a series of wide steps cut into the sandstone. A handful, including Mace, rode their horses down the steep slope, but the majority of us dismounted and guided our horses alongside us. The sandstone steps had crumbled into sand from years of use. Small wooden boards prevented the sand merging into a slippery slope, but I still needed to concentrate on my footing and keep a tight hold on Bolt's bridle. My shoulders were aching from the strain and my hand had cramped on his reins by the time I reached the bottom, but we all made it down without mishap.

The tide was out, resulting in the beach stretching a long way ahead of us. Large rocks gathered at the base of the cliffs, getting progressively smaller the closer they got to the tideline, which was marked by a small barrier of smooth boulders at least fifty paces from the cliffs. Beyond that, the beach was smooth with packed golden sand, occasionally interrupted by long, narrow pools of seawater that had been trapped as the tide receded. Grey seabirds waddled along the edges of these pools, poking for beach worms.

The final warmth of the sun was lost as we descended the cliff, leaving the chilly sea breeze to predominate. I was set the task of gathering driftwood, but wood was scarce on this tranquil coastline and I travelled some distance from the group in search of beached timber. The sounds of orders being shouted drifted on the breeze heading away from me. I had only collected five or six small items by the time I turned to find I was completely alone on the beach. The coastline had curved round to hide the group from view, although the trail of my footprints could be seen extending far into the distance. I had walked in a diagonal line towards the sea, and the water rolled slowly to meet me. The tang of saline tickled my nose as I watched the waves ease forward before being pulled back to the ocean. I placed the wood on the ground beside me as I sat and watched the hypnotic rhythm. Unconsciously, my breathing slowed to match the pace of the waves. Slowly in, slowly out, pausing before repeating.

I turned to the sound of a noise to my left. The light had dimmed so that I could barely see the figure approaching me. I squinted to gain a better look but could not make out the features until he was within ten paces of me. I recognised the voice first as Kutan hailed me.

'Tallen! Are you planning on staying out here all night?'

I stood up and brushed the sand off my clothes. 'You missing me, Kutan?'

He huffed in denial. 'Hardly. But there's food if you're hungry.'

My stomach grumbled at his words. 'I wasn't until you mentioned it. Hope it's more than biscuits and dried fruit.'

Kutan smiled, his teeth flashing white in the twilight. 'You'll see.'

We returned to find that word had spread of Mace's return and the villagers had arrived with wood, food and ale. A large bonfire was blazing brightly in the darkening night, with a party atmosphere in full swing as food and drink were passed readily between those who had gathered. I had never seen Mace so relaxed. He was hugged by many of the villagers, with hands lingering on forearms or shoulders.

The smell of roasting meat greeted Kutan and me as we neared the group and mixed with the crowd. Heppra beckoned me as I scavenged bread, meat and ale. She chatted merrily as I sat down beside her. The villagers and soldiers made a large ring around the fire, with an easy mingling of all. Kade sat at the appointed head of the circle with his back to the sea. I was positioned just over a third of the way round so that I could see three people to his right before the fire blocked my view. I tried to concentrate on what Heppra was saying but was frequently distracted by the antics occurring around Kade. His laughter carried easily and mixed with that of the village girls who surrounded him. Tawpin was seated midway between Kade and me. I could see him trying to hold a conversation with a man from the village, but his face was pinched into something resembling an oncoming storm. His eyes darkened as he turned to scowl at Kade with each burst of sycophantic laughter.

Annoyed with myself for obsessing over Kade's behaviour, I made my excuses to those around me and left the fire with a refilled tankard of ale. A small track led me up the cliff to a tussock of grass that provided a viewing point. The distance from the party provided me with perspective and I was soon smiling fondly at the interactions being played out in front of the fire. I relaxed my gaze so the images became blurred, their outlines flickering with the flames. Most shimmered with pale greens, blues and yellows. Kade rippled with a muddy red, paling to a dusky rose before darkening almost to black, and finally settling into a pulsing dull crimson within his lower abdomen. In stark contrast, Drey was bathed in a rich gold so his outline practically sparkled in the firelight.

My concentration was broken by a sharp curse as Tawpin slipped on the rocks below. I smiled as he struggled to join me on the tuft of grass.

'You all right there, city boy?' I teased.

'Fearsome Father, Tallen.' He sat heavily with a huff of expelled air. 'You pick some rubbish places to perch when you want to be alone.'

'I think you will find the important word in that sentence is "alone".'

He remained silent.

'You could always find your own perch.'

Tawpin continued to look out into the darkness in the direction of the water. I studied the shadows of his face, the curve of his nose, and the early stubble on his chin. I wondered when he had become a man. When had the carefree boy been replaced with this sensible adult?

Tawpin felt me watching him and turned towards me with a questioning frown. I dismissed his concern with a short laugh.

'I was just wondering who this sensible person was, and where my reckless Tawpin disappeared to?'

He returned my dismissive laugh. 'So sensible I've climbed halfway up a cliff to sit on an uncomfortable, damp lump of turf.'

I smiled fondly at him, impulsively throwing an arm across his shoulders and giving him a quick hug. 'I do love you, Taw.'

He raised an eyebrow to mock me, holding my gaze as his face slowly became more serious. 'Why does he still have the power to hurt you?'

'Thanks for drowning the mood.' I removed my arm, quickly raising my defensive barriers by creating a small physical space between us. 'I'm fine.'

'So why are you up here rather than feasting with the others?' He followed my gaze. 'Even now you can't take your eyes off him.'

I resisted the temptation to be flippant with him, maintaining my view of Kade as he raised his cup to salute the small group of girls surrounding him.

'Maybe I just wanted to be alone.'

He sighed in frustration. 'Could you not speak to him? Tell him how you feel?'

'Because last time went so well?! Anyway, what would I say? I have no idea how I feel myself, let alone how to explain it to someone who cannot stand to be around me. He infuriates me. He's acting so childishly. He's being so petty.' I sighed. 'But there's another part of me that knows he's just frustrated. And miserable. And scared. His father doesn't make it easy to fill Kerk's shoes.' I mocked myself with a harsh laugh. 'Now I sound pathetic. Hardly going to impress him.' I turned to look at Tawpin, shrugging in defeat. 'I just want it to be like it was. I miss him.'

'You can't spend your life trailing in his shadow, Tal. It's time you moved on.'

'I know. Well, my head knows but my heart's taking a little more convincing.' I leaned over and lightly kissed his cheek. 'I'll get there. But thank you for caring.'

I could tell his concern would not be so easily dismissed as he raised a hand to brush a stray lock of hair from my face. I frowned at the sudden intimacy, but he quickly reverted to being the friend that he was and let the topic drop. Taking a deep breath, he lightened the mood with a quick grin and a change of subject.

'Well, you enjoy your cliff-face vigil. I'm going for another drink.'

He hesitated before accepting my silence as confirmation that I would not be joining him. I watched him carefully descend the shifting sandstone. I was lucky to have Tawpin as my oldest and most trusted friend, but there was so much I could not tell him. Too many secrets between Kade and me, that Tawpin had no access to. I feared he interpreted my reticence as a personal slight. Sighing, I vowed to make it up to him soon.

The chill sea breeze finally drove me from my sanctuary. Most of the villagers had returned to their homes, with only a handful remaining with the soldiers. The fire had died down to a gentle glow and it was impossible to determine who was who. Several bodies were lying on the sand, close enough to the fire to benefit from its warmth. Those still awake had divided into a number of small groups. Two individuals had walked a short distance to talk privately. I would have to walk past them on my way back to the fire. I recognised the voices before I could see their faces, and stopped.

'Do you realise how much of an idiot you look?' Tawpin's voice rasped with suppressed anger.

Kade's tone was clearly mocking. 'Don't judge others by your own behaviour.'

'I'm not the one carrying on like the local drunk with those girls.'

'I fail to see how that is any concern of yours.' Kade's voice had dropped dangerously low.

Tawpin threw his arms up in frustration. 'By the Halls of the Lower Gods, Kade. How can you do that? How can you do that to *her*?'

I was close enough for Kade to see me over Tawpin's shoulder. Whatever had driven his behaviour tonight, I could tell that it wasn't the ale. His eyes were clear and his mind was crystal sharp.

'You overstep your authority, Equerry.'

The silence was so tense, I almost expected them to start punching each other. Tawpin's body was held so tightly I feared it would shatter. I hardly dared to breathe while the two glared at each other, a contest being fought within their stares.

Tawpin's shoulders eventually dropped in defeat as he pushed past his prince. Kade quickly transferred his disdain to me, raising a challenging eyebrow.

I took the bait. 'You are such a horse's rear,' I said as I moved closer to him. 'No, I take that back. You are a flatulent horse's rear.'

'I'm not really in the mood for one of your tantrums, Tallen. Particularly if that is the best insult you can come up with.'

'Really?' I was annoyed at how he had treated Tawpin, and ignored the warning tone in his voice. 'You surprise me. I thought you would be in a jolly mood. Your evening looked like it was going well earlier. From what I saw, you looked like you were getting pretty much everything you wanted.'

'And you have a problem with that?'

'Yeah,' I snapped. 'When you insist on being so mean. Looks like you've been spending far too much time with Breya. Stop treating people so cheaply. You don't have so many friends that you can afford to drive away those you have. Lay off Tawpin!'

His lips narrowed into a tight, predatory smile. 'Are you threatening me?'

I barked an incredulous laugh, still refusing to see his dangerous mood. 'How could I possibly threaten you?'

He shrugged dismissively. 'True. You are nothing. A necessary evil that I must tolerate. For now.' He leaned in close. 'But step carefully, Tallen. The moment you cease to be useful, I might just make sure you get what you deserve. You've ruined my life. I can easily ruin yours.'

I shuddered at the coldness of his stare. The Kade I grew up with would never have been so spiteful, but a lot had changed since then.

'Breya must be very proud of you,' I said quietly.

I followed Tawpin back to the fire, but lacked his courage to push past Kade.

Chapter Nine

The weather stayed mild as we left the beach, although we saw many signs of the powerful storms that frequently battered the east coast. Plants were restricted to sharp seagrass and spiky gorse as the constant wind blew off the sea. Despite the height of the cliffs, property was set well back from the edges. Buildings were small with low roofs to guard against the fury of the gusts when the winter gales raged. The few people we saw were tanned and weathered, deep creases lining their suspicious eyes. Kade and Hagan made a point of acknowledging all we met, receiving brief but polite responses.

We travelled the coast road for two days before being forced to turn inland as large sections of cliff had crumbled onto the beach. A few had slipped down to balance precariously, waiting for the next storm to allow them to complete their descent. Without a track to follow, the gorse and seagrass stabbed and cut the horses' legs, and the decision was taken to turn away from the coast even though it would mean extra days of travel. Away from the constant erosion by the wind, the land quickly returned to viable farming. The countryside changed to a more managed landscape as we rode further west, before having to turn north again. The recent prolonged rains were still evident, with many fields flooded near streams and rivers. Many farmers would struggle to grow a good crop this season unless the weather dried up soon.

There were several drainage channels dug into the rich soil across this part of the kingdom; long, straight barriers of water that drained the land in flood and provided supplies during drought. Tall banks lined both sides of these ditches, wide enough for the horses to travel in pairs. The murky water was punctuated by reed beds that provided an industry for some, and shelter for waterfowl that startled at our approach. Horse-drawn ploughs cut the dark turf in the fields. The workers raised an arm to us as we rode by, work continuing despite the insistent drizzle that seemed to accompany us. The draught horses' thick legs were being sucked by the heavy soil as they trudged the lines.

Only once were we forced to cross flooded land. The road took us across one of the larger rivers that were slowly draining to the sea. A small stone bridge provided a crossing to allow access to the market town of Wellbrook, and in order to return to the coast we needed to follow this path. While the near side of the bridge extended from the high bank that we had ridden along, the far side was submerged under muddy water. The Wellbrook side had been poorly maintained, and the swollen river had burst the defences in several places. Fields near the breaches had been completely submerged, with the floods in a few places extending for two or three fields from the river. More than one cottage looked to be abandoned as the flood surrounded them. The company halted to assess the risks associated with crossing the bridge and discuss the best way across the submerged path. The water extended several horse-lengths across before the track rose again, but there was no way of knowing how deep it went.

'A swim is just what we need on such a lovely day as this.' Tawpin had been riding next to me, and had halted his horse alongside Bolt. 'I'm already wet from this cursed rain. Submersion in a muddy river would be a delightful change.'

I grunted non-committally, not really hearing what he was saying as I watched Hagan attach a rope to his saddle.

Tawpin slapped my leg. 'Hey. Are you listening to me?'

I turned to face him, relaxing the shoulder muscles I had unconsciously tensed. 'I never listen to you.'

'True.' He cocked his head to one side. 'Are you all right?'

'Yeah.' I gave a small smile of reassurance. 'Just thinking of another time, another place.'

'Oh, now I'm intrigued. Tell me. Tell me now!'

I laughed at his eager face but hesitated before telling him my concerns. We had deliberately not discussed my adventures away from Liegeport, and I was reluctant to share the dangers Drey, Kade and I had faced on our journey across Lindvane. It seemed so long ago.

'It was when I left Liegeport the first time.'

Tawpin grinned. 'The time Kade followed you despite his father's instructions not to.'

'And mine.' Drey had moved Mupp to stand the other side of Tawpin.

'Yeah,' I agreed, grinning. 'Not his smartest move. Anyway, we had entered Lindvane. Everything was going well—'

Drey huffed, not agreeing with my flippant statement.

'Anyway! We had to cross a river, and the crossing was guarded by Hayton's soldiers.'

'Fearsome Father,' muttered Tawpin.

'So, we tried to avoid the crossing…'

'Tried?'

I glared at him in mock disapproval. 'Tawpin! If you keep interrupting, I won't tell you the story.'

He dropped his head in acquiescence.

'The river was swollen due to the rain. We travelled for a couple of days but found no safe way to cross. Kade, being Kade, decided to save the day and swim Mael across. The current was too strong. We nearly lost the horse and the heir.'

I looked over to Drey. He was fully aware of all I had left out. The loss of our supplies, forcing Kade to risk his life again to get more. The use of magick to calm the current and to give strength to Mael's valiant struggles, neither of which was enough. The fight with the soldiers when forced to use the crossing. The first time I had killed someone.

'This is different,' Drey said quietly. 'The river is calm. The flood holds little current and I doubt it is very deep.'

I nodded in acknowledgement of his words, accepting that the situation was very different. I turned back to the flood to find Hagan had led his horse into the water. He was more than halfway across and the depth was barely up to his horse's elbows.

Travelling north towards the coast again took us through less managed countryside. Small, scrubby woodlands bordered meadows of tall grasses and wild flowers. The days remained overcast, but the rain had stopped, and the blue, purple and yellow petals opened to catch what little sunlight there was. I spent many hours watching the small birds skimming over the plants after insects. Their tiny wings beat impossibly fast as they released soft chirrups in the excitement of the hunt. I relaxed my vision and slowed my breathing to reveal the currents of air flowing around their bodies as they dipped and dived. Shimmering hues of orange and red suffused their auras. Flashes of gold as the insects released their spiritual essence in the bird. The transference of being completed in a blink of an eye.

A constant presence on the landscape was a strange feature involving two rock pillars set a short distance apart. That distance made it impossible to determine how tall they were, although they must have been extremely large to be seen so clearly on the horizon. Two rectangular slabs of dark grey, with the right one a quarter smaller than the left. Any adornment was invisible this far away, but the flat colour was transformed whenever the sun peeked between the clouds. Flashes of reflected light played over the surface of both pillars, giving the impression of a metallic waterfall rippling over the stone.

I turned to Drey. 'What's that?'

A small smile twitched at the corners of his mouth. 'That is a portal to another time.'

'Oh, thanks for making that less clear,' I retorted sarcastically.

He turned his full attention to me. 'How much do you know of the old Gods? Not just the Sun and Moon. The Lower Gods.'

I frowned in concentration. I had not thought of religion for many years. I had not practised the Druidic rituals since I was a child in Methhold, when my grandfather would lead the festivities. Drey would preside over the sacred ceremonies at Liegeport but I rarely joined him, preferring the company of Tawpin at the Blue Boar.

'The Higher Halls of Eternity are the sole domain of the Sun God and the Moon Goddess. The ultimate balance between creation and destruction. Violence and compassion combined for infinite power,' I recited. 'The Lower Halls are where the smaller deities reside.'

'I'm not sure I would call them "smaller".'

'There are twelve Lower Gods, each responsible for some aspect of existence. These would be prayed to in order to bestow a particular virtue on the individual, or to encourage the Fates to favour them kindly.'

'And who are the Fates?' Drey prompted.

'The legend states that there were originally fifteen Lower Gods. Three broke the tenets of the Sacred Covenant, to honour all living things and protect the...' I faltered.

'To protect the conservation of ethereal energy.'

'The three disgraced Gods were banished to the Underworld and denied the protection of the Sun God and Moon Goddess. They sulked—'

Drey chuckled at the image of divine beings sulking.

'...and became the Fates. Mobis – death. Taranis – torment. Sluagh – abuse.'

'And what are their symbols?'

I thought for a moment. 'Mobis is represented by daemons, horned and hooved creatures. Taranis has the wheel on which he breaks his victims. Sluagh has the skeleton, to represent her undead armies.'

'And what are the names of the twelve Gods in the Lower Halls of Eternity?'

I glared at him in mock horror. 'Ask me an easy one, why don't you?' I sighed dramatically, buying myself some thinking time. 'There's Drunst, the God of Chaos.'

'Trust you to name that one first.'

I grinned. 'Arduinna, Goddess of Hunting. Balloch, God of the Harvest and provider of food. Sucellos, God of Good Fortune and Tawpin's favourite. Camlun, God of Battle.'

Drey prompted again as I ran out of remembered Gods. 'What about the elementals?'

'Oh. Edan, the Goddess of Fire. Muirfuin, the Goddess of the Sea. And there's a Goddess of Air. No… not air…'

'Spirit,' supplied Drey. 'Beathan is the Goddess of the Spirit, or soul. Life essence.'

He waited for me to finish the list, but I could not remember any more. I vaguely recalled that there was an animal one, but could get no closer than that.

'Achaius is the God of Animals,' continued Drey. 'Nathair is the Goddess of Healing and Herbals. Goraith is the Goddess of Peace and Unity. The final one could do with a little more reverence from you. Brennus is the God of Knowledge.'

'Oh! The raven.'

Drey laughed at my enthusiasm.

'Brennus is the raven and Nathair is the snake.'

'Do you remember the animal shamans for Balloch and Achaius?'

I frowned, trying to force the memory. 'Balloch is the badger,' I began hesitantly. 'Achaius is… some animal. A deer? Or a horse?'

'You're guessing. Achaius is a unicorn.'

'Did unicorns exist? You know, when dragons were about?'

'Yes, I believe so. There are many texts from the time of the Ancients that describe unicorns. Very shy beasts.' Drey looked at me and winked. 'Maybe they're still around, hiding in the woods.'

'They would need to be well hidden. I think Selte has hunted every animal in Faulknar's forests.'

Drey chuckled at the thought of Kyllian's hunt master chasing away a beautiful unicorn, preventing it from eating the food provided for the deer, to ensure he could hunt healthy deer rather than weak, starving ones. He would see no sport in that.

'So, are the stones connected to the old religion?' I nodded towards the pillars to remind Drey of my original question.

'Oh yes, the stones. They are located deep within the Fenlands.'

'The Fenlands?' I asked incredulously. 'It would take days to reach there if we rode in a straight line. How big are they?'

Drey smiled knowingly but did not enlighten me. 'The water level in the Fenlands was originally much higher than it is now. The stones were surrounded by a large body of brackish water with only a small island available for the community. It was called the Isle of Serpents.'

'Nathair.'

'Exactly. It was a healing colony. The perils of transporting the sick were more than compensated for by the powers of healing found at the site.'

'It attracted the best healers and the stones guided the way.'

'In part. The stones are made of flint.'

I looked at Drey. 'But flint lies horizontally through rocks. You would never get natural boulders like that. Is the flint stuck on or compressed into other rock?'

'The pillars are solid flint.' He looked at me to confirm his sincerity. 'They have stood as two distinct monuments for as long as anyone can remember. For as long as *anyone* can remember. The oldest records describe them as a natural feature. No one seems to have built them or transported them.'

'But solid flint is impossible.' I could not believe it.

'So is bringing people back from Mobis's Hells.'

I tilted my head in acknowledgement.

'The time of the Ancients was a time of many impossible things. The stones show signs of erosion over aeons; uncountable generations. Yet pure flint is all that is revealed. No contamination by any other material has been seen.'

I was still unconvinced. 'So, you think that these pillars were created by the Gods? By Nathair? Why? Flint is not a healing crystal.'

'But the stone has healing properties. It acts as a conduit, a channel for healing powers. Flint was commonly used as a purge; to clear poisons, particularly of the lungs and digestion.'

'And the pillars?'

Drey smiled at my reasoning. 'The talented healers were attracted to the Isle of Serpents by the stories of miraculous healing. Standing between the stones has been credited with healing everything from skin blemishes to possession by evil spirits. It still holds a reputation for boosting latent talents and promoting recovery.'

I was quiet while I considered this information. 'So, is that why the Lindvanes have taken most of the Fenlands?'

Drey shook his head. 'I doubt Hayton is concerned with the gifts of healing. With Villermir's services, I suspect he will be more interested in destructive powers.'

'The Empathy Crystal.'

'Indeed. Moving mountains and flooding territories seems more suited to his martial tendencies.'

'But healing your injured means more can continue the fight. Perhaps that explains Hayton's lack of restraint when it comes to casualties within his ranks.'

Drey sighed and we lapsed into an uncomfortable silence as we considered the dark motives of Hayton and Villermir.

The countryside changed subtly as we travelled further north towards Kingsport. The empty landscape developed a more hostile undercurrent: woodlands threatened malicious eyes tracking our movements, and empty buildings seemed intimidating. Unconsciously our pace quickened, and everyone became more reactive. The smallest noise spooked the horses, causing ripples of unease throughout the company. Conversation slowed as people scanned the horizon for threats, so that eventually we stopped talking apart from an occasional hushed word. Gestures replaced speech. The slightest movement outside our company was observed and assessed.

I was checking the scrubby treeline when I noticed Tawpin's back tense, noting that this seemed more than the tension caused by the stresses of the last few days. I glanced over at Drey, receiving confirmation that he had seen it too. I slowly moved my horse to walk alongside Tawpin's.

'You all right?' I asked cautiously.

'Yes,' he replied quietly.

Even that small exchange seemed extravagant within the strained silence of the wary company. It was some time before I had the courage to speak again.

'You sure you are all right?'

Tawpin took a long time to answer, and I was considering that perhaps he had not heard me when he finally spoke. 'We are in Kingsport lands. We crossed the boundary to the estate a little while ago.'

I watched his face tense and relax, giving the impression of clouds chasing over it as thoughts swirled in his mind. Many seemed to be painful.

'Home,' I said carefully.

He nodded. 'Home.'

'I can barely remember Methhold.'

He cocked his head, encouraging me to continue.

'Most of my memories involve fire. And ash. And violence.'

'I've never seen what was left of Kingsport after the attack.' His hands tightened on the reins. 'I remember the beautiful city it was, but it becomes corrupted and polluted in my mind. I don't know what to expect when we get there. I know that it will not be as it was; both when I was last there, and after the raiders. But I have no idea what it will look like now. My mind paints pictures of rubble and weeds. The accusing remains of fallen buildings.' He shuddered. 'Skeletons of those who died.'

'Tawpin.' I called his name harshly, trying to break his reverie. 'You could do nothing then. You were at Liegeport at the time, and your responsibilities kept you there. You have nothing to blame yourself for.'

'Even so...'

'Even so. You could offer no help to Kingsport or her people.' I paused to make sure he was accepting my words. 'Now the time is right for you to rebuild the city. And here you are.'

His gaze was still distant as he wrestled with his daemons. His brow deepened for a heartbeat before his face relaxed into a small smile. 'So, with my extensive knowledge of running a city, what would you suggest that I focus on first?'

I huffed in denial. 'You know plenty about running a city, you little street pest. You've been quietly controlling Liegeport for years.'

His smile deepened.

'Most of the merchants would have throttled each other without the mysterious rumours that would have them united against the tanners. And there would have been war between the merchants and the tanners, if they weren't suddenly allies against the dockers. And they would have revolted if the Holy Baila's new scribe had not been blamed for "redirecting the taxes".'

'All right, all right,' Tawpin laughed. 'Point taken. You have to admit that Rimmer has had it coming for so long.'

'True. But he did spend several weeks in the infirmary, just for being the tax collector.'

'Only because he was too scared to leave.'

The smile on Tawpin's face became genuine and I was happy to return it. We spent most of the afternoon discussing the priorities of a new Kingsport, many focused on the ready supply of ale. Tawpin's grip on his reins had relaxed and the tension in his back had dissipated by the time we crested a low hill.

The tension instantly returned as we crested the small rise that had blocked the breeze heading towards us. As we reached the summit the sharp scent of sea air was blown into our faces. We had returned to the coast road and our destination could be seen in the distance. Grey stone stood in contrast to the greens and browns of the encroaching fields; the dark river cutting between the sprawling halves of the city. A quiet monument waiting for the arrival of her duke.

There was a brief discussion concerning whether it would be more sensible to camp for the night and approach the city during the day. Erula's company and I were uncomfortable with spending another night in the unnerving countryside, and Hagan's men were also tempted by a night under cover. Reasoning that an attack was equally likely if we were exposed as it was within the port's walls, Hagan made the decision to ride for Kingsport and we eagerly urged our horses into a canter.

The sun was low in the western sky by the time we reached Kingsport. The road leading to the southern gates was still clear of grass and weeds even after not being used for so long: a testament to how busy this port once was. The wooden gates, however, had long since fallen. Rotten stumps of oak lay jumbled in the archway like skeletal limbs. Most were lying flat, although a few pointed towards the approaching riders like accusing, blackened fingers. Suddenly the idea of sleeping in the fields seemed more appealing, but we were here now, and Hagan did not hesitate to ride into the city. The main street was several horse-widths wide and was well illuminated, although the side streets were already in shadow after less than a horse-length. There were gaps between the stone houses where wooden buildings had once stood. Scorched timbers told of the infernos that had swept through the port on the night of the raid, shells of buildings that had housed the townspeople. In some areas a dark, charred pathway led to the river's edge, with charcoal furniture and broken glass still visible.

The stone buildings had fared better. Dark sockets watched us from windows no longer holding glass. Doors hung ajar, suspended from single hinges, or lay broken on the floor. Grass grew in the cracks, while moss clung to rough surfaces and ivy crept around the corners of the walls. The flint absorbed all the available light, reflecting nothing and looming, malicious and malignant, towards strangers. My back frequently prickled with the thought that archers were about to loose their arrows into my spine.

'No disrespect, Tawpin,' I said quietly, afraid to disturb the silence. 'But this place is really beginning to make me nervous.'

Tawpin did not defend his city, and the company unconsciously bunched together. We rode three abreast, with Hagan and Slicer riding slightly ahead of Kade, who was positioned between them. Dru, Kutan and Mace calmly manoeuvred to protect the rear. All swords were loosened within their scabbards, hands resting on or very close to their hilts. Multiple eyes scanned the rooftops, the side streets, the doorways, the shadows.

A bird exploded in a flapping of wings from a window, two buildings ahead of us. The sudden movement caused a chain reaction within our ranks – people jumped; horses startled. My attention was occupied with controlling Bolt before he smashed into the horses surrounding him, straining my ears for sounds of an attack.

Within five heartbeats all was quiet again. Nervous smiles confessed the anxiety that had built up. Parin and Heppra replaced their drawn swords, and Kutan released a deep sigh before grinning at Dru. We all felt a little ashamed at how easily we had been frightened.

'Time to set up camp,' commanded Hagan. 'Erula, Mace, scout out the building to the right. See if it will hold us for the night. Dru, Kutan, see if the wooden buildings down that side street have any serviceable firewood.'

The four named dismounted and passed their reins to those nearby, while the rest of us stretched out the tension in our backs. Erula had taken less than five steps towards the shadowed stone building when two arrows thumped into the ground at her feet. She yelped and jumped back as the sing of drawn metal filled the air. Fifteen swords were pulled as one, ready for an attack but unsure of where the threat would come from.

Nothing moved. Questioning looks passed between Kade and Hagan, as I looked to Drey for suggestions.

'There are a number of people here,' he said quietly. 'A lot. The attack could be coming from anywhere.'

Several heartbeats passed before we decided that no further attack was coming. Hagan nodded to Dru and indicated the side street where the firewood was to be collected. Hesitantly, Dru stepped forward.

Two arrows drummed into the ground less than a hand-length from his leading foot, which was quickly withdrawn.

Again, we waited, my heart beating painfully in my chest as I strained to hear past the pulsing blood in my ears. The evening light had dimmed so that the only visible pathway was the main track that we were following. Everything else was hidden and the archers could be anywhere. Hagan moved to stand in front of Kade, Slicer and Parin moving smoothly to either side to protect the King-in-Waiting from arrows. None came. Hagan took another step forward. Still no arrows were sent flying.

Hagan turned to call over his shoulder. 'Heppra, take *one* step back towards the city gates.'

She took the one step and was halted by two arrows entering the dirt in front of her feet. The arrows had not been visible until they were embedded in the ground, and only the slightest whisper of wind announced their arrival. We still had no idea where the archers were hidden.

Slicer sniffed noisily. 'Well, that makes it clear, then. We go forward.'

We cautiously moved forward, not quite trusting the obvious invitation to continue. No arrows obstructed our path provided we kept to the main roadway. As the last light from the sun faded behind us, a dim orange glow could be seen from what appeared to be the centre of this half of the seaport. The light grew steadily brighter as we travelled towards it and the darkness deepened around us. The city was completely shrouded by the time we entered a small courtyard serving as a crossroads leading to the main districts of the town and the dockyards.

Five men awaited our arrival. Muris and Etard had their swords half out of their scabbards before Slicer raised his hand to halt them. The men were standing impassively in a half-circle to block our advance; their swords were not drawn and their body postures was relaxed. There appeared to be no obvious threat, although every one of us knew that archers were strategically positioned in the buildings around us. I suspected that there were more armed soldiers nearby to support the archers if we tried to resist their subtle herding of us.

The central figure waited until Hagan was within two horse-lengths before speaking. 'Leave your horses. From here you walk.'

Kade began to protest. 'That's not acceptable. We will—'

'Nothing will happen to you or your horses, princeling.' The man in the middle was clearly in charge. 'Provided you follow instructions and keep your weapons sheathed.'

Kade's voice stayed dangerously calm. 'And if we don't?'

Uncountable numbers of bows with nocked arrows protruded from the windows surrounding us. The soft sigh as sinewy strings were pulled taut caused every eye within our company to turn towards the shadowed buildings. Both first- and second-storey windows contained at least one weapon aimed at us. We would not get far before we sustained multiple casualties: if the soldiers meant to kill, we would not survive the attack.

I focused my concentration in preparation. Swords would not help us here as we would not get close enough to harm the archers. I removed one hand from the reins, letting it hang by my side with the palm pointing forward. A faint tingling sensation trickled across my skin. The buzzing vibrated faster and faster. I was careful to remain still and continue watching the men in front. My palm grew warm with the beginnings of a fireball. Using my mind, I compressed the feeling into a slowly rotating ball, now visible but no larger than the nail on my smallest finger. With each rotation I made the ball denser, compressing the energy to provide the means for the explosion I required, but keeping it small enough to avoid detection until it was too late. The fire grew darker and darker as the power raged within its containment.

No!

The force of Drey's command within my head broke my concentration and the fireball evaporated. I turned to face him with a questioning frown, angry that I had lost the opportunity to defend us if required.

Drey shook his head slightly before continuing. *They have shown no ill intent. Do not provoke them out of fear.*

Mine or theirs?

Drey's frown confirmed that he had heard my thoughts.

With an almost imperceptible nod of his head, Kade agreed to the command. He turned the palms of his hands towards the men, holding them a hand's width away from his body, exaggerating his intention of being no threat and giving the archers no excuse to harm his company. Slowly and deliberately, we dismounted, careful to make no sudden movements. Fear and unease had turned into angry frustration now that the danger had been identified.

The central figure turned and walked down the track, fully expecting us to follow. A small group of youths scampered from the alleys to collect our horses, while the remaining four men who had caused our halt moved to herd us together. Subtly, the relationships of the group were revealed as the man in charge led us down the streets. Kade followed a few paces behind, with Hagan and Slicer at each shoulder. Drey, Tawpin and I were protected in the middle, while Hagan's and Erula's soldiers spread out evenly around us. The four townsmen encircled our group to ensure no one could sneak away. Each had lit a torch as the evening turned to night, restricting our view of the surrounding houses while those hidden within had a highlighted view of us.

I concentrated on the leader as we were led unerringly towards the orange glow at the centre of the port. He was a lean man, smaller than Kade and Hagan, but with a contained sense of power. He reminded me of the rangy hounds at Liegeport that could run all day and still bring down a fully grown stag. The other men in his group were similarly compact, shaggy-haired and stubbled. They wore clothes that had been patched many times, but carried their heads proudly and were not afraid to look anyone in the eye. Defiance was clearly seen in every deliberate step they took. I wondered what they were defying.

The orange glow slowly revealed itself to be a large bonfire, sited at the crossroads within the main square. Golden ash flew into the night sky from the fire, which was at least four paces in diameter. My opinion of the group's organisation grew as I pondered where the timber for the fire had come from. Most flammable materials had been destroyed when the port was attacked. I guessed that driftwood could explain some of the fire's height, but there was a deep earthy smell undercutting the woodsmoke. I shivered at the contrast between the derelict city and the bright, welcoming fire.

We were halted to one side of the fire, so I could see around it to the stone steps of the town meeting hall. The main doors stood empty, as with all the other buildings in Kingsport. The double-door portal was dark in shadow, effectively hiding what was inside. As I strained my eyes to peer into the dimness, I saw the shadows of people within the arches and doorways of the houses flanking the meeting hall. Turning to the buildings nearest to me, I saw men, women and children quietly watching us. Some had bows, most had swords; even the children carried wicked-looking daggers. This close to the border, these people were used to fighting, but why had they gathered in Kingsport? Surely it would make more sense to move further into Faulknar territory, especially with the children.

'You're a long way from home, Prince Faulknar.' A female voice carried clearly from the darkness, the stone walls of the town square providing the appropriate reflection of sound for the giving of speeches from the steps of the town hall.

Kade took a step forward to clearly separate himself from the group. 'So people keep telling me.' His tone was mocking but he had noted the respect given to his title that had been lacking earlier. 'Seems my role is to stay at home and make children.'

The voice remained within the shadows. 'You would make a lucrative prisoner of war.'

Kade barked a short laugh. 'You've obviously never met my father. He'd be glad to see the back of me.'

'You rate yourself too little. Hayton would pay well for your head. I have a small chest that would make a lovely presentation case.'

Kade's back stiffened, but his voice remained quietly mocking. 'If that was your intention you would have struck the moment we stepped into the port.'

'Maybe I wanted to hear you beg for your life.'

Kade finally dropped the mocking. 'That is never going to happen.'

'Perhaps for the lives of your companions?'

Kade hesitated a heartbeat before growling. 'Then it ends here!'

He stepped forward to ensure space for his sword as he drew the steel, and we all drew in unison to support his decision. We would not be held for ransom. We would not be used for political ends. The townspeople mirrored our sentiments. Swords and daggers were drawn all around us. The air around the bonfire crackled with more than the sparks from the fire.

'Hold!' The command rang out around the square. 'You are correct in your assumption that I do not intend to harm you or your company. But I would know why you have come with an armed force to Kingsport.'

Tawpin was the only one to lower his weapon. I turned to see his face creased into a frown, catching his attention and questioning him with a tilt of my head.

Kade answered before Tawpin could respond. 'Just passing through.'

'On your way to where?'

Tawpin took a step forward. 'I know that voice,' he mumbled as he made his way slowly forward.

'And why would that concern you?' Kade asked the voice.

'Friend or foe, your presence so close to the Lindvane border does not suggest comfortable times ahead.'

Kade drew breath to reply, but was halted by Tawpin pushing past him. The prince turned with a questioning expression as Tawpin walked towards the stone steps as if in a trance.

'Leyn?' he said quietly, before repeating a little louder. 'Leyn?'

Movement deep within the shadows slowly revealed itself as a tall, slender lady. A long cloak fell from her shoulders to reveal hunting leathers and a sheathed sword. A long chain hung from her neck to rest between her breasts, the firelight absorbed within the central dark jewel while the surrounding silver glistened like the stars. Her short, wild hair curled around a strong face as she stared at the man who challenged her.

'Tawpin?'

Chapter Ten

The mood within the port changed once Tawpin had been recognised. The archers withdrew, and the number of people dwindled to only a few to support Leyn. She was treated with a quiet respect and was clearly the one who made the decisions within Kingsport. The five men who had stopped us earlier remained with slightly threatening postures, but no further overt hostility was discernible. Leyn invited us into the meeting hall, taking a torch from one of the men to lead the way.

The hall had been damaged during the attacks, with pitted walls and crumbling stone; however the inside had been cleared of all furniture to leave a cleaned reception area once through the open doorway. Darkened rooms could be seen at regular intervals along the sides of the wide hallway. I looked up to see the carved ceiling still intact, with interweaving leaves and flowers. Even though the paint was peeling in places, it could not detract from the craftsmanship needed to make it. The building had once been an impressive one to greet rich merchants and dignitaries. Even now, there was evidence of some pride having been taken to keep the area tidy and free from dirt and dust.

The fine carvings continued on the staircase that led up to the first floor. Intricate swirls of spiral patterns wrapped around the spindles as my hand ran over the banister that was as soft as silk. The dark grain caught the flickering firelight from the torches as it curved gracefully to entice us to the upper rooms. Remnants of a long, narrow rug remained on the stairs and on to the first-floor hallway. Patches of vivid reds and blues scattered among the darkened areas that had been burnt and torn. The scene of a flower garden could be seen faintly, extending the length of the hallway but leaving a border of wooden flooring a handspan from the wall. The right side had been left open to provide a gallery above the reception area below. Metal brackets for torches were attached to the walls in between each of the rooms on my left, so that the landing could be brightly lit if required. I noticed that some of the brackets had melted in places, changing the fine sculptures to misshapen gnarls of iron.

Leyn guided us into the room at the end of the hallway, just before it curved around to the right wing. Candles were quickly lit to provide a warm atmosphere with their golden glow. Several chairs had been arranged into a semicircle around the fireplace that currently stood empty. The long table placed under the tall window was covered in papers and ledgers. A small dagger had been used as a weight to secure one corner of a map of the fens, while a goblet secured the opposite corner. A small pile of clothes was placed in the corner next to a chair, alongside which a sewing basket had several needles poking out of the wicker sides.

'Please. Sit.'

Leyn indicated the chairs in front of the fire. There were not enough for all of us: she and one of her men took a chair each, leaving room for Kade, Hagan, Drey and Tawpin to join them. The rest of us sat on the floor and leaned against the walls, content to hear the conversation even if we were not to be a part of it. I stretched out my legs and watched Tawpin as Leyn continued with the hospitalities.

'Sorry about the welcome.' She smiled apologetically. 'Can't afford to take chances this close to the border.'

'So, I'm a potential threat, while the Duke of Kingsport warrants a comfortable seat by the fire.' Kade smiled to take the sting from his words, although the implied reprimand for Leyn's impertinent treatment of the Faulknar heir remained.

Leyn shrugged easily, rippling her short ash-blonde hair. 'As a duke he merits a comfortable chair, but not a fire as it has taken him so long to return.'

I saw Tawpin flinch as his fears were made public. 'I'm sorry…'

Leyn turned her green eyes towards him, smiling fondly at him. 'Don't be. We understand that you have responsibilities in the capital. Duties to His Grace. Do I recall falsely that you were always ready for a little teasing when you were younger?'

Tawpin groaned. 'Don't remind me. You were a bully and have left me haunted by the jests of you and your friends…' He stopped abruptly, as the ghosts of those that had been lost in the raids drifted into our thoughts.

'Many are still here,' Leyn said quietly. 'Some have left us for safer lands. A few watch from the Halls.' A respectful silence hung for a couple of heartbeats before she broke the tension. 'But there will be time for reflection and remembrance later. Now a celebration is due the return of our duke and the presence of our prince. You have to tell me all the gossip from Liegeport.'

I let the conversation flow over me as my muscles relaxed and I slumped further against the wall. My eyelids grew heavy as the stresses from the ride through Kingsport left my body. The candle flame caused flickering shadows to dance across the room. I watched them lazily as Kade, Leyn and Tawpin's voices floated lightly around each other. Gossamer-pale wisps of air intertwined with the willowy shadows as they chased across the floor. The warm orange flames twisted and turned as the draughts kept a silent rhythm. The arrows of flame turned to tiny fire sprites, dancing in front of my eyes; miniature aerial battles as the gold and red creatures dived around and between each other, coming together, then pulling apart. The details grew clearer so that small wings could be seen pumping the air to manoeuvre the glowing bodies. Folded back along the body as the sprite dived on its victim. Spread out wide to arrest the fall as the victim shied away at the last instant. The creatures grew bigger to reveal midnight-black talons stretched out to tear at the glistening, muscular bodies; forelimbs and hindlimbs slashing as the muscles of the chest strained to pull the wings down and keep the beasts in the air. The thunderous crack as heads collided, whipped back on reptilian necks before slamming into their opponents. Bone-white teeth snapping as the heads withdrew. Both combatants locked in spiralling descent towards the slate-grey mountain crags.

A river of fire flowed over their heads as two sprites, now the size of dragons joined the fight. A bronze behemoth skimmed above the two locked together, its stocky body passing perilously close, but its fiery breath directed towards a smaller rival flying ahead. The flames caused the clouds to turn to steam, circular vortices rotating away from the body of the dragon as it flew through its maelstrom of scorched air. It screamed its frustration: the cry of a hawk but impossibly bigger, filling the crucible within the mountain range where the dragons flew. A screech and a rumble merging to rattle the shale and cause small avalanches of rubble far below it. The soft grey light reflected off the smaller dragon's dark emerald scales. It zipped and flittered, this way and that, membranous wings folding with incredible speed and delicacy. Constantly evading the larger pursuer while threading its way between other groups of dragons. Ripping and slicing. Clashing and barging. The metallic smell of blood mingling with the ash and the steam, making the air heavy to inhale.

The image shattered as my shoulder was shaken. Erula stood over me, laughing as I yawned. She tugged on my arm and encouraged me to stand.

'Come on,' she insisted. 'Let me take you to the room they've set aside for us before you fall asleep in the corner, and I have to carry you.'

I grinned. 'You could carry me anyway.'

She responded by shoving me in the back to get me moving. 'That's never going to happen.'

She linked her arm through mine and guided me through the darkened corridors. There were several rooms on the top floor of the hall: I suspected that these had been previously used for meetings and official business, but they were now commandeered for sleeping areas. We peered into many of these rooms before Erula found the one she was looking for. The spaces were essentially bare of any furniture, with only thin mattresses arranged in orderly lines. Most of the pallets were occupied, although a couple of the rooms were empty. There were no personal belongings that would hint at regular occupation, suggesting that it was more of a casual arrangement; if you find a spare space you can sleep in it. Erula led me to a room two thirds of the way along the right wing. This chamber was smaller than the communal sleeping areas and had only three beds in it. One was a small pallet similar to those I had seen earlier, but I was pleased to see the other two had solid wooden frames to support the mattresses. I almost groaned with my selfish desire to be warm and comfortable, and above any draughts from the door.

The shutters on the window were open and I could see the moon partially obscured by clouds; the light was enough to see despite the lack of candles or torches in this part of the building. I quickly claimed one of the beds, while Erula stood by the window looking over the dark town.

'That was a bit of a strange welcome,' I commented around a noisy yawn. 'Everything was fine once they realised we had Tawpin with us, but before that it was as if they were playing games with us. Why would they do that?'

Erula turned and walked over to sit on the bed opposite me. 'They *were* playing games with us.' She laughed at my indignant frown. 'Some use it as a way of testing their foe. They see how long it takes for the party to figure out where to go. Who in the group makes the decisions, and who listens?

Do they panic? Are they impulsive and reactive? Do they work together as a team, or are there divisions that could be exploited?' She shrugged. 'A lot can be learnt from playing games with people.'

I looked at her critically. 'Is that what you would do? Do you play games with people to find their weaknesses?'

Her lips rippled in a small smile and I had the impression that it contained a hint of pride, as if I had asked an important question.

'We have been known to play with rivals to assess their potential threat.'

'We?' I asked, suddenly realising that I knew very little about Erula. 'You have been repeatedly evasive about where you come from. Are you playing with me?'

The smile grew bigger. 'Of course.'

I felt my anger rise, banishing all thoughts of sleep. I noticed that she was relaxed and did not seem threatened by my accusing attitude, but I felt suddenly uneasy that I had let her into my confidence so freely. I retraced all our conversations, looking for hidden meanings and guarded secrets. Erula had been easy to talk to and had not seemed to consider her words, except in two areas – where she came from and her attitude to my sword. I addressed the easier of the two first. She had no discernible accent and her choice of clothing was an eclectic mix of different styles. Her dark hair and deeply tanned skin would suggest that she originated from a country south of Faulknar, but more than that I could not determine. My knowledge of kingdoms, outside of those Faulknar was currently at war with, was patchy at best. I went for the most southern place I knew, and my guess on first meeting her.

'I would guess at the Travellers' lands,' I ventured hesitantly. 'But further south than where they join Faulknar.'

She gave me a nod of acknowledgement. 'You guess correctly, although I suspect that it has less to do with reasoned deduction, and is more due to your lack of learning beyond that immediately affecting Faulknar.' She laughed freely at my scowl, raising her hands in a pacifying gesture as my frown deepened. 'Relax, Tallen. I am your friend. You have nothing to fear from me.'

I was not convinced. 'But why would you keep that a secret?'

'It's not a secret. I just haven't made the information common knowledge. People have come from all over, both for Faulknar and for Lindvane.'

'Are you telling me that there are Travellers fighting for Hayton?'

'Of course there are. Our northern borders run across both kingdoms. Both of you are a threat to us.'

'Faulknar is no threat to you,' I stated, immediately knowing it for the naive statement it was. 'Kade is no threat to you.'

'Kade is not king yet.' She lifted an eyebrow. 'And to be totally honest, he can be a little… changeable.'

I wanted to argue, I wanted to defend Kade, but found that I could not. Instead I remembered my time in the Travellers' lands, and my encounter with the head of one of the largest families there. One who had ruled as a king, despite claiming no stewardship.

'Eldiss promised he would not fight against Faulknar.'

'Eldiss promised no such thing,' Erula countered sharply.

'And how would you know?'

'Eldiss is my cousin.'

'So, he sent you to spy on us?'

'Eldiss sends people to spy on everyone.' She took a deep breath and continued with a quieter voice. 'He has many cousins and he does not speak for all of us. Despite what he would like to think. Some have simply come for the work, but some have come to see what the kingdoms stand for. Who can we trust? Who will protect our lands and our freedom? I truly hope it will not come to it, but I fear that we shall be forced to join your war at some point. We will not go into that decision blind.'

Erula watched me closely as I considered her words. Faulknar was isolated, while Lindvane had both the Hilman and Gallowgla kingdoms for support. I feared that the Travellers would join them to completely besiege Faulknar, but I could not deny that the choice must be theirs. Kyllian had spies in Hayton's court, and it was accepted that there would be Lindvane spies in ours. Was what Erula was doing so different? My head ached from resisting the urge to shout and rage; from trying to be reasonable. I was starting to feel very tired.

'Tallen.' Erula gently broke into my thoughts. 'I spoke true when I said I was your friend.'

'I know,' I mumbled, wondering if I spoke the truth or whether I just wished it so. 'I would have you at my side when the time comes, but I also hope that the war never touches your home.'

'On that we can agree.' She turned to lie flat on the bed. 'Get some sleep, Tallen. We can talk more in the morning.'

I followed her example and rolled over to lie on top of the woollen blankets. My mind raced with the potential consequences of Erula deciding to fight for Lindvane. Of standing opposite her on a battlefield. Of Faulknar being completely surrounded by enemies. My thoughts circled around the words that had been spoken, and those that had not. Could I trust her not to betray me? Or Kade?

I had not asked her about her manner towards *Saorsa*. How she had avoided holding the blade that had cut other members of her group. Looking back, it seemed she looked at the sword in the same way that Drey did; not with the envy and desire I saw in everyone else, but with an almost religious reverence. I cursed myself as a coward as I eagerly decided that this was a conversation for another time.

I awoke early, having had little sleep and yet come to no conclusions regarding whether my trust in Erula had been misplaced. The shutters had been left open so I could see the morning mist coming in from the sea. It covered everything in a blanket of pale grey and softened the cries of the seabirds as they challenged each other for scraps. I dressed quietly, making sure that the buckles of my baldric did not wake Erula as I settled it over my shoulder, and that my knives remained silent as I slipped them into their holders at the base of my spine. I tucked my sharp dagger into the sheath at my hip opposite *Saorsa*, stashed my small, blunt knife in the cuff of my boot, and even debated whether to hide some poison in my trouser pockets. I decided against it. The poisons I carried worked slowly, so I would not need them urgently and would have time to retrieve them if required.

Quietly, I closed the door behind me and walked along the hallway of the right wing. The detail that had been hidden the previous night was visible in the muted colours of the misty dawn due to a large window that was almost the width of one wall. Broken panes had been repaired with timber, making it seem like a patched sheet, but enough glass remained to illuminate the hallway and highlight the furnishings that still remained. Most of the torch brackets in this corridor were twisted, and scorch marks could be seen along over a third of the wall. The carpet seemed to be a continuation of the garden scene that started on the stairs leading to the upper floor, but much of the pattern had been burnt away, leaving holes through which the boards below could be seen. Despite the extensive damage, the doors to the sleeping rooms were in good repair and the wood had been scrubbed clean. There were two low tables that held stubby candles in carved holders, roughly chiselled but care had been taken over the design and the smoothing of any rough edges. I was getting an impression that the people of Kingsport were making the best of what they had, to give some sense of pride in their home.

Following the corridor round the curve, I peered into the chamber where the meeting had taken place the previous evening. Leyn was sitting to one side of the empty fireplace, the basket of sewing at her side. She was patching a tunic, with a needle sticking out of the corner of her mouth as she worked at untangling a mess of thread. A faded blanket was wrapped around her shoulders to guard against the morning chill. I was able to watch her free the thread and continue with her fine stitching for some time before she noticed me.

'Please,' she said with a soft smile. 'Come and join me.'

I hesitated for a heartbeat, not wanting to disturb her, but she gestured to the chair next to her and I did not want to appear rude. Leyn continued with her sewing as I crossed the room and settled into the comfortably padded chair.

'Did you sleep well?'

I lied easily. 'Yes, thank you. Although I am not sure I deserved the luxury of a bed. A pallet would have sufficed.'

She waved her hand in dismissal. 'Not at all. A bed was the least we could provide for a good friend of our duke.'

'It still sounds strange.' I grinned. 'Tawpin, a duke.'

She laughed quietly. 'I know. As a boy he would avoid anything that carried even a hint of responsibility.'

'He's not changed much.'

'That's good to hear. Although, he seemed competent enough last night when we talked about the factions involved with Liegeport's trade.'

'He's been quietly manipulating the different guilds for years, keeping them at each other's throats so they don't look too closely at Kyllian's taxes. Although, I have to admit his dealings are more like mischief than management.'

Leyn sighed wistfully. 'Some taxes would be nice. We have no trade, so, woefully, no taxes.'

I shrugged. 'You seem to be managing with what little you have. You've treated us very well. You have my thanks.'

The graceful lady opposite me dismissed my comments with a slight shake of her head. 'As I said, your gratitude is not required, although I appreciate the thought. We take care of our own and always welcome extra hands to help with the lifting and carrying.'

'Oh, you'll have some good hands for that. Most of Kade's men are built like plough horses, and work just as hard.' I hesitated before pushing for more information. 'You never asked Liegeport for help. I understand the need to "take care of your own", but a share of Kyllian's treasury could make your lives a lot easier.'

The corner of Leyn's mouth curled in a small smile, and she tilted her head to appraise me and my thinly veiled accusation. She let the sewing sit untouched in her hands, waiting several heartbeats as she considered her response.

'I can see why Tawpin likes you,' she finally admitted. 'You are correct; there are a number of reasons why we did not call on Kyllian. However, you should not assume that this was because we side with Hayton. We do not.'

The reprimand was mild, but the tone suggested the force of character with which she controlled the city. I inclined my head in acknowledgement, and she continued with a milder tone.

'One reason was that we did not want to recall Tawpin before he was ready. He had great fondness for his family and I know their loss will have affected him deeply. He has many ghosts to deal with before he can be comfortable in his home.'

'He did not come willingly,' I admitted. 'Kyllian sent him. Those ghosts are still malevolent.'

She nodded. 'He said as much last night, but for whatever reason he has taken the first steps.'

She paused, maybe hoping that I would be content with her answer, but I prompted her to continue.

'Tawpin wasn't the only reason.'

'No. A greater reason was because we are extremely vulnerable here. We have Lindvane to our south and west, and while Gallowgla has not raided this far west yet, it is only a matter of time. We feared... I feared that asking for Kyllian's aid would be a very public declaration of our fealty. I remain unwilling to draw such attention to ourselves. I have very few soldiers, and they have done their best to train people to defend their homes and families. But we are ill equipped to defend against even a small-scale attack. We have little hope against a sustained assault.'

'I admit that it seems to have worked so far, but it won't last forever.' I sighed at the thought of more harm coming Kingsport and her people. Tawpin would be devastated. 'Kyllian has noticed. It won't be long before others do.'

'I know,' agreed Leyn sadly. 'I feel Tawpin agrees with you.'

'He will listen to your counsel, Leyn. He cares deeply for Kingsport and would value your views on keeping her safe. But he will choose Faulknar over Lindvane when the time comes. He will always side with Kade.'

Leyn tutted. 'I'm not so sure about that.'

I frowned in confusion. 'What do you mean?'

Her cheeks coloured with embarrassment. 'Oh… well… I think I have spoken out of turn. Tawpin told me that in confidence.'

I raised an eyebrow, suspecting some mischief to be had. 'I'm sure he would be happy if you told me. What's going on between him and Kade?'

She fluttered with her sewing that had been forgotten on her lap. 'I've said too much.'

I smiled wickedly. 'You know I will inform Tawpin that you told me, so you may as well tell.'

She narrowed her eyes at me. 'Now I can truly see why Tawpin likes you. Very well, but you did not hear it from me. Tawpin and I were catching up on our separate lives. I talked about Kingsport and he talked about Liegeport. He talked about you so much, I naturally asked if you were courting.'

I choked on my gasp of air, spluttering in my surprise. 'Courting?'

She shrugged her shoulders. 'It was an easy mistake to make. I knew nothing of Kade's command.'

'Kade's what?'

'Well, "command" was not the term Tawpin used, but it amounted to the same thing. It seemed that there was an understanding that you…' she screwed her face up, knowing she would provoke my indignation again, but unable to find a word that would soften the term, '…belonged to Kade.'

It took a surprising amount of willpower to keep my face neutral. 'Really?'

Having begun, Leyn seemed happy to provide the details of the gossip. 'Apparently, he broke the nose of a stable boy who made the mistake of commenting, within the prince's hearing, about how he… admired you.'

'I'm sure Kade was just defending my honour.'

'And another time, after he was married to Breya, he gave a black eye to a guard who he thought was making moves towards you.'

'I did not know that.' My anger was starting to rise and I was finding it increasingly hard not to pace the room.

'I think that was the reason why Tawpin never told you about how he feels.'

'How he feels?!' My mind circled around the thought that my childhood friend could have some sort of feelings for me. That was absurd. He had never even hinted... But then Leyn had just explained the reason why Tawpin would not have said anything. Surely, she must have misunderstood. I recalled all our interactions with a new perspective; especially the night at the beach near Mace's village. 'Oh, Leyn.' I sighed deeply. 'Tawpin is my best friend. I care for him deeply. As a brother. He deserves someone much better than me.'

'Who deserves someone better than you?' Tawpin breezed into the room. 'And is that even possible?'

I burst out laughing at the sudden terror on Leyn's face, as her cheeks glowed with embarrassment. Her eyes darted between me and Tawpin, horrified that he may have heard our conversation. I could not contain my sniggers at her expression. It took her several heartbeats to realise that I was not going to say anything, before she succumbed to a fit of giggling herself.

Tawpin raised his eyebrows at our conduct, scratching at hair still spiky from sleep. 'Why do I get the feeling that you two should not be left alone?'

His comments released another round of chuckles, causing him to throw his arms up in exasperation before flopping into the chair next to me. He waited impatiently for us to get our mirth under control.

'So, what were the pair of you talking about that became so hilariously funny the moment I walked in?' he asked when we had finally mastered ourselves.

Leyn snorted and bit her knuckles to prevent herself from starting to laugh again.

'Just girls' talk,' I replied, smiling sweetly.

Tawpin sniffed. 'I suspect that it would be best for me not to know, then.'

I widened my smile. 'Smart boy.'

He frowned. 'I'm definitely going to have to keep you two apart. Both of you know far too much about me.'

Leyn had bitten her fist so hard that I could see the teeth marks when she turned the hand to cover her mouth, eyes glistening with unshed tears. Tawpin took a deep breath and wisely changed the subject.

'I had a thought to tour the city this morning,' he proclaimed. 'And was wondering if you lovely ladies would care to accompany me?'

Leyn shook her head. 'That sounds like a wonderful idea, but I have commitments this morning. Perhaps this afternoon?'

'Not at all.' I dismissed the suggestion easily. 'You have responsibilities, Leyn. I can keep Taw company. I'm sure he remembers his way around. We can have a nice chat as he shows me the sights.'

Leyn replaced her sewing in the basket and rose gracefully. She laid a hand on my shoulder, leaning in so only I could hear her. 'I hate you.'

I smiled sweetly. 'It was good to talk to you as well.'

She shook her head but was smiling as she left the room. I turned to find Tawpin looking at me with a slight frown on his face. He desperately wanted to know what we had been talking about, but I needed to think about the information Leyn had given me before I would be ready to enlighten him.

'Come on then, duke boy,' I said as I slapped him hard on the thigh. 'Show me your city.'

'Yeah,' he replied softly, rubbing his thigh. 'Let's see what's left of the old place.'

The sea mist still pervaded the port as we left the hall and returned to the square. The bonfire remained as a pile of smouldering embers, adding a smoky scent to the damp air. Few people were around, and those who were huddled into their cloaks as they hurried about their business. We walked leisurely through the wide main streets as Tawpin told me about the markets and stalls that used to line the pathway, selling everything anyone could ever want. He frequently paused to examine a burnt shell of a building or a remnant of wall, remembering how the city had once looked. I allowed him the freedom of his thoughts, watching the emotions cross his expressive face without comment. He slipped seamlessly between the sorrow of things that had been lost, and lively anecdotes about what had been. Despite the destruction we saw, he often had me laughing at tales of Kingsport folk who would relieve unsuspecting traders of their money with stories of mermaids and shape-changing faeries, or would get noblemen drunk on sweet syrups in order to get them to agree to exorbitant prices. He told me a story of a romance between rival families that resulted in a goat becoming the dowry, and of the lives of fishermen being saved one stormy night by the local herb-witch dancing naked down the main street.

The mist had lifted by mid-morning, allowing the sun to share its warmth. More people started to mill around the walkways: chatting with friends and neighbours, exchanging wares and cleaning paths. They greeted their duke politely, if hesitantly. Tawpin charmed and reassured them, apologising for the delay in returning but promising that he would now ensure that their needs were met. I saw some reservation, but most were willing to give him the benefit of the doubt. They remembered his family fondly, and condolences were shared freely as all had known similar losses.

Around midday, an elderly lady generously invited us in for something to eat. She explained that her husband had been killed in the raid along with one of her sons. The other son had left to join Kyllian's soldiers, and while her daughters and their families lived elsewhere in Kingsport and made sure she was sufficiently cared for, she liked her independence and had refused to move into one of their busy homes. Her daughters had ensured that her pantry was well stocked with the basics of flour, cheese, ham and oats. There was fresh and preserved fruit, eggs with random downy feathers still attached, a loaf of bread along with a few small rolls, and a pitcher of wine. Either this woman's family were exceptionally prosperous, or Kingsport were faring better than first appearances would suggest. The grandmother shared her bread, cheese and ham with us willingly, but I noticed that Tawpin ate sparingly so as not to take more of her resources than was polite.

My suspicion that all was not as it seemed was further supported by the internal structure of her house. While the outside seemed to have changed very little following the sooty aftermath of the raid, the inside suggested that violence had never occurred. The floors were scrubbed and clean, with no scorch marks or damage visible. The furniture was sparse, but the main table and chairs looked newly made from timber, while a pair of comfortable chairs near the fire had clean, vibrant upholstery. Time and resources had been used to ensure an adequate level of comfort was maintained, confirming my opinion that Kingsport was not as helpless as it wanted to appear. It seemed that Leyn's plan of not drawing attention to the city extended beyond not asking for help from Kyllian. The whole town appeared to be a facade of poverty and disrepair, while in truth it was still a resourceful and determinedly independent port.

My assumption was further supported when we left the old woman's home, and I assessed the city with a new perspective. Peering in through open doors, I repeatedly saw clean floorboards at odds with external appearances. The occasional glimpse of furniture showed young timber and colourful fabrics. As we made our way to the docks, the commerce of the city became apparent. While Tawpin mourned over the damaged warehouses, the bright colours and gilded statues that were no longer present, I noted the efficiency of those hawking the morning's catch of bass, flounder, crabs and razorfish. They did not mourn the passing of their prosperous heritage, but continued the ancient traditions of fishing and trading. While their clothing may be worn and patched, they were healthy and carried their heads held high. Leyn had managed her city well.

Chapter Eleven

We spent the afternoon by the waterside, recreating more carefree times spent on the shore at Liegeport. The tide at Kingsport stayed close to the sea wall, almost breaching the stone defences at its highest point, whilst receding to reveal scarcely a dozen paces of stony beach. We clambered among the rocks, searching for the egg cases of dogfish that we claimed were the purses of mermaids, and stones with holes scoured through by the relentless scraping of sand that were considered lucky omens by those who worked the north Faulknar coast. We inspected rock pools for shrimp, hermit crabs and starfish, competing over whose pool had the most limpets. We invented stories about the flotsam we found that had been tossed from fishing vessels, and those further out.

By early evening we had exhausted our curiosity and were content to sit on the sea wall, legs dangling over the incoming tide. The rhythm of the waves had a hypnotic quality, and we lapsed into a comfortable silence as we watched the seabirds dance over the breakers. The sounds of the port were muted; no longer full of the cries of merchant ships hailing their arrival and the buzz of activity that was provoked by the promise of new cargo. Now the trading was completed by mid morning, and the rest of the day was spent catching up with friends, repairing nets, fixing furniture and patching clothing. The mood was calm, and I was glad to notice that the strain I had seen in Tawpin's face since we'd crossed into his lands had finally subsided.

'I suppose we should be going back,' I sighed.

'We can stay a little longer.' He turned to face me. 'I've enjoyed today. Thank you.'

I pushed my shoulder against his. 'See, it wasn't so bad coming back. You were right; your people are strong. Resilient. Kingsport will be great again.'

He shrugged. 'Perhaps. There's a lot of work to be done. The jetties have been totally destroyed. Nothing bigger than a fishing sloop can dock here at the moment.'

'Leyn seems to think that is a good thing. She has focused on rebuilding the insides of people's homes. Nothing too obvious.'

Tawpin nodded slowly. 'She said as much last night. She doesn't want to draw unwelcome attention to Kingsport.'

'But you think differently?'

He was quiet for a while. 'Yeah. I think I do. Kingsport was not meant to hide in the shadows. She's too proud for that. And Liegeport shouldn't have to stand alone.'

'If you rebuild the docks, you are likely to get attention from Gallowgla as well as Lindvane.'

He nodded again, more confidently this time. 'I know. But it's time. We have mourned long enough. Hagan and the others will help improve our defences. I'm entitled to a standing guard and the king owes me that. It's time we stood up for what we believe in.'

I smiled at him. 'Your father would be proud.'

He returned my smile, although with more than a hint of sadness. 'Come on,' he said as he swung his legs over the wall and stood on the causeway. 'We have one more stop to make before going back.'

Tawpin led me through the streets towards the far end of the town. The roads grew quieter as we left the docks and the many small market squares. Residential dwellings became the more prominent buildings as we headed south along the swiftly flowing river. Ribbons of dark, gelatinous mud lined the banks as the silty river ran away from the sea, forced inland by the rising tide. As we walked away from the business end of the port, the houses became bigger and mainly built of stone; most were two storeys, a few glass windows remaining intact, and fire damage was less prominent. Occasionally we saw small reminders of cottage gardens with manicured lawns and flowers in bloom, although most green spaces had been commandeered for more practical purposes such as growing vegetables.

Tawpin stopped suddenly as we turned a corner to reveal a grand building shaped to slightly resemble a rolling hill; two storeys of pale stone stood proudly flanked by long, one-storey side buildings. The roofs curved to meet each other like the hull of an upturned ship. A low flint wall enclosed the property, but there were no gates at the beginning of the gravel drive, leaving an open invitation to visit the house. Wide steps led up to a pair of wooden doors, stone pillars supporting a curved lintel with the Kingsport crest embedded within.

'They've repaired the doors,' Tawpin said quietly.

The double doors guarding the house were heavy timber, but plain and functional. The original doors had probably been destroyed in the raid, but the town had taken the time and effort to replace them. I waited patiently as he surveyed his family home, a slight frown creasing his face. I was sure he was revisiting memories of happier times with his parents and sister.

It seemed a long time before Tawpin was ready to step onto the enclosed pathway and walk up to the house. The doors opened easily, and we entered a large reception area that looked as if the raid had never occurred. The wooden floor was polished with wax so that it shone in the light from the open doorway and ground-floor windows. The dark-stained panelled walls were decorated with tapestries that showed no sign of damage or repair. Small tables were scattered along the walls, covered with clean linen and displaying vases of flowers taken from the verges along the driveway that we had just walked. A wide staircase swept up to the next level, the balustrade rubbed dark and smooth. While it appeared as if the raid had not touched the interior of the house, I knew that it had and I was slightly unnerved by the care and attention that had been put into the building. It seemed almost like a shrine to the way things had been. I felt as if I desecrated the place just by being here.

A liveried servant appeared from a side door, carrying a bundle of linen sheets. He startled at our presence but recovered quickly to bow, rising with a big smile. 'Welcome back, my lord,' he said formally. 'I am just about to place fresh sheets in your room. I took the liberty of moving you to the master suite. Would you care to inspect the rooms now? Or perhaps a tour of the house so you may advise on any changes you require?'

Tawpin did not recover as quickly as the servant, stuttering his reply. 'Thank… thank you. Please… continue with your work. I can look around by myself. Thank you.'

'Of course, my lord.' The man bowed again before hurrying up the stairs.

I turned to Tawpin and aimed a lopsided grin at him. 'It is just me, or is this a bit strange? Not just the calling you "my lord" bit, which I will never get used to. But it all feels like you have just come back from shopping at the market, rather than having been gone so long.'

'I know. I half-expect my father to walk through the door, or Elin to run down the stairs.'

Not wanting my friend to dwell on his sad memories of the past, I grabbed his arm and pulled him through the hallway to the corridors beyond. 'Come on then, Duke. Show me your home.'

The house was longer than it was wide, and we passed several grand rooms that had been used for receiving and dining guests. Tawpin explained that both his parents had enjoyed entertaining and had used every excuse possible to host a social occasion. Each room was as well maintained as any in Faulknar's royal house, waiting patiently for its master to return and continue the revelry. At the far end of the corridor, another pair of stout wooden doors opened onto the grounds at the back of the house. From the top of the steps I looked over a large area that would have been the family lawns, where the entertainment of their guests would have continued and the young family would have played. Another low flint wall separated this from a stable yard and paddocks, complete with a number of grazing horses. Beyond this, the estate opened into the fenland grassland with a small herd of cattle nibbling on fields that extended to the riverbank. A few sheep could be seen dotted around the horizon in a view I suspected had not changed for generations.

Time had moved on, however, and the obvious change in Kingsport's fortunes was apparent in the area that had been the lawns. No longer used as a recreational space, the turf had been removed to create rows of turned earth sprouting with a variety of root vegetables. Women and children rooted in the dark soil, harvesting potatoes, turnips, carrots and onions. Another area provided food such as cabbages and cauliflowers, while a third grew tomatoes, peas and runner beans. Tawpin pointed to a secluded area nestled in a curve of the wall, where raised beds caught the last of the evening sun.

'The herb garden was my mother's', he explained. 'She and the cook would spend so much time encouraging the plants to grow. She would be pleased that the gardens have been put to good use.'

I sat on the steps as Tawpin left me to walk among the workers. He made a point of talking to everyone; a comment about the plants, an appreciation of their hard work, an acknowledgement of their commitment, a touch on the arm, a pat on the shoulder, a smile and a tilt of the head. I watched him weave the threads that would bind them to him; saw a glimpse of his future as the duke of these resourceful people, as he led them back into the wars of Faulknar.

Tawpin was unwilling to stay at the house, so we walked back to the town hall as darkness started to take hold. We followed the buzz of noise into a large dining hall where tables and benches crossed the room in long rows. My stomach grumbled at the smells of roasted meat and fish, realising that we had eaten very little that day. I looked around the crowded room for familiar faces, seeing Leyn, Kade, Hagan and Erula at the end of one table. I pointed them out to Tawpin.

'Go and join your lady,' I teased.

'You not joining us?' he asked.

'Maybe later.'

I left him to join the rowdy company of Parin, Heppra, Mace, Dru and Kutan. The food and ale were in plentiful supply, adding yet more confirmation to my thoughts that this town was other than it had first seemed. The mood was celebratory, and I suspected that it was deemed an official feast to welcome Tawpin home. The suspicion I had seen the previous night was well hidden, as the people fully embraced the opportunity to toast their duke and leave their labours until the morning. The evening passed with much jesting and laughter.

It was late in the evening when a scream was heard above the noise of the hall. The room seemed to explode as people jumped up and drew their swords, instinctively moving towards the cry without being aware of its cause. Unknowing of the danger that provoked the alarm, I followed the crowd out of the town hall and into the streets. The port vibrated with activity but I was still unsure of what was happening. There seemed to be no direction to the disturbance. All around the town square, shadowed figures ran. Out of buildings. Down alleyways. Voices shouting for haste; moving in all directions with no apparent focus.

Then I heard it. My stomach dropped as the sound of ringing metal confirmed that we were under attack. I desperately scanned the square. So many faces were unfamiliar. Who was friend and who was threat? I looked round to see Parin and Heppra were also hesitating, trying to determine where help was needed.

The lean man who had escorted us through the town beckoned to us from the far side of the square. 'This way.'

We followed him down side streets, back towards the town gates. We only managed to get halfway to the outer walls before we saw the fighting. Small bands of townspeople defended their city, trying to prevent the advancement of the invaders. The children were trying to avoid the fighting while putting out the small fires that had been set, smoke adding to the confusion. The main threat came from the hand-to-hand conflicts. People fought valiantly to protect their homes, but it was clear that the invaders were professional swordsmen. They presented an organised front, steadily forcing the fight further towards the centre of the port. Kingsport was suffering heavy losses.

I turned to the fighter in front of me, vision restricted to the expressions on his face and the movement of his shoulders. My reflexes responded to his lunge and slice, controlling my breathing to ensure my senses remained focused. Block. Parry. Undercut. He was not much taller than me. Our reaches were well matched, but I was more agile. I twisted under his swing, continuing the circular turn to face his unprotected back, stabbing up through his ribcage and letting the force of his collapse pull my blade clear.

I took a quick survey to locate Parin and Heppra. Parin had paired with Dru, supporting a pair of Kingsport fighters: two bodies lay at their feet. I did not see Heppra.

I ducked as a sword flew over my head, and my attention returned to the fighting around me. An opportunistic slice to the leg distracted my assailant long enough for me to deliver a more meaningful cut along his fighting arm. His strength was much greater than mine and I was forced to slide away from his parries to avoid being forced to my knees. His heavier sword could break *Saorsa*'s lighter blade, so I was made to defend again and again as I deflected the thrust of his attack. I lost control of my breathing, panting as I searched for a weakness. A slight favouring to the right was betrayed as I unbalanced him on the left. I worked this by pushing him further to the right. His weight balanced comfortably on his right leg, he used the momentum of the swing to bring his blade down on mine. At the last moment I stepped to the right, leaving his blade to whistle through empty air. He staggered as his full weight fell forward over his bent knee. In the heartbeat of respite, I sliced my blade under his ribs, aiming for his left kidney and the rich artery that supplied it. The sudden gush of warm blood over my hands suggested that I had got close.

And on to the next. Cutting. Slicing. Stabbing. Bashing. The graceful positioning on the practice fields had been replaced by primitive, animalistic swinging and slashing. The muscles of my face ached from the rictus snarl that had become my mask. Growling and grunting at the dehumanised daemons that I needed to kill before they killed me. Blinking away the sweat – or blood – from my eyes. I did not care which. It made no difference. The only things that mattered were keeping my legs moving and my arms flying. Staring into the eyes of my opponent. Feeding off his energy. Using it to find his weakness. Slashing the throat. Cutting the hamstring tendons. Stabbing through the heart. Opening up the face from eye to jaw. Move on to the next.

Suddenly my view was clear. I swung round, fearing that the enemy had broken through. I was ready to defend my back, but there were no invaders behind me. I checked all quarters, noting that I had travelled almost to the city walls. A few dead bodies lay around the breaks in the stone defences, both townspeople and attackers. I noticed for the first time that the invaders had all been clothed in black, an unfamiliar crest stitched onto their upper sleeves over their right arms: a fiery orange oval with flames licking the surrounding black background. A chill raced down my spine as I was reminded of Kade's vision of his brother being murdered by men dressed in black.

The grey of pre-dawn was starting to lighten the sky, highlighting three men and two women standing several paces from me. All were looking dazed and deflated as they searched for signs of further attack, unconsciously wiping blood from their faces and hands. I noticed more than one deep cut that would require Drey's herbs and medications. I huffed in dry humour at how quickly I had changed my role of killer to healer.

'We should get back to the square,' I suggested. 'They'll gather there.'

Nobody voiced their agreement but all followed me lethargically towards the centre of the town. I quietly searched my tunic for a clear patch to clean my blade, and when I could not find one I made do with wiping *Saorsa* on the backs of my leggings. It merely served to smear the residue.

'Have they really gone?' asked a timid older lady. I turned to see her pleading with the man beside her, a deep cut scarring her face and her blade stained with blood.

'Yes.' He nodded. 'They've gone.'

He placed his arm over her shoulders and held her close while she visibly shook, guiding her numbly round the bodies of both invaders and defenders. A couple of young boys collected the blades from the fallen while checking for survivors. The older boy calmly slit the throat of a mercenary when he found one still breathing. I sighed sadly, rubbing my forehead between my eyes as a headache started to press against my skull.

A significant crowd had gathered in the main square by the time we arrived, and it was some time before I could find the faces I was searching for. Tawpin was with Leyn on the town hall steps. Drey was attending to the wounded, guiding the injured and their helpers to a small building to the left of the town hall. He had already enlisted the help of several children to act as fetchers and carriers. Erula stood a short distance away from me, using several more children to offer water to the fighters who had gathered in the square. I found Kade standing beside Hagan; from a distance he appeared unharmed. I made my way to Erula, touching her arm to let her know I was there as she talked to a couple of men. She turned and greeted me with a smile, which I returned hesitantly, still a little uncertain of our relationship after our conversation the previous night.

'It's good to see you,' I offered.

'It's good to see you too.' Her smile widened before she gathered me in a quick embrace, dissolving my concerns about her welfare and our friendship. 'You well?'

'All good. You?'

She touched the right side of her chest gently. 'Swine caught me across the ribs with his pommel. This will be a glorious bruise with a fine range of blacks and purples in a couple of days.'

'I hope you made him pay.'

She grinned wickedly. 'I sent him to Mobis for appropriate judgement.'

'Good for you.' I grinned back before scanning the crowd. 'What about the others? Etard is over there, looking sore but intact.'

The smile melted from Erula's face. 'I haven't seen Iffan or Heppra, but the rest are well. Muris has been taken to Drey's makeshift infirmary with a nasty head wound. Drey says it's mostly superficial, looks worse than it is, but she's confused and her eyes won't keep still. Parin has got some cuts and bruises but nothing serious. She's gone to look for Heppra. Seems we were a lot luckier than the people of Kingsport.'

I frowned. 'They seem so unprepared for fighting. I understand that they're not professional swordsmen, but after so many years of border skirmishes I would have thought they would have been… well, better.'

'These are people defending their homes. They fight as best they can, but they are not used to attacks of this type. Talking to the townspeople, they are used to opportunistic raids. Sabotage. Small groups only. This was different, in numbers as well as strategy.'

'Could Lindvane know we are here?'

She held my gaze, confirming that she had suspected the same thing, but before she could reply, Parin pushed her way through the gathering crowd to reach us.

'I can't find Heppra. I've looked everywhere and I can't find her.'

Parin was clearly agitated as she tugged at Erula's sleeve. She frantically scanned the square in the vain hope that she had overlooked her friend, and that Heppra would appear. Erula took her hands and waited for Parin to focus on her.

'Where have you looked?'

'Everywhere.' The words rushed out so fast that I had to concentrate to understand what she was saying. 'We left the town hall together when the alarm was first raised. I thought she had stayed beside me but she must have followed Hagan to find Kade. The fighting was almost upon us so I didn't have time to check. I should have checked. I should have checked. But she should have stayed with me. Why didn't she stay with me?'

'Parin!' Erula cut in to halt the ramblings. 'Where have you looked?'

'Erm...' Parin rubbed her head as she tried to organise her thoughts. 'We were on the west side of the town. Dru drove them towards the northern city walls. The warehouses were running with soldiers. So many. I called for her. Thought she might be inside. I checked all the bodies on the way to the square. I couldn't find her. I couldn't find her.'

'Parin, she could be anywhere. It's a big city. You've only covered a fraction of it. I'm sure she'll turn up soon.'

Parin returned to her frantic searching of the crowd. 'Why isn't she here? Why isn't she here?'

Erula gently shook the younger woman's shoulders. 'Why don't you go and check with Hagan? Maybe he saw her in a different part of the town.'

Parin nodded vacantly. 'Yeah. Yeah, all right. I'll ask Hagan. Or Slicer. Slicer knows everything.'

She wandered away towards Hagan and Kade. The two men seemed to be having a disagreement, with Hagan frowning as he pointed at his prince.

Kade held up his hand to conclude the conversation and I saw Hagan's shoulders slump in defeat.

I placed my hand on Erula's back. 'I'm going to check on Drey; see if he has need of an extra pair of hands. Do you need anything?'

The tall, dark-haired lady smiled sadly. 'I think I'll keep an eye on Parin.'

The square was starting to quieten as people turned to attend their own needs after the trauma of the attack, and I passed easily through the sombre crowd towards the small group of people around Drey. He seemed to be prioritising those who came to him. As most received clean linen for bandaging and small samples of ointments, he would run out of his supplies quickly and I should check the store of dried herbs to see if I could produce more. The more obviously wounded were guided towards the building behind him.

I had made it to within five paces of him when a shriek pierced through the low hum of the crowd. I turned to where Kade and Hagan were standing at the south side of the square. Hagan was leaning in towards Parin, talking in her ear, although she did not appear to be listening. The crowd in front of them parted as a tall man, who had been talking to Erula earlier, approached them from a side alley. His shoulders were hunched forward as if he was carrying something, but I could not see through the crowd to see what it was. I dared not think too hard about it. I knew what I feared and would not tempt the Fates by forming the thought. After an intolerable wait the man finally made it into a cleared space in front of Kade, Hagan and Parin. I could see what – who – he was carrying at the same time as it was confirmed to Parin. She collapsed to her knees with a sob that echoed around the now-silent courtyard. The man gently placed Heppra on the ground in front of her, resting her limp head on Parin's lap.

I pressed my aching back against the cool wall, rubbing my tired eyes with the heels of my hands. My bottom was growing numb from sitting on the stone floor, but I didn't care. It had been hours since I had last had the opportunity to sit down. Keeping my eyes closed, I curved my back away from the wall, feeling the bones of my spine click as the muscles contracted. My hands moved to my shoulders to tread the final knots out of the tense muscles there. I sighed deeply, relaxed my muscles and folded into the wall for support.

'You did well today.'

I opened one eye to see Drey standing in front of me. Annoyingly, he had been working harder than I had but showed no signs of my tiredness. I grunted at him in reply.

'You're welcome to the compliment.' He grinned and stretched out his hand. 'Come on. There's work yet to be done.'

My groan was more heartfelt as I used his hand to haul myself to a stand. All the muscles I had tenderly relaxed spasmed back into fists, but I rolled my shoulders and focused on what Drey required of me.

'I thought we had attended to everyone. Who did I miss?'

I followed Drey out of the dim side room, expecting to turn right into the infirmary. Instead he turned left, exiting into the town square.

'You missed no one. All the wounded are being taken care of. The people of Kingsport are glad to focus on helping the living rather than those who…' He rubbed the back of his neck absently, suddenly looking very tired.

'Do they need more supplies?'

Drey was leading me away from the town hall where we had left our supplies.

'Surely I don't need to go herb-picking already?'

Drey smiled at my obvious reluctance to go gathering medicinal plants in countryside that could still be harbouring hostile intruders. 'No, you don't need to look for any herbs. I need to teach you something, and I'm not sure we have much time to spare.'

I huffed dramatically, the sound echoing off the empty buildings to amplify my displeasure. I felt a little guilty at sounding ungrateful after so many had lost friends and family members. 'Now, Drey? The sun is about to set. That means we've been up two full days without sleep. Surely my education can wait while I sleep for a couple of hours… couple of days… couple of weeks…'

'I fear there will be few chances for us to sleep in the coming days.' He hit me playfully on the shoulder. 'Fortunately, we don't have to sleep to recover our energy.'

'Speak for yourself.' I followed him into a small wooden shack. 'I'm completely drained and need to sleep forever.'

A conspiratorial smile lifted the corners of Drey's mouth. He held his palm upwards and a small orb of pale blue light illuminated the corridor as we walked to a bare room at the back.

'Show-off.'

I startled as Kade emerged from the shadows near the empty fireplace.

'We leave tomorrow,' he instructed Drey.

I replied, despite his marked ignoring of me. 'Leave? We've only just got here. And I think these people could do with our help, don't you? The raiders will have gone to ground by now. There's no telling where they will be. You can't abandon Kingsport when Lindvane mercenaries are freely killing them.'

Kade turned to look at me with a stare that accused me of being the most stupid person he had ever met. 'I won't be leaving them unprotected. The whole point of coming here was to leave a fighting force to protect the town and its people. It will just be us going deeper into the Fenlands. Remember?'

I dropped my shoulders in submission, feeling embarrassed and foolish. I had forgotten.

Kade turned back to Drey. 'There is no more valerian root.'

Drey harrumphed as if his suspicions had been confirmed. 'I thought you would give away your supplies. Not sure that was wise, but understandable.'

'We leave before dawn,' Kade commanded as he left the small room.

I turned immediately to Drey, suddenly suspecting the reason for Kade's volatile mood swings. 'Why does Kade have valerian root?'

Drey ignored my question, instead instructing me to sit in the middle of the room. He used a small piece of chalk to draw a circle on the floorboards around me. At the four cardinal points he drew the four elemental signs: for east, a triangle in a square; south, a pentagram; west, an inverted arrowhead; north, three parallel wavy lines. At the eastern point Drey breathed, '*Cead*' over his rose quartz before placing it to bisect the chalk circle. The white chalk mark fluoresced in a bright blue, leaving a ghost-image burned onto my vision after it settled to a gently pulsing pale blue dome.

Drey sat opposite me. 'You feed from your energy field when you use magick. This weakens you and you need time to recover. It is ineffective. It's time to learn a more effective way to gain energy.'

Drey's voice developed a soothing tone that relaxed me as soon as I closed my eyes. Breathing deeply, I concentrated on the rhythm, relaxed my muscles, emptied my mind except for the images conjured by Drey's words. With each in-breath I imagined growing taller as my posture straightened. With each out-breath I imagined stretching my arms and legs. I imagined that I had a tail growing out of my spine and extending with each out-breath. The pointed, scaly tip reflected the inverted arrowhead drawn in chalk at the western point of the circle, pushing its way through the floorboards, down into the dark earth. Further and further. Burrowing deeper and deeper.

The dark peat merged into drier soil, still dark but now with identifiable roots and stones. Pebbles worn smooth. Jagged rocks. Pushed to the side as my ever-growing tail muscled its way through. I could feel the slide of the earth over my flat scales; the muscles flexing and contracting as I rippled through the ground. Soil turned to rubble. Rubble turned to rock. It took no more effort to force a path through the compacted rock than to move through the peat and soil. As easy as thought. Streams of quartz glistened through the stone at irregular intervals. Some seams were thin, while others were the width of my arm. Light from an unknown source bounced off their surfaces, playing muted colours of silver and peach over my scales. The rock became warm, then hot. Vibration hummed through the stone and into my tail. A sensation that felt like insects crawling over my skin invaded deep into my muscles, shaking sleeping tissue into attention, enticing them into anticipation; expectation.

I crashed through the final layer into an enormous cavern boiling and bubbling with lava many leagues below. Flames exploded to a height five times that of a man. Sulphurous gases swirled as yellow smoke. Acrid clouds drifted on the currents of hot air rising from the pit. A heat haze gave everything a shimmering veil, seemingly melting the very air within the cavern. My tail stretched further and further, swishing left and right like that of a mildly irritated cat. I expected the heat to singe my scales, but it was not unpleasant. It was invigorating. Stimulating. Welcoming.

Hesitantly I touched the molten rock. I breathed in, and energy rushed through the nerves in my tail. Crashing through the base of my spine. Racing up my backbone. Bursting into my brain, and exploding as a fan of opal droplets above my head. I breathed out, and the hum of energy settled in my solar plexus. Spreading warmth throughout my tissues. Causing needle-stabs in the tips of my fingers, my toes, my nose. I smiled as the energy gave me the feeling of invincibility. Of being able to move mountains. Of being able to fly. I breathed in again, drawing upon the power to spread out behind me, not as a fan but as wings. Slender limbs straightened from my shoulder blades. Iridescent membranes attached to the sides of my chest, stretching to become taut as the limbs extended fully. The faint buzz of power as it flickered over my wings.

'I think that's enough for now!'

Drey's disapproval broke into my concentration and the wings dissolved as the energy returned to my solar plexus.

'Concentrate on your breathing. Let the energy flow up with the in-breath. Allow it to flow back into the earth with the out-breath. Take no more than you need. Give thanks for the gift. Withdraw your ethereal tendrils. Let your consciousness guide you back to my voice.'

I took one last breath in, held it, and then opened my eyes on the exhalation. 'Whoa.'

Drey raised an eyebrow. 'Indeed.'

I followed his gaze to the pale blue dome hovering above us. Lightning streaks of orange flashed across the surface. A faint smell of acid tickled my nose.

'That was a lot of energy you raised,' Drey said quietly. 'The dome barely held to contain it. The good people of Kingsport nearly had more to worry about than Lindvane raiders.'

He looked at me with a strange expression. There was almost a hint of admiration. Awe. Maybe fear.

'You never fail to surprise me, Tallen. How did you contain all that power?'

Chapter Twelve

Before dawn I went looking for Tawpin as I had made the promise to say goodbye to him whenever I left on an adventure. I was not looking forward to it, but a promise was a promise and he deserved to know I was leaving.

It seemed that I was not the only one lacking sleep. Tawpin and Leyn were standing over a table covered in paper and ledgers. Empty cups stood to one side, along with a plate with a discarded crust that appeared to have been there for several hours. I stood quietly in the doorway, watching him discuss the needs of the town. His town. He looked tired, with swollen eyes and tousled hair, but his attention did not waver from the task at hand. Arrangements were being made for the increased food requirements now we had arrived with fifteen extra mouths. Extra security was organised for the docks where fishing boats were still able to operate. The final bridge between the north and south sides of the town was to be barricaded to prevent more Lindvane mercenaries from crossing from the northern territories. Communal dormitories were suggested for the children to increase their safety should there be further organised attacks.

Eventually Tawpin stretched and saw me leaning against the door frame. He flashed his toothy smile at me, making my stomach flip with sudden guilt.

'Good morning,' he said, finishing the stretch of his back muscles. 'Have you come to help with sanitation?'

Leyn playfully smacked Tawpin on the arm. 'I hardly think that's the reason Tallen has come to see you.'

I was thankful when she collected the plate and empty cups and made her excuses to allow me to speak to Tawpin alone. Again, she was proving to be a lady who knew people and was astute enough to satisfy their needs without them having to be openly expressed. I was beginning to really like Leyn.

'So, if you haven't come to help clean up my town, what have you come for?'

I stalled. 'You and Leyn seem to have everything covered. Looks like you two will be a good team.'

Tawpin tilted his head to one side. 'Yeah. She has a good handle on things. Knows what needs doing and how to get it done. I'm just trailing along behind her, really.'

'Don't sell yourself short. I've been listening for a while. You held your own.'

He was not fooled. 'What brings you here at this time of the day, Tallen?'

I gave a small smile. 'Time to say goodbye again.'

'So soon?' Tawpin frowned. 'I thought you would stay for a few days at least.'

'You know Kade. Always in a hurry.'

Tawpin smiled and nodded, but he soon returned to business. 'How many will you be taking with you? Kade will be taking Hagan obviously. I could do with Mace to lift a few buildings. Dru and Kutan would be nice to rally the troops—'

'No, Tawpin,' I interrupted. 'All the troops are for you. The companies were always for you, to help rebuild Kingsport. To protect you from… everyone.'

An uncomfortable silence held for a few heartbeats as I watched Tawpin's frown deepen. His jaw worked the muscles at the base of his face as he came to terms with the inevitable.

'You know it has always been the three of us,' I apologised. 'And you know your need is greater than ours. It is just a reconnaissance mission. We need stealth, not strength. That's the whole reason I'm here. Not good at strength, but pretty good at hiding. And with the attack last night—'

Tawpin held his hands up in defeat, smiling at my nervous rambling. 'All right, all right. I understand. I don't like it, but I understand.' He walked around the table and gave me a quick hug. 'If I say be careful, will you listen?'

I grinned back. 'Probably not. But then you were the one who led me astray all those years ago.'

'Oh, so it's my fault now?'

'Oh yeah.'

We grinned at each other, and he punched me playfully on the shoulder. 'Well. You're probably right.'

'You know I'm right.' I leaned into him. 'It should only be for a couple of days. I think Kyllian just wants to check the loyalties of those deeper in the swamps.'

Tawpin did not look convinced. He returned to the table, resting against its edge as his frown returned. 'If I know Drey, he will want more than a look. Kyllian has lots of settlements along the border. Why worry about this one? I feel Drey's meddling in the choice of this particular group. Still not sure why Kade's here, though.'

'Maybe Kade is in need of some of the healing waters on the Isle of Serpents?' I pushed gently to see what Tawpin knew of Kade's use of valerian.

'Maybe,' he said non-committally. 'Perhaps Kyllian is hoping the waters will cool his temper.'

I sniggered. 'If only it could be that easy.'

Tawpin returned my smile, before I watched it slowly fade. 'Be careful, Tallen.'

I wrapped my arms around his shoulders and gave my old friend a prolonged hug, before turning to leave.

'And take of those old and young fools,' he called as I left the room. 'Scarily, you are probably the most sensible one of the three!'

We left Kingsport quietly, leaving behind the horses that would struggle in the marshy soil. The dawn was still hidden behind the horizon as we walked soundlessly down the town's streets. No one stirred to see us leave. A light rain started to fall as we travelled west into the countryside, with the smell of wet earth creating a warm musk as the dark peat was compressed by our feet. As the faded sun rose slowly above the ocean, the landscape diluted into watery tones of grey: a washed-out painting of flat farmland. Hedgerows huddled against the strong sea wind, while brave seabirds battled the turbulent gusts and often flew backwards.

We were heading towards the imposing twin pillars of flint that had dominated the landscape for several days. Even in the subdued light of the rain, the stones glistened; dark beacons enticing wanderers towards their majesty, and tempting them with their mystery. With no other significant landmark, I found myself watching them as we moved imperceptibly closer.

I wondered when they had appeared, and how they were formed; impossible structures that seemed as smooth as glass and as dark as a pool at midnight. Ripples of light played over their surface as the sun danced between the scudding clouds; one moment looking as hard as granite, the next flowing like ink, seeming to change its appearance as the Gods changed their minds.

When not looking at the stones I watched Kade. His stride was sure, his limbs moved freely, his feet striking the ground rhythmically with purpose and determination, but there was a tension in his posture and a slight frown remained to crease his forehead, and the anger lingered in his eyes. His mind wandered in a landscape that caused his face to momentarily soften before hardening once more, undulating like the rain clouds above. I watched Kade fighting with a decision he had not yet accepted. Our path seemed to be taking him in a direction he did not want to go. I wondered if his concerns were for the kingdom or more personal matters.

'I wonder how they will view our arrival.'

Drey startled at my voice after the silence had persisted so long within our small group.

'I mean, from what you said I don't think they had many visitors before the war. With Lindvane on their borders I doubt anyone would voluntarily enter the fens.'

Drey signed sadly. 'It's true the Fenland people have not been the most welcoming of late. But it is not without reason.'

I decide to push Kade. 'For a start, Kyllian has just left them to deal with Hayton on their own. They can't be too impressed with the Faulknar family.'

Drey gave me a questioning glare, but Kade did not take the bait.

'The king has his reasons,' Kade said quietly.

I pushed harder. 'You defending your father now? That's a first.'

Kade continued to look ahead. 'The Fenlanders have been able to look after themselves for generations. They are not without protection. It has always been their choice to stand alone.'

I let Kade continue in his dark mood, content that it was not the thought of meeting the Fenlanders that troubled him. I turned my curiosity to Drey.

'What does Kade mean, they are not without protection?'

Drey's voice dropped as he adopted his storytelling guise. He began by reminding me of what he had told me earlier; that the two pillars of flint were conduits used to increase the power of the healers who gathered there. Their reputation grew, so that people would travel for months to benefit from the knowledge and skill of the Fenlanders. It had been a peaceful, sacred place for many generations.

As is the nature of people, those who visited the community were not always looking for benign healing and spiritual cleansing. The power of the stones attracted those who wanted to use them for more malign purposes. Initially individuals came to try to harness the energy for their own needs. Being surrounded by water, the Isle of Serpents could control the small numbers who had ill intent by refusing passage on the small ferries used to transport pilgrims. The community outside the sanctuary would often recognise and turn away those who meant harm. Even within the island, individuals could be dealt with by traditional means or those less obvious.

Power always comes with a consequence, with two sides to every coin. Many herbs that can be used to heal, can also be used to kill. Energies that promote regeneration can be reversed to hasten decline. Creation is the sister of destruction. There are stories of those who travelled to the island in their prime, to return aged and haggard. Those with energy to spare returned dull and unresponsive, frozen in a world unconnected to our own. Spiteful people became altruistic. Vengeful people preached forgiveness. Everyone returned from the island changed. Some were no longer recognised by their families.

For all the power on the Isle of Serpents, they could not hold back time. Individuals became small groups; small groups became large ones. Lone entrepreneurs chancing their luck became organised and more determined gangs. More energy was being spent on deterring those wanting the power than helping those who needed healing. The Elder Council decided that they needed to act. A permanent solution was required to prevent those not invited to the island from accessing the stones, and the power within the flint from being used to cause untold harm to the community and the wider world.

The decision was made to protect the stones and close the Island of Serpents to visitors, but the power required to isolate the island was unprecedented. Hundreds of the most powerful Druids, shamans, priests and priestesses were needed to control the storm that was released from the stones. Day turned to night and all light was extinguished across the three kingdoms for more than a week. People went mad believing the light would never return. Chaos and violence ran unchecked through the cities and hamlets alike. The dark side of humanity was released to destroy what generations had built. To take what had been hard earned. To dishonour those of pure spirit. The daemons of the Seventh Hell seemed to have been unleashed to play with any they chose.

The silence that returned with the light came like the passing of a hurricane. The world held its breath as it surveyed the damage done. People looked to their neighbours in shock at what they had done only moments before; appalled at what they had seen and who they had become. Terrified that things had changed irrevocably; that love and compassion had vanished so far from the earth, they would never be found again. Then the sound of a robin floated on the breeze. The small bird could not be seen but its song travelled the length of the three kingdoms. It was heard in the fields, in the streets, in the barns, and in the houses. Everyone heard the achingly beautiful tones and felt their hearts beat again. The world released its held breath and colour returned to their lives.

And the island had gone. The lake surrounding the sanctuary was gone too, with only the two flint pillars standing alone above an enveloping mist. Two sentinels casting judgement on those who saw them, to remember their shame and be forever unworthy of accessing the power that was held within the stones. The persistent fog covered a maze of boggy marsh waterways. Those foolish enough to enter were instantly lost in the twists and turns taken by the only safe path through. Numerous dead ends led to brackish water pools that sucked any living creature into their peaty depths. Swirls of vapour and carpets of algae made the ground seem solid until stepped upon. Nothing escaped these liquid graves. Stories were told of fae creatures that stalked these murderous marshes; spirits that appeared to entice strangers further and further into the swamps. Voices of loved ones, long dead, pleaded for them to stay. Familiar faces floated in the murky waters, reaching ghostly fingers towards their kin. Strange lights flickered in the haze as banshees screamed in the wind that blew at night. Very few people ventured into the marshes.

'And that's where we are going?' I asked as Drey grinned mischievously. 'Great.'

It was another two days before the peaty ground out of Kingsport turned marshier and started sucking at our boots. A further day and a half and the first boggy pools formed alongside the pathway. The reeds were small and sparsely clustered to begin with, but then became taller and thicker until they were as high as my shoulder. The wind whistled through the stalks as a dull drone; the smell of musty, stagnant water adding to the ominous feel of the place. I found myself jumping at the birds startled by our approach. Just when I thought it could not be any less welcoming, the skies darkened, and a drizzly rain soaked even slightly exposed skin.

We made camp early that night, huddling under damp blankets and morosely listening to the moaning marsh reeds. Kade was still reluctant to make eye contact, much less talk. Drey seemed very interested in checking his supplies for water damage and replied with single words when asked questions. I was content to watch the fire as fire sprites writhed and danced hypnotically within. I threw a small piece of dried meat into the flames, smiling as the sprites tore the offering apart; fibres thrown up to join the sparks floating into the night.

A flicker of movement flashed in the corner of my peripheral vision. Turning my head for a better view, I saw Kade twitching nervously. He seemed unaware of his fidgeting fingers and his trembling legs. His perpetual frown had deepened, his eyes shifting from side to side without moving his head, as if he was watching a fencing match or a bird darting over a stream after insects. I found myself intrigued by the numerous small movements, trying to find a pattern or a common rhythm between fingers, feet and eyes.

Kade suddenly cried out, causing me to jump and Drey to drop his packet of dried herbs. Drey held up a finger to my questioning frown, warning me to stay quiet.

'No... no! We have to do something. We have to help them.' Kade's eyes had rolled back in his head, so that the firelight flickered against the white globes. His head shook slowly as his fingers and feet twitched. He seemed to be in a dream, but sitting upright. I watched as emotions contorted his face, as visions only he could see played in his mind.

'Tell me what's happening,' Drey instructed quietly.

'The town is on fire,' Kade replied. His eyes were still rolled back as his fingers flexed as if to grab a sword. 'The people are screaming. There's so much noise.'

I looked back at Drey. I had heard this tale before when Kade had foreseen the death of his brother. Why would he be reliving it now?

Drey shook his head almost imperceptibly. 'What do you hear?' he asked gently.

'So much noise. People screaming. Buildings crashing down. Flames racing up the sides of the warehouses. Timber exploding in the heat. A bell ringing. Warning. It's too late for a warning. She's already here. Can they not see her? Can they not hear her?'

I couldn't help but ask, 'Who? Who's there?'

Drey lifted an eyebrow at me but kept quiet.

'She'll destroy everything. She doesn't care. People are burning. By the Gods, people are burning. They are jumping into the bay. The docks are gone. The grain has gone. The city is in ruins. No one seems to know what to do. We have to help them.'

Kade ducked as if something had flown over him. 'Fearsome Father. She is so big. How are we supposed to stop her? How can we possibly stop her?' He covered his ears. 'Mobis's mercy. That roar. That scream. My chest feels like it will shatter from the vibration. The horses are in a blind panic. They will trample the troops. This is chaos. Total chaos. Oh, Gods. She's coming back around. She's flying straight at us.'

I turned to Drey. 'Flying?'

He shrugged apologetically, but we both turned back to Kade as he screamed.

'She's burned them. She's incinerated them. The whole left flank is gone. A thousand souls sent to Mobis's Hells. How can I stand this? How is my heart still beating? One fiery breath and a whole army is consumed. She's brought an apocalypse. This is the end of everything.'

Kade shuddered violently as his eyes rolled back to their normal position. He stared vacantly at the fire for several heartbeats before lifting his gaze to Drey. The older man's face creased in quiet concern as the horror slowly left Kade's eyes. After what seemed like an age, Kade took a deep breath and turned to me; accusing, daring me to judge him. I didn't know what to say. What could I say? I searched his face: he required no sympathy from me.

'So?' I turned to Drey. 'Breathing fire. Flying monster. Anything you'd like to tell me?'

Drey had the grace to look sheepish. 'Yes, well. Perhaps there are a couple of things that need explaining.'

'Do you think?' I shook my head. 'How long has this been going on for? Is this why you brought me back to Liegeport?'

Drey glanced at Kade for permission, which was granted with a small nod. Drey kept himself busy making a tea of peppermint and willow bark in order to avoid looking at me.

'Kade started having visions a few months after you left. They were infrequent to begin with; easy to distract through concentration and breathing control. But they got more insistent and harder to suppress.'

I turned to Kade. 'And you've been taking valerian all this time?'

Kade nodded as Drey continued.

'After Kerk, it was hard to dismiss as imagination. But how could it be a premonition? No one has seen a dragon in generations.'

'And you thought, *If only we knew a Dragonslayer!*'

Drey raised an eyebrow in submission. 'Seemed like too much of a coincidence for me. We did some research and... well, you know what we found.'

My mind was racing. They were taking this seriously. They were talking about dragons as if they were discussing birds of prey. This was ridiculous. This was crazy. But as I looked at the two men, their faces were scarily serious. It sent chills racing down my spine.

'Do you know when this is to happen?' I looked at Kade. 'Do you see me?'

Kade shook his head. 'We never see you.'

'*We?*'

A look passed between them.

'Drey has seen it too.'

I turned to glare at Drey, my head tilted in accusation.

'I've had the same vision for many years,' he confirmed quietly. 'Well, not this exact vision. Not from Kade's viewpoint, but the dragon's. Setting Liegeport aflame. The deaths.'

'How long?'

Drey looked at me apologetically. 'Since before Laken found you.'

'Before *you* found me,' I retorted unkindly.

I placed my head in my hands, as if that could stop the thoughts from slamming around my skull. It had all been planned. I had been manipulated from the very beginning. But for what? I could no more stop that dragon than I could turn the sky green. How could they possibly think I could stop a dragon?

But then, I had brought Kade back from Mobis's Hell.

Step by step the marshes took control of the land and we were corralled into a narrow strip of tufted grass with stagnant pools either side. The cold water soaked through our boots as we squelched through the mud. I wasn't sure whether the oppressive gloom came from the rising mist, the low cloud or a combination of the two. The dampness caused clothing to chafe and conversation to be stilted. I commiserated with myself on how pointless this journey was: how much my feet hurt, how my back hurt, how my shoulders hurt. I put one foot in front of the other, staring at Kade's calves in front of me, resenting him for placing the burden of solving all the world's problems on me. He was the King-in-Waiting. Let him deal with the dragon.

I don't remember being aware of when the voices started. They crept into my consciousness as the damp crept into my muscles, whispers at the edge of my mind persistently making hints and suggestions. This was a total waste of time. The whole mission was pointless. We would find no information here that could be used to defeat the Lindvanes. Nothing useful at all. Yet again I was being sent off to do the king's dirty work; punished for being a thief, but compelled to use those skills when it suited. Always looking for a way I could be used. Always happy to put me in danger if it would get him something. Always the reason being that I owed him; I had a debt that needed repaying. Well, I didn't owe anyone anything when he took me from Methhold. It didn't stop them taking me. Didn't stop them making me owe them. One big plan to make me owe them.

I was grabbed by the shoulder and jerked backwards, falling into Kade. My mind raced to catch up with the new sensations flooding my brain.

'Look where you're going,' snapped Kade as he pushed me roughly away from him. 'You're going to get yourself drowned.'

Drey was several paces ahead of us. I must have fallen behind, lost in my thoughts. The short reeds and tough grasses around the murky pond had been crushed. I had been walking towards to the water when Kade grabbed me. The greasy scum floating next to the shallow bank convinced me that it would not have been pleasant to fall in.

'Keep an eye on her,' instructed Drey, turning away and continuing on the narrow trail. 'You know what it's like here.'

Kade grunted in what I assumed was affirmation, before pushing me ahead of him. I felt his eyes boring into the base of my spine, adding new tension to my overworked muscles. We soon fell into the rhythm of walking again and the monotony of the pace encouraged my mind to wander. The faded greys of the landscape coalesced into swirls and shapes. Before long I was seeing faces and heads floating effortlessly in the breeze over the water.

The air through the reeds called my name, inviting me to join them. The faces solidified into features I recognised. Those fallen at Kingsport. My stomach cramped as I saw Heppra's face shimmering towards me, ghostly fingers beckoning.

I turned away, only to look over another patch of misty water. More figures glided. Faces from my past, tempting me with suggestions of companionship and acceptance. Kerk and Jeck cajoling. *Come join the party. Relax for a while. Just a for a moment.* I took a deep breath, knowing it was not true. How could it be true? But I could not block the voices. The faces smiled at me. Laughed at me. All I had to do was join them. As simple as that. Join them and everything would be fine.

I couldn't stop my cry of pain as Laken appeared out of the gloom. He said nothing; just gave me a small smile that promised all was going to be fine. He was here now, and I didn't have to worry any more. Without thinking, I moved towards him and the security he offered. Once again, I was nine years old and my only concern was pleasing him. Of course I went to him.

The splash of water as my foot slipped off the bank snapped me back to reality. A heartbeat later Kade grabbed me under my arms, dragging me back as I slid down the muddy edge. I sat shaking, not sure whether it was from the shock of coming so close to being sucked into the marsh and trapped by the underwater weeds, or from the loss of Laken, again.

'For the love of Mobis, Tallen.' Kade hit me on the shoulder hard enough to hurt. 'Put your damned defences up.'

'Leave her be,' countered Drey, squatting in front of me to look directly into my eyes. 'You were no better on your first time. If I remember correctly, you had to be carried.'

He winked at me as Kade replied indignantly, 'I was eleven years old!'

Drey cupped my face in his hand, ensuring he had my full attention. 'It's not just your barriers. Your senses are feeding you false imagery that your brain is only too happy to form into images to tempt you. Concentrate on what you know to be real, not what seems to be.'

He gave Kade a stern glare as he stood and continued walking. Kade helped me up and slipped his arm around my waist, his hand resting on my hip. I concentrated on building more layers for the barriers around my mind while Kade led me forward. He was walking slightly behind me due to the narrowness of the trail, but his touch was gentle as he breathed out his frustration.

'It's different for everyone, but there are common themes,' he explained quietly. 'For me it's music. No surprise there, I suppose. People I have known tempt me in with beautiful singing. The reeds play melodies that I could spend forever listening to. The key is to look for the falsehoods; the bits that are wrong.' He gave a small laugh. 'Easy to do when Kerk is serenading me. Never in his whole life did he sing a note in tune.'

I smiled at the image of Kerk singing out of tune. The figures still floated in the air, but Kade's voice gave me an anchor point, allowing them to stay at arm's length, no longer wearing the faces of those I'd known and lost. Perhaps these were the faces of those snared by the malevolence in the marshes, the souls trapped forever in this watery wasteland. Their faces became more cadaverous than before, showing the decay of uncountable ages with eyes too large, cheekbones too prominent and fingers too long. I still startled at movements at the periphery of my vision, still questioned whether that was my name being called, but I concentrated on the small details I knew to be true. The warm touch of Kade's hand on my waist. The feel of cracked leather under my fingers where they touched my sword belt. The rough fabric rubbing against my shoulder where I pressed into Kade's chest. The sucking at my boots from the boggy tussocks of fibrous grass. The cadence of Kade's tone as he talked about imps and sprites that lurked at the water's edge and spun tales of mischief and mayhem.

We eventually came to the end of the trail, and a small wooden jetty that extended several paces into a wide expanse of water. The track continued straight and uninterrupted to the left and right, but there was no obvious means of crossing. Drey dipped his hand in the water, swirling his fingers slowly before removing it and wiping it dry on his breeches. I removed my backpack, letting it fall to the ground with a quiet thump before I collapsed with a louder whack next to it. I stretched out my back and hips, earning a satisfying crack as the joints realigned themselves.

'So is this the end of the road?' I asked no one in particular. 'We've trudged through this watery hell to be thwarted by the river that everyone knew was there.'

The shadows and their whispering had ceased but I was starting to get an ache behind my eyes from trying to peer through the gloom. Kade offered me some dried meat before sitting opposite me on the jetty. Drey huffed at my poor impression of his navigational skills as he reached for some meat from Kade. I took the opportunity to question him on how he expected the islanders to know of our arrival.

'Did you speak to them with your mind?'

'No.'

'Can they see through the mist?'

'No.'

'Can they predict the future?'

He refused to answer, raising an eyebrow in expectation of me figuring it out for myself. I looked to Kade for help, but he was just as unhelpful. I sighed in resignation and tried to remember what Drey had told me about the Isle of Serpents. My mind was still concentrating on the images and emotions I had just experienced in the marshes, remembering only the stories of fae creatures he had used to scare me. I took a deep breath, quietened my mind and refocused. The island was a place for healers, so herb-witches and Druids would be attracted to it, but as far as I knew they had no special abilities for communication. Drey could not expect me to know of all their talents, so it must be more obvious than that. Kade relaxed against his pack and closed his eyes, obviously not impressed by my blatant stupidity. What did I know about healers, Druidic lore, Gods, Goddesses… or Ancients?

'Aqualine!' I shouted excitedly. 'They have power over water.'

'Indeed,' Drey confirmed. 'Not only can they control the flow of water; to a degree they can communicate with it. The water recognised the auric signature of my hand and will project an image of me to the Aqualine watchers on the Isle.'

'That's very impressive. How many Aqualine are there? Are all the Aqualine on the island, or are there others in the three kingdoms?'

'There are a few on the island, but I'm not sure how many are spread around the kingdoms. Few are direct descendants and have the full range of abilities of the first Aqualine. There were some here last time I visited, and even with diluted bloodlines their talent is more than enough.'

'You weren't lying,' I conceded. 'This island is very well protected. If anyone was fool enough to walk more than a hundred paces into this swamp, they would soon be lost to the twists and turns of the treacherous walkways. Failing that, they would lose their minds to the marsh wisps and spend eternity listening to the calls and pleas of dead loved ones. If you made it as far as the river, you would only be able to reach the island if the water knew you.' I shook my head. 'It's a wonder anyone makes it to this place of healing.'

Drey chuckled at my surmising. 'The marshes will be kinder to you once you've been on the island, and you now know what to expect. But yes, the island is well protected.'

We lapsed into a comfortable silence as Kade dozed. The water lapped gently against the wooden struts of the jetty, becoming as hypnotic as the images had been. I thought about the Aqualine. Real Ancients. Did they know about Dragonslayers? Did they know what I was supposed to do if we ever found the dragon of Kade's vision; of Drey's vision? Were there Firewalkers on the island? Were there Empaths? Did they know about the Empathy Crystal? So many thoughts raced through my mind. I could barely comprehend how it all related to me.

The slapping of the waves grew stronger and soon I could hear the rhythmic splashing of oars against the water. Before long, a small, round boat emerged from the mists. The dark brown colour of the craft made it almost indistinguishable from the water below it, but for the fold of white being pushed before it. A small figure, cloaked against the damp, sat in the centre of the boat. I frowned, trying to imagine how all four of us would fit in there. The vessel was almost at the jetty before I saw three similar boats following it.

Drey caught the light rope that was thrown and quickly tied off. The slight person jumped easily onto the jetty and folded back her hood. Thick ginger hair was tied up in a loose bun on top of her head. She had an open face, and smiled warmly at Drey.

'Master.' She extended her hands and clasped his outstretched ones in friendship. 'It is good to see you again.'

'You also, Cait. I'm glad to see you well.'

She turned to Kade, giving him a small, respectful bow. 'Well met, Lord Faulknar. I hope Your Grace's journey through the marshes was not too arduous.'

Kade smiled broadly, clasping her hands in greeting. 'It was awful, as well you know.'

She shrugged. 'As to be expected.' Still smiling, she turned to me. 'Welcome, Dragonslayer. We have felt your presence and are honoured you have come to visit us.'

I turned to Drey. 'Thank you. But it wasn't really my idea to come and visit.'

She flapped her hands in dismissal, leaning in as if taking me into her confidence, and winked. 'I know Drey likes to make the decisions. But talk of your reasons for coming can wait. Let me get you to the island for comfort.'

The small brown boats were unlike anything I had seen before. They were roughly two paces wide, circular and shallow. A plank stretched from side to side to offer a place to sit. I only saw a paddle in Cait's vessel.

'They are called coracles,' the young woman informed me. 'The shallow base allows us to navigate through the marshes.'

Drey and Kade were already settled in their vessels, and cautiously I crawled into the one remaining. The wide, shallow hull provided stability and I saw a thin cord connecting the four craft, although I was not convinced that Cait would be able to tow us all with her one paddle. Untying the cord anchoring us to the jetty, Cait jumped lightly into her coracle and used the paddle to push away from the bank. With no visible effort, we were soon trailing behind her like a row of ducklings. She used the oar more for steering than for propulsion, making small adjustments to ensure we remained on course. Within a few heartbeats we were clear of the mists, and the sun reminded us that we were halfway through spring. I turned to see the marshes still covered by a thin fog, while the island ahead was bathed in warm sunshine. A cold shudder trickled down my back as I thought of the magick needed to sustain this deception.

I turned back to the island in front of us. The flint pillars reflected the light as flickering shards of diamond. The curve of the island could be seen as a green carpet of grass highlighted with purple and yellow wild flowers, while small birds darted after insects. It was a startling contrast to the grey and lifeless marshes.

Suddenly I was splashed in the face with cold water. Drey laughed freely and even Kade smiled, while Cait looked totally innocent for a heartbeat before grinning mischievously at me. Another splash turned my attention to my left, where a water sprite floated above the river, its body shimmering with rainbow colours as it moved in the light.

'Sorry,' she said without any noticeable remorse. 'Couldn't resist. You looked so serious.'

I tried to be annoyed but couldn't help smiling at the sprite's cheeky nature. Translucent serpents swam alongside the coracles, ducking underneath to emerge on the other side as they twisted around each other.

The sprite was joined by a handful of others that played and danced in the waves caused by the boats. Their carefree spirit was contagious, and I found that I welcomed the release from the stresses of the previous few days. I settled further into the small boat as we moved swiftly towards the Isle of Serpents.

Chapter Thirteen

We tied up at a jetty similar to the one we had just left. The coarse grass grew almost to knee height either side of a small gravel track, with wild flowers dotted within releasing their subtle perfume onto the gentle breeze. A small copse of stunted trees grew to our left as we walked towards the flint pillars that dominated everything. Cait led us confidently away from the river, which was soon hidden from view. The trail was direct and well tended, leaving a clear path in stark contrast to the mazes of the marshes. It was not long before we heard the voices of those resident on the island.

The hamlet was a rough collection of small, round huts, thatched roofs overlapping wattle-and-daub walls. Each was standing on a low platform of timber struts so that it rested at the height of my shoulders. Apparently, the river occasionally flooded so the houses were raised to protect those inside, along with their food stores and small supply of personal possessions. The people of the hamlet appeared to be mainly women and children, although several men were also involved with the duties of the community. Most were dressed simply in cloth leggings and loose-fitting tunics, but these were occasionally decorated with scarves, shawls or neckties to add splashes of colour that rippled through the community.

Cait led us to a slightly longer, but no taller, building to one side of the gathering. A small fire was lit in front, with a few people sitting around it chatting companionably. As we drew closer, I recognised the smell of distilling herbs. At our approach, everyone stood up and made polite excuses before leaving, so that only a small woman with curly red hair that looked impossible to control remained. Her face was round and friendly, and she wore a big smile as she looked at Drey. She came towards him and enveloped him in a firm, overly familiar hug. Kade and I looked at each other and grinned as the embrace lasted several heartbeats longer than was comfortable. When they eventually pulled apart Drey looked suitably flustered, causing the woman to laugh heartily.

'Drey, it's so good to see you again. Welcome back to the Isle of Serpents.'

Drey stepped a few paces away to compose himself. 'Thank you, Sutha. I had forgotten your enthusiastic greetings.'

She laughed again, turning to Kade. 'Welcome back, Your Grace.'

She inclined her head, respectful of his status, and I was surprised to see him return the gesture.

'Well met, Sutha. Thank you for hospitality once again.'

She inclined her head once more in acknowledgement of his statement, but then her eyes narrowed as she appraised him more closely. She turned to Drey and I saw concern in her eyes.

'You were right to bring him here,' she said quietly.

Drey nodded quickly before changing the subject by gesturing towards me. 'May I present Tallen nic Duane. Tallen, this is Sutha nic Aine. She is the caretaker of the Isle and Mother Priestess to the initiates training here.'

Sutha turned to me and smiled. 'That's a very official welcome. I feel obliged to do the same.' Again, she inclined her head in respectful greeting. 'Welcome, Dragonslayer, Daughter Empath and Moon Warrior. We have been looking forward to your arrival.'

I looked to Drey for explanation, but he deliberately avoided eye contact. 'Are you sure you mean me?' I asked.

She laughed indulgently. 'Oh yes,' she said, and I had the feeling that she would talk to me about this later, although I was uncertain whether it was my heritage or my lack of understanding that she would be speaking to me about. 'Let me look at you.'

Her eyes grew soft and she focused on a point slightly away from my head and shoulders. Her gaze moved slowly up and down, and a slight crease folded her forehead. After a while she let out a quiet sigh. 'You are so like your mother,' she whispered.

'You knew my mother?'

She smiled sadly. 'She studied at the Isle for many years before she met your father.'

'Did you know my father too?' My heart was racing with the thought of learning about the people behind the memories I cherished.

'Sadly, I never met your father,' Sutha said gently, reaching for my hands as she saw the disappointment that must have shown on my face. 'But we will talk more about your mother later.' She winked at me. 'We are ignoring the boys.'

I startled, having completely forgotten that other people were present. I had been captivated by Sutha's reassuring manner and the promise of information about me and my parents. I realised, belatedly, that this woman had significant power of her own.

She turned back to include Drey and Kade, gesturing for them to sit next to the smouldering fire. 'You're looking well, Drey,' she said with a mischievous smile. 'These two keeping you young?'

Drey huffed. 'Ageing me rapidly would be more truthful. But how are things here? There seem to be fewer acolytes. Are you safe?'

'We have our protections, as well you know. We are safe enough. But yes, we have fewer trainees coming to us these days.'

'And yet you still refuse to acknowledge the war and help us?' said Kade sharply.

Sutha's reply was equally terse. 'You know we refuse to take sides. We swear no fealty to kings. Kingdoms come and go, but the Isle remains. The knowledge we have here is for all.' Her tone and facial expression softened. 'However, we also cannot stand unaffected while the natural balance is corrupted. What Villermir is doing with the Empathy Crystal involves us all and is causing disruption throughout all the kingdoms. Weather patterns are shifting, as well as the changes to the energy within the ley lines. Migratory birds and sea mammals are being thrown off course to starve. Birds are drowning, whales and porpoises are being stranded on beaches thousands of leagues away from their normal migratory routes.'

Drey nodded solemnly. 'I've noticed the energy changes in people, too. Wounds that take longer to heal. Coughs that linger for months. And a general malaise that can waste the life out of the healthiest.'

'We do what we can, but it is becoming increasingly harder. Villermir is getting more confident and his range is getting further. It's not just the border that is affected. We have had reports from Hilman that rivers have dried up in one area, while a few leagues away floods have devastated crops. Southern Lindvane has had mudslides and rocky cliffs where the land was previously flat.' Sutha's face briefly clouded with anger before she looked at

Drey in concern. 'That madman is messing with powers he has no idea of. I fear a catastrophic backlash that we will not be able to control.'

Drey's expression did not inspire confidence. 'Particularly if you are down on acolytes?'

Sutha sighed dramatically and tossed her head in annoyance. 'Don't get me started on that particular subject. Idiot priests of Baila. It is an insult to call them priests. Lie-masters would be more truthful. People are too scared to send their sons and daughters to us for fear of contamination.'

Drey smiled at her outburst. 'It is an effective strategy. Reduces our strength while increasing his.'

'Humph. It's preventing good talent from learning their heritage, is what it is.' Sutha turned to Kade. 'At least we still get those from Faulknar.'

Kade dipped his head in acknowledgement of the softening of Sutha's tone of voice. He continued in a conciliatory manner, perhaps as an apology for his earlier accusation. 'Villermir targets people's fears while promising them salvation if they follow his guidance. People want to be told what to do, and Villermir has taught his priests well in telling people what to do. The only way is to follow the official word from Baila, prevent free thinking and ensure obedience. The goslings following the goose.'

'That makes it difficult to convince them to listen to more rational thinking,' agreed Drey.

We were all silent while we thought of the consequences of the encroachment of the religion that led so easily to the ostracising of those outside the order, and encouraged fanaticism. Physical threats were relatively straightforward to deal with, while ideology was insipid as it wormed its way into people's subconscious. The teachings had become unquestionable facts within a generation.

'What is the latest intelligence from Lindvane?' asked Drey when the silence became uncomfortable.

Sutha gave a small smile. 'It seems hard to keep a secret these days. The scouts mainly bring back confirmation of what we already know. Occasionally we get warning of future raids into Faulknar territories.'

'And what do you do with that information?' Kade was back to his accusatory tone again.

Sutha gave him a cold stare of derision. 'What do you think, Your Grace?'

Kade shrugged. 'With you not taking sides…'

Sutha huffed in contempt. 'We take no sides when it comes to fealty. We do not stand by as people are slaughtered.'

Drey raised his hand pacifyingly. 'We appreciate your position, and the need to stay impartial, Sutha.' He glared at Kade. 'Ignore my prince's passion when it comes to defending his people.'

'I appreciate your diplomacy, Drey. And I do understand your frustrations, Your Grace.'

Kade dipped his head in acknowledgement once again, although I did not see any acceptance in his body posture as Sutha continued.

'We cannot afford to antagonise Hayton; even less Villermir. While they think we are unconcerned with politics, we can continue to work against the more destructive effects of the magickal interference. Make no mistake, with the power Villermir is gaining from the Empathy Crystal, if he sees us as a threat he could extinguish us in a heartbeat.'

'You think he has grown that powerful?' I asked, suddenly very afraid.

All three turned toward me, having overlooked my presence as I had quietly observed up until this point. All had expressions that reflected my worries. Quietly, Sutha answered me.

'Yes, I do.'

I awoke early the next morning after a restless night. The mist hung low in the air, giving the community a hushed and expectant feel. The few people already awake quietly went about their chores with hushed greetings. I sat outside the lodge I had spent the night in, holding a warm mug of tea. I watched the calming scene as the sun rose behind the two flint pillars to cause sparks of silver light in celebration, songbirds heralding the day. I had almost finished my tea when Kade joined me, sitting down heavily with a deep sigh.

'Sleep well?' I asked, already suspecting the answer.

Kade looked at me with a head tilt and a raised eyebrow, causing me to smile at him.

'No, thanks for asking.'

'Me neither. I've been trying to think about how to stop Villermir, but I keep being lost in thoughts of Burford.'

'It's not a time I choose to discuss.'

'I know. But if he is getting more powerful, how can we hope to stop him?'

'You,' stated Kade seriously.

'Oh, please. Don't start that again. I still don't believe that dragons exist. And there is no chance of me slaying one!'

'Like you didn't bring me back from the dead?'

'I thought you said you didn't want to talk about it?'

Kade smiled sadly. 'You are stronger than you know, Tallen. Who knows if dragons still exist, but Drey has had visions for years. Now I'm having the same visions. And you're here. And you can do things that have not been done for generations.' He sighed. 'Maybe I'm hoping for a solution that is not there. But I'm not sure how else to win this war.'

I was surprised by Kade's sudden admission of possible defeat. He was usually so confident, and I had never doubted that he would win and Faulknar would be victorious. The realisation left a heavy lump in my stomach.

'You will win, Kade,' I reassured him. 'You are cleverer than Hayton and you are braver than Villermir. People will come to help you.'

Kade snorted. 'Where are they now? We lose ground daily. Countless lives have been lost...'

'That is not your fault, Kade. You cannot think like that.'

He turned to me, looking haunted; seeming so distant. 'Then whose responsibility is it?'

'Your father's, for now.'

Kade huffed.

'He is the king right now, and therefore he has the responsibility. He makes the decisions and accepts the consequences. Yes, one day those will be yours—'

'If there's anything left.'

'...but for now, you have to let him carry that burden.'

'And when did you become so wise?'

I shrugged and gave him a small smile. 'When it stops me thinking about how scared I am of Villermir. I can't think about the war and all the pain it causes people. Villermir scares me enough. If I think about all of it, I'm worried I'll go mad.'

Kade was quiet for a long while before finally taking a deep breath and visibly shaking off the weight of his thoughts. 'Well, if we are going back to Mobis's Hells, we can at least go together and do it in style.'

I grinned. 'And take that son of a diseased goat with us!'

We lapsed into companionable silence and I had finished my tea by the time Sutha joined us. She was dressed in formal robes of dark blue with a paler blue satin lining visible in the hood. She wore plain leather sandals, but the hem of her dress could be seen beneath her cloak to reveal a bright orange decoration. She smiled warmly at Kade and me as we sat side by side on the short grass.

'Blessed morning to you. I hope you slept well.'

Neither Kade nor I could contain the smirks elicited by her comment.

'Thank you,' I said diplomatically. 'Your hospitality was truly appreciated.'

'Nicely avoided,' countered Sutha. 'I think we all slept poorly after last night's conversation. But enough of that. Today is for lighter matters.' She inclined her head towards me. 'Tallen, I promised you a conversation. Would you come with me to the towers?'

My stomach flipped as I rose to join Sutha and thought of going to those impossible shards of flint. Their imposing presence shouted a history beyond my understanding and of a power before the Ancients. I felt unworthy of the honour of being in the same space. Who knew what mysteries they held? What would they reveal about me?

My internal rambling was halted by Kade making to follow us. He had not taken three steps before Sutha turned on him. 'You cannot come with us, Your Grace.'

Misunderstanding the harsh tone of her voice, I reassured her that I didn't mind him coming, and that she could talk freely in front of him. Sutha's tone softened when she talked to me, but her posture was still adamant.

'Our conversation is not the reason he cannot come to the towers.'

'Then what is it?' Kade demanded. 'I have handled the towers before.'

'But you were not then, what you are now.'

I was confused. 'I don't understand. How can he be different? Surely it cannot be because he's King-in-Waiting?' Was this part of not taking sides in the war?

'It's because of what happened at Burford Hythe,' stated Kade angrily.

My heart turned cold. Here was yet another problem created by my instinct to save Kade, my selfish desire to continue to have him in my life. Once again he was paying for what I had done.

'There is a shadow around you.' Sutha's eyes lost focus as she looked at Kade, assessing his aura. 'It is interwoven with your energy lines so that it is hard to see the person underneath. There is no way of telling how it influences you.'

'Oh, I know how it influences me,' Kade snapped. 'The cursed visions started after Burford.'

Sutha mocked his statement with a sharp laugh. 'Don't fool yourself, prince. The visions have nothing to do with the shadow, and you know it. Do not deceive yourself into believing your abilities are other than your own, however distasteful you find them.'

At that, Kade turned on his heel and stamped away from us. Having been so wise earlier, telling him he should not feel responsibility for things out of his control, I could not take the same advice and dismiss the guilt I was feeling; knowing myself to be responsible for his current pain and frustration.

'You did an incredible thing, bringing him back,' said Sutha quietly.

I was wondering how she knew what I was thinking, when I realised that I had subconsciously been rubbing the scars on the backs of my hands. 'I'm not sure Kade agrees.'

Sutha sighed as we continued walking towards the flint towers. 'It would be unrealistic to expect Kade to be unchanged. Drey tells me he is more moody and shorter of temper.'

'The loss of Kerk and his sudden rise to King-in-Waiting could explain that.'

'Do you really believe that?'

I thought about it for several heartbeats. How well did I know Kade since I had returned from the cottage? He had been effective at avoiding me in Liegeport and on the journey to Kingsport. He had practically ignored me before then.

'I don't know,' I admitted. 'He has been more sullen, I suppose. But so much has happened over the last few seasons or so. And with the war getting more serious. And apparently he's been taking valerian for months.'

Sutha tutted. 'That will not have helped, but I can understand his motivation to control his visions. According to Drey, his father pays him no attention and the last thing Kyllian wants is a gifted seer for a son. But I fear that Kade is listening to Drey less and becoming more isolated.' Sutha touched my arm, and I turned to face her. 'He needs you, despite his manner. Can you be there for him as he navigates his way?'

I frowned at her suggestion that I would do otherwise. 'Always.'

'Good.' She smiled encouragingly before attempting to change the subject. 'And how are you dealing with all this?'

I was not ready to leave the matter of Kade just yet. 'Do you think that his visions are because of what I did?'

Sutha sighed. 'You know the Druidic path. You know the progression he needs to go through. Maybe the incident at Burford Hythe accelerated the process.'

'So you think he will be a Druid? I didn't think there was a history in his family.'

'It doesn't always follow that there is a familial connection. Drey is very careful about his friends and most are very talented in something.'

'If Kade's visions come anywhere close to his bardic talent… It will send him mad.' I had a terrible thought. 'Not to mention that his father will be furious!'

Sutha nodded sadly in confirmation. 'Like I said, watch out for your prince. He has challenges pressing on him from many sides.'

We walked the rest of the way to the pillars in silence, as I fermented the idea of Kade being a Druid. Much as I hated Kyllian declaring his support for the Baila faith, it had prevented the war from becoming a religious crusade. If it became known that Kade was developing Druidic talent, Hayton, with Villermir's counsel no doubt, would use every weapon he had to turn the people against their prince. It would split the kingdom in two, with those with Baila fighting those with the Gods. Lindvane could sit back and watch as neighbour turned against neighbour, and Faulknar tore itself to pieces.

We were several paces from the flint when I felt a tingling against my skin, like the prickling of a stinging nettle but not unpleasant. Relaxing my vision, I saw four ley lines radiating from the towers. Pulses of soft blue veins travelled along the lines, fading as they got further away, and bled into the surrounding earth. Traces of blue flickered in every plant, animal and person on the island. A thin pathway took us to the pillars, which were not smooth as I had assumed from looking at them from a distance. Countless shards of flint poked from their surface, looking sharp enough to cut flesh. Various tones of grey mottled the stones.

'Clear your mind,' instructed Sutha.

I slowed my breathing and concentrated on the feel of the breeze on my skin. I gave a small nod to confirm I was ready, prompting Sutha to take my hand and lead me into the area between the pillars. A slight resistance was felt initially, then all I felt was calm. The tingling had ceased, and although the pillars only stood to two sides of us, the wind seemed to blow around rather than through the stones. The space in between felt totally protected.

Sutha gestured to a spot at the centre where a circular space, perhaps seven paces across, had been cleared of grass and covered with reed stalk rushes. I followed the older woman's lead and sat on the surprisingly comfortable ground with crossed legs and spine balanced. Sutha sat opposite me, our hands relaxed on our almost touching knees and our palms facing upwards.

'What do you feel?' asked Sutha quietly.

I took a deep breath, exhaling slowly. The first sense to create a thought was hearing; a soft hum as the breeze played around the towers. I smiled at the memory. 'That sound. It reminds me of a small bowl my grandfather had. When you rubbed your fingers around the edge it would hum like that.'

Sutha nodded. 'Family it is, then. The stones can do many things. They can take memories and share them with others. We will not be able to interact with those we see, but we can observe. Why don't we start there? Which memory do you want to see first?'

I answered without thinking. 'My father.'

Sutha rocked forward slightly, to place her palms on top of mine. I closed my eyes, not really knowing what to expect. Her breathing slowed and I instinctively matched her rhythm.

She huffed in annoyance. 'Can you let down your barriers?'

'Oh, sorry,' I spluttered. I had forgotten that I had raised them when travelling through the marshes, and I had subconsciously maintained them once upon the Isle of Serpents.

The background vibration from the stones became stronger and thicker as soon as I relaxed my protections. For a moment I was lost in the currents that swirled around the area in which we sat. I forced myself to take a deep breath before composing myself again. I imaged the hallway of doors that Drey had taught me to accept entrance into my mind, and smiled as the door representing Sutha turned out to be a reed-woven door with red flowers interwoven throughout.

Sutha raised an eyebrow at my projected younger self. 'You don't like visitors, I see.'

I shrugged. 'It gets busy in here sometimes.'

'Think of your father and we should get to see him.'

My stomach fluttered with anticipation as I decided what memory I wanted to share. I had so few of my family, and even fewer, it seemed, of my father. I chose one, opening the plain timber door to reveal the scene for

Sutha. I was running through the meadow outside the village, just in front of the forest. It must have been late summer as the grasses were yellow and there were small blackberries on the bramble bushes. I would have been about five or six years old. Tanned, stubby legs poked out from beneath my tunic as I giggled in pleasure. My younger self turned to see my father, who had been pretending to be a bear and was chasing me.

The scene froze before I could clearly see my father. The vision of a slender woman wearing a black cloak coalesced in front of the observing me. The woman was close enough for me to see her face: the milky-white complexion, the soft rose of her lips, eyes so pale a blue that they were almost translucent. Silver hair framing her delicate features.

The image vanished, and my head swam dizzyingly as I was suddenly sitting opposite Sutha in the circle between the pillars. The priestess had gone pale and was visibly shaking. She removed her hands from mine and wiped them over her face.

'Merciful Mother,' she breathed. 'I had never thought I would see...'

I was confused by Sutha's reaction. 'She is often in my dreams. And she was in a vision I had with Drey once.'

Sutha laughed nervously. 'I can see why Drey keeps you close by. You continue to amaze.'

I frowned, getting more confused. 'I don't understand. Who is she?'

Sutha looked at me as if I had grown an extra head. 'Tallen. She is the Lady. The Goddess of the Moon.'

'Don't be silly.' I easily dismissed her comment. 'Why would I be seeing the Goddess?'

'I don't know. But you are. And it seems she does not want you to remember your father.' She took a deep breath. 'Perhaps we should try something a little safer. How about one of my memories of your mother?'

My disappointment at not being able to see my father, even in a memory, was muted by a flutter of excitement at the thought of learning something about my mother. At my nod, Sutha returned her hands to mine and we slowed our breathing as before. The memory sharpened into an autumnal scene of orange grasses and mischievous winds. A group of young women was sitting on brightly coloured woven rugs around a small, low-burning fire. My breath caught as I recognised my mother, younger than I remembered her, talking to the gathering. Her face was open and inviting, smiling at comments made by the others as she demonstrated weaving a straw dolly.

'Ma,' I breathed, taking a step forward before I remembered that she could not see or hear me. She had no notion that I was seeing her.

'Your mother was a good teacher,' Sutha said gently at my shoulder. 'If she had stayed on the Isle, she would certainly have made a respected elder. People listened to her. Would talk to her.'

'Why did she leave?'

I felt Sutha's breath change as she smiled. 'Your father.'

I wanted to turn to question Sutha, but was loath to take my eyes from my mother, deftly helping one of her students correct a weave. 'My father was here? I thought you said you had not met him?'

'Your father never came to the Isle of Serpents. By the Gods, that would have caused a stir. Drey had warned us about you, and still the place was an ants' nest when we felt your arrival. No, your father never came here. Maeryn returned to her village during a bout of scarlet sickness, met your father there and did not return to the Isle. It was a great loss to us.'

'Maeryn,' I breathed. I had not known my mother's name.

'Do you know the meaning of your family name?'

I frowned at the sudden change of direction. In the old tradition, a girl's family name came from her mother, as boys took their father's name. Still, it seemed an odd time to raise this subject, when all I wanted was to know more about my mother. Maeryn.

'It means black,' I stuttered. 'As your name, Aine, means light.'

'That's true, but it only tells half the story.' Sutha's tone softened as if this was a tale she had told many times to different people. The words had been rehearsed, although the specific names might often change. 'Many students who come here have ancestral talents. Like Cait, who you met on your arrival. She is descended from many Aqualine, but her heritage is not true. Her bloodlines have been diluted over the centuries, and so her power has diminished. There are others, like me and you, who have pure bloodlines that can be traced back to the Ancients. There may only be one true talent per generation, but there is always one. These are given the title of the ancient family names.'

I turned to Sutha in shock, temporarily forgetting my treasured mother. 'But there are so few who carry the old names.'

'I know. We are a dying breed, Tallen. The number of true-born gets lower every year.'

I turned back to the tranquil scene of my mother weaving. 'My mother was a true-born? But Villermir said she was a healer. How could she be a true-born?'

'Pah! What does that man know?' Sutha sighed. 'The Gods are good at keeping their secrets. And after seeing the Goddess, I suspect that she is actively involved in controlling who knows what about your abilities and bloodlines. You mother was a true-born, as was your father. Which makes you very special.'

'I'm not special,' I protested.

Sutha breathed a mocking laugh. 'So you believe.'

I considered her words for a moment. 'So, if the names are an indication of talent, what are you? What does Aine signify?'

'Your mother was an Empath, as am I.'

'Is that why I can touch the Empathy Crystal?'

'Possibly, but I think it is more than that. I'm not sure I could touch the stone without getting burned. I suspect your father's heritage has more than a little influence in it. Still, your mother was a powerful Empath. She understood people, as is the way of Empaths. However, the talent appears differently in different people. This is reflected in our names. Aine, light. My family has an ability to see the light of any situation. The good in people.'

'Like Villermir?'

'Huh, I may find that particular soul difficult. But yes, I understand his motivations. But most people are not that dark or light. We have good and bad threaded throughout us. Some people find it difficult to see their kinder nature or brighter soul…'

I had the feeling she might be talking about my refusal to believe that any talents I had could be beneficial, and not just harmful to those I cared about. 'And Duane?'

'The dark. I knew your mother better than you, so I will explain her gifts. You can see that she had a way with people and was a good teacher, but that was not what made her special. There was a reason I showed you this memory. Watch Kareme, to the right of your mother.'

I moved my focus to the right and saw a young woman, hardly more than a girl, concentrating on weaving her straw dolly talisman. Her round face was pinched in a scowl as the stalk would not bend as she wished. As she got more frustrated, her fingers fumbled the fiddly threading and her expression turned to anger. She pursed her lips and was about to throw her talisman into the fire, when my mother placed a hand on her arm. The girl snapped her head up, ready for a spiteful retort, but her anger faded as she looked into my mother's face. A placid smile eased the younger woman's frown lines as my mother gently guided the girl's fingers to repair the damage and correct the weave. The girl looked up at my mother with the most beautiful smile of gratitude.

'Kareme came to us after she had been rejected by her family. As her talents started to show, people became scared of her visions and she was ostracised from her village. Kareme learnt to trust the community here but was always quick to believe the worst of herself. That she was worthless and no good. She would grow angry with herself and take it out on others; a dark stain on her soul. Your mother saw that hurt and rubbed the stain until there was virtually nothing left. Kareme became a valued teacher in her own right, thanks in no small part to your mother's understanding and care.'

'So that's the heritage of the Duanes,' I said quietly. 'I'm not sure I will be any good at soothing anyone's dark soul.'

Sutha turned me to face her and placed her hands in mine. The vision faded, and we were back between the towers. We both instinctually gave a deep sigh to cleanse the remnants of the memory.

'I fear your dark path will take you on quite a different journey. I suspect that you will use your talents to discover blackened souls, but I doubt that understanding will be your gift when it comes to dealing with these threats.'

Chapter Fourteen

I left Sutha at the flint pillars and thought about what she had said as I strolled back to the settlement. Was I drawn to the dark side of people? I didn't think I was drawn to the darker side of Kade but then, I did understand his frustrations and motivations. Most of the people I spent time with were professional soldiers who killed for a living. Both Tawpin and I were thieves. Maybe there was a dark stain on my soul that attracted a similar taint in others.

I was about halfway to the community of huts when I felt raindrops fall on my face. I looked up to see a clear sky as more raindrops fell onto my forehead. This time the drops were larger, and I had to wipe my face before the water trickled into my eyes. I looked down to see if anyone else had seen or felt this strange phenomenon. Cait was sitting with her back to a boulder, plaiting some grass stems, grinning at me. She made a small gesture with a finger and instantly I was shaded from the sun. I looked up to see a large dome of water suspended an arm-length above my head. The small woman was grinning mischievously at me, ready to release the volume of water and drench me. I was not going to let her get away with that, so with little more than a thought I produced a fireball the size of a baby's head.

'You willing to play this game?' I asked.

She laughed and moved the water away from my head. Unable to resist, I sent the fireball into the water. Steam hissed as the water evaporated into mist by the heat.

'Impressive fireball,' commented Cait.

I sat down next to her. 'Yeah. Not sure what happened there. I can't usually make them that big. Or that easily.'

'It will be the towers. You must have felt their power.'

I nodded in agreement.

'They give a boost to the natural talents of everyone here.' She smiled. 'Still, that was a nice fireball.'

I shook my head. 'I saw the energy in the ley lines from the pillars. I didn't think it would affect me. We've only been here a day.'

'It's almost immediate. Seems once you step onto the island, the energy seeps into you. Most people feel a difference within half a day.'

'Is everyone here talented, then?'

'Mostly. There are a few who come for healing, but generally it's those who want to study here.' Cait frowned sadly. 'The elders say that it used to be different. That folk would ride for days to be healed on the Isle of Serpents. That people – lords and ladies, not just commoners – would send their children here to study the old religion and learn herb lore. But not now. The marshes deter most people. Those who make it to the Fenlands, anyway. Many more follow the new religion of Baila, or are too scared to show that they don't.' Cait was quiet for a few heartbeats, before adding, 'Seems we are to be forgotten like the old Gods.'

I frowned. 'Do you really believe that?'

Cait shrugged. 'I don't know. That's what the elders say. Some were here before the new religion became so common.' She gave a short laugh that contained no humour. 'Seems strange, calling it the new religion when I've never known it to not be there. It sometimes feels like Baila is as old as the Moon Goddess and the Sun God.'

I felt cold, thinking that the old Gods could be completely replaced with Baila; that religion that had caused such misery and hatred. I remembered being in Methhold, being surrounded by the old Gods and acceptance. The raid on the village had been caused, in part, by the religious differences between Lindvane and Faulknar. Memories of my home, awakened by Sutha in the towers, felt betrayed by Cait's pessimism.

'Surely it is up to us to ensure that Baila doesn't succeed in driving out the Gods? How many of you are here? Can't you go back to your villages and show the people how powerful the Gods can be?'

'How do we show them?' asked Cait, looking at me as if I was naive. 'I come from Lindvane. I will be stoned as a heretic if I show them what I can do. My mother had to smuggle me out of the kingdom.'

'But she did smuggle you out,' I persisted. 'She must still believe. How many more are like her; staying silent, but quietly resisting Baila?'

We were silent for several heartbeats as we considered the plausibility of maintaining the ways of the Gods and the Ancients, while time moved us ever closer to the dominion of Baila. My mind wound me into spirals of doubt that I was not prepared to accept.

I changed the subject. 'So, are all the students here Aqualine?'

Cait smiled at my obvious tactic but was happy to follow me into less depressing talk. 'There are a few of us, but mostly students come to study the old ways in general, learning herb lore and childbirth, as well as some of the more basic magicks.'

'Sutha mentioned that you inherited your talents from your mother.'

Cait laughed. 'By the Gods, no. My ma can hardly walk through a door without injuring herself. We would be permanently soggy if she had power over the elements.'

'Then your father?'

She shook her head. 'No. I'm not sure where the gift comes from. Of course, we lived in Lindvane so they could just have been hiding any talent, but they seemed as shocked as I was when I started making water fountains in the washtub.'

I giggled at the image in my head. 'Oh, that must have been something to see. None of your family had any hint?'

'No. My whole extended family was boringly normal. I had no idea what was possible, until I came here.'

I shook my head. 'I don't remember much before the raid, but magick was normal for my family. Mother, father, grandfather. Especially on festival days.'

I absently experimented with the new skills afforded me by the energy of the flint and created a fireball that split into two before spiralling to the ground. Sparks rained from the fireballs so that they dissolved before hitting the ground. Cait grinned and sent a plume of water into the air. It caught the sunlight, and rainbows flickered as the water swirled. I added a small gust of air, causing the water to rotate as a miniature tornado. Cait added another stream of water, which I also twirled, the two water spouts spinning around each other.

'Fire and air?'

I smiled and, feeling like showing off, added a small number of pebbles, piling two or three on top of each other and making the handful of piles jiggle underneath the water as if they were dancing. 'Drey is a good teacher,' I confessed.

The presence of the flint energy was making it very easy to control all the different elements. I had not worked with multiple forms before, but all I had to do was think about what I wanted the fire, air and stones to do, and they did it. I doubted I would have been able to do anything as complicated away from the Isle.

I found Cait easy company and was soon asking her questions about her magick. Although Drey had explained the basic principles of the elements, much of what I did was instinctual and I found it difficult to understand what I was doing most of the time. I wondered if it was the same with Cait and her control of water.

Cait thought for a while before answering. 'I know what you mean,' she started hesitantly. 'It feels as natural as breathing. An extension of who I am. It's hard to put into words.' She laughed at my frown. 'But I shall try. It's almost like having a conversation, like talking to Muirfuin, but it is not as simple as speaking to one being. And I wouldn't presume to ask the Goddess for anything. It's like you are talking to all the individual droplets of water, all at the same time. Suggesting what shapes to make, or how fast to travel, or…' she grinned at me '…who to soak.'

'Does the water ever talk back?'

'Sometimes. It's more of a feeling than words. I feel acceptance for what I am asking, or anxiousness. I'm sure I would know if what I was doing was unacceptable.'

'And do the sprites talk to you?'

Cait frowned at me. 'You see those?'

'Yes,' I replied, confused at her question. 'Doesn't everyone?'

She shook her head with a short laugh. 'Of course, you would see them. You're a Dragonslayer.' She shook her head again. 'No, Tallen. Not everyone sees them. It took me several month cycles to be able to even glimpse them.'

'So, you didn't create them? The water sprites and the serpents? They're real?'

She slowly tilted her head at me. 'You have so much ability, with so little knowledge.'

'Is that a compliment or an insult?'

'There are creatures that live in all the elements. I see those that live in water, but cannot see those of fire, air or earth.'

'I've seen fire and water, but not air or earth. Mainly fire.'

Cait nodded. 'That sounds true. Air creatures are supposed to be so flighty that it's really hard to give them form. Often, they are just flickers at the edges of your vision, or shadows that catch your eye. It is said that earth spirits move so slowly that we don't recognise them as living beings. You just get impressions of a face or a body, but they don't seem to move so you ignore them. You're lucky to be able to see two elements.'

I sighed, playing with a blade of grass between my fingers. 'There is so much I don't know. And even less that I understand.'

Cait grinned at me. 'I think that is the point. I was totally overwhelmed when I came here. At least you have Drey, and the memories of your family, to guide you. This was all so new to me. Sutha has spent a lifetime studying these things, and she says she still doesn't understand them.' She punched my shoulder playfully. 'We have no hope!'

'I think Drey is so caught up in his fantasies of this wonderful Dragonslayer who will bring back the Gods that he forgets that most of what I've done has been pure luck and a large helping of panic!'

'You sell yourself cheaply. Sutha and the other elders have been buzzing like bees at the thought of your arrival. You have control of all four elements, which is not a gift offered to many.'

'I just wish I knew what I'm supposed to be doing with all these "gifts". What is the point of me having them? Why is Drey so reluctant to teach me everything I need to know?'

'Your abilities already outshine most of those on the island, and you admit that you know a small part of what you are capable of. Just imagine what you could do with a lifetime of training.'

We spent several days on the island, learning all that they were willing to share. Kade would often spend his mornings with Drey and Sutha, in a hut away from prying eyes. I had no idea what was happening during these sessions, but Kade would often emerge in a fouler temper than when he went in. He would pass the rest of the day by isolating himself from the community, sitting alone by the river. In a reversal of our natural roles, while Kade sought solitude I enjoyed the company of the students as they went about their lessons. I relished the opportunity to learn, without the pressure of being the only student. Although I was careful not to be too eager to show off my skills, it was clear, even to me, that I possessed abilities that were not common in this selective group of talented scholars.

Cait started at the beginning, taking me to the lessons that were primarily for the young children of the community, but also contained a handful of older youths and sprinkling of adults who had come to the Isle later in life. These sessions taught the fundamentals of herb lore; identifying plants that could heal and purge, the benefits of tinctures and infusions, the strengths and dilutions required for safe practice. Cait explained that many would not progress further than this class, returning to their homes as herb-witches and herbalists to help their local communities. The information had been drummed into my head by Drey many years ago, so we soon moved on to the next level of learning on the Isle.

These teachings took place in a hut on the outer boundaries of the settlement, so that the noise from day-to-day activity was less intrusive. The students learned meditation techniques and the ways of channelling the energy from the elements. Although there was a smaller number in this class, most had some latent talent for the elements and a large proportion were destined to become healers. Only four had some ancestral link to the Aqualine or Firewalkers, and none had the strong bloodlines of a direct descendant. I saw no Empaths or Dragonslayers, reminding me again of how different I was; emphasising why I found many of the exercises practised here easy, while others struggled.

We spent a whole day with the scholars of this group. Cait had graduated from this level several seasons previously, but she welcomed the chance to review her basic methods and highlight the bad habits she had lapsed into. I initially felt self-conscious at the buzz of murmured conversation that accompanied my arrival. I was uncomfortable with the attention I received, as several openly stared at me and whispered behind their hands. They had the grace to look away, embarrassed, whenever I caught their eye, but I was grateful when the tutor regained the focus of his students and the lesson began. It was not long, however, before I was the one staring as the pupils practised breathing techniques and explored the auric field of their partner. I was lost in the shimmering of colours that played around the students as they manipulated the energy fields. I had to be gently reprimanded several times to follow the teacher's instructions, as he guided his group and explained processes that I followed instinctually.

Listening to the young man's quiet tones, I felt the energy currents surrounding me like ripples on a wind-blown lake. I heard the almost silent hum as they vibrated the air around them. Tiny whirlpools were created as they connected with the physical structures of grass, stones and insects. Blending with the auras of the people around me, the faint hum harmonising with individual energy currents as the students shaped and guided the air. Shimmering tides that sparkled with jewelled droplets of amber, rose, gold, silver, azure, turquoise and lilac. The corona around each learner radiated throughout the open-sided hut, extending beyond my visual range to cover the whole island. The colours changed subtly as they interacted with the energy sources of the elements around them; darker when touching earth or stone, more intense when touched by heat, paler when brushed by air, sparkling when enveloped in moisture.

I was mesmerised by the interweaving tapestry of colour, and felt such joy at my tingling senses. The exquisite harmonies of the vibrated air that tickled my ears and energised my brain. The gentle warmth of my skin that felt like a hug of acceptance and safety. The smell and taste of sharp, freshly cut grass, salty sea spray and warm baking bread coating my nose and mouth and spreading throughout my muscles. The glow of pure motes of light dancing to an ancient, timeless beat that pulsed through every particle of creation. I drifted blissfully on the undulating swirls of energy, gently swaying and twirling like a feather on a summer's breeze; the colours of my aura dissolving into the rainbow surrounding me as I touched the essence of everything around me.

I was jolted back to an awareness of others, within a hut on the Isle of Serpents, by a gasped intake of breath. I opened my eyes to see the building glowing with a rainbow hue, as the sun would shine through a jar of coloured glass beads; countless different shades that grew darker as they neared the ground, and paler as they touched the rafters. Students who had an affinity with water sparkled like the flame of a candle, while those who connected with fire glowed with an intensity that hurt the eye when looked at directly. Some were lost in the spectacle, but most were looking at me with open mouths. The tutor was staring as if stunned, and Cait was grinning at me like a madwoman.

'Oops,' I apologised, melting the colour into transient sparks before returning the room to its normal appearance.

The teacher smiled, nodding his head in acknowledgement of what I had just done. 'Thank you, Tallen. You have very visually demonstrated the different tones that are associated with the range of energy signatures emitted by the elements.'

It was decided that we should take a short break, while everyone grounded themselves again and refocused on their own abilities, rather than on my interruptive show of light. The lesson moved on to the use of crystals as a tool for guiding energy or promoting healing channels. The tutor asked the students to show him their personal crystals, to determine the effects of the cleansing task they had been set. Crystals had been placed in the clean, flowing current of the river or left for a night under the gaze of the moon to clear them of stored energy. All the stones looked clear and gleaming to me, although I had little knowledge in this area. Drey was never without his rose quartz and used it frequently in his healing and rituals, but I had never used one effectively despite Drey's many failed attempts to find a crystal appropriate for my use.

'And do you have a crystal?' the teacher asked after he had examined Cait's aquamarine pendant.

I shook my head. 'I don't use crystals.'

'Why not? They can be very useful to empower runes and sigils, as well as provide focus and grounding.'

I hesitated. 'I tend to break them.'

There was a ripple of giggling from a group of younger students, as the tutor frowned in confusion.

'What do you mean?'

I shrugged, a little embarrassed to admit my difficulties with the stones. 'They tend to go cloudy when I use them. The surface becomes pitted and cracked. If I use them more than once, they tend to shatter.'

He stared at me for several heartbeats, his dark brown eyes searching my face for some sign of deception or mischief. Finding none, he shrugged his shoulders before going to retrieve a small woven basket containing crystals of different colours, shapes and sizes. 'Show me.'

He extended the basket towards me and I selected a crystal from the top. It was a clear quartz, a little shorter than Drey's and a lot thinner. It had milky-white edges where it had been polished to a point, leaving the centre of the stone as clear as water. I slowly rotated the rock so that it caught the light, holding the base gently between my thumb and first finger. It was a pretty stone and cast shards of rainbow colours as it moved, but within a few heartbeats I watched the frosted edges move towards the centre of the crystal as if a cloud had formed at the heart of the rock. The surface of the stone became roughened as tiny craters dotted the edges. Small cracks radiated from the points, more numerous in the areas where I touched it. I closed my hand over the stone to hide it from the wide-eyed stares of the students.

'I see,' the tutor said, tilting his head to one side. 'How very interesting.'

He turned to walk to the front of the class, explaining that the currents in our bodies are passed to the crystals that we use, causing clouding and requiring their regular cleansing in fresh water and natural light. I relaxed as the group's attention was taken away from me, listening to the tutor describing the different energy sources that could block the clarity of the crystal's power, and how that might result in impaired conduction or even harmful energies being released from the stones. I thought of the Empathy Crystal, doubting that Villermir would be conscientiously releasing trapped currents from within its heart. How far had he corrupted its natural powers just by being around it, not to mention his sullied use of its abilities?

I cursed loudly, using phrases that would have had Drey cuffing my ears, and provoked another outburst of giggles from the youngsters at the front. My hand opened to reveal the shattered crystal, shards of rock embedded in my palm and smears of blood coating the frosted splinters. Saddened that I had destroyed the pretty stone, I dismissed the requests that I visit the healers, and spent the rest of the lesson sulkily pulling fragments from my hand.

Cait thought it was best if we moved on to the third and last level of training on the Isle; healing. The teaching hut was close to the one where I had learnt about the different types of crystals, but was smaller in size and enclosed on the side that faced the settlement. It provided some privacy for those working inside, and those being treated. There were only five students in this group, mainly older men and women who had progressed through the other two stages and were ready to complete their studies as healers. I noticed that all had inked an image of a snake, partially curled to form an S, on the base of their neck or on their inner wrist. Cait explained that this represented their service to Nathair and the healing arts. When they had finished their training, they would travel the three kingdoms as healers and advisers. Some would go as far as the Travellers' lands and be called a *zaratos* in their culture. After years of service, perhaps one or two from each group would be initiated as acolytes of the God or Goddess. Very rarely did they progress to become a Druid.

I frowned. 'I've never seen a snake mark on Drey.'

Cait shrugged. 'They say that Drey took a different path. He certainly didn't study here, but there are other places to learn; other ways of becoming a Druid.' She grinned. 'Some say he was born an old Druid, all wrinkly and cross. Instead of crying like a normal baby, he would spit curses.'

I punched her playfully on the shoulder for teasing, but the class started before I could question her further. The teacher had a faded snake mark on her wrist and, if I stared at her grey-blue eyes for too long, she had the same hypnotic gaze that I had seen in Drey and Sutha. She had a quiet voice that had everyone leaning forward to catch her every word, but she exuded a confidence and authority that made me feel safe and protected.

The session was mainly theoretical as the tutor explained some of the common diseases and the ways of managing them. It was clear that the symbols and runes used in the healing process were known by the students, and I had to concentrate to remember the sigils used by Drey. The first time I had seen the characters used was when Drey had delivered Eldiss's nephew; a difficult birth that required the baby to be turned before it could be born safely. I had seen Drey use the magick a few times after that but, as I had never performed the rituals myself, he had not seen the need to explain what he did. I was totally absorbed by the discussions of presenting symptoms and energy corruptions that would allow correct identification of the diseases present; the progression of these signs that would indicate whether any interventions were helpful or harmful. I memorised each condition described, and was occasionally able to recall which herbal infusions or tinctures would be appropriate from years spent with Drey. I was fascinated by the use of symbols to channel the power of the elements towards correcting specific dysfunctions or stimulating the body to produce its own healing properties. The complex interplay between the different characters to create a mesh of internal and external energies, which could be used to provide a matrix for the specific healing requirements of the individual. I sat open-mouthed as I absorbed as much information as I could, from both the tutor and her students.

It seemed no time at all until a break was called for the midday meal. I turned to find Cait beaming a wide, toothy smile at me.

'What?'

She shrugged. 'It seems that we have finally taught you something.'

I returned her smile. 'There is so much I don't know. You are so lucky to have all this knowledge around you. How do you remember it all?'

Cait laughed and held up her wrists, showing me their inner surfaces. 'I don't need to. See, no snake. The healing path is not for me. Only one element, remember?'

I shook my head, slowly understanding. 'So, these are those who have control over all four elements? There are so few.'

She nudged my shoulder. 'Told you, you were special.'

I frowned at her, still not believing I was anything different, but finding it harder to hold on to that belief. I spent the break looking for signs of the snake, to confirm that Cait was exaggerating about the lack of those who had full elemental control. I accepted that most would be travelling the kingdoms, but even so, in a community that attracted the most gifted, that numbered over a hundred scholars, I saw fewer than twenty who carried the mark of Nathair. I returned to the class with a new understanding of how lucky I was to be part of this exclusive group.

For the second session that day, we were joined by one of the elder residents of the Isle. Her neck was distended by a large lump of tissue that had ulcerated and was leaking a sticky, yellow-tinted fluid. The mass had been growing steadily over the past three moon cycles, and she had started to lose weight despite ointments and teas. It had been decided that she would need more invasive methods, and she had agreed to allow the students to perform the healing. I thought about which student would be most suited to the task: Meech was calm and methodical, Lier was more intuitive, Polara was skilled but hesitant, Grav was a little too confident – Malic would be the one I would choose. I was unprepared when it was suggested that I should come forward.

'Oh my.' The elderly lady fluttered her hand in front of her mouth.

I moved my horrified gaze between tutor and patient. 'I don't think that's a good idea.'

The teacher dismissed my concerns. 'Please,' she said calmly, gesturing towards the old lady.

I shook my head. 'You realise that I have never done this before?'

The older women reached for my hands. 'I would be honoured.'

I looked around the group to see faces of expectation and excitement. I was sure that word of my exploding crystal had spread, and these people were keen to see what would happen when a Dragonslayer used her powers.

'You have to start somewhere,' encouraged the tutor. 'I will be guiding you all the way.'

With a sigh, I stepped forward and clasped the old lady's hands. She had a firm grip, and I smiled at her confidence in me. I guided her to a low pallet that had been brought in, helping her to get comfortable and arranging her arms by her sides and her legs together. I placed a rolled cloth under her head to support the position of a slightly extended neck. I placed a hand on her shoulder, and she nodded to confirm that she was ready to begin.

'First we will place Veeta in a sleep state so the body can work without the concerns of her mind. Tallen, could you draw the symbol for sleep on the inside of her forearm?'

The teacher handed me a thin stick of charcoal while I gently rotated my patient's wrist to expose the thin skin of her inner arm. Careful not to smudge the markings, I drew the outline of a spiral containing three rings, starting at the centre and ending in a small tail pointing towards the head.

'That's good,' murmured the tutor. 'Now use your crystal to activate the rune.'

I raised my head, tilting it to one side.

'Oh. Yes,' she stammered when she had realised what was wrong. 'I heard about that. Well, I'm not sure what to do next. I've never encountered someone at this stage who could not handle a crystal. The symbol requires fire and earth to activate it, so perhaps if you—'

She was interrupted by a collective intake of breath. As she had been considering different options to replace the crystal, I had pondered that charcoal was burnt wood and perhaps the wood could be the focus of the earth element, so I just needed to add some fire. As I pictured fire burning the charcoal spiral, the symbol on Veeta's arm momentarily glowed orange before seeping into her tissues.

I slowed my breathing to match hers, connecting our auras so I could see the tangled web of trapped energy surrounding the mass in her neck. A small part of my mind travelled the length of Veeta's body to ensure there were no other discrepancies; releasing energy in one part, renewing tissue in another.

'I'm sure Veeta would appreciate having the body of a twenty-year-old, but that is not our focus for today. Concentrate on the ulcerated lump.'

The teacher's voice arrested my corrections, and I withdrew from the elderly lady's body to inspect her aura. It glowed with vitality, but there was still a stain over the region of the abnormal growth.

'Control the flow of your energy and focus on the tissues of the neck.'

I extended into Veeta's tissues again, finding the webbing that had caused the lump to reproduce out of control. Energy was being absorbed from the surrounding structures to feed the mass. Black tendrils coiled around the vessels of her throat, pulsing in time with her heartbeat. I shuddered at the feeling of decay that emanated from the site, as it prodded against my own energy fields, looking for a way to enter my body.

The session that morning had taught me the symbols to use, and I did not wait for instruction before drawing the patterns and shapes needed to correct the flow of energy to the area. I drew individual sigils of interlocking circles, triangles or squares onto the skin of her arms and neck. Patterns created to guide the elements in supporting healthy tissue while suffocating the diseased; shrinking the corruption and diluting the stench of decomposition. Clear colours threaded through the region, bringing fresh energy to the damaged tissues. I weaved the filaments through muscle, cartilage and skin. Shades of yellow, green, red and blue grew more vibrant as they connected with others of their colour. A bright azure blue predominated as the black and browns of the diseased flesh were absorbed and transformed by the healing energy I guided into their coils.

Once I was content that all harmful currents had been removed, I slowly withdrew my touch and inspected Veeta's aura to confirm her energies were flowing freely. Her aura hummed with a pleasant tone and pulsed in shimmering waves that were free of unnatural taints. I blinked to focus my eyes on the physical world, noting that her neck once again followed the normal contours with no wounds or ulcers evident. The skin was a little pinker than the surrounding area, but I was happy that I had healed her condition as much as I was capable of doing. I was also more than a little relieved that I had not exploded her as I had done with the crystal.

'Well done,' someone breathed in the silence that hung heavily in the hut.

I breathed over the symbols I had drawn, confident that the moisture in the air from my breath would be adequate to provide the air and water needed to release the spells and the energy contained within them. The images faded under the skin, and I smiled as Veeta blinked herself awake.

'How do you feel?' I asked gently.

She lifted a hand to her throat and felt the healthy skin that had previously been sore and weeping. 'It's a little tender when I touch it, but otherwise I feel amazing.'

She placed one hand over her mouth as she clasped my fingers in her other one. Tears caused her eyes to sparkle as she looked at me, unable to find the words she wanted. I smiled at her, understanding her difficulties in thanking me for such a gift as that I had been able to give her.

Chapter Fifteen

I spent most of my time with Cait, although she had her own duties to attend to and I did not want to distract her during these times. The community was welcoming and never made me feel like I was imposing on their hospitality, but I still felt like an outsider and often chose to spend my time watching the activities of the Isle from a distance. It was during one of these times that Sutha came to find me. I had seen little of her since the visit to the flint towers; her time was often taken up with her responsibilities to the Isle, and her mornings were spent with Kade. Despite the many thoughts she must have been juggling, she had a manner that made you feel like you were the centre of her attention whenever you were around her.

She smiled at me as she curled her legs and gently sat beside me. She raised an eyebrow at the straw dolly I was struggling to make, knowing it had been prompted by the memory she had shown me of my mother's teaching.

'I need a little practice,' I explained as I held up the partially completed, slightly rotated box shape.

'Yes, well, if you will pick one of the most complicated patterns...' she gently mocked. 'And it looks fine to me.'

I continued feeding the dampened stalks of reed through the loops of the widening cage, content to let her watch me work. 'It keeps my mind busy.'

She laughed quietly. 'Indeed. I hear that you have been causing quite a commotion in lessons.'

I avoided looking up. 'Sorry about the crystal.'

She dismissed my concern with a flick of her hand. 'I think the Isle will be talking about that for quite some time. Although, I have to admit that I'm more pleased with Veeta skipping around the island like a young maiden. I believe you were meant to heal her neck, not her chronically aching joints.'

'The energy from the flint helped.'

She harrumphed. 'You sell yourself cheaply. Drey has given you the minimum of training, and still you accomplish these feats with ease.'

I stopped weaving and placed the dolly on my lap. 'I am happy here. I would spend the time to complete my studies here, if I could.'

'And we would be honoured to have you.'

The unspoken words hung suspended in the silence between us, and I felt the weight of my unknown future weighing heavily on my shoulders. After a while Sutha sighed, accepting that I was unwilling to proceed with the conversation.

'And yet, that future is not for you.'

I nodded. 'The king owns my future.'

'And Kade?'

I thought for a couple of heartbeats, before nodding again. 'And Kade. But I can't shake the feeling that I have unfinished business with Villermir. I can't leave the Empathy Crystal with him.'

Sutha inhaled deeply before releasing the breath as a long sigh. 'When you first arrived on the island, I gave you three titles. Dragonslayer from your father's bloodlines. Empath from your mother's. And Moon Warrior. I was a little presumptuous to name you that, but seeing the Goddess in your vision has confirmed my suspicion. I feel convinced that she has chosen you.'

I looked up at the older woman to see her serious face contained a hint of something else; fear, or maybe reverence. The hairs at the base of my skull were tickled by a breath of cold air.

'I have not heard the term before. What is a Moon Warrior?'

'The title goes back almost to the time of the Ancients. They were individuals chosen by the Goddess, known as Moon Warriors, or by the God, known as Sun Guardians. These incredible fighters were said to defend their deity from all human threats.'

I frowned. 'Why would a God need defending?'

She tilted her head at me. 'Do you not feel that your Gods need defending? That their powers are being eroded by the teachings of Baila?'

'I suppose. But are you saying that the Goddess has appeared in my dreams to let me know that I have been chosen to serve as her warrior? To do what?'

Sutha shrugged. 'That I don't know. But I feel that Villermir and the Empathy Crystal are involved somehow. What I do know is that the energy currents that are running through the earth are no longer balanced and in harmony. They have become chaotic and destructive. Care and stewardship of the land has been replaced by ownership and exploitation. We are seeing more corruptive diseases, like that of Veeta's neck. Perhaps your role is to heal these ailments.'

I tensed. 'Veeta was a test?'

Sutha's face creased in an apology. 'No. That was not the intention. You are here to learn, not to be assessed. Veeta is one of so many who are developing these lesions and growths. I'm sure you saw the dark threads of corruption woven into the tissues. I find I am unable to dismiss them as unrelated to the corruption seen in the ley lines and energy fields.'

'Villermir scares me,' I stated, leaving unsaid the fear that I would be unable to control the damage he was doing, much less stop him.

'He scares me too. But he must be the key to this. He is the most powerful of all Baila's priests, and he has mastered some control of the Empathy Crystal. Perhaps he is just a place to start.'

I sighed at the enormity of the task she had just given me. 'I'll make a deal with you. You fix Kade and I will try to stop Villermir.'

She barked a quick laugh. 'You make a hard bargain. Your prince is proving to be more of a puzzle than I first thought.'

The Mother Priestess of the Isle of Serpents gave me a quick, firm hug, before standing up and brushing dried grass from her skirt. She smiled sadly down at me. 'I know you don't think you are capable of doing what I have just asked you to do. But you are the best chance that we have. You have all the resources of the Isle at your disposal whenever you need them.'

She walked away, leaving me to ponder whether she had just agreed to go to war. Not for Kyllian. Not for Kade. Not even for Faulknar. But for me.

The sun had almost completed its descent, when my stomach growled in hunger. I walked over to the communal firepit where a porridge supplemented with berries was almost constantly on the go. Flat breads were also available, and I helped myself to some along with a handful of dried meat.

It was not long before Drey found me, and informed me that I was needed at a meeting in which the scouts were planning their next foray into Lindvane. I followed him to a small, round hut on the outskirts of the settlement. The door faced the river and it would be unlikely that any conversation could be overheard by accident. The space inside was dark after the sunlight outside, but my eyes soon adjusted. The patch of bright light by the door faded into an area that could comfortably house two families. Padded mats were placed in various spaces throughout, allowing private conversations to be had by smaller groups, as well larger gatherings. I recognised Sutha sitting with three other people who looked like they could be the ones who made the decisions for the Isle. Kade was seated to one side, with several younger men and women from the island. My assumption that these were scouts was confirmed by Sutha as she introduced me to those present. I nodded in acknowledgement to all as I sat with Drey, next to Kade.

'Thank you for joining us,' began a lady near Sutha, whose hair had just started to grey. 'For those who have not met our guests previously, may I present His Grace, Kade Faulknar.' She extended her hand towards Kade, who bobbed a nod in return. 'Our honoured friend and Druid, Drey Haelan.'

I looked at Drey, more surprised at his family name meaning healer than the proclamation of his rank as Druid. It had always been assumed but never confirmed.

'And Tallen nic Duane.'

There was a quiet murmuring among the scouts at the mention of my full name. I now appreciated the significance, and the rarity, of it. Not even Drey, who was the most talented person I knew, had the ancient bloodline title. It made me proud of my family and the legacy they had given me.

The man who sat between the initial speaker and Sutha spoke next. His hair was completely grey, and his face was weathered and lined by his years. His posture was a little sagged, as if sitting took effort, but his voice carried with authority and everyone paid attention when he spoke. 'While we preserve our non-involvement when it comes to the war between Faulknar and Lindvane, we nonetheless keep informed of Hayton's plans wherever possible.'

He looked at Kade while making his opening statement, while Sutha looked at the floor. It was clear that the conversation between Sutha and Kade had been relayed.

'Tarlee, your team came in this morning. What news?'

A young woman, perhaps a handful of years older than me, spoke next. She spoke hesitantly, but was shown equal respect to those who had spoken before her. 'There have been a number of reports of strange weather to the south of Lindvane. Rains have fallen more heavily than in previous years. Crops have spoiled. Livestock have foot rot. Two smaller rivers have changed course.'

The man to her right nodded in agreement. 'Similar reports have come in from the west. I saw with my own eyes a fissure in a meadow. The crack was as wide as my arm and the difference in height between the two sides was as high as my knees.'

The elder man considered these reports, before turning to another scout. 'Fennan, what news from the north?'

Fennan was a small, wiry man who sat, quiet and unassuming, within the group of scouts. It was easy to overlook him, although the northern border between Lindvane and Faulknar was known to be particularly troublesome. I suspected that he was very useful for obtaining information through blending in and going unnoticed.

'Much the same. Uncharacteristic weather. Violent storms that come from nowhere.' He shrugged, dismissing the environmental concerns. 'Usual stuff.'

'There's more?' prompted the older man.

The scout slowly shook his head. 'I'm not sure. We travelled back via Bream. Expected the town to be busy with spring trade. But this was different. There was a buzz to the activity. Whispers and glances. The town seemed nervous.' He shrugged again. 'Probably nothing.'

Sutha spoke for the first time. 'We have come to trust your hunches, Fennan, even if you don't.'

Fennan dipped his head. 'Aye, my lady. It just didn't feel right.'

'Perhaps another visit would be wise,' suggested the woman who had introduced us. She turned towards Drey. 'I understand that your visit here is more than social.'

'That is true, my lady,' agreed Drey. 'The king wanted to learn from your scouts to see if such techniques could be utilised elsewhere in the kingdom.'

The woman smiled self-deprecatingly. 'Our techniques are not that special, my friend. We watch, we listen. We leave without being noticed.'

'That may be so, but you repeatedly return with valuable information and, from what I hear, remarkably few casualties.'

'As I said, our aim is to leave unnoticed. However, if you and His Grace feel it is worth the risk, our scouts would be happy to accommodate you.'

'You are most generous,' Drey replied. 'But only Tallen will be going.'

I felt the atmosphere change within the hut, as everyone seemed to hold their breath. The scouts looked at the elders. The elders looked at each other. Their glances held discomfort and perhaps a hint of fear. I looked at Drey for answers, but he maintained his stare at the elders, daring them to disagree with him.

It was the man who finally spoke. 'I'm not sure we understand your request. The scouting raids are for tactical information, generally regarding elemental misuse but occasionally information that may benefit more military concerns. We use no magick on these missions.'

'I am aware of that. Tallen has a number of talents; some more mundane than those she has inherited. She is the right person to go with your scouts.'

There was another exchange of glances between the elders. Another few heartbeats of tension before Sutha spoke.

'You must appreciate our concerns, Drey. Someone of Tallen's abilities has not been seen in centuries.'

Drey's posture softened slightly as I finally realised why the tension had arisen. While Drey and my king were happy to place me firmly in the path of danger, it would appear that those on the Isle were not.

'I do understand your concerns,' he said. 'But Tallen has a duty to her king as well as her ancestors. We all pray for a speedy end to this war, when we can be free to pursue our desires rather than our obligations.'

The elders seemed a little deflated by Drey's comments, but I could see reluctant acceptance of his words. I was not one of their students. They had no influence over what I was tasked to do. Eventually, all the elders gave their nod of agreement.

Fennan gave a quick nod as well, before turning to me. 'We leave at dawn. Pack lightly.'

Fennan was true to his word. The sun had barely peeked above the horizon when we left the Isle. The early-morning mist hung low to the ground and there was a chill in the air as we gathered at the small jetty. I had left my sword with Drey, preferring a smaller blade for the quiet raid. My sword would draw too much attention and was too big for the close-quarter skirmishes within town alleys. I also took two throwing knives sheathed at the base of my back, gaining a brief nod of approval from Fennan my choice of weapons.

We were joined by two other scouts. One was small and stocky, with such short brown hair that I could see his tanned scalp. His body posture was open and confident as he rested his hand on his sword hilt. The other was taller, but wiry and cautious like Fennan. We nodded quiet greetings before boarding our individual coracles. The men paddled confidently, but I struggled with the technique before deciding to cheat. Using the command of water taught to me by Cait, I easily guided my small craft after the others.

As Drey had promised, the journey back through the marshes was much easier than that to the Isle. There were still flickers at the edge of my vision that made me turn my head to find nothing there. The wind rustling through the reeds still sounded like voices. I actively avoided looking into the bogs, where faces stared at me with dead eyes. However, despite all that, the feel of the place was less malignant than before. It was unnerving but not hypnotic, and I was reactive but not fearful.

It took two days to cross the marshes and arrive at a small fishing town on the north coast, where the people went about their business unaffected by our arrival. When I commented on this, Fennan explained that the people of the Isle often used the town as a crossing into Lindvane, which was just the other side of the cove. The town was trusted due to Evan, the small and stocky scout, having family here. We were to spend the night with his parents and young sister.

We spent a comfortable night in the easy familiarity of Evan's home. His younger sister was perhaps seven or eight, and followed her older brother around like a puppy. She had his hair colour and dark brown eyes, but was shy and avoided talking to us if she could. His parents chatted easily, playfully teasing the other scout, Daw. It was unusual for me to be in such a family setting and I felt slightly out of place, unsure of what to say or how to fit in. I missed the buffers of Kade and Drey, who were much better in social situations than I. Despite the warmth and the comfort, I was glad we were to leave before dawn the following morning.

Evan's father owned a small rowing boat with a single sail. It was a tight fit but all five of us managed to find space in the boat, with Evan manning the oars while his father handled the sail. The surface of the water was deceptively calm. The currents were strong in the bay and it seemed that the men worked for ages before we made any headway away from the beach. We were about a third of the way across when the currents ceased, and we were able to glide on the control of the sail alone. I huddled deeper into my cloak to avoid the chill of the pre-dawn as we made our way closer to the Lindvane shore. The sun was just touching the horizon as we landed on a pebbled beach hidden by tall cliffs. We disembarked quickly, allowing Evan's father to swiftly leave the Lindvane beach. He had blended in with the first of the fishing boats leaving the Faulknar shore before the sun was only half visible.

Fennan led us to a sandy path that climbed up the cliffs. The nesting seabirds cawed noisily at us as we disturbed their roosting. I was unsettled by the noise, but the scouts continued with no obvious concern, and as we reached the top of the track, I could see why. Empty land extended as far as I could see, which was a good distance over the flat heath with no trees or hedges to obstruct the view. The wind blew directly off the sea and the grasses bent in its wake. A kestrel hovered away to the right, but otherwise the area looked devoid of life.

'Most people avoid this area,' Fennan explained. 'There is easier access along the coast so there is little need to come this way.'

We set off at a lope that was easily maintained and covered the ground quickly. We took a direct route west across the meadows, keeping in single file to avoid trampling the grasses and wild flowers too much and leaving obvious evidence of our passing through. We had travelled for most of the day before we saw any signs of civilisation, starting with a defined dirt road.

'How are we going to do this?' I asked as we slowed our pace to a walk.

'We'll join the main road into Bream and blend in with the market traders,' Fennan explained.

I frowned. 'I don't really do blending in.'

Evan laughed quietly. 'I'm not surprised, with those eyes.'

I rolled my amber eyes at the familiar comment. 'And when we get to Bream?'

Fennan scowled at my questioning but answered anyway. 'Daw will check the markets. The three of us will head to the King's Head tavern and listen to the gossip.'

I was not overly impressed by the plan. It did not play to my strengths, and I had a suspicion that sending me to learn the techniques of the scouts was a cover for some other plot Drey was hatching. I doubted anyone of importance would be drinking in a spit-on-the-floor tavern, and suspected that weather changes would probably be the most exciting news we would hear. Still, it would be a place to start.

We reached the market town around noon, the road having become busy with traders, farmers and a general mix of people. I kept my head down and looked at the road to avoid meeting anyone's eye. As with any other trading town, most people were more concerned with their own business than with their fellow travellers. Oxen, donkeys and horses jostled for position. Carts ran indiscriminately over toes. Geese and chickens protested loudly at being barked at by dogs. The scene was usual market-day chaos.

Once through the town gates, the crowds thinned and ambled towards the main square, the merchant houses or the livestock arenas. Daw slipped away with the market traders while Fennan, Evan and I followed those heading toward the merchant houses. The streets were busy, but tidy. There was some pride in this place, with doors neatly painted and windows cleaned. The drainage channels along the edges of the pathways glistened with fresh water, and I suspected that someone was paid to flush the gutters with water each morning.

Fennan saw me looking. 'Minor crimes against Baila are punished by working for the town. Cleaning the drains, covering the midden heaps, sweeping the streets and clearing general debris are all forced labour in the name of penance to the Holy Baila.'

Much as I hated to admit it, the system seemed to work. Liegeport could do with some of this type of punishment.

The King's Head was a medium-sized, single-storey tavern tucked between two merchant houses. The baying from the livestock arena could be heard above the cries of the merchants selling goods from the open fronts of their buildings. As in Liegeport, most merchants lived above their warehouses, while the front walls consisted of wooden shutters that could be folded back to open up the lower floor for customers to browse and buy. Clothing, housewares, weapons, jewellery, ornaments, food – all types of goods lay jumbled side by side as we walked past them to the tavern.

Just as Fennan was about to enter the tavern, I touched his arm. 'I'll be back soon,' I informed him, disappearing into the crowd before he could protest.

After a quick scan to check that I was not being watched, I ducked into the alley beside the tavern. This had not been given the services of those who had in some way offended the prevailing religion, with rotten vegetables and other waste scattered throughout, and I was fairly confident that no one would come this way unless they had to. With another quick check, I used an upturned crate to provide the extra height I needed to lift myself onto the roof. As I approached the tavern, I had noticed that this building had tiles that overlapped the walls by half an arm-length. Lying on my stomach, I could see under this ledge, and I smiled. As I had suspected, there was a gap between the walls and the roof that allowed the smoke from the fires inside the tavern to escape. With a bit of wriggling, I was able to crawl through this space and balance on the beams that ran across the tavern. I now had access to the inn's loft space, and it was easy to navigate towards the noise of the main room. Pulling my small, blunt dagger from my boot to lever out the tacks, I moved a plank to one side and was able to see into the bar area. I could not hear the details of the conversations at this height, but I was not interested in the weather. I would happily leave that to Fennan and Evan. I was looking for clues in body posture. Those who were nervous. Those who were tense and jumpy. Those would be the ones with something to hide.

I saw Fennan and Evan settled at a table in the corner. They had picked a good spot that was near to the counter but not too close. Both men had their backs to a wall so they could see most of the room. Furtive glances allowed them to keep an eye on the drinkers without drawing attention or meeting anyone's gaze. They sipped their drinks so one tankard would last a long time. I soon dismissed them and scanned the rest of the tavern.

I ignored most within the room. The usual fare of merchants, farmers and guards filled the tables and leant against the counter. The serving girls were kept busy refilling tankards and bringing food from the kitchen. The scent of steaming bowls of stew reached me in the rafters and my stomach growled in complaint. Hard cheese, dried meats and dark bread were also being taken freely as the temperature in the tavern was warmed by so many people. People jostled each other and fought for the girls' attention, but it was early in the day and tempers remained controlled. Later I knew there would be fights, and I wished Tawpin could be here to join in the inevitable brawls.

As I swept my gaze over the tables, my attention stopped at a couple of thickset men. Their heads bowed together over the wood in deep conversation, sly glances were frequently darted to ensure they were not being overheard. Their posture alerted my curiosity, but as the darker one turned to face into the room a memory flashed in my mind. I knew these men. I had seen them before. I thought hard, trying to place the scene of the memory into context. A tavern. Rainy night. Liegeport? No, not Liegeport. Where else would I have been in a tavern?

The memory snapped into clarity. We had stopped in a tavern just before getting to Kingsport. Those two had been there. A chill ran down my spine. It was too much of a coincidence to have seen them on the road in Faulknar, just before we were attacked in Kingsport, and again here in Lindvane. They had to have something to do with the raid on Tawpin's port.

As I was watching the two men, a flicker of movement at the corner of my eye drew my attention to the door. A low buzz of murmuring announced the presence of the new arrival; a small, unassuming man dressed in the robes of Baila.

'Now, what are you doing in a fleapit like this?' I muttered.

The acolyte was obviously uncomfortable in the tavern environment and shuffled his way through the crush, straight towards the two men I had been watching. Upon reaching their table, the acolyte used his back to shield his actions, but from my vantage point in the roof I could see clearly as he removed a small pouch from within the folds of his robe. He placed the pouch on the table and slid it towards the darker of the two men, who snatched it greedily, opening the drawstring to drop a few coins into his palm. Smiling appreciatively, he nodded to the acolyte, who then scurried out of the tavern.

I quietly left my perch on the beams and jumped down into the alley, joining the main street just as the acolyte disappeared into the crowd to my right. I hurried after him as fast as I could without drawing attention, using glimpses of his robes and shaven head to confirm that I was still following him. He weaved through the market and around the livestock stalls, heading towards the stone temple now visible above the other buildings. The building was modest in size but expertly decorated with winged figures and stylised sunrays. The dominating ethos of the religion was demonstrated by a large bell tower that rose from the centre of the temple. Pale stone was topped by a roof covered in expensive silvery tiles that reflected the sun to create a dazzling corona, making it painful to look at in the bright light of the clear day.

I felt the familiar repulsion as I neared the temple, and swiftly ignored it. A few worshippers were entering and leaving, so I managed to slip into the building without undue attention. Staying in the shadow of the wall, I followed the acolyte to the front of the temple and a door to the left of the altar. I checked to see all were piously bowed in prayer before sneaking through the door into a dark corridor. The acolyte entered a room about halfway along. Between me and the door I needed were several cells that had no coverings, so that I would be visible to anyone who was in one of these. Slowly I advanced to the first pair of cells, one opposite the other across the hallway. I said a silent prayer to the Fates and was answered when the stalls were empty. I moved to the next pair, also empty. Only three more pairs to go. One of the next cells contained an acolyte, but he was deep in meditation and I was able to pass him without notice. I was not so lucky with the next set of cells. Both were occupied, with men sitting on plain cots reading scrolls of scripture. They were positioned side on to the doorways so they would only need to look up and they would see me.

Taking a deep breath to slow my breathing, I watched the two study their texts. Such was the religious devotion of Baila acolytes that neither raised their head for several heartbeats. It took several more heartbeats to convince myself to take the risk. In the end, the desire to know what was in the far room overpowered my anxiety. I willed myself to walk as normally as possible past the cells, hoping that the play of my shadow would be dismissed as just another acolyte walking the corridor.

I quietly let out my held breath as I reached the far side without incident, and almost walked straight past the final pair of cells. I halted just in time to see the final occupant facing the far wall, kneeling and rocking in prayer. Timing my pass for when he was leaning forward, I crept past the final obstacle to reach the door that the acolyte had taken. I pressed my ear to the wood and heard a soft buzzing, while the faint acrid smell of crackling energy tickled my nose. I definitely wanted to see what was in here.

I opened the door slightly to see into a plain room. There were wood-panelled walls, a functional table, and a pair of plain rugs on the floor. Small slits of window dotted the top of the far wall, to allow a little light into the room. The acolyte had his back to me, but I could see the edge of his right hand resting on a roughly cut, pale yellow crystal. It was about the size of a man's fist and rested on a cushion of gold velvet. There was a faint shimmer surrounding the rock, which radiated along the acolyte's wrist until it disappeared into the sleeve of his robe. The small man was visibly trembling.

'I understand,' he said, making me jump. 'And I have done as you asked. But I am concerned that the priests here will find out and—'

He stopped mid-sentence and waited. I could not see anyone else in the room and did not hear any other voice. I chanced opening the door a little further.

'Yes, Your Holiness. I appreciate that your rank supersedes theirs. I just don't see why we can't tell—'

Again, a pause. I looked round the room to find no chairs to accompany the table. A single chest and an untidy stack of scrolls was all that could be seen.

'Of course, Your Holiness. I remain your faithful servant. I will attend to it right away.'

The one-sided conversation appeared to be over, as the acolyte covered the crystal with a gold velvet cloth and placed both this and the cushion in the chest. As he walked towards the only exit, I quickly scanned the first pair of cells on the far side of the door. I sent sincere gratitude to the Fates when these were revealed as empty, allowing me to slip into the nearest one just as the acolyte walked into the corridor and strode back towards the main temple.

I waited until all was quiet again before returning to the door and slipping through. The buzz of energy was stronger within the room and it was clearly coming from the carved chest. Resisting the obvious temptation, I started at the table. There were no drawers in it, and the surface contained only a lamp and a candle. I quickly ignored it and moved on to the scrolls. Most were lists of items I did not recognise, but one contained a map of the three kingdoms with images added at some of the larger towns, cities and ports. I stuffed it into my waistband and moved on to the chest. As I reached for the catch, blue sparks leapt towards my fingers, stabbing with a thousand needles. I cursed myself for being a fool. Of course, it would be protected. In the air above the latch, I quickly sketched the neutralising sigil that I had occasionally seen Drey use. I dragged through the invisible currents to form a character something close to a stylised acorn and tried again.

I smiled at my own cleverness as I was able to access the chest with no further incident. The cloth-covered crystal was placed in the centre, and the persistent buzzing emanated from it. Scattered around it were other ornaments and artefacts: old wooden idols rubbed smooth over time, metal amulets containing coloured glass stones, engraved tankards and stone knives. None radiated power like the crystal, so I paid them no further attention. Leaving the cushion behind, I picked up the cloth and stone. It was surprisingly light, and the rough surface allowed a secure grip. Folding an edge of the cloth back, I turned the crystal to catch the light. 'Pretty little thing, aren't you?'

Arguing voices came from the corridor, and my heart raced as I thought of being trapped by Baila's priests. They would stone me as a heretic, or, worse, they would hand me over to Villermir. I could not let that happen. Not again. Cradling the crystal firmly, I moved to stand beside the door to shove it hard as the two men entered, sending them stumbling across the room. I barely had time to recognise the acolyte from earlier, who was with an older man in the banded robes of a priest, before they fell in a tangle of legs, arms and robes.

I bolted out of the door and ran down the corridor, not caring any more if those in the cells saw me. I crashed through the door into the temple, thumping into a warden who was standing on the other side. Losing my balance, I staggered to one side and lost my grip on the crystal. Shocked worshippers stared as I blundered into the altar in order to retrieve the crystal. Candles were knocked over, igniting the aromatic oils contained in shallow dishes and causing the embroidered cloth to burst into flames. The fire spread to the robes of the priest standing behind the altar. As he flapped his arms, fanning the flames, the altar overturned and the fire crept along the oiled floorboards.

Shocked at the carnage I had wrought, I was nevertheless pleased that the worshippers were much more concerned with trying to help their priest and salvage their relics, than chasing the thief who had burst out of the temple doors and disappeared into the market crowds.

Chapter Sixteen

I slowed my pace as I mingled with the shoppers outside the temple, trying not to draw any further attention to myself. I kept my head down and weaved my way through the stalls. Even covered in the cloth, the stone was drawing too many glances, so I dropped it in the deep inner pocket of my cloak and held it close to my body. I hunched my shoulders and tried to make myself as small and inconspicuous as possible. I was only a few paces from the end of the street when the first murmurings concerning the temple began. Not looking back, I used the distraction to steal a small loaf of bread and a handful of baubles that glistened in the late-afternoon sun. Handling the stones calmed my breathing as the murmuring turned to muttering, which turned to gasping and pointing. The first scream was heard just before I turned right at the end of the street, and as I turned back to look at the temple, flames were starting to escape through the door that I had recently charged through.

'Oh, horse dung,' I cursed, increasing my pace and turning the corner at the fastest speed I could go before slipping into a jog.

I burst through the door of the King's Head, not caring whether I was noticed but ensuring I kept my back to the table of those I recognised from earlier. Fennan and Evan glared at the commotion I made as I approached them.

'We have to go,' I hissed before they had a chance to speak.

'Where have you been?' growled Fennan.

'We're supposed to be keeping quiet,' pleaded Evan.

'For the love of Mobis.' I was having a hard time keeping my frustration from raising the volume of my voice. 'Will you just trust me on this? We need to go. Now!'

With a final look between them, Fennan and Evan finally agreed to follow me out of the tavern. Once outside, they were left with no doubts as to the reason for my urgency, as the shouting had reached this far from the temple. People were gesticulating towards the fire, which was now visible above the houses. Greedy flames licked out of the bell tower's slits, while black smoke curled into sky. The mood had changed from surprise to anger, and I suspected that word had travelled that this was not an accident. Ignoring the questioning looks from the scouts, I urged them on.

'We need to find Daw and leave before they close the gates.'

It took forever to find Daw in the confusion of the markets. I was practically jumping on the spot with nervous energy by the time he came running up to us. The atmosphere was starting to get ugly as people heard that someone had deliberately started the fire in their sacred place of worship. That a stranger was the cause of this desecration, this defilement. The townspeople were shouting, and shoving people they did not recognise. Arguments and small scuffles were starting all around us, leading to the town guards coming in to keep the peace. Dogs were barking, donkeys were braying, and geese were honking. By the time we reached the gates, the guards were just happy to let people out of the chaos, thereby reducing the number they had to deal with. We found it easy to slip through without incident.

The journey back to the coast was uncomfortable. The men barely spoke to me, other than to accuse me of starting the fire and ruining the whole mission. My protests that it had been an accident fell on deaf ears, as they pointed out that I should never have been anywhere near the temple, and that I should have stayed with them and remained inconspicuous. They repeatedly told me that the whole point had been to stay unnoticed, until I retreated into silent sulking.

We made haste through the Lindvane countryside, being careful to avoid used paths and trails. We constantly looked over our shoulders, cursing the open landscape that meant we could be seen from afar. Farmers working in the fields became spies ready to inform Lindvane guards or soldiers. Being seen by market travellers threatened exposure and entrapment. Tempers were short and conversations restricted to harsh sniping at each other.

We arrived at a small fishing village as the light was starting to fade into dusk. Fennan had informed us that we would have to risk the village rather than head to the sheltered cove that we'd used previously, as we were ahead of the rendezvous time arranged with Evan's father. He looked pointedly at me when talking about the risk and the need to change plans. I found it easy to ignore him at this point as we hunkered down and waited for night to fall.

The scouts were efficient at avoiding the wooden shacks that bordered the small harbour. Only one dog barked, and soon quietened when we posed no threat to it or its property. The fishing boats were moored to a small quayside, but these were too big for us to handle. Evan selected a moderate-sized rowing boat, taking the oars as the rest of us settled in the bow or the stern to balance the weight. Evan rowed with strength and skill, and we arrived back in Faulknar as dawn was turning to morning. After landing at Evan's home village, we sank the rowing boat so that no trace was left of our visit to Lindvane, and no link could be found between Evan's family and their neighbours. We stopped only for a hot meal and more supplies before carrying on to the Isle of Serpents. It was almost a relief to return to the marshes, where I finally let go of the fear of being attacked by Hayton's soldiers.

Drey and Sutha were waiting for us when we docked at the small jetty. Neither looked happy to see us, and we were taken straight to the meeting hut to report on what had happened and why we had returned so soon. Kade joined us as we entered the hut, wearing a light shirt that was open at the neck. He had a questioning look with a hint of an amused smile aimed at me, which I ignored. My emotions fluctuated between fear, disappointment and anger as we joined the two other elders who were sitting on cushions in a corner. The nine of us settled into a rough circle. Anger became my dominant emotion as the scouts started to explain what had happened.

'Tallen deviated from the plan and disappeared before we entered the tavern,' began Fennan. 'We had to leave before we could gather much information.'

At a restraining glare from Drey, I bit my lip to avoid interrupting the scout's report, but could not avoid fidgeting with frustration.

'What did you learn?' asked Sutha with a placating tone.

'The farmers are complaining of higher taxes, probably to pay for the summer campaign. Mostly the fees are in coin, but grain and horses are also being taken.'

Evan joined in. 'This is at a time when the ground has been unusually dry. Water is just running off the surface of the fields rather than penetrating through to the crops. The farmers are really starting to struggle.'

'The markets are still busy,' added Daw. 'The soldiers are bringing all manner of goods back from raids and are happy to sell for the coin they can spend in the tavern or on the local girls. But food is getting scarce and the prices are going up.'

Fennan resumed his report. 'The buzz we felt earlier was still there. Still hard to define but there is definitely something going on. People were cautious. Guarded. Nervous. It seems some Baila acolyte is paying more attention to people's private lives than is comfortable. A few children have been taken to the temple and returned changed.' He shrugged. 'We did not find out how they had changed.'

Everyone was quiet for a time while they considered the implications of the information coming from Bream. I continued to fidget, but no one was paying attention to me. Eventually Drey asked for my findings.

'What do you report, Tallen?' he asked quietly.

Before I had a chance to reply, Daw said, 'Apart from setting the local Baila temple on fire!'

I impatiently tolerated the shocked gasps and accusations but could not avoid the disappointment in Drey's face. I had embarrassed him in front of his friends.

'It was an accident,' I said hurriedly. 'I didn't mean to.'

'Just tell us what happened,' Drey prompted.

I took a deep breath and looked at the floor as I tried to recall all that I had seen. 'I was in the tavern—'

'When were you in the tavern?' interrupted Evan. 'You didn't come in until after the fire.'

'I was there when you first went in,' I explained. 'I was in the rafters.'

'What?' Daw spluttered. 'Why?'

'I can watch people's postures better when I don't have to worry about being seen. People act differently around those they don't know, even when they are sitting in a corner trying not to be noticed.'

Fennan started to voice an objection, but Sutha stopped him with a raised hand.

'So, what did this tell you, Tallen?'

'Much the same as has already been said. The people are wary. They kept to their own groups and did not mingle freely with others.' I looked up at Drey. 'I saw two travellers I recognised.'

Everyone started paying attention at that, including the scouts, as I continued.

'We saw them in the tavern we stopped at before arriving at Kingsport.'

Drey nodded to confirm that he remembered the tavern.

'I'd wager that they had something to do with organising the attack. Being there, and again at Bream, is too much of a coincidence for me. The timing of the raid was perfect. Someone knew we were there.'

Drey and the elders nodded in agreement.

The elder man asked, 'So how does this result in the temple being set on fire?'

'While I was watching these two, a Baila acolyte entered the tavern. Now, I'm not familiar with all their practices, but it seemed an odd place for him to be. More so when he gave a pouch of coin to one of the travellers.'

Drey growled low in his throat.

'So, I followed him when he left. Sneaked into the temple after him. Hovered by the door that he entered.' I frowned in recollection. 'It was the weirdest thing, but he seemed to have a conversation with himself. He was talking about not letting the priests know; saying he was worried about being caught, but he would continue with the plan.'

'And the fire?' Drey prompted again.

I frowned at losing the trail of my thoughts. 'I was discovered. As I was leaving, I accidently knocked over the altar candles.'

I looked apologetically at Drey, but his earlier disappointment was replaced by a slightly amused raised eyebrow.

'And now we can't go back to Bream,' persisted Daw.

'I don't think it would be safe for anyone to go to Bream any time soon,' stated Sutha. 'I think we all agree something is brewing there, and maybe more remote means are advised for monitoring this situation.'

At a nod from the other elders, the scouts took this as the conclusion to the meeting. Shallow nods of respect were made before they rose and left the circle. As Kade and I rose to join them, Sutha spoke.

'Not you, Tallen. We have more questions for you.'

I looked at Kade, who gave me a wink in gleeful anticipation of the telling-off I was about to get for deviating from Fennan's plan. As he turned to leave, I saw that his collar had fallen down a little, revealing inked spirals at the base of his neck. I had no time to question him, however, as Drey commanded me to sit down.

'So, you accidentally set fire to the Baila temple?'

'Honestly, Drey,' I pleaded. 'It really was an accident.'

'And why were you there?' he persisted.

'I told you, the acolyte had approached the travellers I had seen in Faulknar, and I thought I would follow him to see what he was up to.'

I was confused by Drey's line of questioning. I had already told him this. Looking at the three elders, it seemed I was the only one who did not know what Drey was searching for. The three had matching expressions of frustrated expectation.

'And once you were there...' Drey prompted.

I frowned, concentrating on what information Drey could be after. What hadn't I told them? Then I remembered the map. 'Oh, I found this,' I said as I removed the parchment from my waistband and handed it to Sutha.

She ignored it, placing it on the ground beside her as Drey sighed impatiently.

'We can all feel it, Tallen.'

I suddenly realised that I had become so accustomed to the energy buzz that I had felt initially from the stolen crystal that I was no longer aware of it. Having received nothing but mild curiosity from the scouts, I had totally forgotten that others with power would be able to sense it too. I reached inside my cloak and placed the crystal, still wrapped in its cloth, on the floor between us.

'I've felt a few crystals with this kind of energy,' said Sutha quietly. 'But this seems different. There is a catch to the energy signature. It doesn't seem to flow freely.'

'Humph,' grunted Drey contemptuously. 'If it is being used for Baila, I'm sure it is not being used for its natural function.'

'And you say you overheard this acolyte talking to himself?' asked the male elder. 'Was the crystal visible?'

'He was touching it,' I explained. 'And it seemed more like a conversation than him just talking to himself. There were pauses, as if he was listening to someone else.' I shrugged. 'Of course, he could have been listening to his own daemons in his head.'

I looked at Drey to find him looking back at me. I suspected that we both remembered how Villermir had manipulated my thoughts. Perhaps he had a similar control over this acolyte.

'Have you touched it?' Drey asked.

When I shook my head, he nodded as if confirming something to himself.

'Well, there's only one way to find out what this thing does.' He reached forward and took the crystal. Hesitating for only a heartbeat, he folded back the cloth and placed the palm of his hand on the stone. His forehead creased in concentration, and the rest of us held our breath. I was not sure what I was anticipating – flashes of lightning or booms of thunder, perhaps – but Drey was silent, with only a small frown to suggest that anything was happening.

Suddenly, Drey drew back his hand with such speed that the stone rolled off his lap and onto the floor. His eyes had widened with the shock of something that had been revealed. I reached forward to pick the stone up, but Drey shouted and I froze with my arm extended.

'No,' he commanded me. 'Don't touch it. Don't you ever touch it.'

'Why not?' I asked, withdrawing my arm and rocking back to sit on the cushion. 'What did it do?'

Drey remained silently looking at me, and I started to fear what he was going to say. That somehow the crystal was connected to me, and that was not a good thing. As he hesitated, Sutha gently prompted him.

'What did you see?' she asked quietly.

Drey broke eye contact with me to look at Sutha, and then the other two elders. 'I didn't see anything. I heard someone talking.'

'Auditory resonance,' breathed Sutha. 'I have not heard anyone talk of that for such a long time.'

'They were angry. Complaining about not contacting them on time.' Drey took a breath and resumed looking at me. 'It took a while to recognise the voice. It's been a while since I heard it. I don't know why it took me so long. I should have known he would be behind this.'

It started to become harder to breathe. My chest refused to expand so my lungs could inflate. I started to tremble; wanting Drey to confirm my fears, but so scared that he would.

'The voice was Villermir's. And I think he knows where we are.'

I don't remember leaving the hut, but found myself outside leaning against the rough wood. I repeatedly swallowed against the nausea that threatened to empty my stomach contents onto the floor. I waited a long time before my heart stopped thundering in my ears.

It had been so long since Villermir had been a physical threat that I had almost forgotten what it was like to feel him reaching for me from a distance. I had almost forgotten how the mere mention of his name could cause my whole body to tremble and my palms to become slippery with sweat. I took a deep, shuddering breath and tried to calm my raging panic. There was nothing I could do about it. He was not here, yet. I would just have to wait to see what move he made next.

I distracted myself by going to find Kade, who was sitting on the little jetty with his legs dangling over the edge. His feet were barely above the surface of the water. He heard me approach and turned to face me with a big grin.

'So, how much trouble did you get into?'

I smacked him playfully on the shoulder as I sat next to him. 'I didn't get into trouble, actually. I brought back some important information, a map and a pretty stone.'

I tried to smile, but Kade saw through it to the effort it took.

'A pretty stone, huh?'

'Yeah, well, it was pretty until I found out what it can do.'

'Well, what does it do?' he prompted after I hesitated.

I swallowed hard as I felt the burn of acid at the back of my throat. Again, Kade noticed, causing him to persist quietly.

'What does it do, Tallen?'

I sighed, trying to make light of my dread. 'Apparently, it can communicate with people over a distance. Apparently, it can communicate with Villermir. Apparently, Villermir now knows where we are.'

Kade stayed silent as I refused to look at him. The silence became uncomfortable and I soon broke it by abruptly changing the subject.

'Anyway,' I began. 'That's not why I came to find you. What is it that black splodge on your neck?'

Kade grinned. 'Black splodge?'

I grabbed his arm to turn him around. 'Let me have a look at it, then.'

Kade pushed his shirt up at the front so that its collar fell down at the back, revealing the pattern marked on his skin. Black ink traced swirls that connected the points of his shoulders and extended to the base of his neck. Thicker lines developed into intricate knotwork, with runes and sigils dotted throughout.

'Did you have this just to annoy your father?'

Kade pulled his shirt back into place and turned back to me. 'No, it was not just to annoy my father.' He grinned maliciously. 'That's just a welcome bonus.'

It was Kade's turn to be quiet as he seemed to debate whether to say more. I waited patiently until he had made his decision.

'The tattoo will be permanent, but the power of the runes and sigils will fade over time.'

I frowned in confusion. 'What do you mean, their power will fade over time? They are more than decorative, then?'

He looked at me with a small, self-deprecating smile. 'While you were busy with your lessons, Sutha explained why I was not to go to the towers. About the shadow that was following me.'

Pimple-flesh lifted the hairs on my arms as I thought about Sutha's words to me, and how I could attract souls stained dark. 'That's what you were doing with Drey and Sutha? In the mornings?'

Kade nodded, before reaching out and tentatively tracing the scars on the backs of my hands. 'It seems that both of us have brought back wounds from what happened at Burford Hythe. Mine are not so visible, but they are there just the same. Sutha was worried that the flint would amplify the effects of the shadow. They've been working on removing them, or at least controlling them.'

'What shadow? What is it doing to you?' I was starting to get worried.

Kade shrugged. 'She doesn't know. Maybe nothing.'

'Kade. You did not get someone to stab your neck and permanently mark your skin over nothing.'

Again, he flashed the hint of a self-mocking smile. 'It didn't hurt that much.'

I raised an eyebrow, daring him to evade further.

'I don't know. Everything seems so difficult. Too much effort. I just get so angry.'

'I noticed,' I teased, shoving him with my shoulder to take the sting out of my words. 'Did you really want to kill me that day in the training arena?'

'No, not really.'

'Thanks very much. That doesn't sound too convincing.'

He gave me a more genuine smile. 'Well, you can be annoying. But seriously, I was angry at you. So angry at you.'

'Why? I'd been away for almost two years. How could I have annoyed you when I wasn't even around?'

'Exactly. You left.'

'I didn't really have a choice. Breya made it quite clear—'

'And when did you start listening to Breya? Everyone has a choice, Tallen. And you chose to leave.'

'Oh yeah, everyone has a choice.' Our voices had risen in volume. 'Just like you chose to marry Breya.'

I knew I had gone too far as soon as the words left my mouth. I waited for Kade to throw back something equally hurtful, but instead he took a deep breath.

'I suppose we both had reasons to be angry,' he said quietly.

'We did. Langdon was quite angry too.'

As I had hoped, my comment had broken the tension and gained a chuckle from Kade.

'Yeah. He was a little angry.'

We sat quietly, and the silence was more comfortable this time. I still had questions but was loath the break the calm. In the end, as always, my curiosity won.

'So,' I began, causing Kade to give a groan. 'Does the tattoo make you less angry?'

'If it does, it seems to be working. I haven't pushed you into the river yet.'

'I'm not that annoying!' I claimed indignantly.

'Yes, you are! But regarding the tattoo… I don't know. I suspect it's a little early to tell. I've only had it a couple of days. But things seem a bit easier. A little less heavy.' He turned to look me in the eye. 'We will deal with Villermir. I won't let him hurt you again.'

I was not sure how he was going to be able to do that, but I was grateful for the sentiment. I smiled at him in appreciation, nudging him gently. This time I was happy to let the silence linger.

The dream that night came with a force I had not experienced for a while. The mountain walls seemed closer and lower. Waves of malicious feelings oozed out of the rock and caressed the back of my neck. My muscles spasmed intermittently as I maintained the tension, hunching my shoulders and making myself as small as possible. I forced myself forward, previous experience having taught me that to linger would prolong the agony.

The noise was next to arrive. Tough skin slithering over the stones. A rhythmic swaying of sound. So very slowly getting closer. The click of claws. One. Two. Three. Four. So very slowly getting louder. The rasp of breath being inhaled. The rumble of breath being exhaled. The faint smell of the forge. The hint of warmth brushing my face. My legs trembled as I took one faltering step after another, eyes straining to see images half-seen. Shadows moving at the edges of my vision.

I heard Villermir's voice and turned. It was a mistake. Solid rock blocked my path and squeezed me towards the granite now at my back. Villermir was whispering. Taunting. I was trapped and had nowhere to go. Knowing it would not help, I could not stop pressing against the mountainside, hammering my fists until blood smeared the stone. Using the pain as a focus to control the panic running around my head. Trying to ignore the floor rocking under my feet.

I woke up with my blankets tangled around me. Heart hammering against my chest. Breath rasping in my throat. The ground was still rocking. I looked around the sleeping hut to see the walls shaking back and forth. My boots and water skin had fallen over. I stumbled out of the hut. It was still night, but the moon was full and the scene around me was clear. Thatch from the roof had fallen off many of the smaller huts, while dried peat tiles had been shaken free from the larger huts, including the one I had slept in. People were standing around looking confused, searching for someone to tell them what to do. Another tremor shook the island. The force was strong enough to knock us to our knees. The quake lasted for only a few heartbeats, but the Isle of Serpents held its breath, waiting for another shake. There was no wind, and the silence in that moment seemed to expand to fill the whole world.

Then, very quietly, we could hear a hum. We looked at each other to determine if anyone knew what the sound was as the hum became a hiss, then a roar. We turned towards the river as a wall of water twice the height of the tallest hut rushed to smother the island. I could see the debris of branches and broken fences being tossed in the froth of muddy water as it raced towards us. I barely had time to register the danger before the river engulfed the island. I was submerged in the maelstrom and thrown against the wall of the hut, my back slammed against the crude stones, forcing the air out of my lungs. Resisting the urge to take a breath, I scrabbled my fingers against the wall, trying to find purchase as the water threatened to tear me into its raging torrent. My nails ripped but I managed to find the corner of the hut and hold on to the ragged overlap of timber. My lungs felt on fire and my head was pounding with the blood pulsing at my temples. Red spots were starting to dance in front of my closed eyelids as my mind screamed that I needed air. I was fighting every instinct I had, and barely holding on.

Then the river finally subsided. I was dumped on the ground as I gasped and wheezed in an attempt to satisfy my tortured lungs. Wiping my face with trembling hands, I forced myself to inhale before coughing liquid from my throat. It took several rapid heartbeats before my breathing eased and I was able to look at the devastation around me. Many of the smaller huts by the river had been completely destroyed. Most were scattered and broken over the ground. A few had been washed away completely. People's belongings lay entangled in jetsam from the river and debris from the shattered buildings. A few of the islanders were lying or sitting on the grass, which was now covered in a layer of mud. All looked shocked and bewildered. The nighttime scene threw the trauma into a shadow play; silhouettes of puppets with their strings cut, ruins of buildings with ragged outlines and fallen roofs.

I looked for people I knew. Sutha was there, comforting a group of people. She seemed to be examining someone's forehead, and I suddenly realised that people would be injured. I stood and walked towards the nearest group to see what help I could offer. Two young women were sitting dazed, although they responded appropriately to my questions so I knew they did not have head injuries and it was just the shock of the event. They had a few scratches and a number of bruises but were otherwise unharmed. I moved to another group and again found them dazed with only superficial injuries. By the time I had moved to the third group, closer to the centre of the settlement, I heard the cries and groans of people suffering with more serious damage. I was not surprised to find Drey already among them, helping those who needed him most. Many had head wounds or gashes to their arms. A few lay unconscious. I touched Drey's shoulder and gave him a warm smile, which he returned.

'You well?' I asked.

'A few bumps and bruises, nothing more.'

I squeezed his shoulder before removing my hand. 'You tough old goat,' I teased affectionately.

Looking around the island, it seemed there were fewer people than before. I turned back to Drey. 'Kade?'

He shook his head once before determinedly returning to those he could help. I followed his lead. I would not think of it, and I would concentrate on those in front of me. What clothing was available was torn into strips to make bandages. Fires were made to boil filtered water, which was then used to cleanse wounds. Anything that was found that provided rigidity was used as a splint. Casualties were bandaged, cleaned, splinted and supported. We dealt with each as they arrived, trying not to think of those not being brought in.

The light was brightening towards dawn by the time I finally saw Kade. I felt weak with relief and had to lean against Drey to stop myself from crumpling at the knees. Drey slipped an arm around my waist in support, giving it a quick squeeze.

'Go,' he said, knowing I would go to Kade. 'You've done your share.'

Kade was carrying a large bundle that turned out to be my soaked blankets and carry-pack. Dropping these at my feet, he handed me my sword and throwing knives. I grinned at the absurdity of him turning up with my weapons.

'I found these in your hut,' he explained dismissively. 'Thought you might want them back.'

'You know me so well.'

I couldn't stop grinning, knowing it was ridiculous but unable to control myself. I was so relieved that Kade was standing in front of me. His shirt was ripped at the shoulder, its edges stained with blood, the skin showing through red and swollen, but I could not see the cut. His sleeves were rolled up and there were bruises on his lower arms. His knuckles were bloodied and there was a slight catch to his breathing, but he was basically unharmed. All three of us had managed to survive with only minimal injuries. Kade nodded his head in the direction of the large group of people sitting in the middle of the muddy patch that was the central area of the Isle.

'How are they?'

'Most are well. Shaken and a little frightened. Bruising and cuts, some of which are deep. A few broken bones and blackened eyes. A handful have had bad knocks to the head and are still unconscious.'

Kade nodded in acceptance. 'You well?'

'Yeah. I'm fine. Had the wind knocked out of me, but I got off lightly. You?'

He gave me a small smile, knowing that I had already appraised him as a healer. 'A few cuts and scrapes. The hut saved me from the worst of it.' He took a deep breath. 'I've been with Gency.' He nodded towards the elder lady who had attended our meetings, both before and after my trip into Bream. 'We have been gathering the dead. We don't know how many have been taken by the river, but Gency estimates about a third of the community are missing, including Forst, the other elder from the meetings. The old man probably didn't make it.'

Kade looked at me. He twitched his hand toward me before changing his mind. His face creased in concern.

'I'm sorry, Tallen. Cait is one of the dead.'

Chapter Seventeen

We tended the injured. We helped erect shelters. We tidied the island. Despite this, it was soon obvious that we had outstayed our welcome. It was never spoken aloud, but the stolen glances and whispered comments ensured that we got the message. It was too much of a coincidence that the quake and subsequent storm surge had happened so soon after Drey had connected with Villermir. All knew what the Baila priest was capable of. They had been monitoring his increasing strength over many seasons, but this was the first time he had directed his aggression at the island.

Sutha came to find us as we were gathering our supplies in Drey's sleeping hut. She had brought some of the few items that the Isle had left, which Drey graciously refused.

'I'm sorry we have to part like this,' she said softly. 'Once the shock passes, people will realise that you are not to blame. You will be welcome here when you choose to return.'

The priestess gracefully included Kade and me in the offer, not just her old friend, and Drey took her hands to gently kiss her knuckles.

'I'm so sorry for the damage to your community, and for those you have lost,' he said. 'But you are strong, and you will recover from this. Villermir is destroying many communities and many lives. We all have to do what we can to stop him.'

Sutha nodded. 'I will try to ensure that the new council member is more favourable to direct action. We will do what we can to prevent major changes to the energy lines. I will push for more information on how we can control any damage.'

Drey kissed her knuckles again before releasing her hands. 'Thank you.'

Sutha left us and we continued packing the small store of sundries salvaged from the flood. Blankets and clothes were wet but serviceable. Food was ruined but we could scavenge along the way. Weapons had been collected by Kade. Drey wrapped the stone taken from Bream in his blanket and placed it securely at the bottom of his sack. I was a little nervous about taking it with us but knew it could not be left on the island. It was not long before we were ready to leave. As we left Drey's hut, we found two scouts and four others waiting for us.

'Sutha sent us,' explained the elder of the scouts. 'Me and Aitken will guide you to Stanton. Geffin and Gen have studied the element of air. Tem and Helien are Aqualine. Between us, we should be able to get you to where you need to go.'

'We are grateful,' said Drey, 'but this is unnecessary. I'm sure you are needed here.'

The smaller scout, with a mess of curly dark hair, grinned. 'Sutha was very insistent.'

Drey nodded in submission. 'Then you are most welcome.'

The scouts guided us to the northern marshes when we left the island. The reeds turned into tufts of coarse grass as we travelled further from the Isle; the stagnant water turning brackish, before finally becoming salt marsh as we neared the coast. As the scent of salted air grew stronger, small terns startled at our approach, shrilly calling the alarm and breaking the silence of the deserted flatlands.

The salt marsh ended at Stanton, a moderately sized fishing town. Aitken took his leave to return to the Isle, while Puk, the taller, older scout, confidently took us to a shack at the far end of the town; acknowledging the few people who were around with a nod of the head or a wave of the hand. I kept the hood of my cloak up so that nothing notable, such as my eyes, would be remembered after we had left. It did not seem that I needed to take the precaution, however, as nobody paid us much attention.

A man came out to us as we approached the shack. The family resemblance was clear as he shook hands with Puk. He nodded a welcome to the small group before him, taking a prolonged look at Kade. After a few heartbeats he turned away, making no comment.

'You after a boat, then?' he asked Puk.

'Aye,' confirmed Puk. 'Enough to stand the crossing.'

The fisherman nodded as I looked questioningly at Drey. I had assumed that we would be heading back to Kingsport, or even Liegeport. 'The crossing' suggested that we were headed north across the open sea. The open sea that was patrolled by the Gallowglass.

Drey gave a small nod and then refused eye contact. I had to be content to wait until we were alone to ask him directly what the plan was, as it seemed we were not to return to Liegeport just yet.

We were led to a small bay that was hidden from the town by a sandy cliff. A ramp extended into the sea, but most of the fishing boats were moored some way off the shoreline where the water was deeper. A fleet of rowing boats were pulled up onto the shingle and tethered to large boulders that acted as wave breakers. As our gear was loaded into the small craft, I guided Drey to one side so we could talk privately.

'So, we are not going back to Liegeport, then?' I demanded.

Drey had the grace to look uncomfortable. 'Well... no. Not just yet.'

'So where are we heading?'

Drey hesitated for several heartbeats. 'Initially, we are going to the Holy Isle.'

I felt my mouth drop open. 'The Holy Isle? Are you mad? That's days away, across open sea that is crawling with Gallowglass pirates.'

Drey sighed. 'I am very much aware of that, Tallen. But there is something there that I need.'

'Something that you need? Something that is worth risking our lives? Risking the King-in-Waiting?'

'Yes,' replied Drey quietly, taking the strength from my argument.

I moved on. 'So, assuming we don't get murdered by pirates, drowned by massive waves or eaten by sea serpents, where are we going after you've collected your *something* from the Holy Isle?'

'There are no such things as sea serpents.'

'Really? You tell me there are dragons. I've been to Mobis's Hells. We've just come from a place that can make memories become reality. And you tell me there is no such thing as a sea serpent? That's where you draw the line?'

Drey gave a small smile. 'Yeah.'

'Great. So where are we going after the Holy Isle?'

He shrugged. 'That depends on what we find out on the island.'

I waited for him to elaborate, and when he remained silent I groaned in frustration. 'You're not going to tell me, are you?'

He grinned mischievously. 'Why worry about things that are yet to come? Let's worry about the murdering pirates first.'

Once our gear was loaded onto a rowing boat, Puk's relative returned to Stanton to gather his crew. Puk rowed us out to the waiting fishing boat; it required two journeys before we were all safely aboard. The vessel was large: at least eight paces wide and easily double that in length. There was a large mast in the centre, holding the mainsail that was currently curled neatly at the top. Pairs of oars lined up along the port and starboard sides of the central deck, while benches extended across the full width of the boat, with boxed-in sections between them to house any fish that were caught. Small indentations had been worn into the ends of the benches from countless rowers over the generations. The oars were currently stored along the timber sides of the boat, stacked one on top of another and held in place with thick rope. At the stern and the bow, rough wooden planks had been used to make a small covered section for off-duty crew to shelter or sleep away from the wind and rain.

The crew arrived during the late evening. The eight young men were normally involved in fishing but would primarily man the oars on our journey north. They were quiet and efficient, storing their gear in the covered area at the bow. The evening was calm, and we only required the unfurling of the sail to launch us at the turning of the tide and send us out into the Northern Sea.

After a sleep in the stern, fitful thanks to the movement of the waves and the rolling of the boat, I awoke early and listened to the quiet breathing of those around me and the muted conversations of those few who were awake. The soft grey light that came before the dawn crept slowly into the stripes of sky that I could see through the planks above me. A few random cries from the seabirds broke the rhythm of the slap of waves against the hull. The birds were hoping for an early meal of cast-off fish: they were left disappointed.

I wriggled awkwardly out of my blankets. The timber overhead was too low for me to do more than sit up, so I had to crawl between those still sleeping. Fortunately, numerous nights spent squeezing through rooftops and alleyways had trained my body to move in confined spaces without disturbing those nearby. I managed to escape the covered stern without waking anyone.

The chill to the morning felt crisp and fresh. I raised my face to the breeze, closing my eyes and savouring the slight sting of the briny air. The smell of the sea reminded me of Liegeport; of home and of safety. The thought jarred harshly with the knowledge that we were in the Northern Sea along with Gallowglass pirates. The serenity of the moment vanished, and I turned to distract myself with the activity occurring on deck. Four of the crew were quietly performing their duties; tidying the ropes and spare canvas, washing the deck of the salt that had dried on it overnight, waxing the oars in readiness for the day's rowing.

Puk was standing near a small brazier that was heating a kettle and, seeing me watching, he smiled and held a mug aloft. I did not need to be asked twice. As I approached him, he held out two mugs of tea and indicated behind him, where I saw Kade leaning against the port wall. I smiled my appreciation to Puk before joining my prince. By the rigid set of his shoulders, I could tell he had been there for some time.

'Here,' I said, offering him one of the mugs.

Kade startled, even though I had not been overly quiet in my approach. 'Thanks.'

I shrugged. 'Puk's idea.'

We stood in silence while I enjoyed the warmth of the slightly bitter tea. The sea extended as far as the horizon in all directions. Small caps of white crowned a few of the waves, but the water around us was calm. A gentle swell rocked the boat and gave some impression of movement. I had no landmarks to tell me where we were, but I was confident we were heading north when the sun rose slowly from the waves in front of us. Its arrival was heralded by an infusion of dusky pink reflected off the clouds, before the radiant sphere peeked above the sea to bathe the day in light. Spears of gold sped along the horizon for several heartbeats as the sun paused, before fully emerging and proclaiming a new day. The Father Sun in all his glory.

I sighed deeply as the magick of the sunrise was replaced by the normality of the day. 'You been here long?' I asked Kade, already knowing the answer.

He grunted a non-committal reply and we lapsed into silence again. It was several heartbeats before I pushed again.

'The tattoo not helping with your sleeping?'

'It helps.'

When he did not elaborate, I groaned in frustration. 'Merciful Mother, aren't you the chatty one this morning?'

Kade signed in annoyance and poured the dregs of his tea over the side. 'Did you want something, Tallen?'

'Well, now that you've asked.' I gave a cheeky grin and hoped that he would be easily distracted from his bad mood. 'Do you know where we are going?'

He turned to look at me, confused. 'What?'

'Do you know where the boat is taking us? I had thought we were going back to Liegeport, to report back to your father, but we're going in the wrong direction.'

Kade continued to look at me for a couple of heartbeats, then returned to gaze over the sea. 'We're going to the Holy Isle.'

'Yeah, Drey told me that—'

'Then why ask me?'

'Where are we going after that? I don't believe this is just a fun trip across the water. Surely we need to inform the king of what we found out about Villermir?'

Kade turned back to look at me, a small kink to his mouth suggesting the beginnings of a smile. 'Drey wouldn't tell you?'

'No.' I pouted as Kade mumbled something that sounded like 'coward'.

'You won't like it.'

I narrowed my eyes in suspicion. 'Why won't I like it?'

The smile crept briefly across his lips before disappearing again. 'Drey wants to go to the Holy Isle to look at some ledgers. Apparently, there is an old tome that mentions the Ancients. There is a suggestion that there may be evidence of a dragon.'

I stared at him, open-mouthed. 'A dragon? You are seriously telling me that this is all about a dragon?'

He nodded.

'Oh, for the love of the Lower Gods. And you're all right with this? You are the King-in-Waiting, Kade! You can't just go off following myths and folk tales. Do you have no concept of the danger you are putting yourself in?'

'Drey believes that our visions are prophetic, and I agree with him. There will be a dragon, and she will destroy Liegeport if we don't stop her.'

I raised my arms in exasperation. 'Stop calling it "her". Mobis's Hells, Kade. Do you know how insane this sounds?' I shook my head in disbelief. 'How in the Heavens did you convince your father?'

Kade studied his hands for a heartbeat. 'He doesn't know. He thinks we are staying on the Isle of Serpents.'

'Oh, this just keeps getting better.'

'He won't be expecting us back for some time.' He gave a bitter laugh. 'He expects the healers there to "cure my affliction". He knows what the visions signify. He knows that being a seer is the next step in becoming a Druid.' He turned to look at me with real concern in his eyes. 'We can't let this become a war of religion.'

I held my face in my hands as my mind swirled with a multitude of horrible ways in which Kade could die: at the hands of Gallowglass pirates, captured by Lindvanes and paraded as a trophy by Hayton, tortured by Villermir, drowned by the ocean and eaten by sea serpents. Dragons did not feature heavily in my concerns.

I sighed, forcibly ignoring those thoughts. 'Well, let's just hope that Breya has a healthy boy so that when you get yourself murdered on this ridiculous quest, there is another heir to the throne.'

Kade frowned at me. 'How did you know about that?'

I shrugged. 'Suspected more than knew. Breya was putting on weight, so either she ate too many pastries at the festivals, which is unlike Breya, or you got her pregnant.' I shuddered dramatically. 'Which is not a pleasant image to have in my head!'

Kade snorted contemptuously. 'Not sure it was me that who got her pregnant.'

'What? You can't be serious?'

He shrugged. 'She spends more time with Rolyan than she does with me.'

'For which you should be grateful.' I shook my head in disbelief, starting to understand why Kade had been so attentive to the serving girl in Faulknar. 'Those two have many things in common, but Breya is not stupid. She is vindictive, but she is ambitious. Listen to me, Kade; she would never risk the baby growing up to look like Rolyan.' I grimaced. 'Poor kid. Having his ugly face as your own. Imagine if it was a girl.'

Kade snorted as he tried to contain his laugh.

Later that day I was startled awake by a large wave slamming into the side of the boat. I had dozed, propped against the bow with my legs stretched over the planks of the sleeping area and the sun warming my face. It had started its westward descent as I straightened my back against the timber side of the boat. Yawning at the abrupt interruption of my slumber, I watched as Geffin and Tem, who had positioned themselves behind the water barrels, were helped up by Gen and Helien. Tem staggered slightly on standing and was quickly supported by Helien. They stamped their tired legs and rolled the tense muscles of their shoulders, while Gen and Helien settled into the positions they had vacated. It was not long before the waters calmed again, and the vessel picked up speed. The wind filled the sail with a snap, forcing the boat in the direction required with only minor adjustments by the tillerman to keep us on course. I felt a slight tingle on my skin, hinting at the effort needed to maintain the magick.

I stood up to stretch my back, turning to rest on the rail. While the sea near to the boat was calm, with only the waves we made pushing through the water, white caps told of rougher waters further out. The sea had turned a darker grey, looking more menacing. On the horizon I could see a few black dots, and I frowned as I wondered what they could be.

The sun had moved further west by the time the black dots revealed themselves. One of the fishermen shouted the alarm, and all eyes turned to the east. Five long, sleek vessels were heading for us. Large, square sails embroidered with a black dragon sent chills down my spine. It seemed that dragons were to be more of a threat than I had anticipated, albeit ones from Gallowgla.

Those who had been resting scrambled onto the deck as the pirates raced toward us. We may have harnessed the element of air to send us north, but the natural weather was blowing strongly from the east, sending the Gallowglass ships towards us at a terrifying speed. Tem and Geffin rejoined their colleagues in an attempt to outrun the dragon ships, but the boat rocked unsteadily when pushed to move at a speed greater than it was designed for. They stood as helpless as the rest of us as we watched the pirates close the distance.

It took frighteningly little time for the Gallowglass ships to join us. Their single-level vessels were so much longer than our fishing boat; intimidating from a distance, and terrifying up close. The noise of the warriors' battle cries added to the terror; the bashing of axes on shields, the hostile posturing, the harsh, guttural shouts of insult and promised aggression. All were designed to unnerve their opponents, and it was working. The fishermen were not trained for battle, and their faces drained of colour as their hands shook.

We were outnumbered and I did not fancy our odds in hand-to-hand combat. Gripping the hilt of *Saorsa*, I knew that we would lose if the pirates came aboard. I searched for Drey and Kade further along the port rail. Kade was determinedly studying the ships, assessing their strengths and looking for weaknesses. Initially, I could not locate Drey, but then I saw him standing further back, feet braced against the swell of the boat. A slight haze surrounded him, and I cursed myself for being a fool. We had magick.

As Drey gathered the friction in the air and his hands started to glow a pale blue, I formed a large fireball and send it hurtling towards the nearest ship. It fell short, fizzling out in the water several arm-lengths from its target. The warriors laughed and jeered, but I had assessed the distance and drift. The second fireball landed in the middle of their deck, setting the clothes of the closest warriors aflame.

While I rained fire onto the nearest vessel, Drey sent sparks of lightning arcing over the water onto another ship. Splinters rained down on the Gallowglass as panelling exploded. A second bolt slammed into a warrior, causing him to twitch and jerk uncontrollably before collapsing onto the deck. The warriors aboard the ship under Drey's attack hesitated in confusion. While they could fight the flames of my assault, there was nothing they could do against Drey but shelter behind their shields. I suspected that they were not used to taking a defensive role.

Tem and Geffin followed our lead, each picking a ship. Geffin gathered the air into a funnelling whirlwind, forcing it towards a Gallowglass vessel. The sail snapped backwards and tore down the centre, straight through the dragon emblem. The vessel rocked violently, causing the warriors to scrabble to find handholds and avoid being tossed over the side. Water flooded the ship, sweeping several of the pirates overboard.

Tem corralled the sea into a shimmering wall of water. Fish and debris were gathered into it as it raced towards her chosen vessel. The water crashed into the Gallowglass ship, destroying its side and studding its warriors with shards of wood the size of my hand. The pirate ship lurched towards the sea, water rushing in through the hole caused by the impact. The warriors knew their vessel was doomed and jumped into the water to avoid being trapped on the ship. Many were sucked under when the ship sank.

The barrage of fire, water, air and lightning delayed the pirates' frontal attack, but there were only four of us who were free to work magick against the Gallowglass, and they had five ships. While we concentrated on the vessels in front of us, one had slipped behind and was approaching from the starboard side. Kade's shout of alarm was immediately followed by the dull thud of grappling irons. The Gallowglass warriors quickly and efficiently brought their ship alongside our boat and boarded us. Without thinking, I turned towards the more immediate threat and drew my sword. Moving to stand alongside Kade, we gave each other a quick, fatalistic look before advancing on the swarm of warriors. Drey, Kade and I were the only ones with weapons, and the fishermen were left to grab the oars in an attempt to beat back the intruders. The Gallowglass laughed at their ineffectual assault as they desperately defended their vessel. They laughed as Gen tried to hide, falling over as a large, bearded pirate roared and lunged at her. They laughed as Geffin and Helien raised their fists. They laughed as another brute grabbed Tem by the hair, pulling her head back into an unnatural position.

'You sank one of our ships,' he grunted.

His words were heavily accented so that we could barely understand him, but his intention was made horrifically clear when he raised his axe and smashed it into her skull. Bile rose into the back of my throat as he dropped her onto the deck, blood and tissue spreading over the wood.

We all stood in shock for a heartbeat, and then bedlam erupted. Both male and female warriors were attacked with equal vehemence. We were determined to remove the mocking snarls from the pirates' faces, as our fishermen bashed their skulls with the oars. Kade, Drey and I slashed with swords and stabbed with knives, but the Gallowglass were well armed with short swords, axes and shields. It was only ever going to end one way.

Unsurprisingly, those from the Isle fell first. I saw Helien hit in the face with a shield, blood pouring from his nose before the butt of an axe sent him thudding to the floor, unmoving. Geffin and Gen were similarly unconscious, or dead, within moments of the pirates boarding. The fishermen fought bravely, but they too were soon overwhelmed. A couple of the pirates were downed by an accurate blow to the head or face, but many more fishermen were felled by fatal wounds to the belly or skull; axes biting into flesh that was unprepared for such abuse. Spilled blood and other bodily fluids made the deck slippery and fouled the scent of the sea.

I saw Drey battling with a female pirate before falling over the side of the boat. I had no time to register this before a warrior came at me with axes in both hands. My retreating feet had to avoid becoming tangled in rope or bodies, while I furiously fought his twin attack with my one sword.

Metal screeched as he trapped *Saorsa* with one of his axes. I ducked to avoid the other one swinging towards my head. Taking the opportunity to push him off balance, I released *Saorsa* and carried the momentum of the swing towards his face. His reach was greater than mine and I only managed to slice a superficial cut on his cheek. He was quick to come back at me, and before I could recover from my swing, he smashed me full in the face. I heard the crack as my cheekbone gave way under the pressure. I staggered backwards, catching my foot on the deck and falling over. I heard another crack as my head hit the railing. My eyes rolled up into darkness and I knew nothing more.

Chapter Eighteen

My first awareness was of being slumped at an unnatural angle. There was a constriction across my chest that made it difficult to breathe, and held me at an angle to the floor. The rolling floor. I was still on a ship. I could smell the sea air, and my face felt gritty from the salt in the spray. I tried to open my eyes. The left was swollen shut and my cheek felt at least twice the size it should have been. My right eye felt glued together, but with a bit of effort I was able to open it a crack. The muted light sent shards of pain into my skull and I quickly closed the eye again. The pain in my head subsided to a dull pounding as I assessed the rest of my body. Cold metal enclosed my wrists, with a rigid pole between them that restricted movement to small adjustments. My leather bracers were gone, exposing my scars, and already the abrasive spray had started to chafe at my skin. Rope bound my upper arms to my chest, which in turn was tethered to an upright pole that I assumed was the mast. Easing myself into a more natural sitting position released the pressure on my chest and made breathing a little easier, but awoke a tapestry of aches and soreness in my ribs. My hips and legs were cold and numb, having had the circulation to them compressed for too long. Trying to move them into a more comfortable position resulted in needle-stabs throughout the muscles. A small groan escaped my lips, alerting those around me to the fact that I was conscious again.

'Ah, good,' said an accented voice. 'Your bash on the head was not so serious, hey?'

Forcing my right eye open again, I squinted against the light and the pain it caused. Standing in front of me was a large man, or rather two large men. I tried to focus as the warrior and his ghost image weaved in front of me. Shaggy brown hair hung past his ears and touched the collar of his stained leather gambeson. His beard was separated into two, with metal rings containing the two tails. His face wore many blue tattoos, and a number of scars. He knelt in front of me and laughed as I pressed myself into the timber pole at my back. There was nowhere I could go and very little movement was possible. His grin widened at my pathetic struggles to avoid him grasping the back of my head. Holding a handful of hair, he forced my head back, the movement causing my vision to swim and the two images of the pirate's face to shimmer as they crossed over each other. I swallowed to discourage the stomach acid trying to leak up my throat. He waited until I opened my eye again before holding a horn cup to my lips and dribbling cold, crisp water into my mouth. He allowed me only a couple of mouthfuls before removing the cup. I tried to follow it but was soon stopped by the ropes that bound me.

'No puking allowed on my ship.' He laughed again, before standing and walking behind me, out of view.

The water weighed heavily in my stomach as the boat rose and fell to the rhythm of the waves and the strokes of the oars. It was not long before I closed my eye again and drifted back into unconsciousness.

I awoke next to the afternoon sun in my face. While the rays warmed my bruised flesh, opening my eye caused intense stabs of white flame. I had to squint so that my eye was barely open in order to reduce the pain to tolerable levels. My vision still had ghost images that swim in and out of focus and made it difficult to concentrate on a single object. The hair on the back of my head was stiff; matted with blood, I suspected. Looking around the deck revealed the efficient operation of a Gallowglass pirate vessel. Both men and women were manning the oars, rhythmically moving back and forth without the need for a drummed pace-setter. Their movements were powerful and synchronised, allowing the ship to glide through the water with some speed. I could see five pairs of rowers on either side of me, and I assumed that an equal number worked behind me. There were no covered areas for shelter, with each rower's blankets rolled their inside shields that rested by their sides. Short swords and axes were within easy reach, allowing a change from rower to warrior within a heartbeat.

I could see no one from Faulknar on our boat, and heard nothing but the oars slicing through the water. Slowly turning my head, I could just see the prow of another Gallowglass vessel, but was frustratingly unable to detect anyone on board. I suspected that all four remaining pirate ships had survived and hoped there were some from Faulknar had survived aboard them. Then I remembered Drey falling overboard, and my stomach lurched. I was not sure whether I hoped he had been captured by the pirates or not. At least if he had he would be alive, but I had no way of finding out his fate, so I shut it away in a corner of my mind for when I was able to do something about it.

The warrior level with my right shoulder said something in a language I did not understand. The harsh sounds were clearly mocking, however, and I turned to see a leering grin splitting his black beard. As with all the pirates, male and female, his face bore several blue tattoos with angular shapes. He also had an old scar that ran from his temple to the base of his left nostril. He spoke again, gesturing crudely, and causing the female warrior behind him to laugh and clap him on the shoulder so hard that he was pushed forward. Other rowers also laughed at me, clearly enjoying the jest made at my expense.

The tall, brown-haired captain walked forward to stand in front of me. He spoke to his crew in their own language, prompting another round of laughter before they all focused again on their rowing. He turned to face me. 'He says he likes angry girls,' he said. 'Snappy. Like a spitting fire.'

I just glared at him, to which his reply was to widen his grin.

'You do not help yourself by being angry. Nothing you can do, so relax. We will be in Freisholm soon. Maybe we keep you. Have new life with us, yes?'

I curled up my legs and spat, aiming at his feet, but the thickened mucous barely missed my own. Quick as a striking falcon, he slapped my bruised face so my head slammed back into the mast. Explosions of colour flashed across my vision as tendrils of molten lava spread across the back of my skull.

'You dirty my ship,' he barked, before marching behind me to the bow.

I concentrated on keeping very still to prevent the fluid from my stomach joining my spittle on the deck.

The warriors did not row at night. While they rested, the sail caught what wind was available and only one pirate was awake to steer the vessel. I slept in brief snatches; too uncomfortable to rest, too tired to stay awake. I had been given very little water and no food, so that I felt weak and light-headed.

Although by the third morning my headache had receded to a dull throb and my vision had cleared so that only one image of everything was visible, I felt that if the ropes had not been restraining me, I would not have had the strength to stay upright. Perhaps this was part of their plan. I would have very little fight left in me when we arrived at our destination: Freisholm.

The captain came to me again, as he had each morning, to give me a couple of swallows of water. This morning, however, I was distracted by *Saorsa* tucked into his sword belt.

'Drink,' he said gruffly, knocking the cup into my teeth. 'Today we make land. Need your strength for big gathering.'

I was too thirsty to refuse the water, but continued to glare at him. He ignored my silent protest while I studied his eyes. Irises that I had taken to be blue were rimmed by a band of white, giving his gaze a strange and unnerving quality.

'That doesn't belong to you,' I snarled as soon as he moved the cup away, my voice little more than a whisper.

He grinned. 'I disagree. I think she suits me.'

He drew the blade. The sigh of the metal being released from the scabbard caused everyone to look. The morning sun sent rays of red light reflecting off *Saorsa*'s ruby eyes. I waited for the slip that would cut the pirate, but the darkness I usually saw when someone else handled the sword was missing. The dragon's face looked almost content.

'We have an understanding, I think,' the Gallowglass continued, while rolling his wrist and twisting the blade to catch the light. 'We used to have dragons in Gallowgla, many generations ago. The people remember. The people miss the dragons.'

We made land later that day. I was facing the stern of the ship so could not see it approaching, but I felt the increased energy in the strokes of the oars and heard the rising noise levels as the pirates anticipated getting home. As with everything else, the mooring was handled efficiently, with half the oars being stored as the tide carried the vessel towards the shore. The remaining rowers were used to control the speed as the tillerman made adjustments to the direction. I felt the bump against the dock as the captain came to cut the ties securing me to the mast. As I was unable to raise myself, he easily lifted my upper arm and turned me around. Concentrating on keeping my balance, I offered no resistance as he bound my upper arms behind my back, forcing the iron bar restricting my wrists painfully into my stomach.

As I was turned around, I could see Freisholm outlined in mountainous majesty. Three peaks stood dominating the skyline, with a semicircular valley in front of them that had been the base for the coastal town. Tall, straight trees covered the sides of the mountains, their silvery bark reflecting the afternoon sun before a crown of green poked triangularly into the sky. Grey rock was scattered between the clusters of trees; large boulders lay at the base of the peaks, getting smaller until they became the fine pebbles of the beach. These stones had been used in the construction of the dwellings within the settlement. A long, two-storey building with timber poles for a roof lay at the centre, surrounded by four rings of similar but smaller huts. Concentric quarter-circles radiated from the main building, all facing the sea and made of the grey stone from the mountains with caked mud forced into any gaps that could cause draughts. The construction looked like the stone walls used to keep sheep contained on the moors in Hilman. The people, dressed in leathers and furs, gathered in a packed earth area in front of a wooden jetty that extended several boat-lengths from the shore. The wealth of the Gallowglass, of which Tawpin had told me many years ago, was not evident, but neither were these poor fishing folk; their clothing was finely tailored, their dwellings well maintained. The community gave the impression of prosperity despite the harshness of the terrain.

Small fishing boats were moored against the timber docks, as well as ocean-going vessels. The three battle-scarred pirate ships and the one carrying me were tied up next to each other, and I could see who was aboard. The ship nearest to me contained two of the Faulknar fishermen, Puk and Gen. The next one held Geffin and another three fishermen. I did not see Helien on any of the vessels. On the last ship was Kade. I almost stumbled when I saw him, but was saved by the pirate's grip on the back of my tunic. As we were marched onto the jetty I could get a better look at him, and we managed a quick glance at each other before he was pushed ahead of me. Watching his back, I could see a slight limp and a hitch to his breathing suggesting damaged ribs. His arms were restrained in a similar fashion to mine, with iron shackles binding his wrists and rope drawing his elbows together behind his back. I had seen bruises on his face and a cut above his eye, but he looked generally unharmed. His temper, however, was murderous.

The pirates were in jubilant mood as we were all marched to the central area where the Gallowglass had gathered. They clasped forearms and patted each other on the back, talking animatedly in the language I did not understand. Puk, Gen, Geffin and the Faulknar fishermen were restrained by ropes around their wrists that were tied behind their backs. Rope nooses hung around their necks to join the small groups from each ship together. The collars caused them to jostle each other when they walked. The indignity of wearing rope collars seem to hurt more, and cause more anguish, than any discomfort from the chafing. Many eyes were already dead, having lost their fighting spirit.

At the centre of the clearing stood a couple who obviously held the power in the village. The man was tall and muscular, and looked capable of using the axes that hung at his waist. His leather leggings looked soft and supple, while his fleece-lined gambeson sat over a finely embroidered tunic. A heavy silver torc encircled his neck. Angular blue tattoos covered half his face and accentuated his blue eyes. Standing next to him was a thin but muscular woman. She also had an axe at her waist, along with a short sword. She wore a long, straight dress that was as finely embroidered as the man's tunic, and the slits up each side showed leather leggings underneath. The outfit was stylish, but also looked capable of allowing free movement if required. She had a finely woven silver torc around her neck, ending in dragon heads with dark stones set within. The black stones also appeared in her long silver necklace and a couple of her many silver rings. They flashed in the sunlight as she crossed her arms.

We were led to stand in front of these two, while the other villagers gathered around us to make a large circle. The Faulknar fishermen and those from the Isle of Serpents were herded into a group slightly to the left, while Kade and I were positioned slightly to the right. The Gallowglass pirates positioned themselves between us, and it was becoming increasingly clear that our fates would be different to those we had sailed with.

'You have done well,' boomed the man in charge, his words translated by a smaller man standing beside him. 'You have collected our prize and brought extra with you.'

The man with dark hair who had sailed with Kade grunted in affirmation as he gestured towards Gen and Geffin. 'Two are Windtalkers,' he said, his speech sounding nasal thanks to a misshapen nose that I suspected had been previously broken.

The chieftain dipped his head in response. 'A bounty indeed, Harke Calderson. They will fetch good price at market.'

'I look forward to receiving my share,' Harke replied, to the laughter of those gathered.

The chieftain's eyes turned flinty. 'Perhaps.'

With a gesture from the chieftain's lady, two men departed from the crowd. The remaining villagers muttered between themselves, many comments seemingly aimed at Kade and me as they watched us while talking behind raised hands. Some stared with open hostility. A few looked at Gen and Geffin, apparently impressed by their ability to control the wind. I appreciated that this would be helpful to a seafaring community.

Before long, the men returned carrying a large metal brazier. When placed on the ground it stood at waist height and was as wide as a man's forearm was long. Thick logs and a liquid that smelt like pine resin went into the brazier, flames soon licking at the rim. One of the men poked the fire with a long iron rod, which had a flattened end to it so it could stand upright when placed on the ground. Sparks danced into the air as the logs were agitated, and the heat generated was soon radiating across the clearing. The poker had turned red hot.

The chieftain gestured with a wave of his hand and the pirates nearest the two groups of noosed prisoners pushed them roughly forward, causing them to stumble towards the smoking brazier. Swords were drawn and the ropes binding their wrists were cut. No one moved, being adequately controlled by the rope collars and the threat of violence from those around them. The first fisherman was knocked to his knees, his wrist grabbed and forearm extended. Another firm grip locked his shoulder, effectively restraining his arm.

'Hear this,' boomed the chieftain. 'You belong to us now. No matter how many owners claim you, remember that you were taken by Freisholm. Your lives are first and foremost mine!'

With this, the man holding the poker removed it from the fire and placed the glowing iron on the inside of the fisherman's forearm. The stench of charred flesh wafted on the breeze as the man screamed in agony. His struggles were ineffective against the two muscled warriors and the rod was held in place until it had penetrated deeply. When it was finally removed, angry welts striped his skin; three vertical lines with what appeared to be spear heads pointing toward the wrist. The man wept unashamedly as he was hauled back onto his feet and the next captive was selected. Puk struggled desperately, knowing what was to come, but once again, the pirates easily subdued and restrained every member of the group until all had been branded, and the air was thick with the smell of burnt tissue. The wrist restraints were no longer necessary to contain the prisoners. All had the look of utter defeat and followed meekly as they were taken from the gathering.

I shifted uneasily as our crewmates were taken away. Only Kade and I were left. What would the Gallowglass have planned for us? I looked around the crowd; suddenly all appeared hostile, malevolent. I glanced at the man who had interpreted for the chieftain, noticing for the first time that he had been branded with the triple spears. The scars were faded but the mark was still clearly there. Scanning the gathered villagers, I saw several with the brand. I wondered briefly whether they could be potential allies, but their clothing and their stance reflected the Gallowglass so much that I suspected their allegiances were more with the pirates than with us.

The chieftain gestured to Harke, who aggressively pushed Kade forward. As Kade struggled to maintain his balance, I instinctively stepped forward to assist him, scared that he was about to be branded. My brown-haired captain clamped his arm across my chest in an iron embrace, as he rested a knife at my throat.

'Stay still, little she-wolf,' he whispered in my ear. 'Your prince brought this on himself.'

I felt chills run down my spine and shivered against his grip: they knew who we were. They knew Kade was the Faulknar prince. I prayed to all the Gods that they would consider him too valuable to kill. Not even I could believe that this would stop them hurting him.

Kade got control of his balance again as Harke hauled him away from the brazier. The crowd parted to reveal a medium-sized boulder, as high as the women's knees. Kade was stopped in front of this, and my mind spun so fast with terrifying possibilities that I could not coalesce them into a prediction of what could happen. Harke removed the binds from Kade's elbows, and the King-in-Waiting immediately turned to swing his shackled hands into Harke's belly. The pirate easily stepped aside from Kade's sluggish movements, bringing his elbow down on Kade's exposed neck. Kade dropped like a stone and I initially feared that he had broken his neck, but within a heartbeat he was struggling upright again. The big man laughed at his uncoordinated attempts, clasping the iron rod of the shackles to return the prince to the stone. He shoved Kade to the ground so close to the boulder that his knees banged against the rock. Kade scuttled ungracefully backwards as Harke moved to the other side of the boulder. Nodding to a burly man nearby, the pirate handed him the shackles. Kade's arms were extended over the stone so that his sword arm rested on the uneven surface, while the other dropped slightly to one side.

'In case you feel like causing more trouble,' Harke grunted.

Removing his axe, the warrior reversed the handle so that the crosspiece of the axe rested in his palm. Raising the weapon high above his head before brutally bringing down the thick wooden handle. The valley echoed the crack as Kade's forearm shattered.

We were taken to another cleared area that had been hidden behind the final row of houses. The appearance of this was similar to the one facing the sea, but the feeling was very different. Lying under the imposing shadows of the mountains, the space seemed cramped and menacing. The buildings faced away from the space, as if they had turned their backs on what happened there. Along one side were barn-like structures, and there were a few stocky ponies grazing the scrub nearby. The main feature, however, were the cages that swung in the breeze, creaking ominously. Thick timber posts stood twice the height of a man. Balanced between two posts was a cross-pole, with two metal cages that were slightly longer than a person's torso hanging from it. There were four sets of these timber frames, each holding two empty cages.

Kade and I were led towards the middle set of these cages. Kade had turned grey and I could see sweat beading on his forehead. He swayed slightly as he walked, hunched over his smashed arm that had already begun to swell. I could not see any bone poking through the skin and hoped that meant there would be no infection. We were separated so that, although I was next to Kade, there were two timber poles between us and I could not see him as well as I would have liked. A stool was provided to aid our entry into the cages. I watched Kade struggle with his balance before I was taken to the cage that would house me. It was impossible to stand straight inside it; my back was almost bent double as I entered, my shoulder pressing painfully against the top bars. The ropes restraining my elbows were cut, releasing my arms but causing excruciating needle-stabs as the circulation returned. The cage door slammed shut before I had a chance to turn around. The door was locked and the Gallowglass left without saying a word.

Getting even slightly comfortable in the cage took some manoeuvring. I settled on pressing my back to the bars, while sitting with my feet jammed against the far side and my shackled wrists resting in my lap. I had thought to lower my legs through the bars at the base of the cage in order to stretch them out, but I was reluctant to force my knees through the gaps in case my legs got stuck. It was not long before welts had formed on the soft tissue of my bottom through being forced through the holes in the cage floor, and my leg muscles cramped from being held in the flexed position for too long. The wind swept down from the mountains, causing me to chill and shiver soon after being left in the desolate surroundings.

As afternoon drifted towards evening, activity returned to the clearing. People came carrying kindling and logs, building a number of small fires around a larger one in the centre of the arena. I was tortured by the smells of roasting meat as several swine were spitted over the smaller fires. Casks of ale were opened, with all helping themselves to the liquid. By night-time, the atmosphere was one of celebration, with laughing, dancing and singing; it felt like a clear mockery of the position Kade and I were in. As if they were showing us the joy of their freedom, while we were caged like animals. They totally ignored us as I hugged my knees against my grumbling stomach.

The mood changed as the moon floated high in the sky. The revelry had continued for some time but, at some unseen trigger, the people became sombre and there was a growing feeling of anticipation. Voices were hushed and groups huddled together, with some hugging while others held hands. A drum began a slow, steady beat before it was joined by a single male voice, chanting unknown words over and over. The pairing of drum and voice was hypnotic. I felt my heart synchronise with the beat. A chill ripped through me, and my responding shudder rocked the cage.

A movement at the edge of my vision caused me to turn my head, as a man dressed in only a loincloth walked out from the side of the large main building. He was strong and healthy, his muscles and face painted with clay-water; spirals, circles and angular patterns all merging in a manner that confused the eye when looked at for too long. As he passed in front of me, I looked for slave branding but could see no blemish or mark.

He was followed by a man and a woman in long, dark robes, who were in turn followed by a number of people wearing similar but shorter robes. The man was tall and had long grey hair. I assumed he was some form of elder or spiritual leader. The woman next to him was small and stooped, using a stick to support her tottering steps. Her face was as wrinkled as a crumpled leaf. For some reason, I could not take my eyes off her. She was frail and unimposing, but I sensed power from her. I feared her.

The small group halted before the large fire. Ruby flames picked out the white markings from the clay, causing them to writhe and squirm like angry serpents. The man in the loincloth sat cross-legged on the ground and was handed a large circular dish, which he placed in his lap. One of those who had accompanied him moved to stand behind him, gently cupping his head. The music stopped, and an expectant silence hung in the air.

The robed, grey-haired elder stepped forward to stand directly in front of the painted younger man. I did not understand the words he said, but the ritualistic posturing was familiar. He raised his arms to invoke the Gods. He gestured to the magnificent mountains. He held his arms wide to gather the ancestors. A silver knife flashed in the firelight as it appeared in his hand, and faster than I could blink, he swiped the blade from one side to the other. It took a less than a heartbeat for the crimson to show and for me to realise what had happened. The lethally sharp blade had sliced open the painted man's throat with no more effort than it took to swipe at a fly. The man rocked forward slightly, but was held in place by the person at his back, his head over the circular bowl so that it collected the blood that had started to pour from the wound. The crowd murmured in rhythmic chanting, and the power within the arena almost crackled. My attention was drawn back to the old lady, who looked at me with clear eyes. She seemed to grow a head taller as her back straightened, and she appeared much younger as her posture strengthened. I relaxed my focus, expecting to see the blue power currents familiar to me when magick was being worked. The air was clear, with bright auras being the only visual evidence of the power that was palpable. This was not the magick I knew. This was older, more primal magick. The crone smiled a toothless grin at me, knowing that her display had scared me.

It may have been the lack of the valerian that Kade had been taking for so long. It may have been the stress of our situation. The fish broth was sustaining but weak and bland. The wind was chilly and relentless. And then there was the fact that Kade was caged, and the unconquerable fear he had of being contained. It may have been the delirium of fever, caused by the damage to his arm. Whatever the reason, over the following days Kade's dreams and visions became more frequent and more violent. It was strange that, after so many years of having night terrors, hearing Kade suffer caused me equal distress. I felt frustrated, angry, helpless.

Some were easy to dismiss as dreams. Although I could not see Kade clearly, these occurred at night when all was quiet. They often involved remembered scenes and feelings from Burford Hythe. I knew that Kade did not consciously recall the images from Mobis's kingdoms, but his dreams involved him shouting about daemons and shadows chasing him. Having pieces of his soul flayed by claws and talons. Running and running and running. Others I recognised from our travels through Lindvane or Hilman, or verbal fights with his father. But some were less easy to dismiss as dreams; occurring during the day when others were about. These often involved battles and fighting, sometimes as part of an army, defending Liegeport; sometimes on his own, as a challenge or test. The dragon attack on Liegeport was a regular theme, but some I did not understand at all, with landmarks and people unfamiliar to me. Sword fights in forested glades. Storms in the middle of the ocean. Maybe prophetic visions. Maybe personal fears.

One Gallowglass guard was particularly superstitious about Kade's attacks. He grumbled, in a heavily accented voice, about the curse of the Gods, and Kade being possessed. This prompted much laughter and teasing from his fellow guards, but he insisted that evil spirits had inhabited the Faulknar prince. He was uncomfortable during day shifts. He was visibly fearful during night shifts. It was a moonless night when he finally decided that he would no longer guard us during the dark hours. Those of Freisholm were understandably confident that their village was safe from raiders and escaping prisoners. The sea guarded one exit while the mountains guarded the other; both were unsurmountable without local knowledge. Consequently, we only had one guard on duty at night, and I suspected even this was more to prevent us from harming ourselves rather than to avoid any possibility of escape. With only himself for company, the guard's fears were given freedom to torment him and he startled at every noise and sudden movement.

I had fallen into the rhythm of dozing during the day and being awake for most of the night, when it was quiet and peaceful. I felt the need to watch over Kade as he slept, even though there was nothing I could do to protect him from the pain he felt or the horrors he encountered in his dreams. Often, they would start with trembling or twitching, the squeak of the cage swinging on its chain alerting me to his increasing distress. This night the Fates had delivered a particularly apt vision to play into the guard's fears: the daemons of Mobis's Hells. The guard paced up and down, mumbling to himself as Kade twitched and turned in response to the images only he could see. He startled as Kade cried out on seeing a daemon; graphically describing the sharp teeth and claws, the dead, soulless eyes, and the putrid smell of its skin.

The guard cried out himself as a woman approached with a horn cup of warm spiced mead.

'By the Gods, Frick. It's only me.'

He replied to her in the language I did not understand.

'Please, speak in the words of the Lindvane. I need the practice. I want to understand what they talk about when he comes.'

'I don't understand why you want to listen to his conversation. He is not helping us. Just them.'

'Hush, Frick,' she pleaded softly. 'They get rich. We all get rich. Here.'

She passed him the drink, which he took appreciatively, sighing as the warm liquid settled in his stomach. She smiled seductively as she ran her fingers along his jacket collar.

'It's cold out here. Why don't you come home?'

She saw his eyes flick to Kade and me.

'Where are they going to go? If they were going to cause trouble, they would have done so by now.'

Frick hesitated, obviously tempted. 'But the other guards…'

'They don't need to know.'

She moved her hand lower, making it very clear what was on offer for him at home. He hesitated a heartbeat longer before allowing her to lead him away.

It must have been the seventh or eighth morning when two guards were sent to fetch me. I was helped out of the cage, staggering the first few steps as my joints struggled, stiff following the prolonged flexion. It was the first time I had been able to get a good look at Kade. He sat huddled at the back of his cage, gently cradling his injured arm. His skin was flushed, with sweat darkening the hair framing his face and neck, but he shivered as if cold. Purple splotches were scattered over his cheeks and down his throat. His arm was swollen, large plum-coloured bruises interspersed with angry red tissue. His hand was almost twice its natural size, compressed by the iron shackles that restricted the blood supply to his fingers. More concerning than any of that was that, for the first time, I could see a small wound on the inside of his forearm. Tiny pieces of white bone showed through the inflammation, and I knew the discolouration of his flushed skin was from the poisons flowing through his blood.

I was taken to the large building in the centre of the village. There were four steps that led up to a set of double wooden doors, which were carved with trees and beasts of the forest. I was taken through these doors and into the main meeting hall. Even early in the morning there were several Gallowglass within, drinking and eating. I saw slave markings on those who were serving and cleaning. A few of those seated also carried the brand of the three spears, but had another welt running straight through the marking. Perhaps these were slaves who had earned their freedom, or maybe there was a hierarchy of slaves within the community. At the far end of the hall was a dais, on which stood two ornate chairs covered in furs. The chieftain and his lady sat on these chairs and watched me coldly as I was escorted through the hall towards a side chamber. A young man with a blue fish tattooed on his face whispered into the chieftain's ear as I passed. On a small table behind the two chairs were Kade's sword, many of our knives and various other items that had been looted. I noticed that *Saorsa* was not with them.

I was walked through the hall to a chamber to the side of the raised chairs, which was separated by a hanging sheet of leather. The room was dim and stuffy, with a musty odour that tickled my nose as I walked in. A small bed and table were pushed against the far wall, and a delicately carved chest stood proudly at the foot of the bed. Shelves lined two of the walls, laden with glass bottles and dried herbs and, on one of the shelves, a golden crystal.

A rattling laugh startled me as I had overlooked the old lady sitting in a chair in the corner of the room. The gloom had hidden her and the young girl with her, and I suspected that it was not by accident. On gaining my attention, she rose with the help of the child and came into the middle of the room where there was more light, revealing her to be the old woman from the gathering on the first night. The shaman who seemed to look through me. The one who frightened me.

The girl translated as the old crone spoke.

'I see you recognise the crystal. Very useful. Very useful stone.'

The girl placed a cushion on the floor, exposing her slave mark, before helping the old lady to be seated. She sat in front of a small firepit and gestured for me to sit opposite her. I hesitated, but was forced to the ground by the guard at my back. The second sentry had lowered the leather hangings over the small window, shutting out the light and leaving the room in almost total darkness. I heard the shuffling footsteps of my wardens as they hurriedly left.

The shaman clicked her fingers and the firepit was filled with flames, quickly dying back down to a soft glow as the logs warmed. The old woman continued to stare at me, her clouded eyes reflecting the rosy glow from the fire. They seemed to swirl in the flickering light, becoming hypnotic, drawing me into their hidden depths. I hastily looked away and found the yellow crystal again.

She cackled her bitter laugh. 'It draws you to it. It wants your power.'

I croaked a reply, having to cough to clear my dry throat of the lingering incense in the air. I repeated my statement. 'I know what it is.'

'Do you?' she mocked. 'The crystal is becoming more versatile in the hands of a master. Villermir is exploring more uses all the time.'

At the mention of Villermir, I reflexively clenched my fists. She noticed and grinned, revealing her remaining stained and rotting teeth.

'Yes. You do well to fear him. I understand that he has many plans for you. I doubt any will be enjoyable for you.'

I concentrated very hard on controlling my face, on not showing the terror of what my mind was suggesting about my fate. I could not control the slight trembling that racked my whole body. 'And Kade?'

She waved her hand dismissively. 'He will make Freisholm rich when he is auctioned to the kings of Lindvane and Faulknar. He is no concern of mine.' She tilted her head like a bird. 'But you. Villermir wants you very badly. Now, why would he want a small thing like you? Your eyes are a clue, I feel.' Her eyes relaxed as she appraised more than my physical appearance. 'There is something of the raven about you. Thought? No; you are cunning but not deceptive. Memory? Yes. Memory. You are a reminder of the past. That is why you have the sword? Is that why Villermir wants you?'

She waved her hand at the young girl, who scuttled off to rummage through the carved chest. She continued to interpret as the crone chatted freely while waiting for her attendant to return with whatever she had been sent for.

'You were foolish to take the crystal with you,' she said while rolling up her sleeves to reveal tattoos of bird skulls and feathers. 'It was how Villermir knew where to find you. Where to send us.' She chuckled to herself in amusement. 'He was not happy to lose it to the bottom of the ocean. Seems he take a lot of energy to attune new crystals. His influence is growing ever bigger. We can but hope that he spreads himself too thin, yes?'

The slave returned carrying a small sack, and removed a leather pouch to hand to the crone. Walking around us, the girl placed bird skulls at the four cardinal points: a hook-beaked raptor skull behind the shaman, a small hedge bird to her left, a woodpecker to her right, and a corvid behind me. Various-sized bird bones were placed between these skulls to create a protective circle. I knew what was coming, and pre-emptively strengthened my mental barriers. The old woman placed her hand in the leather pouch, withdrawing pinched fingers. She hesitated for a heartbeat, smiling as she caught my gaze, then threw the powder onto the fire.

I rocked backwards in surprise as iridescent blue flames erupted from the fire, reaching towards the ceiling. My back slammed into the protective circle that had become a physical barrier, knocking the air from my lungs. My reflexive gasp drew in a large breath of the smoke, stinging my nose and throat. It caused me to cough and draw in another lungful of the incense. My eyes streamed as I tried not to inhale more of the substance, while my lungs spasmed. The chamber had grown very hot, and I was sweating as my vision began to blur. The room spun dizzyingly, making me nauseous as I fought to maintain my balance.

The shaman was suddenly inside my head. It felt like a ferret tunnelling through my skull, trying to find the rabbit. I instinctively tried to chase it, only for it to repeatedly twist out of my grasp. I spent frustrating heartbeats on this futile game before logic returned to me. I stopped chasing and visualised the hall of doors. I concentrated on a thick oak panel covered in iron straps, rivets and bolts. I trapped the ferreting presence behind it, breathing easily for a couple of heartbeats before the creature behind the door started to sound more like an enraged bull. The door vibrated with a deafening thud. The beast rammed against the oak again with a sickening blow, pushing the barrier a finger-length closer to me. I stepped away – one pace; two – before backing into a stone barrier. Afraid to turn to look, my fingers explored the rough texture of rock. My heart raced as feelings from my dreams collided with the shaman's pounding on my defences. The stone cell was getting smaller and smaller. I squeezed myself into the furthest corner, watching as the door crept closer and closer.

Suddenly, my back burned as a toxic, gelatinous material oozed down the walls. It ate away at my clothing and irritated my skin. Blisters erupted on my hands where I touched the floor. I scuttled away from the wall, but moving too far brought me uncomfortably close to the door, still rocking on its hinges with each blow. I huddled in the centre of the cell, balanced on the balls of my feet to avoid as much contact with the noxious substance as possible. Just as I thought I had conquered the effects of the slime, the ooze turned into uncountable scurrying beetles. My breath became ragged as the insects scuttled over the stone, climbing over each other and running over my feet. I tried to stamp on them as they came towards me, but the ceiling had dropped so low that it was difficult to balance in such a stooped position. Tears stung my eyes as I tried to concentrate on the fact that these were just images in my mind. The creatures were not real. It could be worse. They could be...

Spiders descended from the ceiling on gossamer strands. I felt them falling down the back of my neck. I felt them crawling up my legs. The rivets holding the hinges and locks of the oak door were giving way. I couldn't concentrate on the barrier when the spiders were landing in my hair. I scratched at my head, my face, my arms; blood oozing from the welts I had made. The spiders were increasing in size. I could see their reflective eyes; hear their sharp mouth pincers clicking.

The crone's mocking laugh echoed around the walls of the stone chamber. 'Fear is your greatest weakness.'

I screamed with a raging mixture of anger, fear, frustration and despair. I pushed out my barriers as hard as I could, forcing the spiders, the beetles, the walls, the door away from me; shoving everything backwards with as much strength as I could muster. A blinding white flash filled the cell, causing me to close my eyes tightly to avoid painful stabs of light driving into my skull. Red motes danced on the inside of my eyelids as I shielded them with my raised arms. I waited several heartbeats for the explosion that had to follow, but gradually the light faded, and I opened my eyes to see the dim chamber at Freisholm. Streaks of blood dripped from my wrists where I had pulled against my shackles and ripped the skin. Flickers from the embers made my scars look like living flame.

I looked at the crone opposite me. Her face was a mask of anger, but she could not hide a hint of alarm. The child was crouching between the bed and the decorated chest, her face white and her eyes wide.

'Fear may be my weakness,' I told the shaman quietly. 'But you should still be careful if you want to provoke it.'

The old woman screeched for the guards and they rushed in to drag me roughly out of her chamber. I was held firmly by my arms as I struggled to regain my footing. The heat of the hall and the jeers of the warriors within created a sea of mocking faces as I fought with the vertigo caused by the shaman's smoke still in my lungs. I remained outwardly submissive as I tried to keep up with the marching pace of my captors, but tried to use the opportunity to observe the interactions of the warriors away from the structure of their boats. Frequent moving between groups was evident in the short time it took to travel the length of the room, so perhaps alliances were not fixed. It gave me a small amount of information to consider when planning how to get my weapons back.

We were almost at the door when we passed a stocky woman with braided blonde hair hanging almost to her waist. She was companionably shoving the male warrior next to her, raising her right leg as she kicked his shin to reveal the worn leather binding of my smallest dagger poking out from the top of her boot. I knew getting that back would be a challenge, but that would be where I would start.

Chapter Nineteen

The chieftain of the coastal community only came to visit once during my time in the cage. The day was overcast, and his arrival scared away the large black rooks that were noisily pecking for grubs in the grassland arena. Lazily, I turned my attention from them to what had disturbed them, immediately focused when I saw the tall man walking towards me. His elaborately embroidered tunic and silver torc were gone, but his blue eyes still demanded the respect due to his station. He walked briskly from between two huts, paying no attention to the old man hurrying to keep up with him. The elder had long grey hair that bounced against his shoulders as he struggled to match the taller man's pace, and he was dressed in a plain tunic over faded woollen trousers. It was not until he raised his head that I recognised him as the one who had led the ritual on the night of the blood sacrifice.

The two men stopped level with Kade's cage. Kade remained sleeping and was oblivious to their inspection of him. I leaned forward in my enclosure to let them know that they were also being observed, but the chief only stared at me for a couple of heartbeats before dismissing me as irrelevant. The old priest did not even bother to note that I was there, sniffing noisily to catch the sickly-sweet scent of Kade's infected arm. They had not brought the small interpreter with them, so I could only guess at their conversation, but their posture suggested that there was a disagreement between them. The leader pointed sharply at Kade's arm, turning his hand over as if it supported what he was saying. The priest shook his head, dismissing the comments with a flick of his hand. The tall warrior kicked the cage, and the sudden movement woke Kade with a cry. I saw his eyes dart nervously as his brain fought off the effects of sleep, clenching his jaw against any further displays of pain. I banged against the bars of my cage in frustration.

'Leave him alone,' I shouted. 'He needs healing.'

I was not surprised when the two men ignored me, but I was unable to do anything else to help Kade. He glanced at me sadly before returning his attention to those in front of him; carefully holding himself as still as possible in the gently swinging cage, but glaring at his captors with quiet, impotent rage.

The chieftain slapped the priest on the shoulder, and gestured abruptly to Kade again before walking off without a backward glance. The Gallowglass elder looked at Kade for several heartbeats, a frown creasing his forehead, before following his leader. I called after him in desperation.

'Help him,' I shouted, but the priest gave no indication that he had heard me.

'Leave it be.' Kade's voice cracked, and he coughed to clear his throat and force the words out with more strength. 'They will do what they want to do, with no influence from us.'

I banged my fists against my forehead in frustrated anger. 'They have to do something, Kade. You're burning with fever. You can't...'

I stopped. It would not help to tell Kade how sick he was, or how desperate our situation was. He gave a faint flicker of a smile, knowing his position better than I did.

'I am well aware of how bad my arm is, Tallen. It is being most insistent on the issue.'

I tried to reassure him with something positive – we would be rescued before his infection got any worse; I would think of a way to get us away from Freisholm; the Gods would not let anything happen to him. But I knew them to be false hopes, and that Kade would take no comfort from empty words. We sat in uncomfortable silence as I watched Kade's face contort with the effort of maintaining his own falsehoods; that his arm did not pain him as much as I feared, and the infection had not spread beyond the immediate area.

Kade had almost drifted off into an exhausted sleep when the grey-haired priest returned. He carried a shallow clay bowl and a beaker, being careful not to spill their contents. He placed the items on the floor below Kade's cage, before retrieving a key from a pouch at his waist that had been hidden by the hem of his tunic. I gripped the bars of my cage so hard that I could see the whites of my knuckle bones through the skin, but could do no more to prevent whatever the old man was planning to do to Kade. I watched, helpless, as the elder bent to retrieve the beaker before gesturing for Kade to drink, forcing the cup towards him when he hesitated. Reluctantly, Kade took a sip of the liquid, his face showing that the taste was unpleasant. The priest continued to glare until Kade had drained the cup, at which point he nodded in satisfaction.

Kade relaxed his back against the bars of his cage while the Gallowglass man collected the clay bowl. Kade tensed as the old man reached towards his injured arm but, following another fierce glare, allowed the wound to be inspected. The man was surprisingly gentle as he removed soaked linen from the bowl and layered strips around Kade's forearm. Flecks of green and brown suggested that the bandages had been soaked in herbs, and I prayed to Nathair that the plants were of the healing kind. Kade's face had paled to an unhealthy shade, and I could see sweat beading on his forehead, but he kept his arm still and suffered the attentions of the priest. After fussing over the final covering, the elder grunted his acceptance of the dressing and stepped away from the cage. He gathered the dropped beaker and added it to the bowl, tilting his head slightly as he watched Kade succumb to a relaxed sleep, resting his head against the bars as his arm lay cradled in his lap. The old man hesitated for a heartbeat, turning to me for the first time to give a quick nod of the head before returning to the main settlement.

The old priest never came to visit Kade again while we were at Freisholm, but I was summoned to attend the shaman woman on two more occasions. The first of these came during the evening after the dressings were applied to Kade's arm. The sun had moved behind the huts, causing long shadows to extend over the grasslands. The three mountain peaks rose into the pale sky, and the gentle hush of the trees could just be heard as the near-constant wind blew through their leaves. I watched two enormous birds, possibly eagles, fly between the two nearest crags; their intricate dance being visible even as far away as they were. I was saddened when the thermal currents took them beyond the summit of the mountains and they glided out of view behind the rocks.

It was not long after the birds had disappeared that the guards came to take me to the crone's chamber. My stomach clenched as I entered the rowdy common room, although I was more anxious about going to see the old woman again. The jeering started as soon as I was taken in, but one of the guards barked at the person who had thrown a tankard in my direction, so that there were no further projectiles. The chief and his lady were eating greasy hunks of meat, but on seeing me the woman dropped her food and snapped a command. The guard to my right shrugged his shoulders and seemed to apologise or claim that it was nothing to do with him. She clearly gestured to me and the double doors that we had just come through, but again the warrior only shrugged; at this point we had passed beyond her line of sight and I was quickly bundled into the shaman's oppressive room.

The room was dimly lit despite the leather hangings at the window being drawn back and hooked around nails in the wall. The hag sat on a wooden stool, small and unimposing, while her young attendant sat cross-legged on the carved chest. The old woman's dark eyes glinted as she grinned her toothless smile at me, cackling quietly. I avoided her gaze and looked around the room, not knowing that I was looking for the yellow crystal until I could not locate it. The firepit was also absent, with only the dark ash left behind within the small indentation in the floor. I was not fool enough to believe this would make things any easier for me; it just seemed that the sorceress was to use a different method this time.

At a flick of the hand, the girl picked up the small leather pouch beside her and climbed off the chest. She impatiently shooed the guards away, and they happily took their leave through the leather door. I stood awkwardly, not knowing what I was required to do or where I was to stand. The girl ignored me as she placed the bird bones and skulls in a large circle around the room, although she waved me out of the way when I interrupted her design. I was tempted to take the opportunity to follow the guards but, with a room full of warriors waiting to lynch me, I decided against it. Instead I moved as far away as possible from the shaman, hoping she would forget me in the dim corner.

The hag cackled again, before grunting some unintelligible words.

'She will not forget you are there,' interpreted the child.

I stretched my back, happy to stand upright while the circle was completed with ash that the girl had collected from the firepit. She used the dust to connect the bones and enclose the centre of the room in the circle, with the old crone requiring a few adjustments before she was finally satisfied. She rose slowly from the stool and tottered towards the small bone in front of her. I was intrigued by her faltering steps and her fragile frame that seemed so at odds with the aura of power that emanated from her. Her paper-thin, veined hands trembled slightly as she leaned forward so that her palm was level with her knees, hovering over the bone. She stood with her eyes closed for a few heartbeats before moving to the next bone, and then the next. When she reached the first skull, she crouched to place both hands around the pale head.

'*Ganga. Finna. Eygja,*' she breathed.

'To go. To find. To see,' repeated the young girl.

The crone turned, as quick as a striking snake, and hissed at the child, baring her teeth and spraying spittle. The youngster threw her hands up and spat some words back at her. A short, ill-tempered conversation passed between the two of them before the girl return to sit on the chest, arms crossed over her chest and a sulky frown on her face.

The shaman returned to the circle, repeating the words *Ganga*, *Finna* and *Eygja* several times before moving on. The process of hovering over the small bones and chanting over the skulls was repeated all the way around. A sensation, somewhere between humming in my ears and vibrations on my skin, became more insistent as she returned to the beginning. The ash seemed to absorb the low lighting, becoming darker and thicker. The air within the room felt denser, and a thin sheen of sweat spread over my skin. As the chanting over the final skull was finished, the circle flashed a dull green, absorbing all the ash but leaving a thread of viridian hanging just above the floor. The after-image from the flash floated in my vision for several heartbeats.

The old woman flapped her hand at the girl as she looked at me, the green glow reflected in her eyes. She raised her lips in a threatening sneer, causing me to reflexively press my back against the wall. As the girl joined her, both walked over to me, being careful not to touch the protected space. The girl was carrying a small bowl and a wickedly sharp-looking blade. I started trembling so violently that I could no longer stand, and slid down to crumple on the floor. Surely, they were not going to slit my throat as they had done to the sacrifice on that first evening? Surely, Villermir would want me for himself? But then, the yellow crystal had gone so perhaps he was not aware of tonight's ritual.

Having nowhere to go, I offered no resistance when the hag grabbed my arm and pulled it forward. Her grip was surprisingly strong, and I felt the small bones of my wrist grind uncomfortably together. She twisted her hold so that my inner arm was pointing upwards, painfully forcing the other wrist to rise. The metal shackles bit into the tender flesh and caused a sticky ooze to seep from the sores, but I paid no attention to it as the shaman took the knife from the girl. I could not take my eyes away from the blade as it glinted in the green glow of the circle. My heart hammered against my chest, trying to compensate for the fact that I was barely breathing. The old woman waited until the girl placed the bowl under my forearm, then quickly sliced the flesh. I felt nothing from the finger-long cut, even as I stared at it; an impassive bystander, watching the blood flow across my skin and collect in the bowl. The woman passed the knife back to the child, and all three of us stood mesmerised as the red liquid gradually filled the bowl.

When the crone was satisfied with the amount of blood collected, she slapped a grubby hand over the wound and pressed hard to staunch the bleeding. I blinked as the proud tissue stung at her contact; it was the first discomfort I had felt since she had made the wound. She wiped her bloody hand on my tunic, before gesturing to her attendant to carry the bowl to the chest. The shaman collected a glass bottle from a shelf and joined the girl, carefully filling the bottle with my blood and stoppering it with a fold of leather. The girl exchanged the bowl, still containing some blood, for the bottle and, ensuring she kept it upright, placed the vial in the chest before resuming her cross-legged seat on top of it. It seemed that her role in this ritual had been completed.

The sorceress carried the bowl to the circle and poured the contents onto a section of the ethereal thread that had hovered since the activation of the ring. The liquid hissed and spat as a red line traced the darker green one around the circumference. Two distinct cords encompassed the inner area, gently pulsing as they floated a finger-length above the floor. The shaman moved to the corvid skull and slowly rocked backwards and forwards as she softly uttered the word '*Bjóda*', almost as if to herself. I felt that, having completed my role in the ritual by providing blood, she had forgotten that I was still there. I should have used the opportunity to leave, but I was mesmerised by her rhythmic rocking and the pulsing of the circle in time with her movements.

I was so focused on the old woman that I failed to notice the white mist that rose from the chamber floor. It was only when the pale, gossamer smoke had risen to the height of the crone's knees that I saw the swirling vapour as it filled the space within the protected circle. The movement of the mist started to pulse in time with the movement of the red-green thread enclosing it, and the woman's rocking. Gradually, the smoke became thicker, coalescing into amorphous forms that writhed like trapped spirits. I shivered, realising that the temperature in the room had dropped considerably, so that my exhaled breath was starting to cloud. Still the sorceress chanted and swayed, chanted and swayed. Her voice was the only sound in the room, adding to the feeling of isolation; that this room had somehow stepped aside from the real world.

A sudden crack of thunder caused me to slam my head against the wall, as I fearfully tried to back away from the circle. The smoke had divided into three distinct forms, solid individuals that were pressed together within the protected space. Muscular shoulders bumped together as the human-like creatures tilted their heads to survey the room, all standing over twice the height of Kade. The smallest was twice as wide as I was, but gaunt to the point of emaciation. The points of its shoulder blades were clearly defined above its rows of ribs, leading down to a pulled-in abdomen. The knobbles of each spinal bone poked through the dark, leathery skin. This figure was rubbed up against one that was a head taller, thin but looking thicker next to its skeletal neighbour. Its skin was equally leathery, but had occasional black blemishes that reminded me of distorted freckles. The final one was built of solid muscle, ripples cascading down its back as its head swayed slightly to appraise the two people in front of it. Two giant horns extended from the back of its bald head, each as thick as my leg and finishing in a sharp point that glistened as it moved. My brain was trying to tell me that these creatures were known to me, but I refused to search for the memory. I sat as small and inconspicuous as possible and looked to the shaman and the girl, who were similarly motionless. It took a couple of heartbeats to realise that the Gallowglass were not frozen in terror as I was, but were as if carved from stone; no trembling, no blinking, no breathing. Again, I shied away from the thought that this was familiar.

'Who dares to summon me?' The booming voice resonated through my head, echoing as if the words bounced around a huge cavern. The horned daemon raised its nose to sniff the air, but it was the skeletal creature that turned towards me first. Her cadaverous face revealed sunken cheekbones and exposed eye sockets. Bright red lips made a disquieting contrast to the dark skin and hollow eyes. 'Dragonslayer,' she hissed. 'Dragonslayer blood.'

All three were naked, and as she turned fully toward me I could see her sagging breasts flap against her chest. Forcefully dragging my eyes away, I looked at the next beast as he turned to me. His facial features were unremarkable, except his grey eyes that churned like storm clouds gathering. He clutched a wooden wheel whose spokes were carved into images of people, and, as he rotated the rim through his hands, these figures glinted and writhed. The final figure turned in my direction and chilled me to the core. The muscles of his neck corded as he moved the weight of his head and horns in a slow arc to look into my wide, staring eyes. His eyes bored into my soul, laying bare all my wrongdoings.

My mind refused to be silenced and thoughts crashed erratically around my head as the recognition of those standing in front of me rose to the surface: the three Fates. Sluagh, the skeletal warrior who commanded the army of the dead in order to avenge those who had been abused. Taranis, the controller of destiny's wheel that would decide which torture and torment your soul deserved. Mobis, the keeper of the dead and the one who would determine the eternal fate of your soul. I was taught that the Fates were impartial; neither good nor evil, as natural as love and loss, or birth and death. I found that very difficult to remember as they loomed over me, notwithstanding the protection of the circle that seemed hardly capable of containing them.

'Dragonslayer,' Mobis boomed. 'Why have you summoned me?'

I didn't. I didn't. I repeated the words over and over in my head, unable to speak aloud and desperately hoping they would hear me as I could hear them.

Mobis held up a hand and instantly quietened my nervous rambling. I blinked at him as he effortlessly controlled my thoughts, causing a small part of my mind to cower how he had broken through my barriers so easily.

'No defences can keep me out,' he replied, his mouth flickering in a brief smile.

Memories ran through my head without any direction or control from me. I recalled the cutting of my arm to collect the blood for the ritual. I remembered the attack by the pirates after leaving the Isle of Serpents. I was taken back to Villermir's use of the Empathy Crystal to torment me. I was shown Kade, beaten and broken at Burford Hythe.

'I know you,' Mobis stated, as he leaned further towards me. 'You owe me a soul.'

My memories vanished with a jolt of vertigo as I saw Mobis nod towards Taranis. Another deafening crack of thunder caused me to blink, and when I opened my eyes the Fates were gone. I was able to wonder at the removal of all traces of the ash, green thread and my blood from the circle, leaving only the dead bones of the birds, when the piercing screech of the shaman snapped my attention back to her. Her face was contorted in angry frustration, causing the young girl to skitter off the chest and cringe in the corner. The crone ignored her as she raged at me, kicking the bones aside as she came towards me spitting curses. As soon as she was in range, she slapped me across the face. Unsatisfied with my surprised reaction, she progressed to raking her filthy nails down the soft skin of my cheeks. I felt the trails of blood seeping from the burning welts she had made.

The noise of the old woman's screaming brought several warriors bursting through the leather flap. Pale faces stared, their eyes darting between me and the hag, unsure of who was in danger and what they were required to do. She redirected her babbling to them, but from their confused expressions and exchanged glances it seemed she was as incomprehensible to them as she was to me. By some form of consensus, it was decided that I had obviously displeased her, and the safest option was to remove me from her chamber. I was marched through the main hall, past several shocked faces of those who were hoping to find out what had caused such temper in their shaman.

I was determined not to return to the shaman again. She had invaded my mind and taken my blood; I was not going to meekly let her remove other parts of my anatomy for her twisted rituals. I knew she would try to summon the Fates again but hoped that the blood she had stored in the glass bottle would be sufficient for her needs, and that I would not be called upon to witness further attempts.

I was given two days to consider my options before the guards came for me again. As before, I was led to the communal hall where I heard drunken singing long before we entered through the double doors. The temperature inside was roasting, as most of the settlement had decided to spend the evening in the hall. I was jostled as soon as I walked in, and my escort had to grab my arms to ensure they did not lose me in the crush. Unwilling to remind the Fates of my presence, I sent a word of gratitude to Sucellos for granting me a full audience for the strategy I had devised. The guards were too busy pushing through the crowd to notice that I was unable to hide my smile at his generosity when I saw the woman with my small dagger.

I was halfway across the room when I stumbled and knocked against a bearded warrior. Unfortunately, he had been holding a full tankard of ale and this was promptly thrown over his neighbour. Predictably, the wronged warrior rose quickly to demand compensation from the man I had stumbled into, who was equally quick to rise to protest his innocence. As the first threw his arm in my direction to indicate that I was to blame, I ducked out of the way and pushed into the guard standing beside me. We both fell in a tangle of legs, crushing the occupants of that bench against the table. More pushing and shoving ensued, accompanied by shouts and curses. I took advantage of the confusion to crawl under the mass of bodies trying to stand, and duck under the table of those I had first disturbed. Before my guards had a chance to miss me, I stood up, causing the table to overturn and throw food and ale over everyone within an arm's length. Further chaos erupted as some tried to escape the flying debris while others roared at me.

Those beyond the initial scuffle were starting to push into the riot to try to restrain me, but only succeeded in causing more shoving and cursing. I ducked, twisted and squirmed between the press of bodies and tried to locate the woman who had my dagger. Many of the warriors had blond hair so I was unable to use this for identification; instead I looked for one who was smaller than most and had a large nose in a pointed face. It took several moments of searching before I spotted her, shouting encouragement and insults in equal measure, at the front of the hall near the chieftain and his wife. I pushed, elbowed, kicked and tripped my way across the room, careful to ensure that there was no clear access to me. I had lost both guards and the warriors around me were easily distracted in fighting each other, so I was able to ensure that none paid close attention to the prisoner sowing discord throughout the hall. Too much ale and too little to do had primed the Gallowglass to relieve their frustration and boredom by pummelling their colleagues. The chieftain shouted for calm but was barely heard above the din as his people clamoured for blood. Punches were being freely exchanged and I received several blows from elbows and knees as I tried to avoid being trampled, keeping low to avoid catching the attention of those around me. The mayhem followed in my wake, as I repeatedly knocked bystanders into the fists of combatants, all the time moving steadily towards my target.

The mood in the hall turned uglier as I reached the group near the blonde pirate. We made eye contact for a heartbeat, her eyes narrowing in recognition, before a sickening cry of pain caused me to turn back to the riot behind me. Someone had drawn an axe to threaten their antagonist, but the close proximity of everyone jostled together meant that the blade had sliced into the smaller man's face. Blood flowed from the slashed tissue, leaving a large gash running from cheek to jaw. The room seemed to stop for the space of two heartbeats, before erupting again in a storm of shouting and fighting. A few others removed short axes from their belts and waved them threateningly, adding to the violence.

I turned back to the dais to find the blonde had moved to stand in front of me, her arm pulled back for a punch. With no time to avoid it, I caught the blow on the side of my jaw and allowed it to knock me to the ground. She succeeded in delivering a kick to my ribs that made me gasp, but on her second attempt I curled around her ankle to trap her leg. The momentum of her swing caused her to fall over me, and we ended up in a tangled heap with legs kicking and arms flying. As I flailed around, I managed to catch her on the forehead with the metal of my shackles, which left her stunned. I scuttled on my hands and knees back towards the double-doored exit, but had not moved more than three paces before someone grasped the collar of my tunic and stopped me from moving any further. I quickly turned and raised my hands, ready to punch both fists into their chest. I stopped when I looked into the face of the shaggy-haired captain, the twin tails of his beard swaying as he shook his head at me.

'You crazy she-wolf,' he mocked.

Using his bulk, he barrelled me through the hall, elbowing the crowds out of the way. He did not slow his pace once we had exited the double doors, but maintained his hold on the neck of my tunic and marched me back to the cages. The few people who were outside the hall took one look at his scowl and decided not to get involved.

He remained silent as we passed a sleeping Kade and stopped in front of my cage. The small stool which enabled me to get in and out was still beside the metal enclosure, and he turned me around before pressing me down to sit on it. He stood in front of me for several heartbeats, his hands on his hips and a frown on his face. I stared at his eyes: the darkness had caused the pupils to expand to almost cover them, leaving only a sliver of bright white iris circling the abyss. The effect was captivating but reminded me of the ethereal fae creatures of whom tales were told on long winter nights.

'Tsk,' he said at last. 'You lucky that they are very frightened of the old witch. Perhaps they won't come and kill you for the trouble you caused. Perhaps they will just break an arm, like they did your friend.'

'I'll take a broken arm over whatever your shaman was planning on doing to me.'

He narrowed his eyes in suspicion. 'She does not waste her time with those who are nothing. I think you are important to her as your prince is to our king, no? What does she want with a little sparrow like you? What does she do to you in that little room of hers?'

I kept sullenly silent, not prepared to remember the details of what happened, much less recall them to him. He may have saved me from the mob and given me an escape from the hall, but despite his gentle talk he was still my enemy. I had no doubts that he would kill me if he felt he could benefit from my death.

He sniffed at my small defiance, succumbing to a brief smile of amusement. 'Perhaps it is better not to share those secrets. I would not want the torment of bad dreams like your prince, hey? She does not play well with others, but those marks on your face suggest you defy her. That is a powerful thing to do. But not very smart.' He paused again, considering for a few heartbeats before continuing. 'It seems you are more than you would appear, little sparrow. Where did you get this sword?'

His hand rested casually on the hilt of *Saorsa*, but I was suddenly as alert as if he had pulled her on me.

'I found her,' I replied defensively.

'Stole her is more truthful, hey? I am doubtful that someone would just leave her lying around for you to find. She has power of her own. She sings to me. She would not let anyone take her, I think. Does she sing to you, little sparrow? Is that what the witch wants from you?'

'I know nothing about power,' I lied, grateful that my voice remained steady. 'It's just a pretty sword. I don't know what you want from me. I just want to go home.'

His face clouded, giving me less than a heartbeat's warning before he slapped my face. 'Do not play me for a fool. You are no fair maiden. You resist a shaman who can summon the dead, and you held a sword that sings to me of power. These things I know. Do not pretend otherwise. What I do not know is, how much of your strength are you aware of? And how much would someone pay to have control over you?'

I felt a cold whisper of wind blow across my neck. He was getting dangerously close to the truth of what Villermir and his crone wanted from me. Fortunately, further discussion was prevented by the arrival of one of the guards who had been given the charge of taking me to the old woman. He barked at the captain, who readily stepped back and allowed the guard to return me to the cage. The guard fussed with the lock, checking several times that it was secure before moving away to stand sentry over me and Kade. He grumbled at the captain, waving an arm to suggest that he should leave. The taller man waited for just long enough to ensure that there was no mistaking that it was his decision, before nodding at me and departing. The guard took up his position as far away from us as he could while still being able to see us clearly, still muttering to himself.

'You need to be careful of him,' Kade said quietly. 'He will find out who you are.'

'I thought you were asleep.' I grinned in the dark, relieved at having succeeded in avoiding the larger threat of the shaman. 'Don't worry. I have a plan.'

'Great,' replied Kade without any conviction.

I waited until the captain was safely beyond the line of huts, and the guard was behind me, before reaching into the waistband of my trousers and removing the tiny dagger. Being the smallest of my weapons, it was the most inconspicuous; no bigger than a table knife and having only a plain leather binding over the hilt to increase the grip. It was the one I used to lever up floorboards or jam into cracks to provide a handhold. It was not sharp enough to be used as a throwing blade or an attacking weapon, but it was one of my favourite knives. Using my nail, I separated the leather bindings on the hilt to reveal my lock-opening tools.

I felt decidedly more optimistic about our situation as I twisted my hand to hold one of the metal pins inside the lock of my shackles. Using my teeth, I carefully manoeuvred a second pin until I felt the *pop*. It was harder to unlock the other end of the shackle as my wrist was not happy to bend the other way. My ligaments complained angrily as I forced them beyond their comfortable limits. Losing feeling in my fingers, I fought to maintain the pin in the correct position while I navigated the other with my mouth. It took a frustratingly long time to release the second lock, but with one hand freed the other shackle was much more easily removed. Some of the sores beneath the iron were deep and I could see raw tissue under the eroded skin. They did not look infected, however, and I readily dismissed them, accepting that there would be a few more scars to add to my arms. The area between the wounds itched, but I resisted the temptation to damage more flesh. I tucked the tools back into my dagger hilt and hid the blade in the cuff of my boot, taking satisfaction from it being there once more. Resting the shackles back in a position that would fool a casual observer, I settled back to wait for the opportunity to release Kade and myself from the cages and get far away from Freisholm.

Chapter Twenty

During the days before the opportunity to escape presented itself, I fretted constantly about my unlocked shackles and my lock-opening tools being discovered, about Kade's worsening condition and the possibility of him succumbing to his fever, and that Villermir would arrive at Freisholm and tear my mind to shreds. My stomach was a nest of snakes. It was four days before Frick came on duty again and, as I had come to expect him to relieve himself of his post early, it would give us most of the night before our absence would be discovered. I had to force myself to stop twitching in frustration as Frick paced back and forth, resisting the temptation to join his woman. I prayed to all the Gods that tonight would not be the night that he found his sense of duty.

Finally, the noise from the hall died down and Frick decided that it was safe enough for him to retire. I wasted no time in removing my unlocked shackles and working at the lock on the door. I was unable to access the keyhole from the inside, so I had to twist my hands through the bars and it took longer than I would have liked to balance the pins and open the cage. I jumped down carefully, holding on to the metal frame so the chain would not screech at the sudden movement. I quickly moved on to Kade, who stared at me with glazed, uncomprehending eyes for a couple of heartbeats.

'Long story,' I whispered. 'Tell you about it later.'

I fumbled around, looking for the stool to raise me up level with the lock on Kade's cage. The points clicked into place easily and Kade presented his shackles to me, clamping his jaw against the pain of moving his injured arm. I removed the irons as gently as I could, but it took Kade a tremendous strength of will to prevent himself from crying out. The effort cost him;

sweat dripped from his forehead and his face had returned to the unhealthy pallor that I had seen on the day the injury was caused.

'Wait,' I commanded, supporting him with one hand while I traced the sigil with the other. Energy seeped effortlessly from my aura to his until his skin colour was a healthier paleness, and his aura shone more vibrantly. 'All done.'

I reassured him as I helped him step down, holding on to the cage to prevent as much movement as possible. Kade wobbled when his feet touched the ground and I grabbed his good arm to prevent him from falling. He swayed for several heartbeats, before regaining his strength and nodding at me to confirm that he was all right. I was required to support more than a little of his weight as we moved silently along the backs of the buildings, skirting the settlement before circling back towards the sea. We headed for a tumble of boulders to the side of the harbour, and I positioned Kade carefully between two of these, satisfied that he was hidden from view on three sides and the exposed side looked over the water. Kade was panting hard from the exertion, and I could see that he was fighting to remain conscious.

'Rest here,' I instructed him. 'I won't be long.'

His eyes widened in alarm as he grabbed my arm. 'Where are you going?'

I squatted down in front of him. 'I'm going to get our weapons. I'm not leaving *Saorsa* behind.'

He hesitated for several heartbeats before nodding in resignation. 'Don't be too long.'

I grinned at him, quietly chuckling at the madness of our situation as I left him in the darkness. I took the direct route back to the hall, dodging between the houses and keeping to the shadows. The night sky was black, with clouds frequently covering the moon. All was quiet as the Gallowglass slept. I crept up the steps to the great hall first, heading for where I knew weapons would be. The door was slightly ajar, and I could see the central fire and some of the warriors sleeping next to it as I peered round the wooden frame. Daring to look further, I saw that the fur-covered chairs on the dais were empty, and breathed a sigh of relief to find that the weapons were still on the table behind them. Between me and the swords were about twenty drunken, sleeping pirates. I sent another prayer to the Gods and pleaded that no one would wake up, before creeping along the edge of the hall. Trying to keep as much distance as possible between me and the many men and women sleeping on the tables and benches, I moved slowly, barely breathing, ever closer to the blades.

I had to pass one last table to get onto the raised platform, but this one was close to the dais and I had to move uncomfortably close to it. Two large male warriors and a female were sprawled across the wooden boards, all three snoring loudly. I edged past, trying to make myself as small as possible, but still managed to knock the arm of the nearest man. I froze as he lifted his head and looked at me with bleary eyes. He gestured vaguely towards his empty horn mug, before mumbling some instruction that I didn't understand. At my hesitation, he slapped me hard on the bottom, before dropping his head to the table with a thump. A heartbeat later he was snoring again, and I slowly released my held breath.

I moved quickly to gather our weapons, buckling Kade's sword to my hip and tucking daggers into my belt. Walking back through the hall, I even took a couple of axes that were lying unattended. I knew that if it came to a battle Kade and I had no chance of survival, but I was determined to do as much damage as possible before they killed me. I would make it very difficult for them to cage me again.

I left the hall without further incident and made my way back to the clearing where we had been caged. I had no idea where the captain was keeping my sword, so in frustration I resorted to searching all the buildings. I moved to the far side of the arena first, towards the barns where I hoped to find Puk, Geffin, Gen and the fishermen: I could not leave them behind. I quickly scanned the rough timber structure but could only find a few scrawny goats who bleated loudly at being disturbed. Disappointed, I tried to think where else the slaves could be. I opened the shutters of some of the larger buildings but found nothing. I investigated the back of the forge, but they were not there either.

I had moved from the more functional areas to the sleeping sections of the settlement, forcing me to admit defeat with regard to finding those who had travelled with me from Isle of Serpents. Either they were well hidden and I was not going to find them, or they had already been moved away from Freisholm to the slave markets further along the coast. My search turned towards finding *Saorsa*, which turned out to be equally time-consuming. I was forced to determine the occupancy of each hut, sneaking into bedchambers in order to confidently dismiss the possibility that my blade was hidden somewhere inside. I investigated at least seven buildings before I stumbled upon the captain's quarters.

It was a small building, sparsely furnished with functional items and little in the way of comfort and personal tastes. A large chest dominated the front room, ornately carved with images of ships and sea creatures. On top of this sat a collection of looted treasures: a large, oval silver plate upon which a number of rings and armbands had been scattered, a pair of decorated goblets, and a heavy gilded shield. I pocketed a handful of rings containing red and blue stones, before moving silently to the back room. My captain was sleeping, his arm draped over a slim young girl and the fur blanket only covering up to their waists. Blue tattoos covered his back and upper arms as he nestled his head into the neck of his companion. I watched their deep breathing for a few heartbeats, making sure they were not aware of my presence before I surveyed the room. Three axes lay within an arm's reach of the bed, and two swords within two paces. I smiled at his readiness for attack despite being safe within Freisholm's bay.

A wink of red light drew my attention to *Saorsa*, lying sheathed across a low chair in the corner of the room. Testing with each step for creaking loose floorboards, I crept over to hold my sword again. Despite the risk, I could not resist the urge to release her from her scabbard and delight in her smoky grey blade whispering softly as she brushed against smooth leather. Once satisfied that no harm had come to her, I re-sheathed her, pushed Kade's sword to my other hip and buckled the baldric where it belonged.

I had spent far too much time searching the settlement. The sky was turning from black to dark blue by the time I returned to Kade, finding him asleep and cradling his arm protectively. I tried to wake him as gently as I could, but he still woke with a start and cried out as he jolted his damaged arm.

'Where have you been?' he demanded. 'You were gone too long.'

'I know. I couldn't find them.'

The anger left him immediately. I did not have to explain who I had been looking for. Kade did not wish to leave the fishermen and those from the Isle of Serpents behind, any more than I did. He nodded, allowing me to help him up. As he swayed on standing, I instinctively transferred more of my energy to him via my hold on his arm. He stood taller and breathed easier almost immediately, but after a few heartbeats he pulled violently away.

'Stop that!' he snapped.

My head was a little fuzzy and I was confused by his sudden sharpness. 'Stop what?'

'Don't give me any more of your energy.' He pointed his finger at me to emphasise his point. 'You need it as much as I do.'

I shook my head, causing my vision to swim, and realised that I had given him more than I had intended. With days of poor food and ill treatment, I had overlooked how depleted my own reserves were. My generosity had left me light-headed and with trembling hands. I nodded my understanding and Kade relaxed, lowering his hand as we supported each other to the harbour. The night was still quiet, and we arrived at the docks without encountering anyone. We stepped onto the jetty, frequently looking over our shoulders, my back itching with the fear of being discovered. I could hardly believe our luck that boats were unattended. I went to the nearest small fishing vessel, checking that the oars were safely stored inside and the canvas sail was neatly fastened at the top of the central mast. I turned around to find Kade missing.

'Kade!' I hissed, scanning the jetty and harbour for him.

His raised hand flapped above the guard rail of one of the ships that had brought us to Freisholm. I scurried off the fishing boat and over to where he was searching on the deck.

'What are you doing?' I asked urgently.

'We need a seafaring vessel,' he replied, continuing to look under blankets and spare shields.

'Maybe, but I can't control this ship on my own. And in case you have forgotten, you are one step away from useless at the moment.'

He looked up as I gestured to his broken arm.

'Kade, this ship is built for sixteen rowers. I'm going to struggle with the fishing sloop that is built for two.'

Kade hesitated. 'If there is a storm...'

I sighed heavily. 'I don't have the energy to worry about problems that may not happen. All I can think about is that with this ship, we'll never get out of the harbour and the storm becomes irrelevant. With the fishing boat, we have a fighting chance of getting out of Freisholm. We'll just have to pray to the Gods that the storm doesn't come.'

'I don't have your faith, but I get your point.' He started walking towards the stern of the ship. 'Help me with this.'

'What now?' I asked as I followed him, getting increasingly frustrated by the delay.

He stopped by a collection of small wooden barrels. 'Water. I couldn't find any food.'

I gave a short, bitter laugh. 'Maybe you are *two* steps from being useless.'

Being concerned with the immediate problem of escaping Gallowgla and the threat of Villermir's arrival, I had totally forgotten about more long-term needs. We each slipped a hand through the rope handles that had been threaded into the neck of the barrel and struggled in an ungainly manner to haul it over the side of the ship, down the jetty and into the smaller fishing boat. The barrel was stowed in the bow, with Kade collapsing in the stern to balance it. There was little wind, so I left the sail folded and untied the craft from the jetty. As soon as it was free, the tide wanted to take the little vessel towards the shore, so I quickly seated myself at the first pair of oars and pulled. Growing up in a port town, I had messed around in boats but never mastered the craft. My strokes were poorly coordinated and lacked strength. It was painstakingly slow to get past the end of the jetty and into the currents of the harbour. My shoulders ached and I was panting with the effort before very long.

'We will never get far enough away by dawn at this rate,' Kade complained.

'What do you expect me to do about it?' I snapped back between puffs. 'I'm trying as hard as I can.'

Kade rolled his eyes. 'Can't you talk to the water or something?'

'Really? I'm not an Aqualine, you know!'

'No? You're not a Windtalker either, but you can control air.'

I glared at him, trying to find a counterargument, but he was right. We would not be clear of the harbour by the time the sun was up and Freisholm woke to find us missing. Sighing in defeat, I used the rhythm of my rowing to centre my mind, relaxing my vision and finally extending my thoughts to the water. Using what Cait had shown me, I visualised the threads of current that wove through the water. Picking up their energy, I encouraged them to push against the boat.

My head snapped up as my mind was forced back, breaking contact with the sea.

'What?' asked Kade.

'It's angry.'

'What do you mean, it's angry? It's water, Tallen. How can water be angry?'

I shrugged. 'I don't know. But it is.' Tentatively, I reached out again, frowning in concentration. 'Tem and Helien...'

Kade tilted his head questioningly.

'They were killed because they were Aqualine.'

Images filled my mind of Helien being murdered and thrown overboard soon after being captured. On my thought of *Why?*, the image changed to show jagged rocks just below the surface of the harbour.

'There's a rock bed just ahead. If we stay on a straight path, we'll rip the bottom out of the boat.'

Kade cursed. 'No wonder they don't bother with security. Anyone approaching, or leaving, would be seen for leagues over the grasslands below the mountains, and the sea is protected by reefs.'

I visualised the Isle of Serpents and the teaching of the Aqualine. I thought of the religion of Baila, and how Kade was the best hope of keeping the Isle safe. I pleaded for help. And waited. One heartbeat. Two. Three.

We began to move. Slowly at first, but then fast enough to create a wave at the bow of the boat. I quickly dragged the oars inside the craft to avoid them scraping on the rock bed as we travelled through, twisting this way and that to avoid the hidden shards of reef. Kade grinned at me in triumph. I glared back, wishing I had as much confidence in my abilities as he had. His smile was soon replaced by a rictus grimace as the boat veered suddenly to the left, knocking his arm. I was forced to grab the sides of the fishing vessel to avoid being thrown about as the boat shimmied around the unseen dangers. Kade and I exchanged looks: we would never have navigated these waters safely.

The sky had turned a lighter shade of blue when the boat slowed and then stopped. We had travelled out of the harbour and were in open water. Freisholm had shrunk to the size of a child's toy, as the waters lapped against the sides of the fishing craft and it rocked gently in the swell. I reached out to feel the water. All was quiet and calm, with no hint of the angry presence I had felt earlier. I was loath to ask more of the sea, grateful that we had been guided through the rock bed, so I gave my thanks, replaced the oars and set my back to the rhythm of rowing again.

Kade settled deeper into the bottom of the boat. Wrapped in a blanket, he had left his injured arm resting gently on top.

'Where to?' I asked before he could fall asleep.

'Head west,' he mumbled. 'Sooner or later we will find land. We can decide to go north to the Holy Isle or south to Faulknar depending on what landmarks we see.'

I smiled at his faith that we would find land so easily, but he had given me an idea with the use of water. I was reluctant to command the sea again, but I still had the wind. Leaving the oars for a moment, I unfurled the sail and fastened it to the base of the mast. Returning to pull against the oars, I imagined little bubbles of air bouncing against the canvas. More and more, harder and harder, until the sail billowed out behind me and we were moving at speed.

I had used wind and oar all day and had taken us far from Gallowgla. The sea was all around us and there were no landmarks to tell us where we were. I had used the sun in my face during the morning and at my back during the afternoon to keep some form of control over where we were headed, but truthfully, I had no idea where we were going. I secretly hoped that we were further north and aiming for Hilman, rather than heading south and risking landing at Lindvane. Mostly, though, I wished we would get there soon. My back ached. My shoulders were sore. My hands were blistered. My head throbbed. I was exhausted.

Kade had been quiet all day. He had occasionally brought me water, but mostly had kept as still as he could. The purple discolouration had returned to his face and neck. From the middle of his upper arm to his fingers was swollen and bruised. He was careful to keep the wound hidden from me, but violet veins radiated from the inside of his lower arm. He had frequent attacks of uncontrollable shivering, despite the sweat that ran down his temples. We might be safe from the immediate threat of Freisholm, but I needed to get him to a healer as soon as I could.

If I was to continue through the night, I needed more energy. Allowing myself to store the oars and give my painful back and shoulders a break, I rested against the side of the boat and slowed my breathing. As I had done in Kingsport, I imagined a tail extending from the base of my spine, down through the floor of the sloop and into the water. Without the confines of a protective circle, my tail was taken by the currents and pulled in all directions and the energy within it was dissipating into the water. I was losing resources rather than gaining them as I had hoped. A frown creased my forehead as I concentrated harder. Resisting the draw of the sea, I focused on the solidity of my tail, wrapping the energy around itself and forcing it through the water, which had taken on the consistency of mud.

I reached the sandy bottom and writhed my tail through this to the solid rock below. Pushing deeper and deeper, through layer after layer, closer to the pulsing energy that lay at the core. The emerging heat encouraged me on. The scales of my tail expanded in the warmth, tingling with the energy that was almost within reach. I smashed through the final barrier, into the chamber of bubbling magma. The sulphurous gases stimulated my sense of smell. The popping of lava and the cracking of rock filled my ears. The heat warmed my flesh as I basked in the radiance of pure energy. The scaly tip of my tail sank into the molten liquid, sending explosions of energy up into my solar plexus. My chest swelled and I felt my wings unfurl and stretch. A smile spread across my face from the sheer exhilaration.

'If you glow much brighter, they will be able to see us in Lindvane as well as in Freisholm.'

Kade's gentle reprimand reminded me of Drey's warning not to take too much and, reluctantly, I withdrew from the lava, giving my thanks for the energy received. I reabsorbed my wings and contracted my tail so that it atrophied back into my spine. I breathed out, producing a small puff of blue light that floated in the darkening air before dissolving. Kade refused to accept any further energy from me, despite me feeling full to bursting, so I pulled a blanket around myself and snuggled further into the curve of the boat side and watched the stars start to emerge as I filled the sail with air bubbles.

The next morning I returned to the oars. My muscles complained, but I soon settled into the rhythm of rowing whilst filling the sail with air. Kade used the nets that were aboard the boat and managed to catch a couple of fish, although even this small amount of movement tired him. He was soon asleep again after only a couple of mouthfuls. As hungry as I was, I could not manage much more than Kade. The texture of the raw fish was rubbery, and the taste was overwhelmingly salty, and fishy, and my stomach rebelled with violent cramps. I placed the remains on the spare bench, hoping that it would taste better dried, or at least taste of less.

The sun was at its highest when Kade woke. He watched me with dull, expressionless eyes while I worked at moving the fishing vessel as fast as I could. I could think of nothing to say to him, so I kept my gaze low and avoided eye contact until my attention was drawn to him as his leg started twitching. I closed my eyes and sighed: I knew what this meant. I waited with a vague feeling of nausea while the trembles worked their way through his body. It still made me jump when he started shouting.

'You, you and you. Take your companies and go over to support the right flank. No, just go and do it. Hagan! Hagan! Come here, I need you to support the rear. Mobis's Hells, man! I don't have time for this. Just go!' Kade ducked. 'Archers! Raise shields.' He was quiet for several heartbeats. 'All right. Regroup. Fill in those gaps. Pages! Get the wounded to the healers. Just move the dead out of the way. We'll deal with them later, if we're not dead ourselves.' He wiped his face with his hand. 'Fearsome Father, this is a slaughter. I can't just sit here. I need to be helping. I need to fight. The throne be damned to Mobis's Hells. There won't be a throne if we don't force them back. There's too many. There's just too many.' He moved his head slowly to the left. 'By the Gods, they're breaking through on the left. Send someone over there. Now!' He became very still. 'Tallen. Oh, Merciful Mother. No. No!' His breathing became ragged as I presumed that he ran or rode toward me. He absently wiped his face again. 'Get out of my way, man! It's not me that needs aid.' He reached out and cradled something in his arm. 'Tallen? Please, Tallen. Wake up. You have to wake up. I need you. I can't lose you.'

His voice cracked and fell silent as tears rolled slowly down his face. I sat as still as stone as awareness returned to his eyes, and with it, comprehension. He looked at me with horror. Terrified by what he had seen. Trying to fuse his vision with what was in front of him.

'It's all right,' I said gently. 'I'm right here.'

He took another shaking breath as tears ran down his face. 'I just want it to stop, Tal. I need it to stop.'

The mood in the boat remained sombre as the clouds built from the east during the afternoon. The wind buffeted from all directions and I felt I was achieving little with my wall of air against the sail. The waves became higher, rocking the little fishing craft so that on every third or fourth stroke the oars floundered in air rather than water. My stomach cramped with the fear that Kade's predicted storm had arrived, and we had no defence against it.

The storm seemed to come towards us at an unnatural speed. Every time I looked up it appeared that the clouds were closer, so that they soon covered the whole horizon and turned the sky dark. Flashes of lightning could be seen ripping across the sky and aiming to strike at the water. Sheets of rain connected the imposing clouds and the angry sea, turning the storm into an apocalyptic vision of Mobis's charging hordes.

'May the Fates take pity on us,' I said quietly. 'Do you think Villermir has discovered we are missing?'

Kade turned to find the storm had closed the distance to the horizon by half since the morning. 'If so, it looks like he doesn't know which direction we have taken, so is ripping up the entire ocean to get at us.'

Iced water ran down my spine. I sat watching the tempest race towards us, unable to move, unable to think clearly. Thoughts of rowing or channelling the wind were gone. I could think of nothing except our impending doom.

A blast of cold wind and the first splatters of rain nudged my mind back into focus. I stored the oars and lashed them down tightly to the floor of the boat, tucked under the curve of the side so no stray wave could dislodge them. Next was the sail. The wind threatened to rip the canvas from my grip one moment, then pull me overboard the next. I struggled with the heavy weight while the rain started pelting me, stinging any exposed skin. I squinted against the onslaught, the gloom as the clouds gathered overhead making it difficult to see.

Kade tried to help but was finding it difficult to rise in the wildly rocking boat. I shouted at him to stay where he was, gesturing to convey my message over the sound of the rain and wind which muffled my voice. The last thing I needed was for him to go overboard, and he soon came to the same conclusion. Frowning in frustration, he could do nothing but sit and watch me struggle. Eventually, I had removed the sail from the mast and dragged the canvas over to Kade.

'Wrap yourself in this,' I shouted into his ear. 'It will keep the worst of the rain off you, and you can stop it being blown into the sea.'

He nodded sadly, silently pleading with me to stay under the canvas with him, but there was still work to do. The waves were now high enough to wash over the sides of the boat. I grabbed a couple of mugs and gave one to Kade. We worked as hard as we could at bailing out the water. The mugs were ridiculously inadequate and there was soon a finger-length's depth of water in the bottom of the sloop.

The storm hit us with its full fury. Lightning crackled overhead, followed immediately by a boom of thunder that rattled the boat and had me cowering at the bottom of the craft. Rain as hard as hailstones pounded against flesh and wood, bouncing in the puddles that were forming everywhere, making movement around the boat slippery and potentially lethal. The waves grew higher, towering above the mast and lifting us high into the sky, before dropping us down again with a heart-stopping lurch. We gripped the flimsy wooden frame to stop ourselves being thrown around or tossed overboard.

My nails tore into the timber as I closed my eyes tight against the horrors of the storm. My wits were about to leave me. I froze, waiting for the mountains of water to tear us apart.

The storm left as quickly as it arrived, racing across the ocean in all directions. The waves rocked the boat violently, but they no longer swept over the sides. Easing my cramped hands from the boat wall, I started bailing out the water from the bottom of the boat and this time it stayed out, the rain slowing to a steady downpour. The gloom remained and I could barely see Kade at the stern. We stared at each other for a long time, neither of us really believing that we had survived. That the little fishing sloop had stayed afloat and in one piece. That neither of us had suffered any more harm than being whipped by the wind and rain.

My nerve finally broke. I stumbled over to Kade and collapsed under his arm as he lifted up the canvas for me to crawl under. I hugged him so tightly that I thought I would crush his ribs, but could not loosen my grip. My whole body shook as I laid my head against his chest, allowing his fever heat to warm me and letting my tears soak into his tunic.

'I can't do this any more,' I sobbed. 'I just can't.'

'Oh, Magpie,' he whispered into my sodden hair.

The tears flowed harder at his use of my pet name that he hadn't uttered for so long. He said no more, just stroked my back in long, soothing sweeps until I fell into an exhausted sleep.

The next morning I renewed my fight against defeat: there was never really any other option. If we were going to die here I would make the Fates work for it, so I removed myself from Kade's embrace and took back the sail. He muttered something incomprehensible, but never really woke up. I resumed my place on the bench and willed my muscles to pull at the oars, having no idea where we were or in what direction we travelled. I put air in the sail to blow us towards my general idea of westward and left the rest to the Gods.

The days and nights began to blur into each other, and I soon lost track of what was what. I fought a constant battle against exhaustion and despair. I took energy from the earth's core as I needed it, having to replenish more and more frequently. I rowed until my body could no longer respond, collapsing into a curled position on the floor of the sloop. Losing awareness of my limbs, I focused only on breathing and forcing air into the sail. Creating the air bubbles. Pushing them into the canvas. Creating more air bubbles.

Pushing them into the canvas. Through all this time, Kade did not wake. His breathing became forced and raspy, but then fell quiet. I did not look to see if he continued to breathe. Of course he breathed. Why wouldn't he be breathing? But I refused to check; fearing the intolerable. Concentrating on creating more air bubbles. Pushing them into the canvas.

At some point I felt resistance against the boat. I created more air and forced it into the sail, but the boat remained sluggish. We slowed as a grinding noise reverberated along the hull. Not having the strength to raise my head and determine the obstruction, I chose to push through it. Gathering my dwindling resources, I filled the canvas until its bindings snapped against the mast. The grating sound intensified, scraping against the timber until the sloop moved no further. I dug deep into my soul, having no more energy to tap into the earth's core. The final scraps were pieced together for one last push.

Hands grabbed my wrists and the energy dissipated back into my muscles. I put up a pathetic struggle, trying to understand how someone could be holding my wrists.

'Kade?' I croaked, confused.

A gentle laugh preceded a reply. 'Kade is fine. He's safe now. Let's worry about you.'

I cracked open my swollen and crusted eyes at the familiar voice. The sudden light provoked tears and blurred the image. I blinked, straining to make out the details. A pair of hazel eyes looked back at me.

'Drey? How can you be here? I saw you go overboard. How did you get here?'

I felt his chuckle vibrate through his chest as he lifted me up and carried me off the boat. How was Drey was walking on the ocean. What was he doing in the middle of the Northern Sea?

'As someone once mentioned, I'm a tough old goat. It takes more than a little water to see me finished. More to the point, how are you possibly here? I suspect the Gods have more than a finger or two in your destiny, Tallen. Always have. Anyway, however you came to be here, here you are. Let's get you inside and warmed up.'

He continued to prattle on as I was carried away from the sound of the tide along a shingle beach. I had no idea where we were, but I no longer cared. Drey was here. All would be well.

Chapter Twenty-One

I awoke with a sense of urgency. Something was calling me. Someone needed me. Kade!

I rose with some difficulty. I felt as weak as a newborn; as insubstantial as the wraiths in the Fenlands. I looked at my arms to find them almost translucent. The blue veins running beneath the skin were clearly visible, the limbs trembling from the small expenditure of energy needed to hold it up. I swung my legs over the edge of the simple wooden-framed bed, fumbling for the cup of water that had been left for me on the small stool within arm's reach. The cold liquid centred me, providing a physical sensation that I could focus on. I took a deep breath and stood to make my stumbling way across the room.

The small, sparsely furnished room that I had slept in led into a corridor of similar rooms. It appeared to be some form of accommodation hall, with barren but private areas for each of the inhabitants. None of the rooms were occupied as I made my way down the passage, being guided by the pull of the urgent sense of being needed. The walls were old, with timber darkened by countless generations of smoke and infused with the hint of recently snuffed candles. They were smooth to the touch from being repeatedly cleaned and brushed against. Shafts of light from the tall, narrow windows striped a floor that was covered in worn rugs; threadbare in many areas.

Opening the plain wooden door at the end, my eyes teared up in the sudden sunlight. The headache that hovered behind my left eye tightened its grip on my skull, causing me to squeeze my eyes closed and raise my arm to cover my face. I had to wait for several heartbeats before I could tolerate the light and see the community set out in front of me. Hearing the crash of waves against a rocky shore some way behind the hut, I looked over three buildings of similar construction to the one I was standing in; long, low timber shelters that were functional rather than welcoming and homely. The style reminded me of a barracks. This was a place of work, not leisure. Seabirds cawed overhead as they wheeled on the thermals and gusts of wind. Short, tufted grass was bordered by low, spiky hedgerows that contained a few scrawny goats. A cat was curled up in a patch of sunlight on the threshold of one of the buildings. No other sign of life could be seen, but a large, dark grey stone obelisk stood dominant on the edge of the settlement. Guarded by a ring of smooth boulders, it cast a powerful presence; not quite malevolent, but it made me feel uneasy all the same; as if I was intruding, warning me not to disrupt the quiet.

The urgent pull on my mind tugged again, drawing me to the building on my left. Little distinguished it from the others but there was a clear pull towards that hut. I followed obediently, savouring the feel of the solid earth beneath my feet and flexing my bare toes in the dirt with each step. I breathed deeply, savouring the scents of mud and crushed vegetation and so thankful that I was no longer floating on the sea.

On opening the door to the building, the fresh, clean smell of the island was replaced by one of death. The sickly odours of blood, infection and bodily waste assaulted my nose and stabbed the back of my throat. I quickly covered my face as my stomach threatened to add its contents to the noxious fumes. The minimal covering of dried grasses on the floor was insufficient, doing little to contain the fluid and nothing to contain the smell. Long benches lined two sides of the single room. A small altar was placed at the far wall, containing candles and a number of shallow dishes. In front of it was a thick, heavy table covered by a stained cloth. Kade lay motionless on the table, Drey cradling his head gently. The old Druid looked tired, with dark circles under his eyes and the beginnings of grey stubble on his cheeks and chin. His hands were covered in dried blood and pus, with similar staining on the front of his tunic. Several subservient men fluttered around Kade, cleaning wounds, removing soiled dressings, and applying ointments to bruising and ulceration. Kade's lower half was covered with a thick sheet, while the men worked on his chest and arms. I knew that they were trying to help, but I resented them touching him. He looked so vulnerable.

I strode towards them, trying not to think about what my bare feet were walking on. Drey shook his head slowly as I approached.

'You should be resting.'

I shrugged a shoulder as I carefully stepped over the protective circle chalked on the floor. 'I felt your need.'

'You exhausted yourself getting here. You don't have the energy required.'

I stared at him, challenging. 'Is there anyone else?'

He looked at me sadly for a couple of heartbeats before shaking his head. 'Then let's do this.'

Drey instructed the men to move away from Kade before invoking the circle. I cleared my mind and steeled my courage for a connection with the core. The protective circle made travelling through the substrate easier than it had been whilst aboard the fishing boat, but it still took concentration and I soon felt sweat trickling down my temples and between my shoulder blades. As I pushed through the soft mud of the island, into the rock, I was joined by Drey. While my energy tail was thick and muscular, covered in shimmering blue scales and ending in an inverted arrowhead, Drey's was a tangle of serpents, writhing and weaving around each other in a mess of pastel colours; apricot, peach, rose, duck-egg blue and spring-apple green. It extended with each exhalation, the blunted heads rotating and boring into the stone through the layers of pebbles from ancient beaches. We continued on through compacted peat from decomposed flora and fauna, then the bedrock studded with crystals and precious gems. We erupted into the magma cave and the intoxicating, sulphurous air swirled around us. Drey's tail of serpents glowed brighter in the poisonous gases, undulating in the ecstasy of the heat radiating from the flowing lava as we raced to pierce its surface. The muscles of my neck, shoulders, back, hips and calves melted as the energy diffused into the tissue.

I opened my eyes as I released a deep sigh of satisfaction. Small wisps of blue energy floated on my breath for several heartbeats before fading. Looking at our hands, Drey's skin glowed with a golden aura of vitality, while my mine was barely visible through the radiant glare of energy. My aura was obscured by the shards of blinding white light.

'Don't take more energy than you need,' warned Drey.

I met his concerned look and nodded in acceptance. Deep down, a primal fear was raising concerns of my own, recalling tales of people being consumed by the energy fields of the earth. Their physical presence was said to be burned away until their individual energy dissolved into that of the universe. I closed the door on these feelings and concentrated on the task at hand. I extended the energy field containing my faded aura and connected with Kade's pulsing, sickly yellow one. My body rocked forward as he snatched greedily at the energy. My vision blurred as I felt sucked into the maelstrom of Kade's auric field, buffeted by gale-force winds.

'Hold steady,' commanded Drey. 'Release your energy slowly. Do not let him take it from you.'

Drey's voice provided a foundation on which I could secure myself. I maintained control of the energy flowing through me into Kade, feeding it to him in a steady stream rather than a raging torrent. I sent feelers of energy through his aura and into the diseased tissues. The blood vessels were engorged and throbbing. The muscles and connective tissue were inflamed and angry. Pockets of foul, dull purple liquid seeped into cavities and between layers of flesh. Overlying all of this were tendrils of black smoke, wrapped around Kade's being like choking vines around a tree. I followed one to the bundle of nerves of the spine, travelling up to the base of his neck to where the tattoo had been inked into his skin. Countless vines coalesced into a seething mass of black, the tattoo appearing to attract and repel it. A coil of material attempted to flee but was drawn back like a fish on a line, oozing hate and malevolence.

Drey gently guided me away with a thought that this was a fight for another day. I returned to the inflamed and infected tissues. While Drey worked on the pools of pus, I created a covering for Kade and his torrid aura; a cocoon of healing that I forced, agonisingly slowly, towards the centre of the infection and his broken bones. Gentle pulsing of my energy field massaged the swollen tissues, breaking down knotted fibres and allowing the energy to flow freely through them. I cleansed the energy stores just above the skull, moving on to the forehead, then the throat. I worked on his heart, solar plexus, abdomen and groin. I unravelled the twists of corrupted vitality, allowing the colours to shine clear and radiant. I was able to move faster as Kade's own healed tissues helped to dissolve the obstructions and restrictions, my role adapting seamlessly between guiding the healing and supporting his own recuperative measures.

Eventually I joined with Drey at the site of the corruption. The wound surrounding the broken bones was seething with foul liquids and congested tissue. The blood ran sluggishly, a maroon taint to the fluid. Areas of necrosis filtered through the flesh, showing as dark voids of death and decay. Drey's steadying presence guided me to the shards of broken bone, enveloping me in a blanket of support as he worked on the damaged tissue. I focused on the white fragments, carefully extricating them from the surrounding flesh. I worked gently to avoid tearing any more muscle or sinew, holding the pieces together like a shattered cup. I glued the fragments together with woven energy fibres, encouraging the bone to replicate and bridge the gaps. Carefully, I threaded new blood vessels and nerves into the reconstructed callus, remodelling the bone to the natural contours of the limb. I watched, critically, as the cavity filled with marrow.

Pulling back, I found that Drey had cleared all the surrounding area of disease and decay, the healthy tissue red but vibrant. Pulling back further, I found Kade's aura to be a more natural yellow. It was bright and throbbing with the remaining inflammation, but able to cleanse itself. I extracted myself from Kade's energy flow, absently noting that I could no longer see the outline of my body despite being able to see Kade's physical form clearly. Skeletal extensions of pure energy rested on his chest, flexing as I moved my fingers. I withdrew my tail from the lava core, feeling myself sway at the sudden removal of energy. I suddenly felt a sensation of my body belonging to someone else as I fell backwards, unconscious before I hit the floor.

The smell of sweet tea permeated into my sleeping brain, mists of enticing nectar beckoning me towards wakefulness. I took a deep breath and opened my eyes. My vision was a little blurred, although it soon returned to focus and showed me the room that I had previously slept in. The steaming mug rested on the small stool, tantalisingly out of reach. My mind was awake, but my body was reluctant to leave the soft embrace of the mattress and blankets. I let out a soft moan at the prospect of having to move.

'Morning, sleepy.'

Turning my head slightly, I saw Kade sitting halfway down the side of the bed. He had the chair tipped back, with his feet balanced on the bed frame. A large leather book was open on his lap, his hands resting on the parchment.

'Morning?' I croaked.

Chuckling quietly, he placed the book on the bed and rose to help me sit up, positioning the pillows behind my back to support me while I drank the treasured tea. Ginger, with a hint of fennel and sweetened with honey. I smiled at the perfect blend that Drey had prepared for me. After so long without appropriate nourishment, the tea tasted like paradise on my tongue but sat heavily in my stomach. I released another deep sigh of satisfaction.

'Better?' Kade asked with a smile.

I rested the mug in my lap, savouring the warmth. 'Much. How about you?'

The smile became slightly more forced. 'Yet another miracle performed by the mighty Dragonslayer.'

'Oh, please.' I dismissed the claim immediately.

We were uncomfortably silent for several heartbeats. What words could convey what had happened, what had been done? It would be easiest for all to avoid the subject.

'As a bonus,' Kade continued, 'I get to be this lovely yellow colour.'

I smiled as I looked at him. His skin was pale but there was a definite yellow tint to his face and arms, and even his eyes were rimmed with lemon. 'It's just your body dealing with the poisons that are left in your system. Your liver is feeling overworked and underappreciated at the moment.'

He grinned back. 'That's what Drey said.'

I compared his arms to mine. My physical appearance had returned but there was an underlying unnaturalness to it. The translucent quality of my skin remained, with the veins easily visible and the fibres clearly defined within the muscles beneath. I took a breath to centre myself before attempting to take more energy from the lava chamber.

Kade interrupted me. 'Drey also said to not let you access the core.'

My concentration faltered as I turned to look at him, a frown of confusion on my face. 'He did not.'

'Yes, he did,' he insisted quietly. 'You've taken too much recently. Look at yourself. You're fading; being held together by energy that is not yours. How long before that energy takes what is due and your life force disperses back into the universe?'

'Oh, now you are being dramatic.'

'Am I? You know this comes with a cost. You're not indestructible, Tallen. Stop pretending that you are.'

I considered his words. I did not like them, but that did not negate what he was saying. 'We don't have time…'

'We have the time,' he insisted. 'There is no alternative.'

I looked at him to see the determination in his eyes. Truth or not, he was concerned that I was over-extending myself, and I had to admit that he had a right to that concern. It seemed I had been running at full speed for too long.

'Very well.' I sighed in acceptance. 'The boring way it is, then.'

Kade leaned back into the chair, picking up the ledger. 'So, do you want to know what I've been reading?'

I settled into the pillows, glad that the conversation had taken a safer turn. 'I'm still surprised that you can read.'

'That's funny. Forget being a Dragonslayer, you should be a court jester. I don't think you need to know about the dragons at all.'

I groaned dramatically. 'For the love of Mobis, Kade. You are obsessed with dragons.'

'As should you be. There are so many histories here. So much detail of how things used to be. There was a time when dragons were an integral part of life.' He ignored my sceptical look and continued enthusiastically. 'Most of the histories are about legal trials and who owed what. Normal, boring stuff. But these scholars have collected an amazing amount of information on all manner of different topics. It seems an old scholar had an interest in the Ancients and the ways of the Empaths, Aqualine, Firewalkers and, most importantly, Dragonslayers. I have no idea where he got this stuff from, but there are ledgers and scrolls dating back generations. I mean, some of these things must have been written only a few years after the dragons disappeared.'

He had a look in his eyes that I hadn't seen in a long time. He was having fun.

I shook my head and smiled at him. 'Really?'

He grinned back. 'Oh yeah. You can read the accounts of the Empaths, Firewalkers and Aqualine for yourself. But the dragons are the main thing. The scrolls talk about five of them flying around the three kingdoms. The descriptions are breathtaking. Muscular giants with wings that could span a village. Dragons with horns extending from their foreheads. Dragons with spines along their backs. Talons that could rip open a horse without slowing the monster's flight.'

All trace of the joy he had started the conversation with had disappeared. A small frown creased between his eyebrows as he was lost in the images the texts had delivered into his imagination.

'The five were different colours,' he continued after a short pause. 'A vibrant emerald-green one. A black one edged in gold along its wings and the ridges of its face. A sapphire-blue one with golden eyes and silver flecking on its scales, so that the skin rippled in flight. Another was creamy white with purple shading along the eyebrows, jawline and spine. The last was an interlacing of purple and red scales, iridescent shades that shimmered when in flight.'

My head throbbed, sending shards of pain through my left eyebrow and up my spine into my brain. I sat very still as Kade spoke the last, vital piece of information.

'That's the dragon of my vision. She's the one.'

He looked at me with a mixture of despair and unbearable responsibility. 'There is an account of her, and the others, destroying the coastal town that was to become Liegeport.'

'So you think that your vision is… what? Some sort of ancestral memory?'

He shook his head.

'A warning not to go chasing dragons?' I added hopefully.

He gave a small twitch of a smile at my desperation, but again shook his head. 'No. I think she is coming to finish what she started.'

The next day I was left to my own devices and, predictably, I was soon bored and eager to leave my sickbed. I rose slowly, but the room still spun for several heartbeats. It felt like ice water pouring down my face as the blood left my head, my heart hammering to compensate. Several deep breaths were needed before my vision cleared and my shaking subsided to a tremble.

Clean clothes had been left on the chair with *Saorsa* and my knives, but I could not find my boots. The cold of the timber floor tickled my soles as I left the room and walked down the corridor. The cool breeze was refreshing as I opened the final door and stepped out into the morning sunshine. Closing my eyes against the bright light, I lifted my face to the sky and soaked up the warmth of the late spring sun. I found a simple pleasure in smelling coarse grass and sea salt, and hearing the seabirds call to each other.

I walked slowly through the green arena that was created by the arrangement of the four buildings, having to concentrate on where to place my feet in order to keep my balance. I headed towards the stone obelisk as simply dressed men quietly went about their business. I received a few nods of greeting, but most were not concerned with my presence, being more interested in whatever tasks they were involved in. I walked past the hut closest to the stone pillar to see Kade practising with his sword at the base of the tower. I sat in a patch of sunlight to watch and critically appraise his healing arm. His strokes were fluid, muscles tensing and relaxing easily under the cloth of his tunic, joints flexing and extending through a full range of movement. Sweat had darkened the cloth at the armpits and the triangle between his shoulder blades, attesting to the effort that it was costing him to perform the routine manoeuvres, but I was content that he was healing fast.

After a while Drey came to join me, smiling as he sat next to me. 'Glad you two are getting along,' he teased.

I shrugged. 'Well, there's not much else happening. And, you know, after you save someone's life you feel protective of them.'

Drey nodded solemnly. 'I believe that is twice you have saved his life now.'

I waved away the compliment. 'I don't like to keep count.'

'I can hear you,' Kade interrupted.

I grinned. 'You keep practising and let the grown-ups speak,' I mocked.

Kade barked a short laugh but did not hesitate in his swordplay. One position flowed effortlessly into the next to create an intimate dance with his blade.

'He looks well,' I commented to Drey.

'Yes, he does.'

At the tone of his voice I turned to find him looking at me with concern.

'But how are you?'

I frowned. 'I'm all right.'

'Your cheek is healing, but you have a nasty crack on the back of your head. How long did you see ghost images?'

I tried to dismiss his worry, but I should have known better. 'I'm fine,' I started, but was halted by his scowl. 'Three or four days,' I admitted, to a disapproving humph. 'But I'm fine now. Just a little tired.'

'I'm not surprised. Any loss of memory?'

'No. Unfortunately I remember everything.' I sighed, rubbing my aching temple. 'Just a headache. That's all.'

'You need to drink more. You are dehydrated. Some food would be helpful too.'

I pushed against him gently. 'I know. In a little while, all right?'

We sat in a comfortable silence, watching Kade flash his sword in the sunlight. It felt good to have the three of us together again, and to know the other two were safe. My breath faltered as I was sharply reminded of those who were not safe.

'I couldn't save them,' I said quietly.

'That is not your fault,' replied Drey, as quietly.

'Maybe, but since I turned up at the Isle of Serpents, three Aqualine bloodlines have been lost. And those are the ones I know about. How many were lost in the flood?'

Drey shook his head slowly. 'You cannot blame yourself for what Villermir and the Gallowglass do.'

'What they did because of me,' I insisted. 'I couldn't find the fishermen, or Gen, Geffin and Puk. They branded them as if they were cattle.'

Drey sighed. 'Gallowgla has always made its money from piracy and slavery. Those are not new professions. To be truthful, much of the three kingdoms' wealth was founded on slaves. We claim we are more enlightened now, and condemn the Gallowglass practices, but we pay our labourers such low wages and give them so few options I sometimes wonder if our system is much better.'

'But we sit here, chasing folk stories of dragons and Ancients when who knows what is happening to them?'

Drey frowned. 'The practice of slavery is inherently cruel and the Gallowglass are hard taskmasters, but slaves are valuable to them. They should be all right until we can get to them.'

'But, Drey, it's not right,' I snapped in frustration.

'There are lots of things that are not right, Tallen. We can't fight them all. We have to pick our battles. You know that.'

'But dragons, Drey. Really? Is that more important than them?'

Drey gave me a look that threatened anger. 'There are countless slaves all over Gallowgla. Are you planning on saving them all, and creating another war for Faulknar to deal with? Or are you just going to save those you know about?'

I opened my mouth for some cutting reply but closed it almost immediately. Drey was right. I was only thinking about those I knew, those who had travelled with me. I had not even considered those who had been taken over the years; fishermen who did not come back and traders who had disappeared. Their stories had remained cautionary tales for me; I had not put faces to them or their families.

'What happened, Tallen?' Drey asked quietly. 'Kade has told what he can remember, but a lot of that time is a blur for him.'

I rubbed at my forehead. 'It was all right.'

'Tallen!'

I sighed. 'It was horrid, but talking about it is not going to change that. It could have been worse. After they broke Kade's arm they pretty much left us alone. I think they were scared of us, or perhaps what would happen to them if anything happened to us.'

'Scared of you, were they?'

'Well, there was one guard who was scared of Kade's visions. Thought he was possessed or something.'

Drey sniffed in morbid amusement. 'And you? Were they scared of you?'

'No. Not really. They mostly ignored me.'

I was quiet for several heartbeats as I tried to organise the memories of Freisholm that I had been avoiding. Drey waited patiently for me to continue.

'What do you know of blood sacrifice?'

Drey tilted his head. 'Blood sacrifice is very old magick. I had not known that Gallowgla was still practising this type of ritual. Their religion reflects the land and its people. It is tough and harsh. Their Gods war with each other and use humans as playthings. But blood sacrifice taps into deeper, and darker, times. Describe it for me.'

I recalled the process as unemotionally as possible; the arrangement of the people, the drumbeats, the chanting and the fire. I described the healthy sacrifice and the collection of his blood, the sigils painted in blood on the face of the priest, and on a selected few within the crowd that reflected the markings on the sacrifice. I stopped abruptly after telling Drey of the drinking of the blood by the crone, my mind shying away from the memory.

'Tell me about the shaman,' prompted Drey when I failed to continue.

'She scared me,' I replied honestly. 'She had real power. Not like you or Sutha. Not like Villermir, even. Something older, more primal. Does that make sense?'

He nodded solemnly. 'There are many types of magick. Some channel the natural energies and involve balance. Some are more primitive and channel darker sources; those released by death and the consumption of blood. It is said that the rituals can summon daemons and release plagues. I am more inclined to believe that they work within the accepted boundaries of magick, but for more malicious purposes.' He paused. 'Was the shaman interested in you?'

I was quiet for a few heartbeats as I considered what to tell him. 'She had a crystal like the one we found in Bream. I'm sure she used it to speak to Villermir. It seemed she was interested in what I was to him.'

I saw no benefit in relaying the attempt at entering my mind. We had been there before and Drey knew how Villermir could freely access my thoughts. I refused to revisit the summoning of the Fates, knowing that Drey would want to know every detail of what I was trying very hard to forget.

Drey waited for me to provide more information, but soon accepted that I was not ready for that. He stood suddenly, brushing leaves and dust from his clothes. He offered me a hand to help me rise, steadying me with a hold on my arm as I found my balance. He continued to hold my arm, gently turning me away from Kade and leading me towards the buildings.

'How do you feel about a little research?' he asked.

'Reading?' I asked, unenthusiastically.

Drey laughed. 'Yes, Tallen. Reading. The library here is incredible. There are scrolls from so many generations ago. Information from so many different sources, on so many topics. You have to see the leather tomes on the Ancients. The illustrations are unbelievably intricate; the colours still vibrant after all this time.'

I smiled to hear Drey nattering happily, even though I did not understand what was so special about a bunch of old parchments. I was not looking forward to spending time with the musty tomes but accepted that my body was not ready for anything physical, while my mind needed stimulation.

We strolled slowly towards one of the huts. I suspected that Drey had slowed his pace to suit mine, particularly when the building turned out to be the area for cooking and eating. Several rows of tables and benches covered half the hall, while preparation surfaces, storage areas and three cooking fires filled the other half. My stomach grumbled in response to the odours of roasting meat and baking loaves. Drey took that as permission to hand me a mug of steaming broth and a sizeable chunk of bread. He continued to describe the marvels of the library while I consumed both, not allowing any morsel of food to be refused. It sat heavily in the base of my stomach, but the warmth penetrated my muscles pleasantly and I gained energy from the nutrition.

When Drey was finally content that I had eaten enough, he guided me towards the final building within the quadrangle. As I stepped inside, I wondered how the four huts that looked the same from the outside could be so different on the inside. The large space of this one had been separated into several alcoves. Lines of shelves jutted out from the walls to divide the area into cosy nooks, where a table and several chairs provided an opportunity for many people to work without seeming to crowd each other. Two long tables, with benches either side, ran the central length of the building and were covered with a scattering of papers and ledgers. A number of men sat, transcribing passages and drawing illustrations from the texts in front of them.

Drey led me to one of the few alcoves that were empty of scholars. He left me sitting while he went to talk to one of the illustrators at the main table. The younger man indicated the section further down the building and Drey went off to retrieve two large books and a few scrolls. He placed them carefully on the table in front of me, his hand hovering reverently over them for a couple of heartbeats. I rolled my eyes, causing him to smile at himself.

'Treat these with care,' he instructed. 'They are older even than me!'

He patted my shoulder before leaving me to my studies. I looked round at the others in the library, all focused intently on their work. They were all men, their ages ranging from young adults to frail elders. All wore simple clothing, many with ink stains on the cuffs of their sleeves. All treated the texts carefully, as if they would crumble to dust at the slightest breath. I looked down at the work Drey had selected for me, suppressing a groan, and picked up the first scroll. The writing was archaic, and I had to concentrate to pick out the words. The curling of the letters joined the words together, with the 'f' and the 's' letters looking similar. It took me a long time to get my head around the style of writing before I could read at any speed. Absently, I rubbed at the left side of my forehead as I read an account of animal sacrifice. Those used were mainly small animals such as chickens or piglets, but occasionally larger animals such as bulls or horses were used to signify a greater cost to the population or an individual. There were similarities with the ritual I saw at Freisholm, with the use of clay to paint sigils on the sacrifice, but there was no mention of what those markings might mean.

I moved on to the next scroll. This one had a more contemporary style and I was able to scan the writings to identify anything of interest. Again, it detailed the sacrifice of animals at the important festivals. It suggested that animals were also sacrificed prior to battles where the Gods of War were to be appeased and encouraged to look favourably on the engagement. The next two scrolls told a similar story, and I soon gave up on those to move on to the larger of the two tomes. The leather of this one was soft and supple, reminding me of a journal rather than an academic text, although its size would prohibit it from being carried far. The text was again ancient, but the illustrations clearly showed the content, making it easy to find what I was looking for. I leafed past images of Gods and Goddesses fighting each other with spears of lightning and hammers of rock. Pictures of mythical beasts such as giant wolves, hideous trolls and massive serpents. Momentous battles involving hordes attacking each other over mountainous regions, or sea battles with fleets of the sleek ships still used by the Gallowglass.

About halfway through the ledger I found an image of a ritual human sacrifice. My stomach clenched at the similarities with what I had witnessed. The text told of the selection of the sacrifice. A young, healthy male was chosen, often up to a year before the ritual, and treated reverently from the time of naming. The best food was given to him, and he was exempt from performing any labouring duties. The one requirement of him was that he stayed in peak physical fitness to please the Gods with his presence. The feasting hall in the afterlife was reserved for those killed in battle, but those sacrificed to the Gods were also offered a place, as favoured servants of the God they were sacrificed to. Clay markings were used to summon the spirits of the ancestors to guide the sacrifice on the path to the Gods' festival hall. Specific deities required specific sigils to gain their attention. The quality of the sacrifice would determine whether the request would be granted.

The next page gave more details about the darker aspects of the sacrifice, confirming my fears regarding the role of the old woman. It stated that the presence of a shaman generally meant that the more malevolent spirits were summoned alongside the favour of the chosen God or Goddess. The shaman would use chanting and the burning of incense to entice the souls of those who were suspended in the wastelands outside the feasting hall; those who could only look in on the excesses and simmer with resentment. Along with those souls, the shaman would summon the daemons of suffering and torment. These daemons could then be used to corrupt the thoughts of those they encountered, causing nightmarish hallucinations and wasting sicknesses.

I stopped reading. I had enough to terrify me with Villermir; I did not want to think about what the shaman could do about destroying the world.

Chapter Twenty-Two

We stayed for several days to allow Kade and me to recuperate, falling into a gentle routine. In the mornings I would rise and spar with Kade. It took considerable persuasion for me to face him over a sword after the incident in Liegeport, but his temper stayed in check as we practised in front of the stone pillar. I was hopelessly outmatched, despite his healing arm. I tired easily and was frequently tempted to draw on the core's energy, ensuring the sessions encouraged the practice of willpower as well as the retraining of my muscles. Kade's injury did not seem to impede him, although he controlled his swing to avoid overtaxing me. His movements were fluid and precise and I was confident his healing was progressing well.

After weapons practice I would help with the midday meal, preparing vegetables and roots before serving to the twenty or so scholars who lived on the island. I ate my meal, trying to pay attention as they discussed their studies with Drey. They talked mainly of herb lore or medical texts, but sometimes referred to ancient customs and the use of Aqualine and Firewalkers. I did not know much about Firewalkers, so I found it easy to listen to them discussing their role in the forging of weapons and the making of armour. It was said that the Firewalkers could heat the forges to extreme temperatures that would temper the steel to be lethally sharp. Blades could cut through rock as easily as they cut through flesh. Armour was created from molten metals that were poured into clothing to allow flexibility, but could also turn arrows, swords and axes. The Ancients were not a warring culture, however, and the Firewalkers would create jewellery and statues that were breathtakingly intricate. The text had illustrations of tiny winged creatures and delicate sculptures that the scholars said were awe-inspiring, despite the illustrator's comment that the images did not do the real thing justice.

After the meal I would help to clear and clean the tables before having the rest of the day to amuse myself. At first, I would often retreat to my room and rest while I waited for the world to stop spinning and my head to stop imploding. After a few days, while the headache remained, I no longer felt light-headed after my sparring sessions with Kade and I was able to function in the afternoons. Several times I descended to the beach to sit alone and play with the elements. Although I was able to create funnels and small walls of water, I always felt that I was intruding and that the sea was reluctant to yield to my requests. It may have been my own guilt, but I was sure that there was some sentience that had still not forgiven me for the deaths of the Aqualine. In the end I returned to the beach for solitude but left the sea in peace. Instead I focused on elements I was more comfortable with – fire and air. Inspired by the tales of the Firewalkers, I attempted to make my fireballs as hot as I could. They glowed red before turning orange, yellow and finally white. I felt the heat on my face and palms even though I hovered them several arm-lengths away. The air shimmered in a vibrating corona, catching the colours of the rainbow as it turned what little moisture was available into steam. I would release the contained inferno into sparks that flew into the air, changing back through the colours of white, yellow, orange and red as they cooled. Occasionally I would blast the fireball into the sand, creating tiny glass beads as the grains melted and reformed. The beads I would pick up in small whirlwinds, to dance and reflect the captured light from the sun, turning the sand into a kaleidoscope of different colours.

Very occasionally, I went to the library.

The summer solstice was celebrated while we were staying at the Holy Isle. Many of the scholars seemed to resent the distraction from their studies, but Drey insisted that the festival was observed, so weapons practice was cancelled for the day to enable me to help with the preparation of the food. The island had few luxuries, so the festival food was much the same as the everyday food but for a young goat that was butchered and roasted over a firepit near the standing stone. The grass was cut around the obelisk to reveal a ring of boulders that surrounded the central structure. Markings had been scratched into the surfaces of these stones to create upright parallel lines in groups of threes or fours, with occasional diagonal slashes through the groups.

'It is an ancient language,' explained Drey. 'One we have lost the knowledge to interpret.'

'Is that why this place is called the Holy Isle?' I asked, brushing the moss away so I could see the markings clearly.

'Indeed. The scholars are very pious in their own way, but the name comes from a time before the three kingdoms. After the Ancients had gone, but before the cities of man. Priests and priestesses would spend their entire lives on the island, living on what was available; mainly roots and fish. They had little contact with the mainland and little was known about their practices here.' Drey sighed sadly. 'They did not feel the need to leave written accounts of their rituals and studies, so that information has been lost.'

Drey retreated to his room in the early evening, saying that he needed to prepare. Kade had as little idea as I had of what he might mean by that, so we refused to speculate and instead helped ourselves to the food that was available. The scholars brewed a type of ale that was sweetened with honey. It had a pleasant effect on the mood and soon the small gathering started to feel like a festival celebration. Seabirds circled overhead, hoping for some morsel to scavenge but not daring to come too close. One young scholar threw a crust to a bird that caught it in mid-air. Cheers of appreciation were generously given, until his next attempt resulted in the crust landing on an elder's bald head and a chorus of mocking jeers.

The sun was a hand-width above the stone pillar when Drey returned. He was carrying a dark wooden staff, around the top of which he had tied the rose quartz crystal that usually hung around his neck. His face was smeared with what looked like clay paint, although the soil on the island was dark and rich, and as he drew closer, I realised that the paint was made from ash. I shivered as the markings reminded me of the Gallowglass ritual, although instead of geometric patterns Drey had drawn one large circle starting at his forehead, travelling down his cheeks and finishing just below his bottom lip. The circle had been divided into four, with lines running from cheek to cheek across the middle of his nose, and from his forehead, between his eyes, down his nose and over his lips. The lines extended beyond the circle by the length of a fingernail. Dots were placed at the four terminal points of these lines. His eyes had been highlighted with paint circling them, reflecting the light and making the eyes deep wells of shadow.

As Drey approached Kade and me, he raised the small bowl that he was holding and dipped his fingers into it. The grey paste glistened as he shook off the excess before drawing circles on our faces. He omitted the large crossed lines that divided his face, instead drawing a single line down our noses. It almost seemed comical, but the atmosphere had turned from that of a slightly drunken festival to one that was darker and more primitive. The ritual felt as old as the stones that surrounded us. I felt apprehensive at the possibility of dark forces being released as they had been in Freisholm, but I trusted Drey without question. I obediently followed him to the standing stone so that Drey, Kade and I formed a triangle around its base. The scholars gathered in a random collection within the boundary stones but left a respectful space around the three of us.

Drey started singing. I had rarely heard his crystal-clear tone since leaving Methhold. The hairs at the nape of my neck and along the length of my forearms stood up as if called by his voice. He started softly, breathing the words of a language long forgotten by most. The lilting melody was almost a lullaby in its gentleness and calm. He raised the octave as he raised the volume; a more insistent vibe, but still relaxing and accepting of those captured by its spell. I felt tears welling within my lower eyelids, not because the music was sad but because it reminded me of my village. Treasured memories of both the ceremonies held there, with my grandfather singing, and my family's funeral eulogy that had been performed by Drey.

My tears could no longer be contained when Kade added his voice to Drey's. Silent streams trickled down my face as the beauty of Kade's harmonies wove around Drey's melody. The air was still and the birds had gone quiet, so that the only sounds were their two voices. Without understanding the words, the tune conveyed elements of joy and hope. From the ceremonies I had witnessed as a child, I knew the solstice was a time for rejoicing for the plentiful harvest to come. The blessings of the Gods and the keeping of the Fates away from those who could be harmed. The love and support from family and friends. I looked at Kade and Drey and knew that I had been blessed this night.

The sun had dropped so that the stone cast a long shadow between Kade and Drey. From my position behind the pillar I saw the shadow trail towards the hut where Kade had been healed; the one that contained the elementary altar. I doubted it was by accident. I closed my eyes and opened my mind to the ley currents that radiated from the stone. One travelled through the hut, while others fed various points of the island. The grass soaked up the vigour emanating from the energy lines and channelled by the solstice ceremony.

Small creatures living within the soil stretched as they felt the warmth of the currents diffusing into the earth. I travelled deeper, exploring the layers and the secrets within. It was unlike my passage to the core, where I prodded my way through the sediment; this sensation wove effortlessly through my senses. Touch and smell became as diverse as the sense of colour – rich, musty odours mixing with ripe vegetation; the different minerals releasing their life-giving nutrients in a cacophony of tiny, tingling sparks and explosions. Travelling deeper still I found a forest of crystals, their colours hidden by the darkness to allow the chiming of their energies to become the dominant sensation. Clear notes tinkled like a universe of crystal peals, harmonies intertwining to create an orchestra of delicate bells.

The cadence of Kade's and Drey's singing changed. Dissonant tones were introduced to guide me back to the surface. Sharper notes to provide clarity and context. The warm embrace of the earth gave way to the fresher air of the island, the scents of loam replaced by the tang of seawater. I opened my eyes to find that the sun had set and the moon was floating over the sea; a pure, watery crescent reflected in the rippling waves. I took a deep breath, grounding myself in the reality of the standing stone and its protective boulders. The men's voices faded into silence, developing into an expectant pause while everyone slowly returned to themselves. A collective sigh travelled through the scholars and, as I looked at their faces in the muted shades of twilight, I realised that many of them had not experienced a Druid solstice before. They wore expressions of awe and bewilderment. Even without being able to commune with the earth as I had, they were still touched by the forces unleashed by the solstice at Drey's summoning. I was sure a new area of research on the Isle had been encouraged that night.

The next day brought the type of rain that soaked whoever dared walk from one building to the next. Desiring to stay dry, I was left with little option but to venture into the library. Understandably, it was busy, with most of the islanders buried within books and under mountains of scrolls. Kade was already there and beckoned me over, sliding along the bench to give me room to sit next to him.

'Look at this one,' he whispered, passing me a ledger with an ornately decorated leather cover. 'I haven't had a chance to read it yet, but I saw some good illustrations of dragons in there.'

I sighed loudly, earning disapproving looks from the others at the table. 'Dragons?'

Kade grinned. 'I've learnt more in a few days here than in all my time spent studying at Liegeport. It really is an amazing place.'

I raised an eyebrow at him, not convinced that this was such an amazing place as he seemed to think, but, resigned to a boring day of reading, I turned to the text. The first page was blank, protecting the parchment from the leather bindings, followed by a full-page illustration of a market scene. The style of dress was unfamiliar, but the arrangement of the stalls and the bustling crowds could have been seen in any town in Faulknar. I turned the next page and skimmed the text for anything exciting. As predicted, the author spoke about trade within this port of Doventon and I quickly became bored. I turned page after page in quick succession, earning an exasperated scowl from Kade, before settling in to read the text more closely.

I was almost at the back of the book, and my stomach was grumbling in anticipation of the midday meal, when I finally found something that related to dragons. There were a number of illustrations as Kade had said, including a particularly graphic one that showed a black dragon resting on a mountain, a half-eaten carcass pinned beneath its talons. Most of the images were of the creatures soaring over settlements or battling each other on the wing, the colours of scarlet, emerald and sapphire vibrant on the page despite the age of the document. The size of the beasts and the ferocity with which they fought was plainly evident, and the text continued on this theme, expanding upon the physical attributes of the dragons; wingspans that could cast shadow over a hamlet, talons as large as a man. I briefly wondered how they had measured them without being eaten, before accepting that seeing a person grasped by a talon would be enough to implant the size of the claws in your brain for the rest of your life. The book went on to describe the cost to a cattle farmer if the dragons flew over. It seemed that they often consumed entire herds before moving on. There were accounts of villages being burnt to ash by one blast of a monster's fire. Each leviathan had a different colour fire that could be expelled from the mouth. Red, orange, yellow, blue or white blazed from gaping jaws. There were dragons with horns, dragons with spurs, dragons with fangs dripping with poison. They had tails that lashed like battle maces, limbs that crushed like fallen mountains, eyes that could captivate and beguile. Their colours ranged from ebony to ice white, warm amber to sharp cobalt. The prose was effusive but there was a clear sense of the danger and beauty of these creatures. Feared and despised, but also respected and venerated. The people who had lived with these fantastical beasts had conflicted emotions about them, which did little to ease my apprehension about what Drey was expecting me to do.

I looked up from the book to find Kade watching me with a strange expression on his face.

'What?' I asked.

He hesitated for a few heartbeats, before shoving the text he was reading towards me. 'I think you should read this,' he said quietly.

I frowned at his odd behaviour but took the ledger. The style was archaic, so I assumed that it was older than the one I had been reading. It talked of five dragons and how they related to the five Dragonslayer bloodlines. It described some sort of link between the creatures and their Slayers, each being bonded to a specific partner. The colours of their skin reflected the stones in the hilts of the swords given to the Slayers. The bearer of *Fírinn*, the sword of Truth, was paired with the blue dragon with golden eyes to match the yellow diamond of the sword's hilt. The white-and-purple dragon was paired with the bearer of *Dlighé*, the sword of Duty with amethyst eyes. The Slayer carrying *Íobair*, Sacrifice, was bonded with the black dragon to reflect the jet within the sword's hilt. The green dragon was bonded with the carrier of *Ceartas*, Justice, with its emerald eyes. Finally, those who held *Saorsa*, the sword of Freedom, bonded with the pink-and-blue dragon. The ruby of the hilt reflected colour change to red and purple shown when that dragon was angered.

I rubbed my left temple as the persistent headache throbbed behind my eye. I continued to read as the description went on to explain the nature of the bond between the Slayers and their dragons. It seemed that Dragonslayers would be aware of their partnered dragon no matter how far away they flew. Attacks on distant villages and towns were known of by the Slayers before messengers could be sent. They would know if their dragon was involved and what the damage had been. I looked up to see Kade watching me closely.

'I feel no bond with this dragon,' I said. 'Are you so certain that your visions are real?'

He replied with a dullness of tone that chilled me. 'Read on.'

The author went on to observe that, stranger than the ability to know where the dragon was at any time, was the apparent link between the creature and the Slayer's health. It was recorded that whenever the leviathan was injured, the Slayer felt its pain. If the dragon died, the Slayer would sicken until they too faded and died.

I felt numb, and turning to Kade I could see this reflected in his blank expression.

'So, this is my fate. We find your dragon, and either it eats me or, if by some miracle I can kill it, I die anyway.'

I slept fitfully that night. I was faced with an impossible decision. Assuming that the dragon existed, I could avoid the situation by running away and leaving Kade and Liegeport to their own fates. But where would I go? And how could I live with myself, knowing that I had sentenced everyone I knew to death? Alternatively, I could go and face the behemoth, get myself killed trying to save everyone, or die anyway if I managed to defeat the monster. My mind raced round and round with no obvious route of escape. The snatches of sleep I managed to get were filled with images of dragons breathing fire and burning villages. Methhold became the target, although I knew that it had been burned by Lindvane raiders, not the purple-and-red monster I was dreaming of.

At some point my dreams turned to the familiar territory of the mountain. I soared over the island, the mountain standing proud on the grassland as the ocean lapped all around the rocky coastline. After circling the sentinel twice, my vision settled on the ledge that protruded halfway up the ragged rock. The dark half-moon entrance stood as a portal to an underworld. I stepped into the darkness and let the damp, cold air brush my face. Taking a breath that felt thick and clammy in my lungs, I started down the tunnel, resisting the urge to place my hands on the walls. Willing myself not to lower my head. Knowing that the stone boundaries were not getting closer, despite my mind screaming otherwise. One foot in front of the other. Always moving forward. Never turning back.

I startled at the sound of the slow, slithering scrape. Scaled flesh being dragged over the rough surface, irregular movement making it impossible to predict when it would sound again. With wobbling legs, I moved closer to the sound, being forced by the left-hand passages to travel deeper into the mountain. The air in the tunnel grew warm, with a trace of rotten sulphur. My lungs struggled to expand and take in the air that I needed. My head became thick, making it difficult to concentrate. I automatically followed the forks to the left, trying to focus on my breathing rather than the terrifying thought of being buried under an unimaginable weight of rock.

My face started to burn as the heat was raised to an uncomfortable temperature. Sweat beaded on my forehead and upper lip, seeping into my eyes and making them sting. Rubbing them made them water more, until tears were streaming down my cheeks. I suspected that not all the tears were a response to my irritated eyes. Frustration at my inescapable situation was burning in my chest as much as the heat on my face. The acrid taste of the air scratched the back of my throat; my nails scraping on the rock as I felt my way along the tunnel. A glimpse of scarlet ahead, before it disappeared around a corner.

My heart raced at the confirmation that something else was in the mountain with me. The clack of claws on the granite floor. The scrape of scales. The quiet rasp of breathing. Cautiously, I reached the corner and peered round. All was darkness. I crept forward, stumbling as my trembling legs struggled to support my weight. Again, a flash of scarlet at the height of my head, before it vanished. Another junction. Another left turn. I turned into the passage and froze. I had time enough to register the massive head in front of me. A blunted lizard nose that was the size of a horse loomed out of the darkness, no more than ten paces from me. The dark purple of its upper head blended into the black of the tunnel, while the scarlet jaw and throat stood out in vibrant contrast. The slit pupils of a cat looked out of orange eyes the size of a cartwheels. Intelligence flared behind those eyes, and an annoyance at the disturbance. It opened its maw to reveal sharp ivory teeth as long as my arm. Fear forced me to pay attention to the small, lethal details such as the serrated inner edges of the individual triangular teeth. The dragon took deep breath in before releasing it in a river of blue fire.

I awoke suddenly, my heart pounding and my lungs gasping for breath. I waited for the agony of molten skin, and it was several rapid heartbeats before I realised that I was awake and safe in my room on the Holy Isle. Sweat had stuck my nightshirt to my back and I started to shiver in the cold early-morning air. Quickly washing my face and neck in the small basin of cold water, I dressed and walked outside to find a few scholars already wandering the compound, preparing for the day. I could smell the smoke from the cooking fires as bread was baked and porridge simmered.

I headed towards the altar building that also served as an infirmary. Drey had stored many of his herbal supplies there and I was hoping to find some willow bark, or at least some peppermint, for a tea. The persistent headache over my left eyebrow and at the base of my skull was getting harder to ignore. In an effort to keep my head still, the muscles of my neck and shoulders were starting to knot. I was tempted to chop my head off, just to be done with it all.

As I entered the hut, the familiar scent of Drey's herbs enveloped me like a hug. A couple of beds had been added since Kade had been brought here, and these had been placed at angles near the tables holding Drey's supplies and the few tools the scholars had for lancing boils and removing teeth. I was surprised to see Drey was already in the infirmary, applying salve to the hand and arm of a young man.

Drey looked up as I approached. 'You're up early,' he said in greeting.

'Could say the same for you.' I nodded at the young man being attended to. 'What happened here?'

The patient grimaced. 'Wasn't looking where I was going. Tripped over and nearly fell into the fire. Splashed oil all over my arm.'

I winced in sympathy. 'That must to hurt.'

The young man shrugged as Drey started bandaging the injured area. 'More embarrassed than hurt, I think.'

Drey sniffed. 'Give it time. This is going to be very sore, for several days.'

I smiled at Drey's characteristic understatement and moved to his supplies, looking for the leaves for a tea. I rummaged through several packages but could not find willow bark or peppermint.

'Something I can help you with, Tallen?' asked Drey in a tone that made it clear I had not handled his herbs with sufficient respect.

Distracted, I continued searching. 'Do you have any willow bark?'

'Why?'

I did not miss his change of tone. Turning with a smile, I tried to dismiss his suspicion. 'No reason. Just thought it might be a good idea to have some around. You know, in case Kade's arm gives him any pain.'

He was not fooled. 'What hurts?'

'Nothing, Drey,' I flustered. 'It's just a headache.'

'Still?'

I cursed myself for saying the wrong thing.

'Sit.'

He gestured the bed that the young scholar had just vacated, as I desperately tried to think of a way to excuse myself.

'Honestly, it's nothing. Just need some air...'

'Sit!'

Submissively, I dropped onto the thin mattress and allowed Drey to press the back of my skull and feel around my cheek.

'The energy you took from the core should have healed your fractures, but let me check to see if any damage remains. Maybe there is some scarring that is causing a blockage in your energy lines.' He sighed in frustration. 'Nothing obvious. Lie down and let me give you a full check-over.'

I lay back, carefully positioning my head on the pillow. I closed my eyes and allowed the pillow to take the weight of my head and support my neck, relaxing my shoulders. Breathing out slowly, I relaxed the rest of my muscles and waited for Drey's touch. As his hands traced my aura, I felt a sensation close to tingling but not as defined. The slightest connection stimulated the nerves in my skin into tiny vibrations. Warmth seeped into the tissues like soaking in a hot bath, but the feeling was gone as soon as Drey moved his hands and directed the stimulation to the next area.

His hands rested over my head for a long time. The increased blood flow subsequently increased the pounding, until the pressure inside my skull throbbed with each heartbeat, while steel rods jammed into the base of my brain. Eventually, I could no longer stand it and sat up to break the connection with Drey. In an instant, I went from having too much blood pounding in my brain to too little. My stomach lurched as the room spun. My vision became bordered by black edges. I gripped the side of the bed and took deep breaths until the room steadied and my vision cleared. I looked up to see Drey scowling at me.

'So, do I get the willow bark?' I attempted a smile.

Drey was not amused. 'Your headaches are not caused by physical factors. Your skull has healed well.'

'Great,' I said, leaning forward to get off the bed.

Drey's restraining hand stopped me before I got very far.

'The pressure is caused by your mind. You are blocking something.'

'Well, no change there, then.' I pressed against his hand, but he held firm.

'We need to address this, Tallen.'

I opened my mouth to protest but was interrupted by the door banging open against the wall. Everyone's attention turned towards it as Kade stormed in carrying a battered leather tome. His hair was tousled and there were dark circles under his overly bright eyes. I suspected that he had been studying all night.

'Saved by my prince with a book. Not the fantasy I dreamt of, but I'll take it.'

I pushed harder against Drey's hand, hoping to use Kade's entrance as an opportunity to leave the infirmary, but Drey was not to be so easily dismissed.

'We are not finished here,' he said, pushing me back onto the bed.

By this time, Kade had walked towards us. Seeing me being restrained by Drey's hand, it took less than a heartbeat for him to deduce what was occurring.

'Tallen, are you hurt? Are you ill?' he asked, with concern clearing his eyes of their earlier sparkle.

'I'm fine.'

'She is not fine,' contradicted Drey. 'But I fear stubbornness is at the root of the problem.'

Kade frowned in confusion, and I took the opportunity to divert the conversation away from me.

'So, Kade. What was so important that you almost broke the door?'

'What?' said Kade, more confused by the sudden change of topic; then, 'Oh!' as he remembered. 'Drey, I've found it!'

'Found what?' I asked.

'I've found out where the Keepers are.'

'Who are the Keepers?'

'The Keepers of the Secret.'

'Kade!' I snapped. 'I have the mother of all headaches that has been hanging around since we left Freisholm. If you insist on talking in riddles and not telling me the plain facts, I swear to the Gods, I will stab you!'

Drey held his hands up. 'Peace. Tallen, be calm. This is the information we came to the Holy Isle for. The Keepers are thought to keep the oral tradition as to where the dragons can be found.'

'Dragon,' corrected Kade. 'Apparently, when the dragons disappeared it was because they were dead. The book says that there was a big battle and all but one of the dragons were killed.'

This conversation was not helping my headache. 'How do you even hurt a dragon, let alone kill it?' I asked flippantly.

'There are details in the book. Their soft spots. Areas of weakness,' replied Kade helpfully.

I rubbed my temples, then stopped as I caught Drey watching me. 'Did he tell you the fabulous news that if I get to kill this cursed dragon, I get to die too? Lucky me!'

Drey's eyes dulled as sorrow clouded his face. He nodded once before turning back to Kade. 'What of the Keepers?'

'Well, according to the book, all the dragons were killed except one. And this one had disappeared. The bonded Slayers knew where their dragons were at all times, but this one's Slayer had been killed in the battle. The sole surviving blood-born Slayer was a two-year-old boy and he wasn't telling anyone where the dragon was. There is no record of the boy after his third summer, but it seems he was sent to the Keepers so that the dragon's location would be kept safe.'

'Why would they keep the dragon's location safe?' I asked, getting more confused by the moment. 'Why not just go and kill the last dragon and be done with it all?'

Drey answered my question. 'The Dragonslayers, and consequently the dragons, were children of the Gods. Among the favoured. There have always been those who felt the dragons should be revered rather than feared; protected rather than destroyed.'

'But they were created to fight Gods and daemons. They were no longer needed. Surely, they were too dangerous to have roaming the world, eating whoever they chose?'

Kade continued. 'And that was what most people thought. It was rumoured that the boy had been sent to the Keepers and they were hiding him. A group went to fetch him back; get him to reveal where the dragon was. But the village resisted. One thing led to another and things got a bit out of hand. Everyone was massacred. As years went by with no sign of the dragon, people assumed that the boy had been killed, and somehow that had destroyed the dragon.'

'And where was the village?' prompted Drey.

'In the Northlands, as suspected. There is so much wild land up there, you could hide a kingdom and no one would find it. As I said, the village was completely destroyed but over time people drifted back and created a new settlement. They named it Little Slaughter to remember those who were killed.'

Drey stood stone still. 'I know where that is.'

Chapter Twenty-Three

We arranged to leave the island the next day. A small boat from the mainland visited on the day after the new moon, but we were not prepared to wait that long. The Gallowglass boat was commandeered for the short trip over the water to the fishing port that supplied the island with food and supplies. Drey made sure to pack plenty of valerian for Kade and willow bark for me. We were warned about the strong currents that ran between the island and the shore and, as I was still loath to ask for help from the Aqualine spirit within the sea, Kade and I battled the oars as the boat drifted south of our target. We had to work hard to keep the bay in sight, let alone aim for anywhere close to it. It took most of the afternoon to land safely on a pebbled beach, before having to walk along the coastal paths back to the fishing village we had originally been aiming for. We were grateful for the long days of sunlight, as the sun had dipped low before we walked into the settlement. We were greeted by an elderly man with a pronounced stoop and using a wooden stick to support himself.

'Welcome,' he said as he extended his hand to Drey and then Kade, giving me a curt nod. 'Name's Rager. We saw you crossing the water. Those currents are strong, yes?'

'We apologise for calling on your hospitality,' began Drey.

The man scowled. 'Faulknar?'

Drey nodded, as Kade looked away from the man in case the connection was made.

'If that causes you concern, we can leave.'

The man considered for a couple of heartbeats before making his decision. 'Nah. You come from the island, so I can guess you are not here to cause trouble.'

'We are not,' assured Drey. 'We thank you and hope to be on our way as soon as possible.'

Rager guided us through the village of small, randomly constructed shacks lining the main pathway down to the sea. Several fishing boats could be seen pulled up high onto the beach and moored to boulders, the low tide stranding them like forgotten toys. A few women stood on their doorsteps with arms folded, suspicious of those who arrived late in the evening. The old man ignored them and chatted amiably while we followed him to a slightly larger building close to the beach. His home was plain but inviting. A pan of bubbling soup sat over a fire with a loaf of bread warming on the hearth, giving the main room a welcoming aroma and making us all realise how hungry we were. He laughed at our growling stomachs and settled us into plain wooden chairs before ladling bowls of soup for us. He refused all offers of help, stating that he enjoyed the company since his wife had died two winters ago. He eventually settled enough to join us when we all had soup, bread and steaming mugs of tea.

'So, apart from somewhere to rest your heads for the night, what can I do for you?'

'We need to get to the Northlands,' said Drey. 'Do you know of anyone trading that far north?'

Rager frowned. 'Maybe up at Hilton Bay. Big trading port about three days north of here. They get stuff from all over; I'm sure there will be someone with contacts in the Northlands. Whether they will be sending a ship, I couldn't tell you.'

'And will it be safe for us to travel?' asked Drey cautiously.

Rager looked as us, considering our situation. 'The war with Faulknar is a long way away. Most of us have no clue as to what the war is about. Decisions made by those in Lindvane are not our concern. That Hilman has sided with them means more taxes and less food in our bellies. Young men are conscripted, to come back aged beyond their years. And those are the lucky ones.' He nodded once. 'If you don't go causing trouble, no one will look too closely at you. And your money is as good as anyone else's.'

The conversation turned to neutral topics such as fishing and the industries of the village. I made my excuses just after dark, spending the night curled in front of the fire opposite Kade. It took both of us a long time to fall asleep, thinking of the perils that could befall us as we trekked towards Hilton Bay. The dull throb of my headache made it difficult to get comfortable and several times I woke Kade with my tossing. We both awoke early, little refreshed by our sleep.

We left soon after dawn, the village already busy with the activities of the day. The boats had already left, but the women and children were hard at work harvesting the clams and sandworms that were already being revealed by the retreating tide. Drey frowned at me as I quickly drank a cup of willow-bark tea. I was not sure whether his concern was for the delay in leaving, or the fact that I needed pain relief so early in the day. I doubted that we would stop until dark and I knew the constant movement was going to aggravate the headache I already had. I anticipated an uncomfortable day ahead.

On leaving the village, I felt the pressures of being in a foreign kingdom. The exertions of the row across the strait and the genteel manner of Rager had dulled my senses. Anxiety quickly returned to pump blood through my veins, making me aware of the slightest rustle in the grasses or the distant movement of a bird. I wanted to trust the old man, but I found it hard not to question his motives. I wondered why the people of the fishing village would not tell the guards about the strangers who'd spent the night there. I started to expect an ambush around every corner, but despite my concerns, the journey to Hilton Bay was uneventful. We arrived at the trading town on the afternoon of the third day, although we had seen it for a long time before walking through the large wooden gates. Tall timber towers flanked the town entrance, each with a covered walkway that allowed the guards to look down on those below. I did not doubt that there would be archers with numerous arrows available should any trouble occur. Beyond the towers, a wall of stone standing three times the height of a man ran as far as the eye could see to enclose the trading centre. Regular slits ran through the stone, again allowing archers to attack any invaders as they approached the town. Hilton Bay gave the impression that it was a martial town, and that it had successfully defended itself for many generations.

The facade finished at the wall. Once inside the gates, the town was much more welcoming and vibrant. It was a warm day and it would have been suspicious to wear a cloak. Instead, I covered the hilt of my sword with the hem of my shirt and ensured my eyes were downcast so as not to encourage closer attention. I need not have worried. The town was bustling with so many sights, smells and colours that it was easy to go unnoticed in the swarming mass of humanity that crammed into the trading port. People of different sizes and shapes pushed and jostled their way through the crowds. Light and dark skin tones mingled with hair colours ranging from purest white to raven black, covering all the different hues of red, brown and yellow. A rich assortment of accents hailed greetings and haggled over prices, acting as a stark reminder of how limited Faulknar's trading had become because of the war. Scents from hot meat pies to exotic spices and new leather goods wove into the briny taint of the sea, tucked out of sight behind the two-storey stone buildings and the large warehouses that stood in between humble timber shacks and lean-tos. It seemed that the hierarchy that existed in most other towns was absent here, as everyone tried to cram their homes and businesses inside the town walls.

We followed the herd towards the centre of the market where street entertainers were amusing the crowds. Fire-jugglers performed alongside dancers, while acrobats turned cartwheels and stood on each other's shoulders. The riot of colour and movement made me feel ill, so I quickly moved on, with Kade and Drey soon following. We continued on to the docks, where the masts of the tall seafaring ships could be seen. The coloured pennants that were attached the crow's nests blew briskly in the wind. I startled when I saw the banner for Gallowgla, causing Drey to turn to see why I had stopped so abruptly. He calmly reassured me that Hilman were not at war with Gallowgla and it was not surprising that they would be present in a trading port of this size. I tried to convince myself that no one would be looking for as no one would believe we had survived crossing the Northern Sea, but my stomach was not convinced. I found it hard to take my eyes from the pirate trade ship as my belly twisted in tight knots. The hull was deeper than those of the agile raiding ships, but there were too many similarities in the lines and the dragon embroidered on the mainsail for me to dismiss it as just another trading vessel.

The town finished at a steep cliff, so that my eyeline was level with the middle of the masts as I stood against the stone wall encircling the bay. Stone steps led down to wooden docks, which jutted out into the water at regular intervals to accommodate the numerous ships roped to iron rings. The walkways were covered with people working at unloading, checking and reloading the vessels. Muscled stevedores mingled with tailored customs officials, and well-dressed merchants wove in between linen-clad sailors as all tried to effectively manage the trade entering the port. Large wooden crates were suspended from ropes attached to timber frames that swung the heavy goods from the decks to the docks. These were then opened to divide the contents among the flatbed wagons of different traders. Cargo from other ships was then loaded into the crates for delivery back onto the ships. The whole scene reminded me of ants in a nest.

After watching the activity for some time, Drey drew our attention to a vessel at the far side of the docks. 'That's our ship,' he announced, pointing to a medium-sized, double-mast boat.

I frowned. 'How do you know?'

'The Northland banner flying from the central mast.'

As with the other ships, a standard was attached to the uppermost part of the mast. This one was divided into four by a large blue 'X', each section bearing a stylised animal – a stag, a rearing horse, a roaring bear and a large hissing cat with its tufted ears lying flat.

'But I thought there was no ruling clan in the Northlands. How can they have a standard?'

'While the clans are ruled independently,' Kade replied, 'there are a number of occasions when they need to speak with one voice. There is a council, of a sort, that negotiates for the Northlands as a whole. The four animals on the standard are reflected in most of the clan markers, so have been adopted as the image that represents all the clans.'

We made our way down the stone stairway and along the crowded docks to the Northland vessel. Animal pelts, woollen cloth and barrels of salted fish were being unloaded while sacks of grain were being carried aboard. A well-dressed dock official was marking a tally book while he and the captain argued over the quantities and value of the goods. We loitered on the docks, watching the activity while the two men haggled and eventually negotiated the tax to be paid.

'You wanting to talk to me?' asked the captain. His accent had a lilting, sing-song quality.

Drey handled the conversation as he explained our requirements for passage to the Northlands, and the specific area where we were hoping to disembark. A fee was quickly agreed, and we were soon aboard the ship amongst the bustle of deckhands securing the goods below deck. The vessel was divided into two distinct areas. A slope allowed easy access to the storage space below deck, with a large cover that could be lowered to ensure the area remained as watertight as possible. Sleeping hammocks for the crew could just be seen lining the walls to either side of the cargo. A small trapdoor in the larger cover allowed access when the cover was lowered. Between this and the stern, a row of basic shelters was available for the occasional travellers who boarded for passage to or from the Northlands. The shelters were wooden structures on three sides, with a lashed and weighted canvas sheet to provide some privacy and keep out the wind and spray. Inside each shelter was a pallet with a small mattress, and a chest for personal belongings. It was basic, but better than the accommodation for the crew. Opposite the shelters was the main structure on the ship. This was a more substantial building with timber enclosure on all four sides. Smoke was coming out of a tin chimney to the left of the structure, carrying the smell of boiling fish. To the right, wooden shutters had been latched open to reveal a stateroom with a large table covered in assorted tools, papers and mugs. The atmosphere on the ship was one of quiet efficiency, with the captain and his first mate generally letting the crew go about their business without much instruction. Everyone knew their job and carried it out effectively.

The plan was to leave the following morning, so Drey and Kade went to purchase some supplies while I settled into one of the shelters. I appreciated the quiet and the dimness it offered, with the sounds of activity being muffled by the canvas flap. I must have dozed, as it did not seem long before Kade and Drey returned, with a young man carrying a large sack walking a few paces behind. He nodded to us amiably before disappearing into his own shelter, obviously joining us on the journey north. I looked questioningly at Kade, who shrugged, before leaning in to talk quietly.

'We noticed him following us as we left the market. The captain seemed to know him as he boarded without challenge. Could be nothing, could be something.'

The tide turned just before dawn and we followed its lead into the dark, cold waters of the Northern Sea. My fear of being betrayed by the people of Hilman was readily replaced by anxiety about the waves, my last two encounters with the ocean having been too traumatic for an easy state of mind. The weather remained kind, however, and I was reassured that the height of the waves was no more than normal for this far north. We saw little of our fellow passenger and the crew treated us with respect, despite our obvious distraction and the additional burden we added to their duties. After the second day, I found that I enjoyed the view of the open water, with nothing to detract from the sea and sky except seabirds gliding on the wind.

Very occasionally I saw what appeared to be a large fish jumping out of the water or chasing the waves in front of the ship. The captain informed me that they were porpoises, and were not fish at all but breathed the air and gave birth to live young just like us. I found myself watching these creatures, fascinated by their apparent joy in playing in the water and showing off to those watching them.

By the fourth day, Kade was complaining about how short-tempered I had become. I had started to avoid direct sunlight as my headache was getting steadily worse despite my drinking copious amounts of willow-bark tea. I often saw Drey frowning at me, and realised that I had been absently rubbing my forehead to ease the pressure that was starting to run from the crown of my head down to the left side of my jaw. The consistent ache was punctuated by stabbing pain up through the base of my skull into the centre of my brain, particularly if I moved my head too fast or twisted it into certain positions. I tried to restrict my movements and use my shoulders to support my neck, but I was still irritable and lacking in patience.

On the fifth day land was sighted and the sense of relief was almost palpable. Our diet of fish stew had become bland and tedious, and the crew started to talk of the roasted meat that could be found in most of the waterfront taverns. By midday, the port was clearly visible, with ramshackle houses scattered amongst trading establishments and taverns. The docks were well-kept but basic structures capable of mooring only a few ships at any one time. The captain would offload us and half his freight, before taking the rest of the cargo further up the coast. As we lingered on the docks, debating the best way to travel further into the Northlands, our fellow passenger walked up to us.

'Follow me,' he said as he passed by, not stopping to see if we had heard.

'Excuse me?' Kade called after him.

The young man stopped, looking around nervously before returning to stand in front of us. 'Horses have been arranged. Follow me and I will take you to them.'

Kade grabbed his arm as the man turned to leave again. 'What do you mean, horses have been arranged?'

The man sighed in frustration, obviously concerned that our conversation would be overheard. 'My name is Storno. I have been charged with bringing you to Little Slaughter.' He turned to me. 'Your arrival was foreseen, Dragonslayer.'

I felt my back tense with the threat of this stranger knowing who I was, but at a shrug from Drey we obediently followed Storno to a small stable yard on the outskirts of the port. The owner gave us a hasty meal of dried meat and cheese while the horses were saddled and made ready. If we left immediately, we could make it to Little Slaughter before dark and Storno was in no mood to stay in town overnight. In what seemed like no time at all, I was handed the reins of one of the small, stocky bay horses who, despite snorting his displeasure and keeping his ears turned in my direction, carried me with little fuss. All the horses seemed to be tough and bad tempered, with each one trying to snap or kick at another if they passed too close. Their choppy gait covered the ground quickly, but the motion aggravated my headache, meaning that I spent the whole journey focusing on tensing my muscles to limit my movements and consequently making the jostling worse.

I paid little attention to the countryside as we travelled away from the port. Specific landmarks went unnoticed, although I was aware of the soft earthen tracks in a landscape of green. Long grasses, thick bushes and a generous canopy of trees gave the impression of a largely unmanaged country, rich in natural resources. Birdsong drifted from the trees as other small birds chased insects over the lush meadows. Horned sheep on the rugged hillsides dispassionately watched our passing, undeterred from their grazing, while hares darted away from our horses' hooves in a loping run. As we crossed a fast-running stream, I felt a strange sensation for a brief moment. It was as if I had ridden through a curtain of glass shards. The feeling was not painful, but my skin prickled with needle-stabs from the top of my head to the soles of my feet. Exposed and covered flesh were equally affected, leaving behind a strange numbness. I looked over to Drey and Kade to see if they had felt something too.

'Little Slaughter has a glamour?' asked Drey.

'It has a number of protections. You would never have found it on your own.' Storno had visibly relaxed, slowing the pace and sitting deeper into his saddle.

'Are they necessary?' asked Kade. 'Are you threatened?'

Storno shrugged. 'We're safe enough. But there are many who would like our secrets. We choose not to be examined too closely.'

It was not long before we arrived at the settlement. A relay of whistles had heralded our arrival, and consequently there was a small party awaiting us. At the centre of the welcoming committee were an elderly man and woman, who I assumed were the village elders. The woman had a stern face, and eyes so dark they were almost black. She wore a long cloak of woven wool containing many different colours, as did the man standing next to her. His was much shorter, however, looking more like a blanket hung from his shoulders. I assumed that the cloaks were ceremonial as the afternoon was warm, and there was no practical reason for wearing them. There was a similarity in the facial features of the two, and he had the same dark eyes. With the elders were a handful of men and women, all dressed in practical leather leggings and tight-fitting leather tunics. All were armed with swords and blades, and a couple had bows slung over their shoulders and quivers of arrows hanging from their belts. All had suspicious and slightly accusatory expressions on their faces. I laid my hand on the hilt of *Saorsa* in response to the implied threat.

'Your arrival has been long awaited, Dragonslayer,' began the elderly man, with a tone that suggested that they were not impressed with my presence. 'And it seems you have brought a Druid and a prince with you.'

Before I could frame an appropriate response, the elderly women turned her back on us. The group parted to let her through as she called back, 'Follow me.'

The group surrounded us, herding us behind the two elders. We were led through a village of perhaps twenty or so round huts. Families stood in a few of the doorways to watch as we passed. The atmosphere was not quite hostile, but I felt my senses alerted to any sudden move. Glancing over at Kade, I saw his hand tighten around the hilt of his sword, suggesting that he also felt uncomfortable. I held on to the fact that we still had our weapons: surely, if they meant us harm they would have taken our blades, although I did not rate our chances if we had to fight our way out of the settlement.

We stopped at the far end of the village where there was a cleared area. Standing in the middle of the packed earth circle was a large man, bare-chested and carrying a long, thick sword. The scars on his face and upper arms stood as a testament to his experience of fighting, and I did not doubt that those who had inflicted those wounds died soon after. His forehead glistened with sweat in the warm afternoon sunshine, and the muscles of his sword arm bulged with the weight of the blade. My anxiety levels increased significantly.

'Time for you to prove yourself, prince,' stated the elder man.

Kade was pushed roughly into the arena before he had a chance to protest. As I stepped forward to support him, my sword arm was grabbed by a woman at my side. She pressed hard into the gap between my upper arm bone and the muscle, causing my hand to go cold and numb. My grip on *Saorsa* faltered and the sword slipped back into its scabbard. The woman eased her grip and my fingers tingled as the blood flow returned to my hand. I glared at her, but she merely raised an eyebrow, knowing there was little I could do. I still briefly considered increasing the threat and forcing my way to Kade, but quickly dismissed it as an unwinnable contest.

The small crowd had closed around the earthen arena, trapping Kade with the larger warrior. They circled each other warily; sizing each other up, assessing strengths and weaknesses. I felt concern for Kade's chances. I did not doubt his skill, but I worried about the strength of his recently fractured arm. Sparring with me was no challenge and in no way prepared him for the muscle behind this opponent's swing. Surely, we had not come all this way for it to end here?

I jumped as the two men lunged at each other, blades screeching as they connected. Kade was using a two-handed grip to counter the strength of the other. His face wore a rictus grin as he fought to maintain the contact, legs braced and back arched. The large fighter grinned as if he was expending no effort at all, while Kade visibly struggled. Kade abruptly broke the connection, sidestepping so the fighter fell forward, which allowed him to swing round behind the man and bring his sword down to slice at his back. The fighter recovered quickly, turning to catch Kade's blade close to the hilt. Another battle of strength ensued, with Kade slowly losing ground. He soon broke contact, breathing heavily as they circled each other again. Kade rolled his wrist, releasing tight tendons and swinging his sword in wide arcs.

Kade's next attack came in quick sequence; a swing to the face, to the legs, to the neck, to the abdomen. The fighter matched his speed but was forced backwards, revealing a hint of a weakness. He had strength but was not as fast as his smaller opponent. Kade pressed his advantage, forcing the fighter back further before the larger man twisted away. Now both men were breathing hard.

Little Slaughter's champion took the advantage for the next round of attack. Hoping to catch Kade off guard, he sliced at his head with a mighty two-handed blow. Kade ducked and danced backwards to avoid a thrust that would have decapitated him. Involuntarily, I stepped forward, but was quickly restrained by the woman at my side. Despite pulling angrily against her grip, I could not dislodge her and was forced to watch helplessly as Kade was herded around the arena. The crowd jeered as it was clear that their champion was winning, but Kade had not finished yet. He dived to the side, his sword swinging to force the other blade away from his back. While the fighter was slightly off balance, Kade kicked at the side of his knee, causing the larger man to crumple to the ground. Despite the mood of the crowd turning nastier, Kade did not press his advantage but stood panting while the muscled fighter got back to his feet. The larger man grinned as he rolled his shoulders, challenging Kade to try to floor him again. Looking relaxed, the fighter suddenly darted forward, swinging his blade at Kade's face. Kade was a heartbeat too slow. The point of the blade sliced his cheek before he was able to deflect the attack. The fighter followed up with a punch to the jaw, sending Kade thudding to the ground.

I cried wordlessly as Kade struggled to his feet, spitting blood. I tried again to break the restraint of the woman holding my arm, and this time she required the aid of the man on the other side of me to keep me from joining Kade. My attention was distracted from the fight as the two elders, standing nearby, held a silent conversation with their eyes. The woman gave a brief nod before turning to leave, resulting in Drey being roughly guided along behind her. At the same time, I was pulled in the opposite direction. My heart thundered as I saw that we were being separated. I fought with my desire to struggle and break free, but worried that I would distract Kade from the fight that was continuing in the arena. The clash of steel rang out as I was taken past the crowd and towards the treeline. I tried desperately to release *Saorsa*, but the grips on my arms effectively restrained them. I tried kicking out, but that strategy proved just as fruitless. I was marched away from Kade and into a woodland that hid the village from view.

I was taken to a round hut nestled in the space between a couple of trees. The structure was obviously some type of detention building, with timber struts over the windows to prevent escape. A wooden plank ran through six iron handles, three to each side of the opening. It was simple but effective. If I managed to slide a blade through a gap in the door, it would take a painfully long time to dislodge the bar. I would be discovered long before I could slide the plank through more than one handle. Inside, the single room was sparsely furnished with two basic beds, a stool, a hearth and a covered bucket. Once the door was closed and barred behind me, the light was dimmed enough so that I could move without bumping into things, but could not see clearly. The lengthening evening, in combination with the overhanging trees, gave a depressing gloom to the room, adding to the concern I had about being separated from Drey and Kade. I fretted about what could be happening to them; worrying that Kade was continuing his fight with the larger man, but dreading that it had already finished with Kade lying seriously wounded. I sat on the bed. I paced the floor. I rattled the door. I lay on the bed. I sat on the stool. I pulled at the window bars. None of it eased my frustration.

It was full dark when they finally came for me. After adjusting to the sudden brightness of the burning torch, I searched desperately for my two companions but could not see anything past the circle of light. I drew my hunting knife in favour of *Saorsa*, but the two guards did not enter the room. They stood to either side of the door while I assessed my options. I could rush them, but I had no idea where the others were and I would be fumbling in the dark. The guards made no attempt to confront me, so it only took a moment to decide to follow them and see where they led me. They moved to flank me, with one slightly in front and one slightly behind, leading me through the woodland to another round hut of similar size to the one I had just left. For a heartbeat I hoped that I would be joining Kade and Drey, but I soon noticed that there were no bars on the window of this hut and no restraining plank across the door. It would seem that this was a secluded meeting place. One far from prying eyes.

My forward guard knocked respectfully on the door before opening it wide enough for me to walk through. The door was quickly closed behind me and I tightened my grip on my blade in preparation for any attack. When none came, I started to relax as my eyes adjusted and I assessed the room. Slim strips of moonlight came in between the two strips of thick material that hung across the window. A modest fire glowed in the middle of the room, highlighting the two elders I had seen earlier; the woman sitting to my left, the man sitting to my right. Both sets of dark eyes were hidden in shadow, so that they looked like deep wells of inky water. They watched me in silence, faces stern, while a young boy placed a ceramic bowl to the side of the elderly man. Firelight flickered against their white hair, making the woman's look like a nest of serpents. The hollows of the man's face projected an image like a skull. Sweat trickled between my shoulder blades; maybe from the heat in the room, maybe from something else.

At a nod from the man, the young boy bowed and then left the room, giving me a slightly fearful look as he went. I was not sure whether he was afraid of me or of what was about to happen.

'Sit down.'

I jumped at the sudden sound as the man indicated a space on the other side of the fire.

'And sheath your blade,' demanded the woman. 'You will not need that here.'

Cautiously, I did as I was instructed, replacing my blade in the holder attached to my belt and sitting cross-legged on the floor opposite the two elders. I peered into the hidden corners of the room to check for potential threats. I could not see any details, but there was no movement and I was content to accept that for now. The elders watched me closely, judging my intentions and appearing to disapprove of my conclusions.

I startled again, reaching for *Saorsa*, as the old woman reached into the ceramic bowl and removed a handful of powder. She tutted dismissively.

'Too reactive,' she scolded. 'Fear is no way to meet a dragon.'

Fear gave way to anger. 'I see no dragon here.' I indicated the powder. 'But I have been here before. I have no desire to inhale your poisons.'

The woman took a breath to reply, but was stalled by the man's raised hand.

'The journey of a Dragonslayer is never easy,' he began. 'But you have no need to fear these herbs. The powder is simply to open your mind; not to allow us access to it. You will walk your dreams to see what they are trying to tell you. Your visions will be your own. No one else will see them.'

They seemed to be waiting for my consent. I considered my position. What would happen if I refused? What if I agreed? Before I made up my mind, the woman blew on the powder. It floated into the flames and exploded into thick smoke. I reeled backwards to avoid inhaling it. My legs tangled and I fell, slamming my back against the floor and forcing the air out of my lungs. The reflexive gasp drew the smoke down into my lungs. My coughing drew the poison in deeper, making my head swim and causing the room to swirl. The flames writhed like a living beast.

I blinked, and opened my eyes to find myself on the ledge on the mountain that was so familiar. I was standing alone beneath a blue summer sky and soft white clouds, but something was different. It took several heartbeats to realise what it was: there was no fear. I considered that for a moment. This was the first time I had visited this mountain without terror gnawing at my insides. It felt very strange.

I took a step into the cave, expecting darkness to engulf me as always, but this time a soft, diffuse glow highlighted the path I was to take. I walked to the back of the cave and took the left fork, following the tunnels as they curved deeper into the mountain. I looked up at the ceiling, able to marvel at the crystals embedded in the rock like glinting fruit in a malted loaf. I gave a small laugh. The comparison did not do justice to the beauty of the sparkling passageway. A beauty that I had never seen before. A beauty I had been blind to while cowering from shrinking walls of stone. This time the walls stood still, maintaining a large tunnel for me to walk upright. The sides stayed where they were and I felt no need to measure their distance with outstretched arms; I knew they were not there to trap and imprison me.

Further and further I travelled. Deeper and deeper. The only sounds were the soft tread of my feet on the sandy trail, the rhythm of my breathing, and the gentle drip of water somewhere in the distance. No horrors awaited me. My heartbeat stayed steady and I walked forward confidently, mildly curious to see what was hidden at the centre of the maze. What was the answer to the question that I had never been brave enough to ask? What was at the heart of the mountain?

The tunnel opened into a massive chamber. Crystal stalagmites rose from the floor to meet sparkling stalactites dropping from the jutting rock face. The light from a central boulder reflected off their glittering surfaces. This domineering rock had the appearance of ice but radiated a gentle heat. The smooth surface was slightly opaque, but clear enough to see what it enclosed; a rough outline, marbled with rose and duck-egg blue. Details became clearer as I approached, revealing the point of a shoulder, the curve of a claw, the sharp point of a horn extending from an eyebrow ridge. The head was the size of a horse, curled protectively over a foreleg with the eyes softly closed. The jewelled scales of the eyelids interlocked to keep out the light radiating from the body. The ribcage rose slowly, moisture glistening on the stone as the breath was exhaled. The tail curled out of sight around the far side of the creature, while the wings were folded neatly along its spiny back.

Without fear, I could marvel at the majesty of the dragon that even in sleep inspired awe and reverence. I was an insignificant mouse compared to the power and presence of this mythical being. That such a creature could exist was beyond my comprehension. That I was standing in its presence was beyond my imagination.

As I walked slowly around the beast, my attention was caught by movement just behind its flexed elbow. A gap in the rock allowed a small patch of scales on its chest to expand and contract with its breathing. I looked closer to see that it was not only the breath that caused the movement. Regular pulses hammered against the skin. The gap in the boulders lay directly over the monster's heart. I took a step back with the realisation. I knew what I had to do. I knew how to kill the dragon.

Chapter Twenty-Four

Kade and Drey joined me in the hut the following morning. Drey was looking ruffled with a creased tunic and dishevelled hair, while Kade had the cut on his cheek, along with a competently bandaged wrist. I was glad to see neither of them were harmed more than that, and gave a small smile of relief at Kade's familiar scowl. We exchanged stories of what had happened while we were apart. Kade's fight had lasted for quite some time after Drey and I had been taken away. Several times he had knocked the fighter to the ground, on one occasion resorting to drawing blood in order to end the challenge, but apparently 'first blood' was not the rule of the game and the fight had continued. Only when Kade had been pushed to his limit and had collapsed, panting, had the larger man extended a hand to help him rise.

Drey had been questioned by the two elders, regarding the conflict between Faulknar and Lindvane. Who did he think would be victorious? What did he think would be the consequence of either side dominating the other? To what lengths would he be prepared to go in order to ensure that Faulknar won? It was clear that we were being assessed for our strength, knowledge and motivation. What was our endgame? What would we do with the knowledge the Keepers had? Could we be trusted with the information and the power it could bring?

Through the telling of their tales, I kept my silence. Eventually, it was noticed and I was called to explain what test I had been given.

'It didn't seem to be a test at all,' I started hesitantly, wondering what the elders' motivation had been. 'It was all a bit strange, really. It reminded me of my time at Freisholm, which made me a little nervous. The old woman said something about not showing fear to a dragon.'

'Did she enter your mind?' asked Drey.

'Are they a threat?' asked Kade at the same time.

I shook my head emphatically. 'No, no, it was fine. They never asked me what I saw.'

'What did you see?' prompted Drey.

'She called it a waking dream. I was in my dreams, but there was no fear. I could look around and see things that I'm normally blind to.'

I paused, not sure whether to continue. My dreams were private, and not even Kade was aware of the full extent of them. I felt protective of the knowledge I had gained. I was uncertain as to whether I was protective of the dragon; it had seemed somehow vulnerable, or was it because telling them I had seen the creature would encourage their belief that this crazy scheme was justified? The men waited patiently while I struggled to determine what to do.

Eventually, I sighed. 'I saw the dragon. Clearly for the first time.' I looked each of them in the eye. 'I know how to kill it.'

We were kept waiting all day. Drey rested on the chair, checking his supplies several times before meditating. I lay on the bed, trying to ignore Kade pacing agitatedly around the small room. With nothing better to do than focus on how my headache pounded with every heartbeat, I found myself getting increasingly annoyed with the flickering movement at the corner of my eye. Each time I asked him to sit down my voice got louder and more abrupt. Each time his response mirrored my volume and spite. Drey somehow managed to ignore the pair of us, other than to periodically hand me willow bark to chew. Gnawing on the green fibres to release the sap provided more of a distraction than any help with relieving the constant pain, but it meant that I could tolerate Kade for a while longer.

We were brought a midday meal of cheese and bread but otherwise did not see anyone else until it was late evening. A young woman came for us as the sky was turning pink to herald a sunset that was hidden by trees. We were taken out of the woodland and back to the settlement, where a central fire had been lit. The villagers were busy loading tables with food and drink, giving the atmosphere of a festival celebration. It was a stark contrast to the suspicion that had met us on our arrival, and we took it as a positive sign. Whatever tests we had been subjected to, it would seem we had passed.

We were led to one of the tables and offered a platter of bread, cold meats, cheese and early seasonal berries. The drink was a clear, light brown liquid that burned my throat before settling as a warmth in my belly. We were then left to mingle with the residents. The people were polite, nodding and smiling in greeting, but we still felt distinctly outside the community and were a little awkward, until someone started playing a fiddle. Like a moth drawn to a lighted candle, Kade gravitated immediately towards the musician, the common bond of music allowing a mutual respect between the two. Kade added his voice to harmonise with the strings, starting with nonsensical words before progressing to more meaningful stories. My prince worked his magick and soon the villagers were enthralled by the melodies he created.

Drey was drawn to an older group of people and was soon joining in with their animated conversation. I was left standing on my own for a while, considering whether it would be judged rude to stay on the outskirts, and if so, which of the groups I should join. My attention was drawn to a group of four young adults, three men and a woman, sitting a short distance from the fire. They were chatting quietly, but every now and then one would flick a hand and the fire would respond with a rush of sparks into the night sky. After a couple more of the fiery drinks, I had enough courage to go and ask if the flying ash was coincidental.

The young woman smiled, her brown hair shimmering around her face as she shook her head. 'I saw you watching us,' she said. 'We thought we would put on a little display for you.'

The smallest of the three men patted the ground beside him. 'Come, sit down and let's show you what we can do.'

Intrigued, I settled next to him just as the fire crackled loudly. The four of them laughed at my startled cursing, but not in a mean way, and I was soon smiling back at them.

'You're Firewalkers?'

The woman smiled. 'We can walk through fire if we really want to show off,' she laughed. 'But nobody round here is impressed any more.'

'Besides,' said the man next to her, 'there are things we can do that are much more fun.'

The rest of the night was spent playing with the fire, and with the benefit of several drinks I forgot my headache and started to enjoy myself. The Firewalkers threw sparks into the air to create shapes and patterns in the night sky. They turned the flames different colours, so that the orange weaved into blue, green, yellow and pink. They made fire sprites dance and play around the glowing logs. They taught me how to sculpt my fireballs into swaying trees and animated animals. I ran my creatures through a forest of rainbow flame as sprites jumped and cartwheeled. Glowing ash spun like whirlpools around the outside of the fire, shadows writhing in their wake. And finally, when I thought that I had seen it all, it appeared that the group had saved their best until last. The four combined forces to create a breathtaking vision that drew an appreciative gasp from the villagers, and left me open-mouthed in awe.

A phoenix rose from the fire. Flames flickered on its iridescent feathers as it hovered above our heads, shimmering with the colours of the rainbow. Its head was a deep purple, while the neck took this purple through the shades of indigo, azure and cobalt. The body and wings rippled through the greens of teal, jade, emerald and lime, before melting into the yellow of the sun. Finally, the tail blended the oranges of flame and sunset with the red of blood. The detail created by the Firewalkers manipulating the flames was breathtaking, before it burst into jewelled sparks that decorated the sky.

Having been released from the mesmerising sight of the phoenix, I turned to find Drey at my shoulder.

'We have been granted the knowledge,' he stated, slightly breathless. 'We will be taken to the dragon.'

All the heat from the fire left my face as the blood drained from my head. I doubted that this would result in a pleasant outcome for me.

Drey wasted no time and arranged for us to leave the following morning. The effects of the fiery liquid consumed the previous evening blended with my persistent headache to create a pressure across the whole of my head, with additional stabbing pains through my temples. My tongue felt coated by a well-worn tapestry and my stomach rolled as if it contained a miniature ocean. I was in no mood for being introduced to a new equine companion. The horses were the small and stocky type that we had used before, but these had an attitude that would have impressed an angry mother bear. They kicked and bit at all of us, but the mount assigned to me was particularly grumpy. I was bitten several times and kicked twice before I managed to settle in the saddle. We adopted a mutual dislike and fought each other at every step. He pulled at the reins. I kicked his flanks. He bucked. I yanked at the bit. It took until mid-morning before we both slumped into a sulking truce.

The day focused on the myriad of different pains that afflicted my body. The slightest movement caused the pain in my head to increase, so I tensed every muscle to try to protect it. This had the negative consequence of making me bounce in the saddle and move my head more. My shoulder and back muscles were soon protesting and cramping. The muscles around my eyes ached as I squinted against the sunlight. By the afternoon I gave up on chewing willow bark as it had no discernible effect on the agony of a bouncing brain within a razor-lined skull. I tried to distract myself by taking in the scenery, moving my head slowly to avoid the disorientation of my vision taking a heartbeat or two to catch up with my head. The woodland engulfed us for most of the day, giant sentinels mottling the light as it dodged through the verdant canopy. Much of the wildlife avoided us, but squirrels cursed us from high in the branches and birds called shrill warnings. Eventually the trees thinned to open into a wide landscape of rugged gorse and hardy heather moorland, with regal mountains standing proudly on the horizon. The scenery was so unlike the flat vistas of Faulknar.

We followed a small stream that wound its way through moorland towards the base of the central mountain. The water trickled over the smooth pebbles and occasionally fish could be seen breaching the surface in search of insects. The horses travelled in single file along a trail only determined by shorter grass and the absence of thorny gorse. Storno had been chosen as our guide, and he chatted freely with Kade and Drey as we rode. He was careful not to talk about our destination or the role of the Keepers, but instead described growing up in Little Slaughter and his travels within Hilman and the Northlands.

The trail had risen gently throughout the day and by the time we made camp we were about a third of the way up the central mountain. The ground was still grassy, with only occasional trees. There was ample space to build a small campfire, and Storno was soon cooking a pair of rabbits he had snared while Kade had collected the firewood. I picked at the food, still feeling nauseous from the jostling of the day's ride and the effect it had on my headache. I tried to make my excuses and retire for the night, but Drey was no so easily fooled.

'Just a moment,' he instructed as I rose to leave the glow of the campfire. 'I have yet to examine the source of your pain, Tallen.'

I sighed, not having the energy to argue with him but dreading the thought of him probing my mind. 'Drey, I'm really tired. Can we do this another time?'

I looked at Kade for support, but I could see his concern and knew he wanted to know the cause of my affliction as well as Drey.

'I doubt you will be any less tired tomorrow,' reasoned Drey. 'We've put this off long enough.'

Storno and Kade watched silently as I returned to my seat and Drey came to kneel in front of me. He asked me to slow my breathing and close my eyes. Talking in a quiet monotone, Drey explained what he wanted me to do, urging me to relax as he inspected my aura and energy lines. Happy that they were intact, he requested that I lower my barriers and allow him access to my corridor of doors. I took a deep breath and opened my mind. I had a moment to wonder at the thickness and complexity of my mental walls before my consciousness was blasted by a concussive force. It was as if my mind had been punched in the guts and all air expelled from my lungs. My thoughts shattered into shards, like pieces of glass from the smashing of a mirror. I was no longer aware of where I was. Of who I was. Of how to get back to being me. Flashes of memory, images I could not understand, feelings that did not seem to belong to me all crowded around me, threatening to dissolve my being into something other.

Far away, someone was calling my name, triggering an awareness, a thought that was just out of reach. I slipped back into the maelstrom, again carried on the currents of images presented, then whisked away. The voice called my name again. This time I recognised it. Drey. Safety.

I reached for the sound. Invisible tendrils drew me towards the full awareness that remained hidden from view. I teased, probed and felt my way towards Drey as he called my name again. I gradually became conscious of who I was and what I needed to do. My barriers appeared as solid granite walls. I added another layer, then another. The whirlwind calmed, all became quiet and I was finally back in control.

I opened my eyes to find Drey directly in front of me. His palms cradled my face as my hands gripped his wrists. It was several heartbeats before I could release my hold. I stared for a while at my shaking fingers, before being able to look at him.

'Please don't make me do that again,' I pleaded.

Drey gently wiped the tears from my cheeks with his thumbs. 'No. I don't think we will do that again.'

The next day we crested the ridge of the central mountain. The wind whipped at exposed skin and lifted the tails of the horses. I retreated into a small bubble, huddling into myself to limit the movement of my head and neck. The small changes in my vision as we rode along were enough to make me feel light-headed and nauseous, so I closed my eyes. Consequently, my horse was left much to his own devices and I was frequently told to catch up when the beast had stopped to eat. Eventually, Kade tired of the constant nagging and returned to collect my reins, leading me like an infant learning to ride around a schooling arena. I no longer cared, appreciating the chance to concentrate solely on anticipating the horse's movements so that I could limit the amount of jostling, and keep my eyes closed. Despite the warmth of the sun, the gusts of wind kept the temperature chill. Drey, Storno and Kade were soon wrapping themselves in their cloaks, making it more noticeable that I was running a fever. The cold air on my hot skin was a welcome sensation, but I caught both Kade and Drey giving me looks of concern. It was getting more difficult to convince them that I was fine.

I was barely in the saddle by the time a halt was called. I was surprised to find that we had travelled so far, seeing that the mountain was behind us and we had stopped by a fast-flowing river in a sheltered valley to set up camp for the night. Kade helped me dismount, catching me as I stumbled on landing. The jolt of that small movement released a weak cry of protest that I could not contain.

'By the Gods, Tallen,' he commented. 'You're burning up.'

I opened my mouth to protest that I was fine, but I could no longer pretend even to myself. The edges of my vision were hidden by black borders, the area of central vision was blurred, and the image seemed to move two heartbeats after turning my head. I leaned into his ice-cold hand that he had placed on my forehead, savouring the numbness that spread across my forehead under his palm and fingers.

'I just need to lie down for a bit,' I conceded.

Kade carefully escorted me to the place where Storno had set the bags and sleeping mats. I curled into a ball, using my flattened sleeping mat as a pillow, while Kade covered me with a light blanket. I waited for the world to stop spinning while I listened to Kade and Drey arguing above me.

'This is ridiculous, Drey. Look at her!'

Drey's voice remained calm. 'I am well aware of her suffering, Kade. I'm afraid there is nothing I can do about it. It does not stem from a physical problem, but from her mind. I cannot go there without doing more harm.'

Kade's voice undulated as he paced. 'The further we go, the worse she gets. We need to turn back.'

'You know as well as I do that we can't do that. You've seen the consequences of not trying this.'

'And what about the consequences of continuing?'

Drey was silent for several heartbeats, allowing Kade to reach his own conclusions. We all knew that there was no other choice. If Kade and Drey's visions were true, Liegeport would be destroyed along with all those we knew there. What other towns and villages would be caught in the blaze of dragon fire? What other horrors would the monster unleash across the three kingdoms?

Drey's voice was very quiet when he continued. 'Kade. You know that there will be no happy ending here.'

The rest of the evening was quiet and sombre. Storno followed our lead and kept his thoughts to himself. I managed to force a couple of mouthfuls of food, and took it as an indication of how ill I must look when Drey did not press the issue. I soon took myself off to an area away from the fire's heat to sleep. I was so hot that I removed most of my clothes before covering myself with the light blanket Kade had given me earlier. I fell into an exhausted sleep before being woken by the insistence of the pain, alternating between these two states throughout the night. The only respite was when Kade joined me under the blanket, his cold body acting as a counterpoint to my raging heat. I pressed my forehead into his chest, as his icy fingers cradled the base of my skull. In this position I was able to find enough comfort to relax my overtaxed muscles and sleep a peaceful slumber for a while.

The next few days passed with the same routine. I was unaware of how many days we travelled, but noted that the landscape gradually changed from mountain, to valley, to heathland, to farmed land and finally to coast. My world had shrunk to the prison of my aches and pains. Kade helped me mount my horse in the morning, we travelled until dusk, we camped and I slept cradled in Kade's arms. The next day would bring a repeat of the process. Each day the pain got a little worse. I spent my time huddled in the saddle, gripping the pommel to stop myself falling as I faded in and out of consciousness. On a few occasions I realised that I had been transferred to Kade's mount, his arms holding me tightly to prevent my collapse.

We spent the final night with Storno in a small coastal town. There did not appear to be much trade this far north and the settlement was quiet and relaxed. As the sun set over the ocean I realised that we had travelled the entire width of the Northlands, from east coast to west. Our hosts were an elderly couple and their grown-up sons, and they explained that there was little beyond the waters except a chain of islands that were not visible from the mainland. These were uninhabited, and few people knew of their existence, let alone travelled there. I was able to concentrate for long enough to determine that this was where we were headed, before succumbing to my narrow world of semi-consciousness. At some point I was given a small milky drink that relaxed all my muscles, and I slept deeply until Kade gently woke me the next morning.

One of the sons accompanied us and we were soon on the water, rowing towards an island that was not visible. Kade continued to support me in the boat, as the motion of the waves aggravated my nausea and I concentrated very hard on not being sick. He started talking to me about the conversations last night, his voice soft and melodic to give it a hypnotic quality that I was able to focus on.

'I'm not sure what Notan is going to tell his neighbours about us,' he purred. 'Still, they didn't seem too bothered about three strangers going for a row this early in the morning. Perhaps there are frequent random occurrences around here, but the impression I got last night was that this is a pretty sleepy town. Not much happens. Life's pretty dull. So maybe he will have to spin some tale about crazy people wanting to see the sea.'

I smiled at his poor attempt to convince me that the people of this part of the coast were quiet little mouse-people, unaware of the bigger picture involving magick and dragons. I felt his muscles relax beside me at the first smile I had attempted for what seemed like a very long time. It was a feeble effort, but it was something.

Kade went on to talk about the island and the responsibilities of Notan's family. 'They have a long history of being the custodians of Wyrm Island. As far back as anyone can remember, they have always known the secret of the island and its name. *Wyrm* is the ancient word for serpent, which seems appropriate as the island is home to a dragon. It's the second island in a chain of six. About once a season, Notan or one of his brothers will row across to check that the mountain is still intact. There is never any sign of the dragon, but it is said that the beast is buried deep within the rock.'

I took a breath to speak, but Kade knew me so well I did not have to frame the words.

'Yeah,' he continued. 'Just as you said. The information just keeps reinforcing what you have dreamt; what you saw in the vision at Little Slaughter. I know you don't want to believe it, and who would blame you, but this just seems too much to be a coincidence. What with your dreams, and mine and Drey's visions, there has to be a dragon in that mountain.'

He fell silent for a while, before continuing in little more than a whisper. 'I'm so sorry, Tallen. You know I would never have wished this for you.'

We skirted around the smaller first island, which was little more than a home for seabirds, with short, tufted grasses. The second island was horrifyingly familiar. It rose out of the sea on sharp granite cliffs, lethal rocks sticking out of the water to catch sailors who were not giving the island the appropriate amount of attention. From the sea, a thin band of green could be seen at the top of the cliffs, before the imposing crown of the mountain thrust into the skyline. The island was much larger than the first; large enough to house a substantial mountain… a mountain large enough to hide a dragon.

Notan expertly negotiated the submerged rocks and landed at a small cove with steps carved into the cliff face. Relying heavily on Kade, I managed to climb the steep stairway and reach the top of the cliff. The final four islands in the archipelago could be seen stretching into the distance: a small, barren island with rocky projections floated nearest; the next was larger with a covering of trees, stunted by the constant sea winds and violent winter storms; and the two furthest were merely blurred impressions of colour.

I turned my back on the sea to look over the island on which we stood. The image froze me to the spot, cold water trickling down my spine in stark contrast to the raging inferno in my head. There it was. The mountain that had haunted my dreams for as long as I could remember. The jagged peak that looked so much like a broken tooth. The sea that separated the island from the mainland was visible on either side. I could even see the track that led to the ledge with the half-moon entrance.

'This is it,' I whispered to Kade, who had come to stand by me and place a supporting hand at the base of my spine. 'This is the mountain of my dreams. This is where it all ends.'

Chapter Twenty-Five

Notan helped Kade make a base camp at the foot of the mountain, then, as there was no safe mooring for the boat, left us with a promise to return in three days' time. Drey brewed a strong tea for me and, while I was happy to just lie in the weak sunlight, it was felt that there was too much time left in the day. Kade supported me as we walked towards the foothills, my eyes almost closed as I concentrated on avoiding the rocks and pebbles that would cause me to stumble. After a while I had moved to the front of our small group, taking Drey's customary place. Years of dreaming of this mountain meant that I knew the way despite much of the trail being covered with grasses and ferns. The path wound around the rock, twisting back on itself several times but gradually rising up towards the ledge I knew would be just over halfway up. I was panting from the exertion by the time we reached the half-moon opening and I sat heavily on the floor, holding my pounding head in my hands. The sun was well past its zenith.

Kade was by my side in an instant, placing a gentle hand on my shoulder. 'What's wrong? Are you all right?'

Rubbing my temples in a vain attempt to ease the throbbing, I looked at the cave entrance before looking up at Kade, confused. 'We're here?'

'Where?' asked Drey, standing a few paces behind Kade.

I looked at one and then the other, frowning at their questioning faces. It took several heartbeats to realise that they were not seeing the entrance that was so obvious to me. I sighed tiredly as I explained the dark opening to the small cave that would be waiting for me when I entered, the centre of which was a little taller than my height and the width over half the length of the flattened ledge that we were sitting on. It would appear that I was to journey through the mountain on my own; Kade and Drey being denied the knowledge of the cave was a clear indication to me that I was to proceed alone. They had the grace to share a look but did not protest too hard. We all knew this was to be my challenge. It was, after all, my destiny.

It took a monumental battle of wills to rise from my sun-warmed spot and approach the cavern entrance. The pain in my head argued that it would be better to curl into a tight ball and forgo any movement. The daemons that lurked in the shadows of the half-moon mouth were cajoling and insulting in equal measure. My logical brain was convincing in its case that this was a suicide mission that had no hope of succeeding. I was no clearer on what would be considered a success: all options seemed doomed, particularly for me. I looked at Kade, and saw the desperation and frustration in his warm brown eyes. I saw the lines across his young forehead, telling of responsibility that weighed heavily on his troubadour's soul. What else was there for me to do but follow the path that had been set for me; the fate that had been determined generations ago? I rose slowly, waiting for the dizziness to pass and my vision to stabilise. Talking a deep breath, I walked towards the mountain. I did not look back at Kade or Drey; I had no words of farewell. I focused on the task before my nerve left me completely; one deliberate step after the other and head held high. I stepped into the shadow.

All became quiet. The sound of the wind had gone. The faint hush from the waves was no more. The birds calling on the thermals had fallen silent. I slowly released my breath, the sound amplified in the stillness. The oppressive air compressed around me as I stood frozen. I was not a dozen steps from Kade and Drey but it seemed they were a world away; perhaps they were. I could not resist the urge, even though I knew what was waiting, and turned to see the open cavern entrance that I had just walked through was now solid darkness. Reaching out with trembling fingers, cold rock rubbed against my skin, confirming that my escape route was firmly closed and there was only one way to go. After so many years of fearing these tunnels, I was surprised to find that I had no concerns about being trapped. As in my waking dream at Little Slaughter, I was able to assess the situation calmly. My head still felt like a giant's hand was trying to crush it, but the insistent throbbing had eased as if it was waiting to see what decision I would take. As if I had a choice. I closed my eyes to avoid straining them by trying to see in the blackness. The spots behind my eyelids that had dazzled previously were transformed into small stars of red and silver. Stretching my right arm in front of me to avoid walking into any obstructions, I reached out with my left to find the barrier that I was to follow. My first hesitant step echoed softly around what I assumed was a large chamber. My questing hands felt nothing but the slight breath of stale air; the hint of a musty scent brushing my nostrils.

One step. Two. Three. Still nothing to hint that I was heading in the direction I needed to take. Fingers stretching as far as I could to find something solid and provide some orientation or guidance. Seven. Eight. Nine steps. A flutter of insecurity awoke in the pit of my stomach with doubts about the reliability of my dreams. Perhaps they had not foretold the path I was to take. Perhaps they were just fantasies constructed by my mind to give me a sense of destiny where there was none. Twenty-four. Twenty-five. Twenty-six. My right hand touched cold stone and I sighed deeply to release the tension that had built. My world had boundaries again; there was an up and a down, a left and a right. It may prove false, but again I had a clear idea of what I was to do next. Confidently, I traced the wall to my left, counting again as I walked sideways like a crab searching for the left rock face. Seventeen. Eighteen. Nineteen. My right hand lost the feel of the mountain, and I waved my arm around to find there was stone to the right, but in front of me and to the left was air. A tunnel? The first passageway? Keeping my feet walking in a line parallel to the wall I had lost contact with, I edged further left, straining to connect to something with my outstretched fingers. After four shuffling steps my left hand connected with the far wall. The image of my route ahead formed in my mind. Assuredly, I stepped forward into the tunnel.

It was a strange sensation to walk into a place that had held such terror for so long, without the panic I normally associated with the labyrinth. My breathing and heart rate remained steady as I was led further into the mountain. Every twist and turn took me deeper into the heart of the stone prison, and at each junction I turned to the left. I soon lost count of my steps and any sense of direction as the path coiled round and round. I found that, without the fear, monotony became the overwhelming emotion, with the only sounds being the soft tread of my feet on the dusty floor and the quiet whisper of my breath.

At some point the texture of the rock became smoother. Small patches in the stone were soft as silk, so that my fingers glided over them. Almost like the sensation of water; slightly cold to the touch. The pebbles became more frequent the further I travelled, joining together to make a seam through the coarse stone. It was as if a line had been painted on the wall to guide me further and further away from the entrance, deeper towards the goal that was waiting for me at the centre of the maze. The next development was the temperature. The air at the cavern entrance had been cool and stagnant but as I walked, the temperature gradually increased. It became noticeably hot after the seam of smooth pebbles and the muscles in my legs were aching, so I assumed that I had been in the mountain for some while. With darkness all around it was impossible to have a sense of passing time and I was warmed by my exertions, but the air felt warm to breathe. My face tightened with the dry heat and there was a strange crispiness to the atmosphere. Eventually it felt like my face was burning, with a sensation of being exposed to too much summer sun. Prickly needles stabbed my cheeks and forehead, while sweat beaded on my upper lip.

A faint light came next. A small pinprick of colour, easy to dismiss as a trick of the eyes. When had I opened them? Step by step, the light became bigger and more distinct. I quickened my pace, eager to return to the sighted world and to look at something other than darkness. The fact that it was taking me closer to my fate seemed less of a concern in that moment. I marvelled at the reflective stones that had guided my way, as tiny prisms of light split into the colours of the rainbow. I gazed at the dazzling spears, as might a blind person seeing for the first time. The colours appeared more vibrant for having been absent for so long, dancing in my vision as I moved closer to them.

The light, and the smooth, reflective pebbles, guided me to another cavern. I hesitated at the end of the tunnel as my vision was immediately captured by the central structure. The warmth of the chamber on my face was a sharp counterpoint to the chill that flooded down my spine. The nauseating stomach cramps that had been absent throughout my travels through the tunnels returned with a sickening intensity. Acidic fluid flooded my mouth, and I swallowed repeatedly to prevent vomiting. I steadied myself against the wall of the passage, taking deep breaths and forcibly looking away from the domed structure. I was not yet ready to make that decision.

The light caused the shadows at the periphery to move, but I had no concerns that others were in the mountain. I knew it was just me and what was in the centre, encased in pearlescent stone. I raised my head. High above me a small circle of paler darkness was studded with tiny stars. The top of the mountain was so far away it seemed that it would take a lifetime to climb up there. I suddenly realised that I had not considered a way out. Logic would suggest that I retrace my footsteps, taking the right turns, but how could I trust that? Without any light, I could travel down any number of dead ends, or travel in circles for eternity until I starved to death. Or got eaten by the…

I turned back to the crystallised dome halfway across the cavern. The pearly white stone was highlighted with the rose and duck-egg blue I had seen in the waking dream. The outline of a giant beast could be seen, curled into a huge ball; hints of scales covering its neck and torso, contours of muscle lying dormant, rounded bumps of spine – a monster encased in ice. I took a step into the cavern, drawing *Saorsa*. The sword sighed as it left its sheath, red eyes flashing in expectation. I heard a faint humming, like the pressure before a storm. The pounding headache returned in time with my thumping heart; a drumbeat to accompany the fulfilling of a destiny. I found myself walking to that beat as I stepped cautiously towards, and then around, the structure. The far side showed the creature in more detail; a tapering tail that was as high as my head, curling around a front leg to balance the arrow-point tip on the dark claws. Claws that were as long as my arm. The head rested further up the limb, the lower jawbones resting either side of the scaled muscle. The dragon's eyes were closed in slumber. Beside its flexed elbow was the small opening that I had seen in my waking dream. It was a little larger than my hand, with edges that were slightly roughened and the scales clearly visible within. The blue shimmered through different shades as the creature took a slow, deep breath in. My heart thundered in my chest at the first movement I had seen from within the encasing shell. I took an involuntary step backwards and raised *Saorsa* in defence, tensed and ready. The scales shimmered again as the chest relaxed and the beast breathed out. No other movement was forthcoming, but I still waited with sword poised, knowing that single breath confirmed that the leviathan lived.

Eventually, I lowered the blade and stepped closer to the stone and the sleeping dragon. The decision had seemed so certain in Little Slaughter, during the journey over the Northlands, even as I walked through the mountain's tunnels. But standing in front of the majestic monster, the choice was no longer so clear. Was this really what I was destined to do? Was this truly the will of the Gods? To destroy the last dragon? To remove a creature that they had created to protect them from daemons? There was no going back from this. For any of us, not just me, but then maybe it was time. The age of dragons had passed and this creature was nothing, encased in stone at the centre of a mountain. Maybe I was doing it a kindness?

I raised my blade again, aiming for the single vulnerable spot exposed by the gap in the crystal. The pounding in my head increased as the tension within the chamber rose. The tip of *Saorsa* trembled as the ruby eyes seemed to look into mine; questioning my decision or frustrated at my delay? Still I hesitated. Something felt wrong. I was not comfortable doing this. I understood the consequences but could not bring myself to plunge the sword into the gap, into the delicately scaled muscle and the slowly beating heart. Was this confusion caused by a glamour the dragon could use to defend itself?

I lowered *Saorsa*, hesitating only for a heartbeat before nodding once. I had made my decision. I sheathed the sword. I would not kill the dragon. I *could* not kill the dragon. The pounding of my skull eased as I accepted the inevitable, the pain seeming to wait for what I would do next. What could I do now? Tentatively, I reached towards the boulder, trembling at the thought of what I was about to do. Finger-length by finger-length, I moved closer towards the dragon, hovering my outstretched hand over the break in the crystal. I took a final breath before plunging my hand in to rest my palm on the warm, smooth scale.

My head exploded. Sensory information was coming from places that I was unaware of. Colours flashed in front of my eyes in shades of orange, red and yellow that I did not know existed. Greens, blues and purples that I had no name for flashed iridescent shapes around my field of view. Sounds ranging from the loudest to the softest, heard in equal clarity all at the same time. Whooshing and whispering and creaking and squeaking swirled around my head, making it impossible to determine where the sound was coming from. The feel of the air against my skin sent sparks along my nerves, creating snowflakes of fire within my tissues. I could taste the scents on the current of air breathed over my tongue; sensory buds popping with salt, sweet, bitter and sour to create a tapestry of sensation. The skin within my nose exploded with fragrances. Fresh, clean smells. Stale, musty smells. Smells of the different rocks within the mountain. The volume of information was overwhelming. My lungs found it hard to function while my brain was trying to understand the sights, sounds, tastes, feelings…

At my thought of feelings, images cascaded through my mind. Valleys I did not recognise. Forests covered in autumn leaves. Herds of deer running through sunny glades. Flying high over mountains sprinkled in snow. Drifting through clouds before rushing low over small villages. People looking like scuttling toys from the perspective of height. Soaring over silvery lakes, feeling the wind caress my skin. Each vision came so quickly, I hardly had time to acknowledge the scene before the flood of sensations accompanying the next one. Hunger cramped my stomach as a group of wild boar ran squealing through the gorse and heath of the moor.

Close your mind to all but my voice.

The voice was deep and sonorous. With the cacophony of noise, from dust motes, to air currents, to mountain stone, to ocean waves, I was unsure whether the sound was in the chamber or in my head. I tried to separate the different sensations into meaningful groups, but it was like trying to grasp water with your fingertips. I could not get a hold on any one thing; each twisting away from me in dizzying spirals of light, noise and texture.

Compartmentalise your thoughts. Remove those that are not yours. Leave your barriers down, but wipe away all distractions.

I imagined the room of doors that Drey had taught me so long ago. Image by image, emotion by emotion, I placed the experiences that were unfamiliar to me behind each new door. Row upon row of plain and simple doors to contain the multitude of information that I had gained in the space of a few heartbeats. Slowly, my thoughts returned to me. I was aware of my own body and my own senses; thoughts and memories that were solely mine.

One of the small doors hovered in front of my mind as an image floating in front of my view of the cavern. I felt a warmth as I imagined reaching out to touch the handle. Cautious, but not overly fearful, I opened the door.

You need to keep this one open if you want to hear me, commanded the voice.

I was unable to locate where the sound originated as it seemed to be everywhere at once, the deep vibrations suggesting a massive chest to create the rich tones. I looked towards the dragon to find her looking at me with dark, velvety amber eyes. Each was rimmed with delicate scales of blue, while ridges above gave the impression of eyebrows that swept into two blunt horns. The nose extended as that of a reptile, with a short length of bone ending in a rounded tip. Darkened nostrils opened in large slits above the mouth, again rimmed in blue scales, with the tips of the canine teeth poking out of the top and bottom lips. A membranous frill accentuated the jaw, with small, sharp hooks projecting from each bony support. Serrated ridges travelled the length of the spine and along the top of the tail to the arrow-point tip, which tapped against the stone floor in a manner that reminded me of a slightly agitated cat. The muscles of the torso rippled under the subtly changing colours of the scaly skin, while the bunched muscles of the upper limbs exuded a powerful strength. Her head rested on extended forepaws, their black claws shining in the small amount of light available in the cavern.

'You?' I squeaked.

She raised an eyebrow. *You do not have to use your mouth. I hear your thoughts perfectly clearly*, she said in my head.

I struggled to order my thoughts enough to form a coherent question. *What was that?* I thought, before asking out loud, 'How can this be possible?'

Which question would you like me to answer first? the dragon rumbled. *Your touch allowed me to finally break through your barriers.* There was a hint of annoyance to her tone. *The images you saw were my memories. Everything I know is now yours. You just have to think your question and the answers are available to you.*

I was reluctant to access the kaleidoscope of emotions and visions that had assaulted me, and fully intended to keep those thoughts firmly behind their doors.

'You speak my language?' It was not the question I wanted to ask, but it seemed a safe option.

The dragon blinked her eyes slowly, giving me the impression that she knew it was not the question I wanted answering. *As my memories are yours, so yours are mine. I see all that you have been. Your language has been familiar to me for some time.* Her gaze was gentle, but there was a challenge lying within.

I took a deep breath. 'You knew my father?'

Of course, she replied softly. *Our connection is now in your mind for you to access.* She waited for me to retrieve the shared memories, but soon accepted that I was not going to do that. *I have known the Slayers in your bloodline since the beginning. Each generation is bonded to me, so that I share their experiences as I do with you now.*

'But I was not aware of you...'

She snorted, blasting me with a gust of sulphurous air and causing me to blink. *Your father should have prepared you for my contact, but he delayed too long. Your natural barriers repelled my attempts at access. The harder I tried, the more you blocked me.*

'The headaches? My dreams?'

Her scales darkened, turning the duck-egg blue to azure and the rose to dusky pink as her muscles tensed. *With the lack of training by your father, and the way Villermir mistreated you, I had no other access. That priest even corrupted them. Stupid ape had no idea what he was meddling with.*

I rubbed my forehead in confusion. 'I don't understand. Why would you want me to have access to your memories; to be able to communicate with you? Surely, that would make it easier to kill you...'

Don't be absurd, she snorted. *As if you could kill me!*

I pictured the vulnerable spot above her heart that I almost pierced with *Saorsa*.

That opportunity will not present itself again.

'But if I'm a Dragonslayer, surely I slay dragons?'

I had the distinct impression that she rolled her amber eyes. *If you insist on denying your intellect, this will be so much quicker if you just access our memories.*

'Excuse me for failing to meet your intellectual standards, but perhaps you could just tell me.'

Humans are always choosing ease over accuracy. Your failure to access our memories is a contemporary example of this. Your ancestors were just as lazy. The Gods created dragons to defeat their enemies. Slayers were created to guide the dragons in which enemies to consume.

I chose to ignore her use of the term 'consume', as the dragon continued condescendingly.

The dragons were used to slay the enemy. People shortened the sentence to 'dragon-slayers', which was then misinterpreted as the slaying of dragons. Such arrogance.

'But then where are the others? There were five.'

The dragon was quiet for several heartbeats. I had almost decided that she was not going to answer me, when a vision was projected into my mind. Dragons flying over Liegeport, but not the Liegeport I knew. The town was smaller and the buildings more basic. People clothed in ancient fashions walked amongst timber structures.

I felt a moment of nausea as the image swung quickly to a wooden tower where four men operated a harpoon bow. They waited patiently while a gold-and-black dragon flew towards them with horrifying speed. They timed their release of the harpoon to the opening of its mouth as the giant aimed to rain liquid fire over them. A chilling roar of pain echoed as the tip of the spear embedded in the creature's skull. I felt my dragon's dull ache of loss as she witnessed its death. I received a brief image of a harpoon embedded in my dragon's left hip, and her tumble to the ground that broke her large thigh bone. I looked to see a swelling still present at the centre of the bone, where the callus had left a thickened area. The dragon rolled onto her left hip, so that her belly concealed that admission of weakness.

'You destroyed Liegeport.'

The ancient town was corrupt. They had forgotten the ways of the Ancients. They had abandoned the natural order. They were opening gates that should remain closed. Your ancestor was charged with cleansing the port. I did what I was requested.

'Kade's vision?'

I have no desire to return to Liegeport.

If I was to believe both Kade and the dragon, there was only one conclusion. 'And if I commanded you?'

I sensed her amusement. *'Command' is not exactly the word. But yes, I would do it if you asked.*

The enormity of that statement weighed heavily. The strength and aggression of a dragon at my disposal, to do anything I asked. I was not sure anyone should have that power.

You have the blood of your ancestors running through your veins. You were chosen by the Gods. You will use your gift wisely.

'How can you be so sure?' I queried.

The dragon was quiet, and I felt that she was expecting me to access our shared memories. I was still reluctant to get lost in the maelstrom of sensations that had assaulted me on our initial contact. I felt that, once opened, I would be unable to contain the emotions that accompanied each image. If the size of a dragon was intimidating, so were their feelings. I was surprised at the responsibility I now felt for this dragon: she felt with a dragon's passion and remembered for a dragon's lifetime. I chose a different line of enquiry.

'So, are you in my head permanently now? Do I have no privacy from you?'

A deep rumble rattled around her chest that was suspiciously close to a chuckle. *You may have kept me out of your thoughts, but I have been fully aware of you.*

I felt the heat flush my cheeks.

However, your barriers are sufficient to keep me out if needed.

I kept the door open so that I could tell when her voice was no longer in my head, and mentally raised my barriers, symbolically adding another layer that was engraved with dragons. Curiously, I felt diminished by the lack of her presence. My senses became dulled and the light in the chamber dimmed. The creature's eyes narrowed, and I smiled as I realised that she was annoyed that I could repel her from my mind. I lowered my walls again.

'Seems my barriers are very effective.' I grinned, surprised to welcome back the sensations that the renewed contact brought.

The dragon snorted, and a cloud of sulphur drifted over me. I gagged at the smell of rotten eggs. I swear the scaly lips pulled into a smile.

'And you can block me?'

Of course, she said immediately. *But why would I? I have been alone for more lifetimes than you can imagine. The only information I gained was from your mind, and the minds of those who came before you.*

'How did you end up trapped in this mountain? Who could capture a dragon?'

It was required, she said simply.

I waited for her to continue, and eventually she did.

After the battle at your primitive Liegeport, where my brethren were destroyed and I witnessed the death of my Slayer, I had no purpose. No direction. I was hurting from more than my broken leg.

She paused, remembering a time I had no wish to intrude upon. Her lids hooded her eyes as she considered how to tell her tale.

I was out of control, but at the time I saw it as freedom. Going wherever I chose. Taking whatever I wanted. Terrorising everyone I could. I may have been the reason for many of the accounts you read of the hatred humans have for my kind. The tide was turning before Liegeport, but I contributed significantly to the downfall of our status. We were the children of Gods, being considered the work of daemons. It was not how it was supposed to be. She reminded me of that.

'Who?' I asked tentatively.

The dragon projected an image into my mind. It was a woman I recognised. A slim figure, dressed in midnight robes with a face so pale as to seem to glow, and eyes of ice blue that appeared translucent. The Goddess who had appeared in my dreams. The one who had prevented me from discovering what lay at the centre of the mountain. Who had withheld the information that a dragon – my dragon – waited for me. The woman who had stopped me from remembering my father.

As my anger started to rise, another image was given. The same woman was at Methhold on the day of the massacre. She held my hand in a circle of calm as the people of my village ran screaming and lay dying. Once more, I smelt the acrid smoke as our houses burned, and the stench of blood and filth as friends were butchered. I saw a look pass between the Goddess and my father, and his brief nod before he handed her *Saorsa* and she turned me away from him. She guided me through the carnage, keeping me shielded from the axes and swords of those fighting under the banner of the boar. She led me to the small building to the east of the village, taking me to a hole in the wall that I was sure hadn't been there on my previous visits to the storeroom. She encouraged me to crawl inside and handed me the blade.

Stay hidden, she commanded. *Stay safe.*

Her words were echoed in the next image of my dragon submitting to being encased in opaque crystal. A Goddess building stone upon stone to create a mountain to cover the slumbering dragon. I saw her carving the maze of tunnels to confound any wayward traveller. I watched as she embedded spells to protect the dragon until she was needed. Until I needed her. Why would I have need of a dragon? My mind reeled with the implications of being involved with dragons and Goddesses. I was a nobody. A thief. These things belonged in tales told by firelight on dark winter nights. They didn't happen to people like me, but the dragon curled up in front of me, looking like some enormous, contented cat-lizard, prevented me from believing the lie. The impossible had happened to me, and while I still had no way of understanding the role I was to play for the Goddess, I understood my responsibility to the dragon. I was to keep her safe.

'Do you have a name?'

The dragon blinked. *We have no need for names. You just need to think of me and I am there in your mind.*

I shrugged. 'I can't keep calling you "Dragon".'

She rumbled with amusement. *You could try 'My Dragon'?* she goaded, with a scarily accurate impression of my voice.

'Do you not have a name?' I insisted. 'Shall I give you one?'

She settled more comfortably on her front legs. *If you insist on using your mouth to talk to me...*

'Humour me,' I encouraged.

I was once given a name. By those of my homeland.

'Home?' I queried, suddenly realising that I had not considered that she would have had a home. The image of a snow-covered mountain range was placed in my mind. A triangular peak emitted a thick plume of pale grey smoke, and I knew this was a fire mountain responsible for a web of heated tunnels below the ice-covered ridges.

They called me Meginvættr-Heitrkaldbalk.

'They called you what?' I stammered.

Meginvættr-Heitrkaldbalk. It means 'strong spirit-creature of the hot-cold mountain'.

'It can mean what it likes. There's no way I'm going to be able to pronounce that!'

You asked for my name, she rumbled, so that I felt the ground vibrate. *And you don't have to pronounce it. Just think it.*

'I can't think it if I can't pronounce it,' I retorted. 'I will call you Megin.'

That's not my name.

'Consider it a pet name.'

Megin raised her lips to reveal her sharp teeth in an unmistakable threat.

'Well, maybe not a pet name. You are definitely not a pet. More an affectionate abbreviation.'

Her lips slowly relaxed and covered her teeth again. I rose and walked over to her massive head, which remained resting on her forelimbs. I had to reach up above my own head to touch her eyebrow ridges. The scales were warm and smooth as I gently rubbed my fingers over them. The rumble that accompanied my touch was almost a purr.

'Well met, Megin,' I whispered. 'I am so honoured to meet you.'

Chapter Twenty-Six

Daylight crept into the small ring at the top of the mountain. I had spent half a day and a full night under the mountain, and I became suddenly aware of being hungry. Megin stood to her full height and stretched her back. She was impossibly tall, and her tail snaked out to scrape against the wall behind her. The pale blue of her flanks faded into the soft pink of her belly as the muscles of her legs bulged to support her massive weight. She snapped her wings out, the loud crack echoing off the rock. I was slapped by the wind of the downdraught as she expanded to fill the chamber. Even in the dim light of the cavern, she was a magnificent sight: power and strength balanced perfectly with beauty and grace.

I need to hunt, Megin stated. *I need to leave this place. Give me the rings that are in your pocket.*

I frowned in confusion before she projected an image into my mind of the jewellery I had stolen from Freisholm. I had completely forgotten that I still carried them.

'What are you going to do with them?' I asked as I placed them in my upturned palm and reached out towards her as if feeding a horse.

Megin stretched her neck, and I looked in horror as she extended her scaly lips towards my hand, mouth open wide. Instinctively, I snatched my hand back and took a couple of steps away from her.

'Mobis's hordes! You're going to eat me now?'

The dragon looked at me as if I was the stupidest creature she had ever encountered. *If you trust me so little, throw the stones in the air.*

Still suspicious of her motives, I did as she asked and threw the rings towards her. With a snap as quick as lightning, she extended her neck, opened her mouth and swallowed the jewels. A short burst of energy travelled up the length of my spine as I watched Megin's scales brighten for a heartbeat. She shook her head, the leathery frill at her neck flapping open.

Not enough, she complained. *I need more.*

'I don't have any more.'

She slowly closed her eyes, as if to summon the patience needed to teach a recalcitrant child. *Go to the quartz seam. Bring me more stones.*

I was about to retort that she could go and fetch them herself, when I realised that the passage was too small for her to enter. With a sigh, I returned to the tunnel, retrieved my small dagger from the cuff of my boot and worked at chipping the crystals from the pearlescent seam. Once I'd removed enough to fit in both cupped palms, Megin informed me that those would be sufficient and bade me to return to her. Throwing one handful towards her, then the other, I shuddered with the shared energy released by her ingestion of the rocks.

'You use the gems for energy,' I whispered, more to myself than her. 'That's why I collected all those things?'

Your instincts run true, she declared. *It's a shame you didn't think to bring them with you.* The dragon shook herself like a wet dog, causing her wings to slap noisily against her sides, before purring, *Time to hunt.*

'Wait! How do I get out?' I spluttered, suddenly afraid of being left alone in the mountain.

She blinked her dark honey eyes at me. *You know the way. You just have to find it.*

Megin flapped her wings; the term did not do the action justice. The muscles of her chest and spine flexed and extended in a ripple. The undulation continued across the membrane as the fingers of bone that supported the wings locked in extension. The downdraught knocked me to the floor and I had to cover my eyes against the flying stony debris that was stirred up by the wind. A second thrust. A third, and her foreclimbs left the ground, while the fourth stroke lifted her hindlimbs. She flew straight up the centre of the mountain, disappearing through the hole at the top. Even in the still air of the cavern the flight seemed effortless, and I wondered at the ease with which she would fly with the wind beneath her wings. It seemed a much emptier place without her, and not just from the loss of her physical presence.

I suspected that the way out of the mountain would be hidden in Megin's memories. I moved to the edge of the chamber and sat with my back resting against the wall. Taking a couple of deep breaths, I emptied my mind and visualised the room with all the doors. My mind was still full of the spectacle of Megin flying, causing a small wooden door to travel towards me at some speed. The door burst open in front of me and I was suddenly lost in a dizzying whirlpool of images of flying. Soaring over mountains. Skimming over lakes and rivers. Diving onto running prey. Dancing on the thermal currents. The rush of wind blasting against my head. The scents of forest and water tickling my nostrils. The vibrant colours of alp and moorland. The sheer joy of being able to move in all directions, with no boundaries or barriers to contain me.

With a significant force of will, I closed my mind to the pleasures of flying and the sensations I felt when feeling through Megin's senses. I must focus my mind on the mountain. A door to my left burst open and, again, I was drowning in a kaleidoscope of images. I felt cold and then hot. The air I was breathing seemed heavy, then light and insubstantial. Barren peaks were followed by lush green vistas. Solitary mountains became uncountable numbers of ridges and valleys. Arid deserts mingled with craggy coastlines.

I slammed the door closed, took a deep breath and tried again. Perhaps I needed to be more specific. I thought of getting home, but my mind seemed to focus on the word 'home'. Once again, I was shown Megin's home range. The snow covering the top halves of all the mountains. The grey rock contrasting with the pristine whiteness above and the scrubby green treeline below. The image lingered for several heartbeats before changing to one of a village that caused a pain in my chest. Methhold lay before me. A bright spring day, with the varied colours of the wild flowers poking through the grasses in the meadow on the outskirts of the village. The mud-and-thatch roundhouses clustered around the central area where villagers were busy preparing the evening meal. Gentle laughter could be heard as root vegetables were peeled and grains softened by being pounded against smooth rocks. Young children chased dogs, paying no attention as they were scolded for running too close to the fires.

These were my recollections of home, not Megin's, and naturally my train of thought wandered towards what memories Megin had of my family, and of my father in particular. The image of Methhold as I remembered it faded and was replaced by another picture. A woman was lying in bed cradling a newborn babe. The man standing next to her, resting his hand protectively on her shoulder, had similar features to my father; dark hair, hazel eyes set in a long face. I realised with a start that the baby was my father. Megin was remembering his birth, although I sensed the connection was through the man as he smiled proudly at his wife and son. This image faded as my mind revealed another picture from Megin's memories. My father was a young boy, being taken into a meadow similar to the one he had taken me to when I was that age. His father held *Saorsa*, and I could see the excitement written all over my father's face. In the centre of the clearing, the larger man stood behind his son and supported his hands as my father took the weight of the sword.

'Be careful, Hael,' the older man said gently. 'Try to keep her steady.'

I watched as my father practised swinging the blade. Very few had swords when I lived in Methhold, and I doubted they were common when my father was young. He was being taught basic techniques for parry and thrust, but there was some skill evident in the way his father was teaching him. It seemed that there was a long history of swordsmanship in my family.

The vision changed again, and this time my father was a little older; perhaps nine or ten summers. The grandparents I had not known were sitting by a fire. My father was on the floor between them, talking to my grandfather as my grandmother sewed patches onto worn clothing.

'Tell me the role of the swords,' prompted my grandfather.

'There were five swords,' my father offered eagerly. 'Each one given to a Slayer to represent their virtue. *Íobair* was the sword of sacrifice. *Fírinn* was the sword of truth. *Dlighé* was the sword of duty. And *Ceartas* was the sword of justice.'

'And *Saorsa*?'

'*Saorsa* was the sword of freedom.'

'Good. Although the virtue of the *Saorsa* Slayers is more about the protection of freedoms. Protecting individuals or states that encourage freedom.'

My father nodded, absorbing this piece of information.

'What more do you know about the blades?'

'The blades were forged by the Gods to stay sharp despite being able to cut boulders in half.'

My grandfather chuckled. 'I wouldn't try that if I were you. But the swords are very sharp. What else is special about the blades?'

My father thought for several heartbeats, while my grandfather waited patiently. 'Oh – the swords are aware of Dragonslayer bloodlines and will allow any to touch all of the blades. Those not of the five bloodlines will be cut and the wounds can become infected.'

The picture faded as my grandfather smiled proudly. The next image was of my father as a young man standing opposite my mother. My maternal grandfather stood in between them in his full Druidic robes and headdress. He was weaving a silk rope over their joined hands and around their wrists in the ancient wedding ceremony, and both looked so happy. I felt tears running down my face, breaking my concentration and dissolving the image. I sat alone in the dim light of the cavern, remembering my parents being happy and carefree. The joy and love that were abundant when I was a child, before Lindvane's boar raiders came.

I was not willing to dwell on that after the beautiful memories of my father, so I wiped my eyes and concentrated on my breathing. At a thought, images rolled back showing me different faces that I knew to belong to my ancestors through my father's line. So many men, and occasionally women, who carried some resemblance in the line of the mouth, or the shape of the nose. It was some time before I saw eyes that were the colour of mine, and Megin's. The knowledge followed a heartbeat later: the eyes of Dragonslayers matched their dragon's eyes, although the shade remained only while there was contact. The connection with Megin had been lost for many years before my father's father had been born, so that his eyes had faded to hazel rather than amber.

You were born with hazel eyes.

My heart slammed into my chest wall and constricted painfully at the sound of Megin's voice in my head.

'I can still hear you?' I stammered redundantly.

Of course. Do you not understand that I am in your mind? Our connection has no physical boundaries. It cannot be dimmed by distance.

'I understand,' I replied grumpily, although I still wasn't sure how my bond with the dragon worked. 'I'm just having a tough time believing this is real.'

She huffed before continuing. *Your link to me was renewed when she took your hand.*

'The day of the raid.'

Your line would have ended then, if the Goddess had not intervened.

It took several moments to accept the thought that a Goddess would deem me important enough to save. That I would be the one to release her dragon. The face of the man with orange eyes was still in front of me: he stood in a grassy glen, *Saorsa* in his hand. A reminder of the history tied into my blood and the legacy I had been charged with.

'He was your last Slayer. The one who fell at Liegeport.'

Megin did not reply, but I felt the tidal wave of her emotions: sadness, loss, grief, something much deeper. There had been no daemons that day, or for several battles before it. The Gods had strayed from their original purpose, using the dragons to enforce their reverence rather than to protect humans from the playthings of Taranis and Sluagh. The dragons had paid a heavy toll for that arrogance.

I questioned how the dragons had become bound to the Goddess. I was shown image after image of Dragonslayers, spiralling back to the time of the Ancients. Tall, graceful creatures who bore a similarity to the humans of now, but differed in subtle ways that were hard to define; a sharpness to the line of the jaw, the long, thin fingers of the hands, the posture and fluidity of gait when gliding over stone pathways. I was taken up the side of a mountain, the snow-covered peak pointing into a blue summer sky. There was no sign of a trail breaking the rugged wilderness of short, tufted grass; not even a deer track to guide a traveller to the peak. My viewpoint tilted over the summit, where the top of the mountain had sunk into a deep, wide basin dotted with caves and steaming pools of murky grey liquid. On more than one of the ledges in front of the caves, scaled creatures about the size of a large dog basked in the weak sunlight; small wings stretched out to catch the warming rays. As one of these lizards took to the air after a flock of birds, it flew over the ledge containing one of blue-pink colouring that was swiping its tail in agitation at the robed figure in front of it. The Goddess extended her hand, a large quartz sitting in the palm. The reptile swayed its head back and forth in conflict, hissing at the woman, whose hand never trembled. After several moments, the lizard reached forward and gently took the stone, throwing its head back and swallowing it. The deal had been sealed. I watched as the Goddess held her hand over the creature's gullet, a silver glow connecting her palm and the crystal inside. The beast grew in size, its body becoming twice as large, and its wings growing to twice their length. Another gem was offered, this time a ruby the size of an apple. Again it was ingested, the residual glow from the first stone activating the new energy source and causing the reptile to double in size once more. I recognised Megin in the curve of the eyebrow ridges, the extension of the horns, and the amber eyes. Realisation seeped slowly through my brain that I was witnessing the birth – the *creation* – of my dragon. So long ago – she must be immortal. No, not immortal. Jewels and precious metals delayed damage and decay, but eventually she would die.

I was reminded that while Megin could live for a very long time, I could not, particularly without water. It had been over a day since I had drunk anything, and I had encountered no sign of water within the mountain. My stomach fluttered at the thought of being trapped underground, slowly dying of dehydration, when another image distracted me from my physical concerns. Megin stood before me, wings held close to her body and head high as she looked down on the Goddess. The Lady wore her familiar black cloak with the hood folded back to reveal its rich purple lining. Her silvery-white hair floated over her shoulders like an icy waterfall. The two stood opposite each other, staring at each other in a battle of wills, although I sensed no hostility between them. Eventually, Megin lowered her nose, blinking her amber eyes in acceptance and relaxing her body onto tucked legs. Her tail curled round in a snap as the only outward sign of her annoyance.

The Goddess dipped her head in acknowledgement. *You know this is the way it has to be*, she said softly. *You will be needed.*

Megin snorted. *Am I not needed now?*

The Goddess approached to lay a hand on the dragon's neck, causing the muscles to shiver at the contact. Megin hooded her eyes and the muscles of her neck and torso relaxed. She settled further into her crouch with a deep sigh.

Your old Slayer is dead, brave one. Your new Slayer is a mere child. It will be many seasons before he is ready to command you, and by then the world will have changed for the likes of us. But be assured, your time will come again. For now, you need to stay hidden. Stay safe.

When? asked Megin, and I detected a hint of fear in the question.

Longer than either of us would like. Such are the ways of men. Their memories are short. They are quick to move on and embrace new ideas, forgetting the knowledge that brought them to this point.

The Goddess moved her hand down Megin's neck to rest at the point of her elbow, where I knew her heart was located. Where I had touched the dragon to break the spell that I was now witnessing being cast. Megin relaxed into a state just above slumber as a soft glow radiated from the Goddess's hand. She continued to talk as the opacity of the crystal started to encase the creature, her scales fading to the palest pink and blue.

Rest well, great one. Your time to fly will come again. You will be needed to protect us once more.

The crystal cage was complete, with the exception of the area where the Goddess's hand rested. She stepped away from entombed dragon, sighing softly as she surveyed her work. After a couple of heartbeats, she turned to look directly at me. Her eyes looked into mine despite the scene having taken place such a long time ago, and I found myself staring at the ice-blue eyes, not wanting to believe that she was actually looking at me. It must be a trick of the angle. Just a coincidence. It became harder to convince myself when she started talking.

You have taken the first step towards your destiny, Dragonslayer. You remained true to your dragon. You have a duty of care to ensure she stays safe now she is free to fly again. There will be those who will try to use her, through you, to cause harm. You need to stay true to your bloodline and resist that pull of power.

I took a breath to ask a question, but the Goddess continued before I had a chance.

You will find many of the answers you seek on your journey, although you still have some way to go. Be patient and listen well.

The image of the Goddess started to fade. I drew another breath, starting to panic that she was not going to give me the vital information I needed to escape the mountain, but again, she answered me without needing to be asked.

You know the way out, Dragonslayer. Follow the left-hand path.

'But wait. How can that be?'

The Goddess was gone, and I was left talking to the empty chamber. Perhaps I had misunderstood her. Perhaps she was giving instructions for the way to the dragon's chamber. But that could not be right, because I was already in the chamber. Maybe the conversation was not meant for me and it was just a coincidence that she had answered my unspoken questions. She had said that the left-hand path was the way out, but if I took that path on entering the mountain, surely I would need the right-hand path to retrace my steps out again?

'That doesn't make any sense,' I complained.

It's an enchanted mountain, Megin mocked. *Why would logic have any place here? Stupid ape.*

'Flying lizard,' I responded childishly.

I waited several heartbeats, determinedly not thinking about Megin. Slowly accepting that there was no other option but to trust in the Goddess and take the left path. I tentatively walked over to the tunnel through which I had entered the chamber, the only one I could see within the cave. The confidence that I had felt travelling into the mountain's labyrinth was gone. My fate had seemed unavoidable – I was unlikely to leave the mountain whether I found the dragon or not – but now things had changed. I had to believe that my destiny was more than just releasing a dragon before starving to death, hopelessly lost within a mountain.

I reached out my left hand and brushed my fingers against the rock wall of the tunnel. Giving myself a quick nod of encouragement, I stepped into the passage and walked confidently out of the chamber. Within three steps I was plunged into complete darkness, with the dim light from the opening at the top of the cavern unable to filter into the passageway. The lack of visual information felt more acute after the vivid images seen through Megin's eyes. The apprehensive fluttering in my belly became painful cramps, my right hand bunching into a fist as I concentrated on keeping contact with the left wall. I had to forcefully reject the desire to return to the chamber, where I hoped Megin would come and rescue me. I knew that this was not an option; too many dreams had taught me that to turn back was to face a solid barrier. I also doubted that Megin would return for me, as her joy at flying free flowed through me intermittently. Despite it making my situation feel worse, I could not begrudge her the freedom she had been denied for so long.

Trailing my fingers over the rough surface, I had walked another five or six paces when I felt the familiar smooth stones that had guided my path towards the centre. My arm had been too high, but now my fingertips tingled slightly as I traced the seam that led me forward. I walked more confidently through the maze as it twisted and turned back on itself. I seemed to be travelling down more often than up, but each time I turned left. I lost all sense of how long I had travelled, knowing only that I had to continue. I was almost at the half-moon cave when I detected the slight breeze of fresher air and a small change in the shade of darkness surrounding me. I increased my pace, eager to be free of the mountain and its maze.

I emerged to the sound of waves crashing onto the rocks, as the first stars were showing in the night sky. I took a deep lungful of the briny air, grateful to be free of the oppressive rock. I stretched my back and shoulders, exhaling in a noisy sigh and smiling at the wonder of what had happened over the previous two days. That I had survived against all expectations. I spent a long time enjoying the space around me, the cool night air and the gentle wind on my face. The rhythmic sound of the ocean absorbed into my body and replaced tension with calm. I felt more alive at that moment than I could ever remember feeling.

Eventually I was ready to descend. I carefully negotiated the weeds and brambles that choked the path, ready to snare passing toes and ankles. I smiled grimly at the potential irony of facing a dragon, only to stumble on an exposed root and tumble to my death. Each time I came around the side of the mountain that looked over the island, I could see the small campfire built by Kade and Drey. The sight initially filled me with excitement and an eagerness to get back to my friends, but as each circuit was completed I started to worry. I had been sent to kill a dragon, and I had failed spectacularly at that. I had been asked to neutralise the threat to Liegeport, and instead I had set the threat free. I did not believe Megin would attack the port, but I did not expect Kade to share my faith in her.

Too many years spent travelling silently meant that I was within the circle of firelight before either man was aware of my arrival. Both jumped up and assumed defensive positions before realising that it was me. Drey relaxed immediately, with a small smile of relief on his face. Kade spent several heartbeats blinking, as if he could not believe I was standing in front of him, finally releasing his sword to slip back into its scabbard as a grin split his face. In two steps he had crossed the distance to me and lifted me in a tight embrace, spinning me round several times so that I was dizzy when he eventually set me on the ground. I needed to hold his arm for balance as he guided me to sit by the fire. Drey handed me a bowl of thin soup that I took gratefully.

'What happened? You were gone so long. We saw the dragon. We didn't think—'

Drey interrupted Kade with a raise of his hand. 'Take your time, Kade. She's not going anywhere.'

'Sorry,' Kade apologised, playing nervously with a blade of grass. 'You look better than you did when you entered the mountain.'

'I am,' I confirmed with a smile.

They both looked at me, expecting me to explain.

'Where do I start?'

Drey grinned. 'May I suggest the beginning? You disappeared into the side of a mountain!'

It seemed such a long time ago that I had entered the half-moon cave. I explained how the dreams had instructed me to take only the left turns, and that my own fears, and Villermir's interference, had turned them into the terrors that had plagued me. The dreams had prepared me for travelling through the enchanted labyrinth to the sleeping dragon. I described how she was entombed in crystal, and how I felt that killing her would be wrong. I tried to gauge their reactions but they stayed still and silent, giving me no clue as to whether they agreed with my decision or not.

'I don't believe that she will attack Liegeport,' I said quietly.

'So, it's "she" now,' Kade mumbled to the fire, before turning to me. 'But you don't *know* that she won't.'

'No,' I confirmed. 'But then you don't *know* that she will!'

'What makes you so sure that the dragon will leave Liegeport alone?' asked Drey, reminding me that he had had the visions too.

I hesitated while I considered how much to tell. Megin's memory of attacking Liegeport floated in front of my view of Kade and Drey. Was the connection between dragon and Slayer a sacred truth? Was this only to be known to those chosen to serve the Gods? What could be the consequences of people knowing of the bond between Megin and me?

'There is a link between us,' I started, choosing my words carefully. 'An understanding. She knows how important Liegeport is to me. And I know how *un*important Liegeport is to her.'

'The texts record that she has attacked Liegeport before,' persisted Kade. 'What's to stop her attacking it again?'

'The texts are correct, but that was a long time ago, Kade. A different time. The city was corrupt. It needed to be cleansed.'

'*Cleansed?!*'

I rubbed my eyes, feeling suddenly tired. 'Sorry. That was a poor choice of word.'

'Perhaps now is not the time for this discussion,' offered Drey, ever the peacemaker. 'You must be exhausted, Tallen. I am glad to see you returned in good health. Tomorrow will be soon enough to worry about what may or may not come to pass.'

Drey walked over and gave me a firm hug before retiring to his bed. There was a short, uncomfortable silence between me and Kade, before he broke it with a sigh.

'I am glad that you are back. And that you weren't eaten by the dragon.'

I looked up to find him grinning at me.

'Regardless of what happens, I'm happy that you are here.' He stood and offered me his hand. 'Let's get some sleep.'

I gratefully accepted his offer, following him to his bedroll a little distance from Drey's. 'Sounds good. I feel like I haven't slept for a week.'

'Well, that's not that far from the truth. You get any sleep in the mountain?'

We snuggled into the blankets, with Kade's arm over my waist while I gently pushed my back into his chest.

'Not exactly. More like my brain has been expanded and stuffed full of information.'

I felt him smile. 'I have no idea what that means, but you can explain it to me tomorrow. Now you need to get some sleep.'

'I'm not sure I can switch off all the thoughts that are hammering against my head. It doesn't hurt any more, but there is so much to—'

Kade interrupted me by moving his hand to stroke my hair. 'Well, let me see what I can do about that.'

The rhythmic, gentle pressure of his touch relaxed my racing mind within the space of two heartbeats, and before long I had floated off into the velvet embrace of sleep.

I did not stay asleep long. I sensed Kade battling with his thoughts, as one moment he was relaxed against me, the next he had tensed and moved away a fraction, only to relax and settle against me once more a few moments later. I tried to keep as still as possible to avoid influencing his internal struggle. I knew he was torn between what he considered to be prophetic visions and the trust he had in me. The need to protect his people and the need to protect me. Had I been offered the same decision? At the time it seemed like the only action to take, but thinking about it now, perhaps I had chosen the dragon's needs over Kade's. I shuddered at a remembered dream in which I had told the Gods that I couldn't betray one over the other. Had I already made that decision? Had I already betrayed Kade?

Kade finally turned away from me and succumbed to a deep sleep at the turning of night into the pre-dawn grey. I rose carefully, so as not to wake him, and wrapped myself in his discarded cloak to protect against the early-morning chill. I coaxed the fire back into life and placed a kettle of water over the flames to heat. The familiarity of the routine allowed my mind to wander, and it was not long before I felt the contented, snoozing mind of Megin.

'Morning,' I whispered, grinning at the ridiculousness of talking to a dragon.

She huffed. *Still using the mouth.*

I shrugged. 'Old habits. You ate well, then?'

Megin stretched in satisfaction, rolling over to expose her bloated belly. *Meat has grown lazy. Spends too much time in the open.*

'Can't really blame them. It's been a long time since dragons preyed on them.'

Stupid meat. Should always be wary.

'Well, I'm sure they will get used to you soon and prove more of a challenge to catch.'

Always too easy, she grumbled.

I smiled at her confidence. Her meal had given her a vitality that had not been present in the cavern. Her scales caught the dim light and sparkled as she breathed. In the full light of day, they would shine brighter than a fish, more iridescent than the feathers of a starling. In response to my thoughts, Megin stretched her wings, locking the bones that supported the membranes and trembling as she tested their limits. She rippled the scales on her back to catch the beginnings of sunlight as she turned her head towards the first rays, eyes hooded in appreciation of the early warmth. She reminded me of a flower, opening its petals towards the life-giving sun.

More meat, she announced as she stood to stretch her legs.

'Really?' I blurted out.

She huffed at my ignorance, before opening her mouth in a giant yawn, cleaning her sharp teeth with her tongue and breathing out sulphurous gas from the back of her mouth. In one graceful leap, she had jumped twice her height into the air. Her wing membranes snapped as she caught the wind and forced it to lift her higher. Within three wingbeats, the trees had shrunk to the size of wild flowers. The clearing where she had rested disappeared from view as she scanned for movement. The rush of air currents brushed against her face and caressed her torso as her wings cut through to channel the wind under her, lifting her effortlessly to soar over the woods and river that lay far below.

A flash of movement drew her attention to the bank of the river. A herd of deer had come to drink. She changed direction as swiftly as a hawk, aiming for the group of seven. Her attention was taken by the large stag with antlers that fanned from his head in thick tines. He lifted his head, sniffed the air and twitched his ears. He could not place her, but he knew danger was coming. A quick warning bark had his hinds running towards the cover of the woods. Megin was flying over the top of them by this point; goading them, harrying them, changing direction frequently to push them towards the clearing that she could see further ahead; her actions mimicking the herding dogs that brought goats and sheep to market. The deer reacted instinctively to her every movement, unwittingly running towards the open space where she could attack. They twisted this way and that to avoid branches and roots. Megin responded a heartbeat behind, always moving them in the direction she wanted them to go.

They broke cover. Nostrils flaring. Mouths open in alarm. Bunched tightly together. Running in a jagged line in an attempt to confuse their attacker. Megin waited patiently for the stag who was at the rear of the group, hurrying his harem to the safety of the copse in front of them. Megin banked to come at him sideways. He roared in pain as the talons of her forelimbs punched into his flesh at the neck and rump. He tossed back his head to pierce her with his antlers, only to have them press harmlessly against the muscle of her foreleg. The speed of her descent knocked the large stag to the ground. His ribs cracked loudly as her weight crushed him when she landed; his final breath coming as a hoarse croak. *Too easy.*

I was startled by a grab at my arm, and turned to see Drey standing over me. It took a couple of heartbeats for my brain to let go of the hunting scene I had just witnessed through my dragon's eyes, and clearly see the image in front of me. I blinked repeatedly at Drey as my mind raced to comprehend the change.

'Tallen, are you all right?' he asked urgently. 'Can you hear me now?'

'Yes,' I stuttered, still a little dazed. I shook my head to dissolve the remaining images of Megin's breakfast. 'Yes, I'm fine.'

Drey relaxed and curled his legs to sit in front of me. He had removed the kettle from the fire and two mugs were steaming with hot tea. He passed the nearest one to me and I drank from it gratefully. The warmth in my stomach dispelled the last of Megin's thoughts and grounded me in the reality in front of me.

'Where did you go?' he asked gently. 'What did you see?'

'Megin was hunting.' The tone of my voice reflected more than a little awe.

'Megin?'

I shrugged. 'It's what I call her. She has a much longer name than that, and it's totally unpronounceable. So, I have shortened it to Megin.'

Drey sat back. 'You've named the dragon? Does that give you control over her?'

I chuckled at the thought of Megin being controlled by anything. 'No. I don't think it works like that.'

'But you feel a connection? She will do what you ask of her?'

I looked at Drey, trying to read his intentions. A man I had trusted most of my life, trusted *with* my life, suddenly felt hostile. There was no accident in his choice of words: 'command' and 'ask of her'. He saw Megin as a weapon. If not against us, perhaps for us.

'The relationship is more like that of a family,' I began, considering my words carefully. 'There is a mutual need to protect. She will not do anything that she doesn't want to do, but she will protect me above all else.' I looked sharply at Drey. 'The same applies to me. I will protect her. Above all else.'

Drey took a deep breath, folding his hands carefully in his lap. I could sense his mind working as he chose a different direction. 'Dragonslayers were not used to destroy dragons, then?' he asked.

'No.'

'But they were used to...' he fought for the right word, 'guide them?'

'As I understand it, yes. The dragons were created to destroy the enemies of the Gods. Specifically daemons. The Gods would determine who to fight and the Slayers took their dragons.'

'But there were no daemons in Liegeport,' argued Drey.

I hesitated again, suspecting where this conversation was leading. 'No. There were no daemons in Liegeport.'

Drey waited for me to continue.

'The Gods had a different need. As I said last night, the port was corrupt. People were turning from the old ways...'

'As it is now?'

'Liegeport is true to the old Gods,' I snapped. 'You know that as well as I do.'

'But if that were to change? If the royal bloodline turned to Baila?'

'Kade would never do that,' I said quietly, losing confidence in my argument.

Drey persisted. 'But if he did?'

I was feeling very uncomfortable. Drey had been my friend and protector for so many years, but suddenly he seemed like my enemy. I understood his desire to control Megin, to use her to defeat Villermir and his armies. I understood so well. I had strong reasons of my own to want Villermir destroyed, but I could not allow Megin to be used like that. It went against everything the dragons and their Slayers were created for.

'The attack on Liegeport all those generations ago was sanctioned by the Gods. No man should use the God-given power of a dragon for his own ends, Drey. We cannot know the will of the Gods.'

I knew it for a lie as soon as the words had left my mouth. Perhaps I had not spoken to the Gods, but the Goddess had spoken to me. I had no doubt that her will would become clear should she have need of my services.

'Are you sure about that?' asked Drey. 'Could it not be the Gods' will that you have found the dragon after all this time? Perhaps they feel it is time to *cleanse* the city once again.'

I flinched at his use of the word I had spoken so carelessly the previous night. The thought of people I knew being consumed by dragon fire was not a pleasant one, and one I refused to dwell on.

'The problems of faith are man-made. We created these divisions, not the Gods. We need to solve them. Megin deserves to fly free, Drey.'

Drey hesitated again as he decided on another direction. 'Do you remember when you asked for money to buy Kade a lute?'

I frowned at this sudden change of topic, unable to comprehend how it was connected to Megin. 'Yes.'

'I mentioned a debt that you owed the Faulknar family for your keep and your training.'

'I remember.'

'I told you that I would let you know when that debt was paid. Tallen. The dragon is your debt.'

I stared at him in shock, my mouth hanging open as I tried to convince myself that Drey was not asking for what he had just asked for.

'You can't ask that! I was willing to go into that hellhole of a mountain for you. I was willing to die in order to kill Megin for you.'

'But you didn't, did you?'

I glared at Drey in disbelief. For a heartbeat he seemed to age in front of my eyes; the lines standing out on his pale face.

'If it was my debt…' he began, before the hardness in his eyes returned. 'But it is not my debt. It is the king's—'

'The king knows about this?' I spluttered. 'How long have you been plotting this?'

Drey continued as if I had not spoken. '…and he commanded that *all* potential weapons should be used at his request to destroy Hayton and any assisting him. That includes your talents, and your dragon. This is the debt that you owe him.'

I had no doubts in my mind. 'Then it would appear that I will not be repaying that debt.'

Chapter Twenty-Seven

The wind played with my hair and the sea breeze filled my lungs as I sat on the cliff looking out over the ocean. My conversation with Drey swirled around my head, repeating and exaggerating his disappointment and my guilt. My internal interrogation left me with no new options. From whatever angle I looked at it, I could not balance my duty to both Faulknar and Megin. I would have to deny my king's request in order to protect my dragon, and Kyllian would view this as treason. I would be imprisoned if I returned to Liegeport, but I could not allow Megin to be used as a weapon against Faulknar's enemies. There were untold numbers of soldiers, cooks, smiths, mothers, fathers and children who were unprepared for her destructive power. They were defenceless against her tooth and claw, much less the firestorm that could erupt from her throat.

I turned away from those thoughts, closing my eyes and focusing on the rhythmic sound of the waves crashing against the rocks far below me. Between one breath and the next, I saw with Megin's eyes as she glided over the water, and felt the power of the thermals as they pressed against her wing muscles where they joined her chest wall. She used the energy of the warm air to add to her lift as she rose higher, then relaxed to drift lower and skim over the gentle roll of the sea. She was heading towards a rocky island at the edge of the archipelago, one that was noticeably devoid of vegetation as the jagged cliffs reached towards a central peak. Her path was leisurely, meandering, as she savoured the flood of sensory information provided by her flight; the ache of muscles that had not been used for such a long time, the salty scent of the water, the caress of the wind as it flowed through the bony channels of her eyebrow ridges and horns.

As she approached the island, a new scent caused a tingling along her nerves. A deep, musky tone was detected below the smell of brine and an iron tang of large blood vessels pumping through muscle. Her flight became more direct as she focused on the pebbled shoreline of a sheltered cove. A colony of mottled seals relaxed in the warm sunshine, their suckling pups mewling as the mass of bodies jostled for space. Megin raced towards them, almost to the breaker waves before they scented her approach. Alarm barks suddenly erupted to echo off the rocky cliffs. A riot of movement rippled along the beach as adults scrambled towards the water, heedless of crushing pups in the chaos. Megin ignored the vulnerable young, leaving them to lesser creatures as she focused on the mothers: the adults' muscular bodies were covered in plentiful fat stores. Their ungainly waddle to the sea offered no challenge, but once in the waves, agile manoeuvres allowed them to dart under the dragon's shadow. They turned direction in a blink of an eye as Megin extended all four limbs, aiming with her front legs while reaching for extra purchase with the back. She watched multiple seals before selecting her victim at the last moment, crashing down on it as the creature broke the surface for air. The mammal was stunned by the concussion of water caused by the force of Megin's splash, allowing her to pierce the skin of its neck with her foreclaws, while her hind talons dug deep into its body to limit the thrashing seal as it tried to break free. Megin strained to trap the air beneath her wings, but most of the effort was wasted as the waves dispelled the energy in violent ripples. The wing tips dipping into the water added to the drag and weight of the dragon, causing her muscles to scream in protest. Another mighty contraction lifted the seal clear of the frothing surf, with a third carrying the dragon up into the thermals. She gave a roar of triumph, bellowing over the cove and causing the seal pups to mewl in terror.

Not wishing to share in the vivid sensations of Megin's fleshy meal, I opened my eyes to my own senses atop the grassy cliff. Despite the primitive violence of the hunt, I could not help but admire the power, speed and dexterity with which she outwitted the seal. I was still smiling with pride as I returned to the camp.

'Glad to see someone is happy about the situation,' grumbled Kade as soon as I was within hearing distance.

My smile evaporated at yet another mood swing from the prince. 'Megin was hunting,' I replied meekly.

'Oh, Megin was hunting,' Kade snapped spitefully. 'Practising her killing skills. How reassuring!'

He dropped his armload of scavenged driftwood to the ground near my feet, with enough force to send small stones stinging into my shins. The tension and frustrations of the last few days were starting to bubble within me, and Kade was offering a suitable target.

'Don't do this, Kade.'

'Do what?' he asked innocently, knowing full well that he was pushing me into a reaction. 'Gather firewood to keep you warm while you daydream with your dragon?'

'She's a *dragon*, Kade.' My volume was rising. 'A mythical creature that shouldn't exist. Excuse me for taking some time to come to terms with that!'

'She's the most dangerous weapon this world has seen in generations.' Kade raised his voice to match mine.

'She's a living creature, not some wooden trebuchet!'

'Don't be so naive. She either helps us or destroys us.'

'Don't be so simplistic,' I countered. 'She has a mind of her own, and to be honest she couldn't give two coppers about our petty land squabbles.'

'Petty land squabbles?!' Kade's voice raised further.

'Her words, not mine.'

'You speak her words now? You her servant now?'

'Don't be ridiculous.'

'Ridiculous? I saw her destroy Liegeport.'

'Visions can be interpreted in different ways...'

'How would you interpret the city being reduced to ashes by the firestorm that erupts from your monster's mouth? How would you interpret the screams of your people as the skin melts from their faces?'

Kade snarled as he stepped close to me to drive home his point, and I was forced to take a couple of steps backwards to avoid colliding with him. I felt a moment of fear as his eyes bored into mine, swirls of inky darkness writhing within their depths. I felt the brush of Megin's consciousness and swatted it away as I would an irritating fly.

Kade's tone carried a hint of nastiness as his volume dropped to barely above a whisper. 'Funny how I never see you in these visions. Where do your loyalties lie, Tallen? Have you been Hayton's spy all along? Villermir's little apprentice?'

'Are you serious?' My anger was fully sparked now, as I pushed firmly against his chest, making him retreat. 'How can you say that? You know what he did to me!'

Kade persisted with his accusations. 'Is that where you went when you left Liegeport? Did you go running to Villermir and Hayton? Did you plot with Lindvane to destroy Faulknar?'

'Oh, you have some nerve talking about plotting! You've been plotting against me my whole life. Drey finding the vulnerable little orphan. The prince offered as a playmate. All so you could use me to get to the dragon. Don't you dare question my loyalties. Your loyalties have always lain with yourself.'

'I've made no secret of where my loyalties lie. The subject under debate is your betrayal.'

'Betrayal?!' My voice rose several octaves as I spluttered the word. 'I've never betrayed you. You just can't handle the fact that I have a new toy and I won't let you play with it. You're a pathetic little boy!'

Kade pushed me hard enough to knock me to the ground. I kicked out at his shins, sending him crumpling to the floor alongside me. We were both up and glaring at each other within a heartbeat.

'Your toy is going to kill everybody you know.'

'There is no reason why she would do that.'

'Unless you commanded her to...'

I pulled at the hair at my temples in frustration. 'For the love of Mobis, Kade. Why would I do that?'

'Because you're Villermir's puppet.' He mimed a puppeteer pulling at the strings of a marionette. 'He's pulling away, controlling you, controlling the dragon.'

I slapped his face. Hard. For several heartbeats we stood still, staring at each other as my hand stung and his cheek reddened. I watched as the dark cores of his pupils appeared to turn into a churning mass of black, streaks of pitch slinking across the abyss, oozing fury and hate. The muscles of his neck and shoulders rippled with barely contained anger. I felt the connection with Megin again, more forceful this time. Danger.

I lowered my voice in an effort to calm him. 'Megin is a free spirit. No one controls her but the Gods. She was not made for the likes of you or I to use. She swears no fealty to kings.'

'But you did.'

The judgement in his words provoked a reflexively spiteful retort. 'The Kade Faulknar I swore allegiance to was not this paranoid fool!'

In a blink of an eye, we had our swords levelled at each other's throats. On the second blink, the sky was ripped by a screech of anger as Megin swept over the island. Her next pass was so low that her downdraught knocked Kade and me to the floor. Kade was soon back on his feet, roaring his fury at the retreating behemoth, waving his blade impotently as she arched gracefully back towards us. Kade changed tactics and withdrew a throwing blade as Megin skimmed over him. It bounced harmlessly off her scales, but his intention was clear, and earned him a swipe of her tail that sent him several horse-lengths across the clearing. He rose carefully, and the protection he gave to his left side hinted at bruised ribs. As he limped his way back, Megin landed, keeping her legs bunched together underneath her body to enable easy lift if required. Her tail swished agitatedly from side to side, flattening plants and small shrubs as she settled. She snorted hot gases over me at my failure to heed her warning.

'You didn't need to do that,' I scolded. 'Kade is not a threat.'

Megin snorted again. *That has yet to be decided.*

'Your dragon tried to kill me!' Kade was red in the face with frustrated rage.

'If she wanted to kill you, you would be dead.'

Kade snarled wordlessly in reply, but my attention was drawn back to Megin as I felt a new emotion from her. A cold, calculating, all-consuming purpose. I turned to face her as she sniffed loudly. The frill at her neck was extended and the hooks at its edge were pointing forward towards Kade. The clear display of aggression was accompanied by a growl rumbling deep within her chest. Sacs at the base of her throat began to swell as she pumped blood to raise the temperature in her mouth. Acid dripped from her jaws as she opened her mouth to expose the furnace.

Daemons!

The word exploded in my mind as I belatedly realised her intent. I swore repeatedly as I used Kade's injuries to force him to the ground and crouched over him. I instinctively held *Saorsa* upright in front of me as I would a shield, knowing it would be an insubstantial defence as Megin opened her mouth, but unable to think of anything else to save us. A jet of red, orange and white flames hurtled towards us. I closed my eyes, clinging tightly to Kade as I waited for our incineration. *Saorsa* was buffeted by gale-force winds and my muscles protested as I fought to hold my position. We were engulfed in a heat haze as we roasted in temperatures hotter than any smithy. Exposed flesh burned and blistered. Eyes stung as tears evaporated into salt. The smell of singed hair and scorched clothing irritated my throat, causing me to choke. Cracking open my streaming eyes, I saw rainbow-coloured flames curved around our prone bodies as the blade deflected their devouring licks. I was close to Kade's exposed neck and watched, fascinated, as the skin around the tattoo he'd been given on the Isle of Serpents rippled. It seemed as if small black serpents slithered away from the runes and sigils. Dark veins radiated from the base of his neck to entwine around his spine as the colour drained from the protective mark like ink left out in the rain.

The onslaught lasted mere moments before Megin quenched the fire, throwing her head back and roaring into the sky in frustration. Using Kade as a support, I rose to glare at her.

'What in the Seven Hells was that about?' I screamed at her.

She straightened her front legs to tower imposingly over us, snarling as Kade shakily stood to stand beside me. I raised *Saorsa* in an opposing threat.

'Don't even think it, Megin,' I demanded, as angry at her as I had been at Kade a moment before. 'I have your memories. You know this sword can cut through your armoured scales as easily as it passes through water. You know my mind. I will defend him.'

For several heartbeats, we glared at each other. I stared down this creature who was larger than any man-made structure I had ever seen. I looked into eyes that were bigger than my head. I stood dwarfed by legs that could crush me like a bug. Yet, it was she who looked away first. She who lowered her head and withdrew her crest.

Daemon, she insisted.

I replied with my mind. *Kade*.

She resisted a moment longer before jumping into the sky. Three wingbeats took her to the edge of the island and out over the water. I turned to confront Kade, but he was already on the path that led to the rocky shoreline. I released a noisy sigh of thwarted temper, turning back to the firewood he had dropped earlier.

It was then that I noticed Drey for the first time. He was standing as still as the stones around him, clutching his rose quartz so tightly his knuckles were bone white. The colour had drained from his face, leaving the lines around his eyes and mouth to show more prominently. He looked old and vulnerable.

'By the Gods, Tallen. She is an impressive creature.'

I walked towards him as he rolled his shoulders and released his grip on the quartz. I stopped within two or three paces, trying to read his thoughts. Was he angry? Was he still disappointed? The anger I had felt at Kade was gone, leaving me tired and sad, and with more than a little shame.

'I have no control over her, Drey.'

'Well, I think you have just proved that to be wrong,' he contradicted.

I rubbed my eyes in frustration. 'Why can't you see? She would have killed Kade. She would have killed me.'

'But she didn't.'

'Because of the sword.'

'Which she probably knew.'

I searched Megin's memories, finding that Drey was right and that she had known the sword would protect me. I breathed out another sigh, this one born of defeat. The freedom of my dragon was not being met with the reaction I had hoped for, and I was doing little to convince Kade and Drey to let her fly free. Instead of showing them the danger, Megin's act of aggression had reinforced their belief that she should be used as a weapon.

Drey stepped forward and gently held my arms. 'I understand your need to protect her. Although it doesn't look like she needs much help there.'

He smiled at me in reconciliation and I found myself replying in kind.

'She does have one or two tricks to protect herself if needed.'

I pulled away from his touch and moved to sit on a large boulder. After a couple of heartbeats, Drey joined me on another rock nearby.

'You're used to dealing with the Gods,' I started tentatively. 'Do you truly believe that this is what they intended when they created the dragons? That we should use their power to settle our differences?'

'I don't presume to know what the Gods intend...'

'Don't give me empty platitudes, Drey. You know more about the Gods than anyone I know. Take an educated guess.'

Drey frowned as he considered his words. 'No. I don't believe this is what the Gods had in mind when they created the dragons.'

I sat back in triumph, but he held up a finger to deny me the victory.

'However, these are very different times. Perhaps this is how it is meant to be?'

'Really?' I leaned forward to re-engage with my argument. 'You believe that we are deserving of an incomprehensible advantage over the Lindvanes? Why? What makes us so special?'

'I believe that Villermir would not hesitate to use the same advantage against us. And I believe that the world would be worse off should Hayton win. He has the Empathy Crystal. Perhaps he has something that is equally powerful. Your dragon may be just the Gods equalling the odds.'

Drey was silent while I considered the consequences of a war with weapons as powerful as Megin and the Empathy Crystal, and the devastation and fear that would cause. I shuddered at the images playing in my head, and shut them deep within my hall of doors.

'Is it easier to believe that all this is a chain of coincidences? You being right here, right now is just a product of chance?'

I shook my head in denial, but Drey continued.

'That your life events have just been a series of random occurrences? The raid on Methhold. Laken finding you and bringing you to Liegeport—'

'You orchestrated that,' I interrupted, but as I said the words, I was reminded of the Goddess's instruction to hide from the boar raiders of Lindvane.

'Perhaps.' He shrugged. 'I was aware of your potential. I was intrigued by the myths surrounding dragons and Dragonslayers. I facilitated your education within Liegeport.' Drey caught my eye and maintained a hard stare. 'But you have developed talents I have no concept of. You have abilities that have not been seen in countless generations. I could never have foretold that. I had gambled on you being able to kill the threat that I had seen in my visions. Now I find that you are the one who will orchestrate Liegeport's downfall.'

I could not hold his stare. I understood his desperation, but his words still stung. 'It just doesn't feel right, Drey. I'm sorry, but it was you who taught me that power comes with consequences.'

'Yes, it does,' he said quietly. 'But you have a duty to your king and his people, a duty to me, as well as to your dragon.'

I looked up at him. 'And a duty to the Gods? Didn't you teach me about the "greater good"? That some things are too dangerous to play with? You tell me honestly if you have never held back from what you can do, in order to protect the balance of natural power. I know you have!'

His silence was an admission of truth. Once again, I stared down my opponent, just as I had with Megin, only this time I realised I was the one in power. I suddenly understood how Drey viewed me now. The student had surpassed the master. There were things Drey could do that I could not, but there were also things I could do that he was unable to. His abilities had been learnt and were, therefore, open to me if I chose. I had learnt this at the Isle of Serpents. I had also learnt that my abilities were mingled with blood and latent talent, and Drey could never achieve what I had done instinctively. He feared me. I relaxed my shoulders and the muscles of my face. I had no desire to intimidate my former mentor.

'I will not let you use Megin in your war against Hayton. Until there is evidence that Villermir has a capacity to match hers, she will not be used in the conflicts of man.'

Drey waited several heartbeats while I watched the emotions play in his eyes; anger at my refusal, disappointment at my betrayal, sadness at the irrevocable change in our relationship, eventual acceptance of his defeat. He walked away from me with no further discussion.

Kade returned to the camp at dusk with a small cache of fish and whelks, which, when added to the broth Drey was simmering, made the meal warm and filling. It had no effect, however, on the atmosphere, which remained cold and uncomfortable. We each sat so the fire was between us and the other two. Conversation barely deviated from the pleasantries associated with eating, and movement was restricted and tight to avoid causing offence or insult. Chewing was mechanical and functional, and I doubted any of us tasted anything. I made some banal excuse to retire early to my sleeping area and was soon followed by Kade and Drey leaving for their respective sleeping mats. Covered by the darkness, I could assess the moods of the other two as they tried to get some sleep. Kade tossed and turned, irritated by even the smallest pebble under his blanket. He rose repeatedly to remove stones and smooth his bedding, huffing noisily as he settled back for a few moments' rest. Drey, in contrast, was a study in stillness, his breaths coming regularly. Only years of experience allowed me to determine that his breath carried the measured rhythm of meditation rather than the relaxed cadence of sleep. I tried to emulate him, relaxing my muscles and slowing my breathing. My concentration, however, was easily disturbed; by Kade tossing, by the sound of the waves, by my own chattering brain. I slept little and woke more tired than if I had never been to sleep.

We ate a cold breakfast and cleared camp with quiet efficiency, waiting impatiently on the rocks for the boat to take us back to the mainland. Just before the sun reached its peak, I saw the small craft bobbing precariously on the swell. Notan was experienced in rowing the currents between the islands and landed the craft a few feet from us with confidence. Kade held the boat close to the rocks, allowing Drey and me to clamber aboard before he jumped in alongside us. Notan nodded to us in greeting, rolling his shoulders before launching once more into the waves.

'You found the dragon, then,' he said by way of conversation. 'And all of you still in one piece.'

Kade grunted. Drey nodded but made no comment. I sank into my corner at the stern of the boat and avoided all eye contact.

Notan could not have failed to notice the atmosphere. 'Well,' he said quietly. 'That couldn't have been easy.'

The rest of the journey was spent in an uncomfortable silence, and we arrived at the coastal town just before dusk. Notan insisted that we spend the night with his family, so we obediently followed him to a small hut set amongst a number of similar cottages. The warmth of the cooking fire and the smell of fish stew met us as Notan opened the door. The sounds of children squabbling and a woman gently scolding them made me hesitate on the threshold. The scene was so domestic. So normal. Had I jeopardised people like this with the release of Megin? I didn't think so, but I didn't *know*.

We were ushered into the main room and seated with mugs of steaming, fragrant tea. The two children, a boy of around seven summers and a girl a couple of summers younger, bickered at the rough wooden table. In no time at all, bowls of stew were placed before us along with chunks of seeded bread. The conversation flowed easily between Notan and his wife, and they soon included Kade and Drey in the simple topics of weather, tides and fishing. I remained silent, finding myself distracted by the images in my head of Megin settling down to rest and cleaning the remains of her meal from between her teeth with her front claws.

'Right, children,' stated their mother, jolting my attention back to the cottage. 'Off to the privy, then bed.'

The young boy made the usual complaints and pleas, trying to stay up later. The girl clung to her mother's leg, twisting the hem of her tunic nervously.

'I don't want to go,' she said quietly.

'Don't be silly,' dismissed her mother, herding her to the door.

'Will the dragon eat me?'

I looked at Drey in trepidation, before the boy commented with a wicked grin, 'Nah, it won't eat you, you're too small. It's more likely to eat your little fat pony.'

His sister wailed in terror. 'Not Blackie. Mam, it won't eat Blackie, will it?'

'Of course not,' her mother reassured her, while glaring at her son.

She guided them both out of the cottage, conceding to her daughter's fears by accompanying them as they left for the communal midden. As the door closed, Drey raised my concerns with Notan.

'Fears of dragons are resurfacing, then?'

Notan nodded. 'Dragon was seen flying over the farms yesterday. Folk have been talking up a storm since then.'

'Any livestock taken?' asked Kade.

'Not yet. People are worried, naturally, but so far only a few stags have been taken.' He shook his head sadly. 'Trouble is, landowners round here take great pride in showing off their venison to the neighbouring lords. Hold hunting festivals every Lammas. Everyone is just waiting for Lord Harson to start taking out his frustrations on us.'

The men continued talking about the rumours and gossip surrounding the mythical creature that had returned from the depths of imagination. I sat listening, slowly realising the seriousness of fear and prejudice against Megin. Even Notan, who had been charged with keeping the island protected, had forgotten his true role and assumed dragons were to be destroyed. It was clear that Megin's incarceration had, indeed, kept her safe.

The children returned, bringing chattering brightness back to the cottage. Bustling activity revolved around trying to get them to bed, and I was able to make an excuse about my own need to visit the privy.

Once outside, I leaned against the timber frame of the hut for a few heartbeats, savouring the quiet and the refreshing cool air. I wandered aimlessly down the main road through the fishing town. Lights burned in a number of cottages, but many were already in darkness, with their owners having to catch the early tide in the morning. I followed a path out into the open fields and salty heathland that bordered the cliffs. I chose no particular direction in which to walk, only allowing the act itself to be something to do, something positive to focus on. I made a point to concentrate on the smells of the ocean and the hush of the night, rather than difficult decisions involving dragons and duty and responsibility.

I was at the far end of a large meadow when I felt the gust of Megin flying silently towards me. She landed with a gentle thud.

Your mind is noisy, she complained.

'I know,' I apologised. 'But it is sort of your fault.'

She huffed. *I am not concerned with your human problems.*

'Well, I am. And maybe you should be too. Things are different from when you last flew. People do not revere you any more. You are a scarily large pest to them.'

She flared her crest in annoyance. *A pest who could eat them all in a mouthful.*

'I think that's the point. They are truly scared of you, and not without reason. People can be spiteful when they are scared.'

I can protect myself.

'Can you?' I thought of the images within her memory that showed the dragons being attacked in Liegeport. 'It won't take long for people to learn to fight you again.'

The thought of Megin being hurt or even killed was unbearable. For reasons I could not explain, the emotions cut deeper than the loss of Laken or my parents. Deeper than walking away from Kade and Drey, which made me suddenly realise that I had already made the decision to not go back. These paled into insignificance compared to the shards of glass embedded in my heart at the thought of Megin being harpooned. I lost control of my breathing. Visions of my dragon bleeding from increasingly violent wounds cascaded in front of my vision. My heart hammering in my chest. Megin throwing her head back in agony. Tears did nothing to blur the images created by my mind. Her chest labouring to take in her final breath…

I'm right here, she said, gently pushing away the images and replacing them with the strength of her heartbeat. *And I can protect myself.*

I sniffed noisily as I wiped at my tears. 'You shouldn't need to defend yourself. You should fly away, far from people. Be free!'

Megin was quiet for several heartbeats and I felt her hold herself very still. *You would send me away.*

It was not a question. She knew my thoughts.

'To protect you. To keep you safe.'

I needed to do more than send her away from me. I needed her to cut all ties with me. She heard my thoughts as soon as I had them. I felt her disappointment, and her feelings of betrayal and abandonment. I seemed to be doing this a lot recently, to those I most cared for. She seemed so vulnerable that the fissure in my heart cracked deeper still.

'To protect you,' I repeated, partially to convince myself. 'They will use me to get at you. Half will want to kill you. The other half will want to use you to kill their enemies. Either way is not a good outcome for you.'

Megin masked her hurt with anger, a defence strategy I knew well. *How little faith you have in me, that I cannot take care of one puny human.*

'I can't take that risk. The carnage when it happened last time; when you lost your Slayer at Liegeport, and they looked for his young son...'

I am well aware of the fates of all my Slayers, she snapped. *I was unable to assist him.*

'I know,' I said quietly, feeling her guilt at not being able to help generations of Slayers while she was within the mountain. 'But I cannot take the risk. To either of us, or those who'd get caught in the middle.'

And how would you make me go away? she asked haughtily.

I shrugged. 'I could order you.'

I expected some acerbic comment, but her silence was as good as a confession. I quickly scanned her memories for confirmation, taking only moments to decide our fates.

'Meginvættr-Heitrkaldbalk,' I said carefully before she had time to stop me, 'I demand that you leave me. That you remove your presence from me, and prevent me from having any conscious awareness of you.'

Her eyes blazed with fury, but she had withdrawn her thoughts from my mind. It was not a command as such, more a formal use of words to convey the undisputable request. She could refuse to comply, but that would sever the sacred bond between Slayer and dragon. With a scream, she launched herself into the air with such force that I was required to shield my eyes from the dust she stirred from the ground. When I lowered my arm, she was gone. The sky was empty and the air was still once again. I yelled at the stars in frustration. This was not how it was supposed to be. How could I have lost everything? Again? I had no home, no companion, and no money. I had only the clothes I was wearing. And my sword.

Saorsa became the focus of my anger. The sword was the symbol of the Dragonslayer. It was the reason Drey had taken me to Liegeport. It was the reason for my orchestrated friendship with Kade. It had led to the selling of my loyalty to the Faulknar crown. It had drawn the attentions of Villermir and his manipulation of my mind. It was the cost of having to send Megin away. I roared with rage, withdrawing the blade from my scabbard and throwing it as far as I could across the meadow. The rubies flashed as it arced away from me. Another accusation of betrayal.

I dropped to my knees, numb and suddenly drained of all energy. I collapsed onto my back, staring up into the black vastness of the night.

'The Gods take my fate,' I shouted. 'I no longer care what you do to me!'

Chapter Twenty-Eight

I lay on my back, watching the stars creep across the dark sky. I did not sleep, but repeatedly poked the self-inflicted wounds of turning my back on Kade and Drey, and commanding Megin to go. I felt numb and empty, without the motivation to do anything, other than watch the stars. No future presented itself that would lead me to a positive tomorrow. The desire to survive, to do an honest day's work, seemed pointless. The energy required to breathe seemed like too much effort.

The clouds thickened as the sky lightened to the grey of pre-dawn. Long, flat strips of fluff would cover the moon for a moment, before she peeked through the gaps that ran throughout. The wind increased slightly with the arrival of the clouds, but it was warm, and I was content to remain where I was until my bladder became too insistent to ignore. I finally had to accept that my night of self-pity was over and it was time to face my future, whatever that was, starting with the routine of satisfying bodily needs.

I rose carefully, groaning at the protest of stiffened muscles as I stretched my back and rolled my shoulders. The timing coincided with the moon emerging from the clouds, so that the pale light caught *Saorsu* as she lay where I had thrown her. The ruby in her uppermost eye flashed accusingly as I walked towards her. The frustration of the previous night was gone, and I knew I would not be able to discard her. She was the only tangible link to my family, and I could not bring myself to lose that despite what she represented. As I picked her up and rolled my wrist, the weight of her hilt in my hand felt right. The runes showed for a moment before being lost again in the dim light. I rolled my wrist one more time for the pleasure of it, before sheathing her back in the safety of her scabbard. I scanned the forest line for an appropriate place to relieve myself, an acceptable path to follow. And froze.

Hidden in the shadows between two large oak trees, a pair of luminous green eyes were reflected at the level of my knees. I squinted into the darkness to determine that the eyes belonged to a grey wolf, perfectly camouflaged in the twilight. I slowly moved away, walking sideways so I could continue to watch for any sudden movements. The wolf stared calmly at me, tracking my movements but making no attempt to either approach or retreat. I was almost at the far end of the meadow when I lost sight of the eyes that had brightly reflected the small amount of moonlight. I strained to hear any sound that might indicate that the wolf had followed me. The night was quiet, with the birds not yet awake to provide alarm calls. I waited several heartbeats before accepting that the wolf had gone.

I pondered the strange incident as I found a secluded spot to void my bladder. How strange that a wolf would be on its own, and that it was prowling in the night before most animals were awake. Perhaps it was hungry and hoping to catch a snoozing meal. It was curious that it did not seem to be bothered by my presence, being neither aggressive nor fearful. I dismissed it as an unusual event that I was happy to forget, and considered which direction to take. Going back to the fishing town was not an option, so I chose a small track that would take me away from the coast. I had not walked more than a dozen paces when the wolf slunk out of the bracken to stand on the path ahead of me. It was less than ten paces away, and I could see it clearly. Its fur was a mixture of white undercoat and black tips, so that it could blend into light and dark surroundings. Its eyes effectively reflected what little light filtered through the canopy, so that their dilated pupils glowed lustrous green as they fixed on me. My heart was pounding, but the canid showed no signs of alarm or concern. It watched me calmly as I stared back. I retraced my steps, slowly, back to the beginning of the trail. The wolf came with me, maintaining the distance between us. I was back where I had started when the wolf stopped. I took a couple of steps further back, but it stayed with its feet still on the track, preventing me from returning that way. I looked around the clearing and found another trail leading off to the left. I took two steps in that direction before halting as a deep grumble vibrated through the wolf's chest. Its lips pulled into a snarl, revealing ivory front teeth and canines. I took a step backwards and the lips relaxed. I took a step forward, and they raised again.

'Seriously?' I asked it, finding it hard to believe that a wolf was commenting on my choice of pathway. 'This is ridiculous.'

Thinking it was going to send me back to Kade, I looked desperately for another avenue while the wolf waited patiently. Observing, but making no complaint if I did not move in a direction it did not want me to go. Eventually, I found a small track, partially covered by bracken and vines. I threw a challenging look at the wolf, daring it to challenge me as I moved in the direction of the trail. It stayed relaxed, matching my pace to follow me to the new pathway. I was forced to take my eyes off the creature as I negotiated the numerous stems trying to trip me, but after several paces, I could no longer avoid looking behind me. I was hoping that the wolf would be gone now I was on the track that it had indicated, but I was to be disappointed. It was still there, tongue hanging out contentedly as I struggled to forge my way ahead.

'Really?' I asked. 'You're just going to let me do all the hard work?'

The relaxed mouth looked so like a grin that I almost expected the wolf to answer me. Shaking my head at myself for talking to a wolf, I returned to battling through the undergrowth on the trail that led further into the forest, listening to the panting predator that was uncomfortably close to my hamstrings.

The wolf followed me as the sky lightened towards dawn and on into daybreak. Seeing it more clearly, I noticed it was thin but otherwise looked in good condition. The eyes, which had looked green when reflected, were a warm yellow. There was intelligence looking out from those eyes, but no fear. Unlike most animals when they were around me, the wolf was calm and not at all bothered by being this close to a human. It maintained its distance, tracking my steps but not rushing me or falling behind. I could see no motive for its actions, but strangely, its presence began to feel comforting as we walked through the ancient forest, startling the birds and the squirrels.

The day followed a simple routine: the wolf followed at a set distance, content to let me lead but giving clear directions, through growls and snarls, each time we came to a crossroads. The trees thinned to glades and clearings, but we never encountered human habitation, neither roads nor settlements. My mind calmed as I concentrated on the trail ahead. It seemed I had no input in the destination, so I was content to wait and see where the wolf was herding me. Surely, it would have attacked by now if that had been its plan, with my exposed back offering a tempting target, but it continued to show no aggression other than when I strayed from the intended path.

The sun had started its descent when the ground began to rise. The peaks of a mountain range lay ahead of us, and it was clear that I was to summit one of the mountains rather than go through any of the valleys between. The trees became smaller with bigger gaps in between as we rose, and by the time we were halfway up I could see why we had avoided the valleys. The light was starting to fade, and pinpricks of yellow were shining from the windows of the villages below. The glint of a river threaded between, suggesting a vibrant trading post on the way to a sea that was some distance away.

Despite the trail becoming easier to follow, with the thinning undergrowth and trees being replaced by bushes and brambles, I was starting to stumble as the light faded to dusk. Although I was not hungry, I had not eaten since the previous evening and I was started to feel light-headed. The furriness of my tongue reminded me that I had not drunk either, and I would have to rest soon, preferably by a water source. I scanned the surrounding area but was reluctant to leave the track, and the hastening dusk did not help me find a stream or brook. I was beginning to think that maybe the wolf had been working on a plan to eat me after all, after it had weakened me by denying food, water and rest. I had heard tales of packs of wolves harrying their quarry until it died of exhaustion. It was a low-risk strategy. Pessimistically, I wondered how long I would last.

I startled as the wolf brushed against my leg. It was the first contact it had made, and I was surprised by the power of the muscle that pressed against my thigh and knocked me gently off the trail into the green bracken. By the time I reacted, the canid had pushed past me and was leading further into the heath. When I failed to follow it turned to look at me, tilting its head to one side as if to query why I had stopped. With no other clear plan of action, I cursed myself for a fool but followed it anyway.

With the evening turning rapidly to darkness and my vision starting to blur, I stumbled over the broad leaves more often than I stepped over them. The wolf waited patiently for me each time I fell, quietly encouraging me to rise and follow. Fortunately, it was not long before I heard the soft trickle of water. My companion dropped its head and lapped noisily as I crashed through the foliage behind it. I didn't hesitate to drop to my knees beside it and drink my fill of cool, clear water from a small brook seeping from between moss-covered rocks. The wolf settled a short distance from the water, circling a few times before dropping to the ground and crossing its paws in front of it. It watched me until I sat a couple of horse-lengths from it, whereupon, seemingly contented, it dropped its head to its paws. I settled down to watch its breathing become slow and regular, and found that my own breaths had slowed to match the wolf's. I was slightly amused at my easy acceptance of its presence as I closed my eyes, but was soon embraced by an exhausted sleep.

I awoke to the warmth of the sun on my face, thick-headed and gummy-eyed. It was several heartbeats before I remembered that I had gone to sleep with a wolf. Snapping my eyes open wide, I held my breath, not knowing what to expect but preparing myself for the worst. Turning my head slightly, I saw that the canid was still lying a couple horse-lengths away, chewing noisily at its nails. Noticing that I was awake, it rose and stretched; first backwards so its chest lowered and its rear end was up in the air, then forwards so its belly was almost touching the floor. It yawned loudly, showing me all its sharp white teeth, before shaking itself. I suspected that the expression on its face was one of self-satisfaction as it waited for me to join it for another day's trek.

That day followed the pattern of the first. As did the next. And the next. At some point the wolf took the lead, and I followed it along paths barely visible through the bracken and brambles of the woodlands, and the gorse and heather of the heath. I repeatedly questioned the sanity of following the creature, but lacked any other credible options and found it increasingly difficult to care. The wolf was confident in leading me to something, and that confidence was strangely comforting. To justify the beast's determination to 'help me', when all logic dictated that it should be looking out for itself, I made up fables and fantasies. Perhaps it was a brave knight who had been cursed by the fae folk to wander the hills and rescue lost souls? Perhaps it was one of the fae folk, tasked with luring travellers to the mythical kingdoms of feast and festival? Perhaps I was already dead, and my penance was to walk the mountains with this strange wolf? Whatever the reason, it would lead and I would follow.

As I grew weaker from the lack of food and the prolonged exertion of walking through the hills, my focus became one of endurance and survival. My senses became those of the wolf, with vision becoming less important than hearing and smell. I reacted to movements of its body; the rising of its nose, the direction of its ears, the dropping of its head. I strained my human senses to detect what had alerted my companion, and in time our responses became aligned. I started to detect faint scents on air currents and small sounds from the scrub; the rustle of grass as a mouse darted for cover, the sweetness of crushed leaves and released pollen as a deer walked through a glade.

Around the fourth or fifth night, as we stopped by a stream to camp, the wolf took off into the shadows of the trees. I suddenly felt alarmed, realising that I had begun to feel safer with its presence than I now felt without it. I had come to rely on its alertness, keen senses and unwavering ability to avoid human contact, even when passing close to the infrequent settlements. The world seemed empty and hostile, and the loneliness opened up the fresh wounds of abandoning Kade, Drey and Megin. I waited impatiently for it to return.

Judging by the descent of the sun and the emergence of the moon, the wolf was not gone long despite my belief that it had left for good. It returned carrying the body of an adult rabbit. I chuckled to myself at my pessimism, when all it had done was go hunting. I still had no appetite and, apart from occasional berries, plucked from brambles that blocked our way, that had sat heavily in my stomach, I had eaten nothing since the meal with Notan and his family. My body no longer recognised the need for food to sustain itself. As a healer I knew I should be worried by that, but I lacked the desire to care.

The wolf padded over to me and dropped the rabbit a short distance from my hand. We stared at each other as I failed to understand what it wanted. It tried to make its intentions clearer by using its nose to nudge the rabbit closer to me, then by pushing it into my hand. I felt my mouth open in bewilderment, seriously starting to consider that I was going mad. The wolf was trying to feed me.

'Kind of you, but no,' I declined, my voice cracking after days of not being used.

As I pushed the offered meal back towards the wolf, it raised its lips in a deep-throated growl. It was clearly reminding me that, no matter how comfortable I had become in its presence, it was still a wolf, capable of ripping open my neck as easily as it had killed the rabbit. My stomach roiled at the thought of raw meat, and I tasted bile at the back of my throat. The wolf continued to snarl, its face contorted to show the primitive ferocity of this wild animal. Slowly, I nudged the rabbit again. Fast as a snake, the wolf snapped at my hand. It missed by a hair's breadth and I felt the force of the expelled air on my skin as the teeth cracked together. I couldn't quite believe that my flesh was untouched as I snatched my hand back.

'Mobis's foul breath!' I cursed. 'Very well. I'll eat the damned rabbit!'

Raw meat was a step too far, so I scavenged around for twigs and bark to make a small fire. I had left my tinderbox with my other belongings at the fishing town, but I easily made a spark to light the dry fuel. Bitterly amused at how comfortable I had become using magick, I soon had the rabbit meat staked over glowing sticks. I assumed the wolf had eaten prior to returning as it ignored my attempts at cooking. The hounds in Bow's stable had salivated over the tiniest morsel of food, shamelessly begging from everyone in the hope of getting a mouthful. After greedily consuming the skin and offal that I removed from the carcass, the wolf crossed its paws, rested its head on its feet and dozed contentedly.

The wolf brought food to me regularly. Mainly rabbits, but occasionally a leg of venison. I ate little, and my body rejected most of that. I understood that any reserves I may have had were being used up rapidly, but the thought seemed distant and unimportant. The wolf kept pushing onwards but I needed to rest more often, finding it harder to start walking again after a break. I was encouraged, herded, pushed and occasionally nipped in order to get me moving again. Each time I questioned why the wolf was so determined to get me to the unknown destination. The journey became a blur of images as we travelled further from my old life. The scenery became a dreamscape in muted shades of green, brown and purple. Sounds were hushed into gentle murmurings. The wolf led me through dense forests that looked like they had been untouched by human hands. Its path wound around mountain after hill after mountain. Only at the top of a particularly high one could any sense of distance be determined. The forest spread as far as I could see in all directions, with the only sign of life being the eagles that sailed on the thermals. We continued on, each night stopping by a water source. The wolf hunted when required, occasionally bringing some meat back for me. I forced myself to eat what it brought and it cleared away all that I rejected.

At some point we stopped at a beautiful waterfall. A section of the mountain had sheared away, leaving a gorge covered in vibrant ferns and colourful wild flowers. Small birds swooped low over the river after insects, while on a branch an iridescent kingfisher sat watching the fish below the surface. I could easily imagine deer coming to drink at the water's edge, if there was no wolf and human to disturb them. The crash of the waterfall was thunderous, but strangely relaxing; the timelessness of the inevitable fall of water from the source river above. The rock face was at least ten times my height, with an ever-present mist causing the stone to sparkle in the late-afternoon sun.

All this splendour, however, was lost on me. I was so tired; bone-wearily tired. Thought was difficult because of the relentless fug in my mind from aching tissues and malnutrition. I had to fight for the concentration needed to place one foot in front of the other, to balance effectively so as not to fall on my face, and to focus on the wolf's back to ensure I did not fall off the side of a cliff. All I wanted was to collapse on the soft ground, curl into a ball and dissolve into the oblivion of sleep.

It seemed no time at all before the wolf poked me in the back with its wet nose. Grunting incomprehensibly prompted the poking to become more insistent. Finally, a nip on the sensitive skin of my buttock had me sitting up to confront the pest, the ensuing rush of blood from my head doing nothing to improve my temper. As my vision cleared, I looked around for the cause of my disturbance, while feeling for a suitably sized rock to throw at its head.

She was standing by the water's edge. The full moon cast a silver sheen over all reflective surfaces, bathing her in a gentle light. Her hood was down, and her white hair fell softly around her shoulders as she looked at me with her ice-blue eyes. Her long, thin hands were clasped delicately in front of her waist, her black robe brushing the lush grass that was just starting to pearl with dew. The wolf padded quietly to her side, pressing itself into her thigh. She dropped a hand and stroked the velvety fur at the base of its ear.

I glared at the canid. 'Seems you are just as annoying in my dreams.'

The wolf's jaw dropped open in its impression of a grin, as the Lady inclined her head slightly.

You are not dreaming, Tallen nic Duane. I stand here to give you comfort that the first stage of your journey is nearly at an end.

'Comfort?' I started to giggle, hearing the undertone of hysteria in the sound.

The merest ghost of a smile played at the corners of her mouth. *You have not lost your mind.*

I snorted. 'Says my imagined Goddess and her pet wolf. I'm just surprised that it took this long. So many people have been stomping around in my head, it's as churned up as a well-ploughed field.'

The Lady frowned at my easy dismissal of her. *I am as real as you are. As the ground you sit on. As real as I was the day I entombed your dragon, safe for when you would have need of her.*

I raised a finger in protest. 'About that. That didn't go so well.'

She shook her head. *Destinies are rarely without cost.*

'Oh, save your platitudes,' I snapped, using the exposed tree roots to help me stand as my anger required more than passively sitting on the ground. 'And you can shove your destiny up your—'

The wolf took a step towards me and I reflexively took a step backwards, pressing my back against the rough trunk of the tree. The animal's hackles were fully raised and its lips were lifted to reveal its teeth in a show of aggression I had not seen before, the growl reverberating in its chest clearly expressing its sudden displeasure. Fearlessly, the Lady smoothed the hackles at its shoulders, calming the storm that had raged in its eyes.

He thinks you should show me more respect, she scolded quietly.

Frustratingly, my brain focused on this new piece of information. The wolf was male. Why had I not taken the time to determine that it was a he? I pressed hard against my forehead with the heels of my hands, forcing my thoughts to concentrate on more important matters.

'You are here to use me.'

Of course, she replied without judgement. *I am a Goddess. Slayers and their dragons were created to do my bidding. You are* my *Slayer.*

She waited while I evaluated the statement, trying to determine what it meant and how it related to my reality.

'But that was generations ago. Deities don't walk the land any more.'

And dragons don't exist? She raised an eyebrow, daring me to contradict her. *Are you telling me you no longer believe in the pantheon of the Higher and Lower Halls of Gods and Goddesses? I am not sure your grandfather would be too pleased to hear that.*

Again, she waited while I sorted out memories, searching for evidence to support her claim, looking for reasons to doubt her reasoning. My brain was frustratingly slow. I refused to believe that there was a Goddess standing in front of me, and that I was arguing with her.

'I don't understand.'

The ghost of a smile returned at my presumption. *You are a rare creature. You have inherited three ancient bloodlines. You are a Dragonslayer. You are an Empath. And you are a Moon Warrior. That is a valuable combination. There is a history to be answered. Three lines of blood energy converging at this point in time. Just when they will be needed. Just as your dragon was released when you will need her the most.*

I could feel the weight of responsibility crushing me again. 'I sent her away,' I pleaded desperately.

Nevertheless, the story is unfolding. The powers will fight over what you have and what you represent. Running and hiding, however tempting, is not an option for you.

I closed my eyes and wished for a different outcome, although I now knew there was no other choice. A Goddess had called me to arms and I could not refuse that, especially after she had scorned my original plan of hiding for the rest of my life.

'What do you need me to do?' I asked quietly.

A celestial war is coming. This is not just about the independence of Faulknar. This is a battle for control of the energy of this land. We believe that the power is too great for any one faction. That is why we have always divided the magicks between different Gods and Goddesses. Baila wants that power for himself, and Taranis is hoping to take control while we are too busy fighting each other. Your prince is going to need all the help he can get.

'I don't know how…'

The wolf has been tasked with guiding you to where you need to be for the next stage of your journey. You have much still to learn. Your powers are only just beginning to develop.

I studied the pattern of earth at my feet, thinking of how insignificant the individual blades of grass were, but how integral each was for the wildlife that lived here. 'I don't…'

I looked up, but she had gone, disappeared with no trace of her ever being there. I tried to convince myself that she had never been there and that I had imagined the whole encounter, but I had found a sense of purpose that had not been there before. I now had a direction in which to travel and a reconnection with a future that may have need of me. I had some idea of what was expected of a Slayer and an Empath, but I knew nothing of Moon Warriors. How were they related to the old religion? What were the expectations involved with that side of my heritage? If my Dragonslayer blood came from my father and my Empath blood from my mother, where did my Moon Warrior blood come from?

I followed the wolf for several more days, but my new-found motivation was no compensation for a body that had been starved of nutrition for so long. My hair had grown and was separated into greasy tufts. My clothes hung off my emaciated frame. My skin was dry, cracked and sloughing off in patches. I was lame from ulcerated blisters, rubbed sores and overtaxed muscles. My vision was blurred and even the palest light stabbed through my eyes into my brain. I was spending more time in an exhausted sleep, and it was taking more persistence from the wolf to get me walking each day. Despite the Goddess's reassurance of my fated destiny, I knew I was dying.

It took several moments for the image to filter into my conscious thoughts, and for me to realise what I was seeing. The wolf had led me to the edge of the forest, opening into a wide, flat heath at the top of cliffs. The sea could be seen as a grey-blue strip extending to the horizon, and vaguely I noted that I must have crossed the entire width of the Northlands.

A walled fortress was the only structure in view. Dark stone walls encircled a settlement that was roughly half the size of Liegeport. A significant number of people would fit within the buildings half-hidden by the outer wall and, as smoke rose from some of the chimneys, I knew the place was inhabited. I became anxious at being around people again, after so long wandering the forests and heaths. I turned to my companion to find he had returned to the shadows of the trees, his body hidden so that only his face was highlighted. He held my stare for several heartbeats, before slowly blinking and turning away to disappear into the undergrowth. It would appear that I had reached my destination and his guidance was no longer required. I found that I was saddened by the fact that he was no longer with me, and suddenly felt very vulnerable.

I stumbled forward into the open heath, squinting in the unfiltered sunlight. I forced myself to ignore the pain as I placed one foot in front of the other, in a manner better described as controlled falling rather than walking. My vision constricted to a small window as blackness crowded in from the edges, sometimes completely obscuring my view of the fort. The heathland seemed endless and the settlement appeared to get no closer; still I pushed on. I concentrated only on the aim of reaching the walls and making it to the place the wolf had sent me to.

I thumped into the wall with enough force to make me stagger back a few steps before falling heavily on my buttocks, another bruise added to my collection of scrapes and sores. I stood unsteadily and felt an egg-shaped swelling in the middle of my forehead. It took several deep breaths until my vision had cleared enough to show that I had veered off the track and missed the gated entrance to the fort. I returned to the wall, using one hand to guide myself back to the centre of the structure. The stone was smooth and cool, and I let it occupy my thoughts as I made my way to the double gates. My exploring fingers found the engraved wood of the first gate and I nearly collapsed with relief. I banged on the gate, shocked by my lack of power and certain that nobody inside would hear. I tried louder, but again failed to summon the strength to make a noise above a whisper. My eyes prickled at the thought of coming so close to the end only to die outside the fort's gates, but I had little water inside me for tears. I stood, wobbling pitifully, in front of the barriers for several heartbeats before I could dig deep within myself, summon the last remnants of my strength and raise my hand for a third time.

Before I connected, the gate opened and an angelic vision stood in front of me. Dark green eyes looked at me from a tanned face, bordered by long blond hair. A thickset frame was covered by a priest's cream robe.

'Sanctuary,' I croaked, before falling forward to collapse into total darkness.

Epilogue

The smoke from the firepit thickened to a dark grey. Acrid fumes swirled in the darkening sky, writhing in time with the chanting from the small group gathered in a large circle around the glowing embers. The thick smoke was contained within the sacred space as it started to form into shapes; grey darkening to black, a flash of red as eyes appeared, yellow teeth at the ripped edges of a mouth. Twisting and turning, the shapes tried to escape from their confinement. They stretched into thick tubes of matter with two legs and two arms. Others flowed into stocky ovoids with four stumpy legs, one at each corner. A third group started to form two legs to support a curved body.

The circle of chanters was forced back as more shapes coalesced from the firepit. The creatures pushed and shoved as they vied for space. Poorly formed heads snapped at insubstantial mist, while stumps of arms punched through gelatinous bodies. Others rushed to the outside of the circle, only to be forced back as if hitting a stone wall. This seemed to result in frustration as they turned on the smoky shapes around them with renewed aggression. The first from the pit became more substantial, causing drifts of smoke to trail from their connected punches. Claws developed at the ends of arms and legs, capable of ripping holes into the developing bodies of others. Snouts lengthened as teeth grew into sharp blades of yellow.

The circle was pushed back again, and a gap opened up. The shadows rushed towards the breach, swarming out into the night. The three different shapes gathered together with others of their kind. Some became essentially humanoid, but at least twice the size of the tallest man. Their torsos were as wide as an oak tree's trunk, with long, cumbersome legs crashing into the earth as they marched away from the firepit. Thick arms swung at their sides until within reach of another shadow, which was pushed or punched out of the way. Round faces elongated into bulbous snouts with yellow canines poking out from behind the upper and lower lips.

Behind these, the second group lumbered. Twice the height of a horse, they were over three times the width of a prize bull. Four massive legs thundered across the ground, churning up clods of dirt as they shoulder-barged those around them. Large, pricked ears rotated, honing in on sounds from potential victims. Gelatinous saliva dripped from square jaws as a rubbery tongue licked at the tusks protruding from the creature's lower lip.

The third group developed wings on their backs. As the two membranous appendages solidified, the shadows leapt into the air to swirl around the land-based creatures. Their two legs dangled from their bodies, equipped with black claws as long as a sword's blade, the thin lower legs distracting from the powerful, muscular thighs. Long, sinuous necks allowed their heads to move in any direction, their mouths sharpened to a point with teeth exposed as they parted their lips to scream. Several swooped onto the bull-like beasts, raking their backs with claws and teeth. The shadow drifted as smoke where it was attacked, but within heartbeats, the form was solid again.

The herd of monsters soon detected the field of sheep corralled at the base of a mountain. Their panicked bleating served only to heighten the frenzy bearing down on them, running and gliding in anticipation of the bloody mayhem. As one, the horde sailed over the pitiful fences to attack the defenceless creatures. Fleece and tissue flew as claws and teeth ripped into the sheep. The metallic tang of blood filled the air as large arteries were torn apart. Entrails mixed with body waste as the daemons gorged on the carcasses, muscle and sinew hanging from their jaws. The killing spree was as effective as locusts crossing a field of corn.

With the sheep decimated, the monsters turned to further carnage. Those gathered for the chanting, until now overlooked, became the next target. As enthusiastically as the giants had descended on the domesticated animals, they now raced towards the humans. Several took steps backwards, as the realisation of what they had summoned started to become apparent. Many mumbled prayers to their Gods.

One stepped forward, waiting confidently for the approach of the murderous tidal wave. Hideous squeals and screeches emitted from the horde as they jostled each other, keen to be the first to sample this new taste of flesh. Eager to rip the limbs from their victims and grind their bones into dust. Impatient to crush their skulls and savour the fatty brains within.

The One raised a bone whistle and blew. The shrill sound pierced the night and echoed off the mountains. The horde of daemons stopped abruptly, pawing at the ground or tossing their heads, like a horse that fights the restraint of a bit. An invisible wall prevented them from moving closer to the humans. Their frustrations were vented on those next to them, slashing and tearing at shadowy skin as the monsters bunched together. Those at the back surged forward and crushed those in front.

The winged beasts were first to realise that the barrier only affected movement towards the humans, who bunched together around the firepit. They soared around the perimeter, unable to get closer but free to move in other directions. Several soon tired of testing the strength of the barrier and flew off to find easier targets. They did not get far.

Before they had reached the edge of the clearing, a thunderous roar bellowed into the night. A streak of red dove down out of the darkness and the body of a dragon dwarfed the flying beasts. The creature was purple against the black of the night, with highlights of red along her underbelly. Her forelimbs stretched to snatch at the monsters, as a hawk plucks at a dove. Her claws scraped along the side of the first daemon she encountered, and it turned away with a deep wound along its flank. The shadowy skin healed before the eyes of those present as it screeched in triumph. The dragon was not concerned; she knew how to kill daemons. She had been created for this.

As the flying daemon threw its head back to mock the dragon, its exposed neck was grasped by a forepaw. The dragon squeezed, causing the shadow to scrabble desperately with its clawed limbs while flapping its wings to stay in the air. Its curved spine was grasped by the dragon's hind feet, claws sinking into the smoky muscle, and, as easily as taking a breath, the dragon ripped the head off the body of the daemon. It evaporated into showers of bilious green sparks that dissolved before they reached the ground.

The daemon horde erupted into a frenzy again, this time in response to their vulnerability to the swooping dragon. They punched and slashed and ploughed over each other in their attempts to escape. The dragon dived and soared, taking a land creature as she dropped and grabbing a winged one as she rose. She took one in each hind foot, leaving her forefeet free to remove their heads. She used her teeth to bite through another's neck before swiftly moving on to the next. Each exploded into iridescent sparks. With ruthless efficiency she massacred the monsters, suffering nothing more serious than a few slices between the edges of her scales. She chased down the last as they tried to flee into the mountains, roaring her triumph as she destroyed them. Circling gracefully against the stars with the exhilaration of doing what she was made to do; the sheer joy of killing daemons.

The One calmly watched the annihilation of the daemon army she had raised from the firepit.

For exclusive discounts on Matador titles,
sign up to our occasional newsletter at
troubador.co.uk/bookshop